"MAY I REMIND YOU THAT I'M ENGAGED TO DANIEL?"

Head held high, Ravenna flung the words at Luke.

"The way you keep repeating the fact, I'm not likely to forget," Luke said sardonically. "But there's one thing you haven't taken into account—*we've* met."

He moved nearer, and Ravenna pressed back against the wall. "Daniel and I can't throw away our love just because—" her face flamed "—because you and I are attracted to each other. A purely physical attraction at that. Well, I don't want you, Luke. I don't need you and—"

Her mistake was that she'd kept on going. In two strides he caught her in his arms, and at the first searing touch of his lips, her own betrayed her. She couldn't hide her hungry response, the arching of her spine, the tautening of her breasts....

Finally he lifted his mouth, his eyes glittering. "You don't want me? You're lying, Ravenna! But your body doesn't lie."

WELCOME TO...

SUPERROMANCES

A sensational series of modern love stories
from Worldwide Library.

Written by masters of the genre, these longer,
sensual and dramatic novels are truly in keeping
with today's changing life-styles. Full of intriguing
conflicts, the heartaches and delights of true love,
SUPERROMANCES are absorbing stories—
satisfying and sophisticated reading that lovers
of romance fiction have long been waiting for.

SUPERROMANCES
Contemporary love stories for the woman of today!

Kathryn Collins

THE WINGS OF NIGHT

A SUPERROMANCE FROM

WORLDWIDE

TORONTO · NEW YORK · LONDON · PARIS
AMSTERDAM · STOCKHOLM · HAMBURG
ATHENS · MILAN · TOKYO · SYDNEY

For thou wilt lie upon the wings of night...
Romeo and Juliet

Published January 1984

First printing November 1983

ISBN 0-373-70097-0

CHAPTER ONE

RAVENNA JONES SMILED at her fiancé, Daniel Rathbourn, in the dim light of the Manhattan hotel restaurant. It was early morning, and the deep blue shadows cast by the towering office complexes opposite the hotel penetrated even to the recessed corner where they sat, as if they were at the bottom of a sunless cavern. But the rich gloom of the canyons of New York held no strangeness for Ravenna—she'd spent four years in the city as a student, learning to love the concrete cliffs that cut the distant sky. She was glad to be back, even though it was just on a stopover.

Her smile deepened as she listened to Daniel and heard the waitress's Brooklyn accent collide with his British tones. He was asking if they served kippers.

"Kippers, mister? Is that some kind of new breakfast cereal?"

"Never mind," he said dryly, and Ravenna smothered a laugh when the chunky woman disappeared with their mundane order for bacon and eggs.

"Daniel, honey, you sound so British and proper. Kippers!"

"It's common breakfast fare in jolly olde England, my dear," he murmured mockingly, "and if you're referring to my so-called accent, just wait till you get to Rathbourn. Your irresistible drawl will be fair game."

She made a face at him. Her years of university in New York had done nothing for her soft Kentuckian drawl. Not that she'd ever tried to lose it. But it certainly was going to stick out like a sore thumb when she got to England. Thinking of this and filled with excitement at their upcoming flight, she eyed her breakfast absentmindedly when it arrived. Then she leaned closer to Daniel on the banquette seating, her curling auburn hair like a bright flame against the darkness of his, her blue eyes serious at a sudden thought.

"Do you think Glynis will like me, Daniel? She's not one of those possessive mothers who don't want their sons to marry, is she?"

"No one," Daniel reassured her, his lips brushing her hair and his dark eyes smiling, "could fail to find you utterly adorable, my darling. Southern drawl included. Not my mother or Luke or Jeremy. Even the servants will fall like flies."

"Servants?" Her voice rose. "You never mentioned servants before!" She looked at him indignantly. "I don't believe you."

"Well, it's true," he said, laughing in turn. "At Rathbourn we'd never survive without them. The place is bigger than one of your father's breeding stables."

"You're making me nervous. I'll bet Glynis

dreamed of your marrying some horsey Brit whose daddy is a duke.''

''And instead I'm marrying a 'horsey' American school teacher.''

''Descended from varlets!'' She laughed. ''And don't call me horsey!''

''When you were born and bred at Elk Creek? You must have been teethed on a saddle horn.'' His brown eyes teasing, he opened wide a menu and kissed her behind its makeshift screen.

They had been engaged less than forty-eight hours, and as Ravenna sank back against the comfortable leather seating to gaze at Daniel, she still saw him through the faint unbelieving haze that had enveloped her almost since the day she'd met him. She'd driven out from Louisville to her parents' horse-breeding farm for a quiet evening, only to be told they had a guest, Daniel Rathbourn, unexpectedly residing in the rear bedroom, flat on his back. Coyote, her wolf-gray Arabian, had stumbled on one of the riding paths and thrown him.

Her first question had been for Coyote, but assured of his well-being, she'd gone on to ask— and she could almost hear herself saying again so casually—''Well, who is he, mom?'' tossing her handbag onto a chair as the familiar ambience of the farmhouse pleasantly enfolded her once again.

They had been in the low-ceilinged kitchen, with its huge stone fireplace, the smell of a roast cooking in the oven and the white corrals falling away on the green hills outside; these things never changed. Her plump unhurried mother, who had raised eight children with far less fuss than her husband had his numerous Arabians and Thoroughbreds, said casually to this, "Oh, a really nice Englishman, dear. In New York on business. He flew down here to see daddy's horses—I think with the idea of buying some. Nothing much to look at, but real nice to talk to. Why don't you take him up a dinner tray and say how do y'do?"

Her mother's deceit had been apparent the instant Ravenna kicked open the door with one foot and swung backward with the tray into the cheerful bedroom that had once belonged to her sister Ginia. The man who answered her hello leaned on one elbow and smiled, as darkly handsome as an English movie actor. He didn't quite fill the shoulders of one of her brother's striped pajama tops—but then they were probably Jamie's, and he was playing for the New York Rangers, after all.

The way the Englishman's eyes widened appreciatively left no doubt in Ravenna's mind as to what he thought of *her*. Suddenly conscious that her body curved beautifully in all the right places in her blue pullover and jeans, that her thick mane of hair tumbled like a sensuous red fire down her back and that her cheeks were flushed to a maddeningly similar hue, she stood staring at him. For a moment neither of them had said anything, and then she'd stuttered, "How's your, um...your back?"

"If you think I look bad, you should see the horse," he'd quipped.

Two hours later she'd suddenly remembered she

was supposed to have joined her parents for dinner and reluctantly tore herself away. At the door he called her back and swore he'd never recover from his fall unless she returned to his bedside the next evening. She'd promised with a laugh, even though it meant driving all the way out from her Louisville apartment again.

"An awfully nice man," her mother had said with an impudent grin when she reappeared.

Now, three and a half weeks later, she was engaged to this "awfully nice man"—to her astonishment. At twenty-two she had fielded several proposals and quite a few more propositions and had even survived a few heartbreaks—the usual romantic ups and downs of an attractive vivacious woman. But she hadn't thought she'd settle down for ages yet. The whole thing had been very sudden, but Daniel was going back to England and wanted her to come with him. And he'd been very persuasive.... She found herself impulsively saying yes, wrapped in the pleasant fog that had seen her through those swift weeks in June.

They had flown into New York the previous morning, after announcing their engagement to her family and calling his in England. In just a few hours they would be going on to London and then the next day driving down to Devon—the county next to Cornwall—to meet his mother at Rathbourn Hall. And then of course they would have all summer to get to know each other better and to plan the wedding, returning late in August to be married on the farm, with two of Ravenna's sisters as bridesmaids. Glynis would fly back with them, they hoped.

"Tell me about Jeremy and Luke," she asked suddenly. "I hardly know a thing about your step-brothers."

Daniel paused to brush back a lock of his dark wavy hair, and she resisted the impulse to reach out and touch it. "Jeremy is at the University of London, or was until the end of the term, finishing his second year. A charming brat who always gets his way. Consider yourself warned. Basically a good kid, though." His voice grew sober, and he looked unsettled. "You won't have to worry about Luke. He's in Africa."

"Why would I worry about him?" she asked in surprise.

"Well. . . actually he and I—we don't always get on well. I'll have to tell you about it sometime." He fell silent, his eyes darkening as if he were remembering something, and she waited for him to say more.

"You may not like Luke, darling," he added slowly, reluctantly. "He's not very. . . civilized. It's his rotten temper."

He looked so serious she didn't dare tease him, and her eyes filled with alarm. Then he laughed again, and drew her close enough to kiss on the temple. "But he's away and won't be back for ages. And Jeremy and Glynis, not to mention my totally charming self, will make up for any failings in the Rathbourn family."

All her other questions were put aside as he

checked his watch, then exclaimed that they'd miss their plane unless they hurried.

The taxi ride from Manhattan to Kennedy Airport was the usual reckless jolting experience, with the large yellow vehicle weaving in and out of traffic. Nevertheless Daniel opened his briefcase en route to study the wording of some contract he and his American lawyer had hurriedly drawn up the previous day, something to do with the purchase of the major shares in a New York-based company. Ravenna knew he had originally come to the States with this as his main objective, as well as to check on previous investments and perhaps add to the Rathbourn stables. These matters had received short shrift because of his riding accident—still giving him back trouble—and even more so because of his precipitate courtship of her.

"I'm worried about the wording of this," he mumbled. "I really should give Wallingford a call from the airport. Do you mind? I know it's a frightful bore." He smiled contritely, and she moaned in mock horror.

"Oh, honey, don't call him! You know what a demon he is for business. He'll make us miss our plane."

"Not a chance," he promised, enveloping her in an embrace that lasted until they were well out of the cavernous streets of Manhattan.

"DANIEL RATHBOURN. DANIEL RATHBOURN. Mr. Daniel Rathbourn." The metallic voice echoed through the loudspeaker system at Kennedy International, as cold and impersonal as if it were whistling down from another planet. It invaded the departure lounge where passengers awaited Flight BA178.

It took a moment for the words to sink in.

"Goodness, darling, they're paging you!" Ravenna exclaimed, suddenly releasing his arm. They were gazing out the window at the runways.

"Damn Wallingford!" Daniel spoke so fiercely a few heads turned their way. "I'm sure it's him," he added more softly. "I'll have to check it out, darling."

She watched in dismay as he walked back toward the British Airways desk. True to his word, he hadn't called Wallingford from the airport, but it looked as if they weren't to escape so easily. Ravenna waited tensely, wondering what this lawyer-cum-stockbroker wanted now, when he was aware they were leaving for England at any moment.

She had met him at lunch yesterday, and her impression of him had been of a man whose business is his passion. He seemed to live and breathe ticker tapes, contracts, terms, clauses, percentages...a tall, large-boned man with a face like a steel trap and a mind like one, too. She had left Daniel with him while she shopped on Fifth Avenue, relieved to get away from the cyclonic whirl of facts and figures.

Trying to keep Daniel in sight now, she was oblivious to the appreciative gazes of two husky young men whose eyes lingered on her curvaceous figure in its knitted rose traveling outfit; on her rich coloring and auburn hair, partially caught back in a barrette that allowed a cluster of curls to fall forward over her right shoulder. Despite her elegance, despite her delicately modeled features, there was something fresh and vivid about her, as if she brought with her wherever she went the vibrant outdoor life of the horse farm on which she'd grown up.

But she had eyes only for Daniel, who was gesturing with exasperation into a desk phone. Their flight was due for boarding in the next few minutes, and she was afraid he'd miss the announcement.

To her relief he strode back to her almost at once, tall and commanding in his gray tailored suit. But when he was near enough for her to see the expression on his face, her heart sank: he was frowning.

His words came out in a rush. "You won't believe this, but Wallingford has managed to put a spoke in our wheels, after all. Or someone has. Jayson and Wharton have made a counterbid for those shares, and we've got to revise our whole position and renegotiate immediately if we're to have any chance at them. Wallingford wants me to drive out to New Rochelle and go over everything with him at his place—says he'll put me up tonight in his guest room." He paused, then placed his hands on her shoulders. "I want you to go ahead to London without me."

She stared at him, frozen with disappointment and remembering her joking words in the cab. Finally she found her voice. "But Daniel, I can't!

I've never been to London, let alone England. Can't I go with you to New Rochelle?''

"There's no point, darling. I'll be closeted all day and night with him. Then I'll grab a few hours' sleep in the morning. I'll get the first flight out tomorrow. I know it's damnable, and I hate it as much as you do, but you'll be much more comfortable at Gordon Square."

She bit her lip and took a deep breath. This was not how she'd imagined the flight to England! "I could go back to the Hilton," she said eagerly.

"The most reasonable thing to do is to go to the town house. It's extremely comfortable, and everything will be ready."

"Your suitcases—"

"They're already taking them off the plane. Please, darling."

At his insistence she gave in with an uncertain smile. "All right...I'll fly ahead and wait for you in London. But you'll call me tonight, won't you?" She lifted her eyes, their long sooty lashes framing sapphire pools, and tried to capture his gaze.

Daniel, busily reaching into his pocket to give her a set of keys, merely said, "Of course." He scribbled the address for her on a piece of paper: "42 Gordon Square, Bloomsbury," and she stared at it unseeingly before stuffing it into her purse. It was all so ridiculous.... Then he was kissing her, a hard brief kiss, his hands gripping her shoulders. Their eyes drank in each other for one painful moment. "Give the address to a cabbie at the airport," he instructed, "and I'll see you tomorrow."

Suddenly Ravenna had the distinct impression that flying back and forth across the Atlantic for him was a simple everyday matter, like moving from Brooklyn to Manhattan was for her. She smiled inwardly. She would have to get used to a jet-set husband! Then he kissed her again, more passionately, and finally turned to walk away. From the back he could be any handsome stranger in an airport, she thought uneasily.... The boarding announcement came crackling through, and she was being swept along with everyone else toward her plane.

ABOUT EIGHT HOURS LATER, somewhat bewildered and very tired, she stood on unfamiliar steps in Gordon Square before a white door with a fanlight window and a triangular pediment above it. The cabbie had told her this was the famous Bloomsbury district and that the writer Virginia Stephen had lived in this very square before her marriage to Leonard Woolf; she had mumbled something in response that sounded as if she were properly impressed. Now she looked up and down the square, surprised to see that the Rathbourn town house was really what they called a row house back home, although its unmistakable air of antiquity and elegance outdid anything she'd ever seen in her native Louisville.

The key refused to work, and she frowned, struggling to see in the deepening dusk. "Number 42," a brass plate said; surely this was the right house!

Lights softly illuminated the interior, casting a warm intimate glow through the apricot-colored drapes on the ground floor and also from one of the rooms above, a bedroom, perhaps. Why was the house all lit up like this, as if someone were already comfortably installed?

But then she remembered Daniel had cabled ahead yesterday to a woman named Annie, to come in and prepare the house for their overnight stay. She was supposed to return in the morning, as well, to check that everything was all right. At the time these arrangements seemed terribly fussy, but now Ravenna was grateful for them.

Finally she got the key to turn, and she entered a small foyer, its paneled walls hung with architectural prints from the nineteenth century. She would take a better look at them the following day, she decided, when she was not so exhausted. She started as she caught sight of herself in the large oval mirror opposite the door. Her eyes were dark with tiredness, her red curls threatened to tumble from their clasp at any moment and her skin, milk white, was drained of its usual honey color. On the plane she'd tried to sleep, but she'd been unable to relax completely. She'd achieved no more than a fitful doze, awaking whenever the flight attendants made yet another announcement.

As she gazed through the open hall doorway into a richly furnished living room in shades of apricot and cream, she imagined Daniel at her side saying, "Well, Ravenna, how do you like it? Let me get you a drink, darling...what will you have?" He'd bring the luggage in and set it at the bottom of the stairs....

She shrugged back her fierce disappointment and entered the lamplit interior, dimly aware of comfortable sofas, graceful antique chairs and tables—and of three thoughts that swam in her befuddled head. "I want a drink, a bath and bed...in that order," she said aloud softly.

She recalled her suitcases and brought them into the foyer, turning the lock in the door behind her. It seemed sensible to leave them right where they were, except for the small overnight piece containing her nightclothes. Even it felt excessively heavy as she searched for the stairs to the second floor, which she discovered at the end of a central hall off the foyer. Feeling foolishly like an invader, she began to mount the carpeted treads. A light had been lit in the hall above by the thoughtful Annie, she supposed.

Halfway up she abruptly turned and went back down again. She might as well locate the liquor cabinet first; it would be downstairs, of course. A sherry would relax her keyed-up nerves and help her to sleep. She had no intention of staring into the dark for hours, counting English sheep.

On the third try she found row upon row of liqueurs and spirits, flanked by several mixes, in a gleaming cherrywood cabinet. Daniel certainly kept the place well-stocked, however seldom he came there. A pang went through her again at the thought of him, far away in New York, closeted with Wallingford, when he should be in London with her,

toasting their arrival. She was beginning to wish he
didn't take his job as manager of the Rathbourn interests so seriously! Automatically she poured her
sherry, then reached to put away the half-empty
bottle of whiskey sitting on top of the cabinet;
Annie must have left it out for Daniel. It was nice of
her, but whiskey wasn't his drink.

Trailing her green trench coat, her suitcase
grasped in one hand and the glass of sherry bal-
anced in the other, she again climbed the stairs in
silence, uneasily aware that she could have heard a
pin drop. No, she corrected herself, she couldn't
have; not with all that carpeting.

On the second floor she located the bathroom
and, without investigating further, set her case
down inside the door and flicked on the light
switch; an explosion of glitter forced her to blink.
Numerous recessed lights picked out the topaz-and-
gold decor with its dark brown fittings. Everything
was in harmony, down to the matching tawny
towels. A masculine decor like that in the hallway,
she decided, rich but decidedly masculine. If she
and Daniel were to live there, instead of in Devon,
she would want to add a few feminine notes. But all
that was still undecided. Daniel had merely said
they would spend a part of each year in Devon and
the rest in London. She assumed he meant in Gordon Square, but somehow she'd forgotten to ask
again.

She opened the medicine cabinet. A man's shaving gear sat neatly on the first shelf, and she wondered when Daniel had last used it. More than a

month ago, for that was when he'd come to the States. Imagine having a shaving kit in London, one in New York and probably another in Devon, too! She would never get used to it all.

Out of habit she closed the heavy bathroom door before she stripped down, shedding her clothes with relief. She found a bottle of scent on a shelf and poured some liberally into her bathwater, then lowered herself gratefully into its warmth, eyes closing in pleasure.

If only Daniel were here, she thought again. Perhaps this night they might have become lovers, since his back was on the mend.... It seemed natural they would want to share their love in every way from the start.

But instead Daniel was spending the night with his stockbroker! She smiled at this, then sighed, easing more deeply into the tub and thinking how the month had flown past. Those long bedside talks while he was an enforced guest at her parents' farm, the candlelit dinners and theater nights later...and then his sudden proposal over a drink at her Louisville apartment. It was amazing how quickly she had taken this step that was about to change her whole life....

She sat up with a start. She had almost drifted off, with the now empty sherry glass poised dangerously near the edge of the tub. Quickly she got to her feet, the froth of bath bubbles sliding down her full high breasts and long slender legs. Her figure had made many people ask her if she was a dancer, but it also gave her trouble with the more forward male students at her college teaching job. Grabbing a huge towel off a shelf, she rubbed herself down, then wrapped it tightly around her, stumbling sleepily into the hall. She remembered her overnight case and returned to extract a silk nightgown of midnight blue, slipping its feathery lightness over her head.

Leaving the case there but gathering up her abandoned coat, she again stepped into the hall. The wider door at the end of the corridor would be a bedroom, she supposed. Soundlessly she padded toward it, swung it open and entered a spacious darkened room. Odd, but she'd thought she'd seen a light from those windows earlier as she'd stood on the steps. Now the room was as black as pitch. Her eyes must have played tricks on her.

In the center she could make out a large inviting bed covered with a dark spread. She loosened her hair from its catch, feeling it fall like a soft curtain down her back, and closed the door behind her.

She wanted only to collapse. The sherry and bath had done their work well, and as soon as she climbed into the wide bed and pulled the covers over her, her eyes closed. The velvet darkness drew around her, then receded, as she slipped pleasantly into a dream.

But the dream suddenly changed. Something heavy in it was pinning her down, and she became wholly awake again, too astonished to do anything but lie there.

An arm had been flung across her, pressing her into the bed. She gasped in astonishment, unable to believe it as a man groaned in his sleep. But when two strong arms closed around her and a voice murmured softly in her ear, she opened her mouth in sheer terror, about to scream but unable to find her voice. The arms pulled her closer to a length of male body, and she realized with a shock that her face was being drawn tightly against a hard naked chest, so tightly she could hardly breathe, let alone cry out.

She struggled to free herself as the man's lips moved in her hair, caressingly yet with the heaviness of sleep. It couldn't be happening; it couldn't. And then she had yanked one arm away and was pushing against his chest, her mouth as dry as sawdust with fear. She tried to scream at him to stop, but the sounds choked in her throat.

She could smell whiskey on his breath...the whiskey from downstairs, she realized in a flash. A sudden spurt of anger lent furious strength to her arms, and all fear drained away as she twisted her face from him and exploded, "For God's sake, let me go!"

There was a moment of electric stillness, neither of them daring to move or breathe as the man in turn came fully awake. He lifted his head, though he still pinned her closely to his chest. Then with one hand he reached out and flicked on a bedside lamp.

"What the devil!" he breathed. "Who are you?" He looked down at her as if he thought he was dreaming.

She stared into gray blue eyes opened wide with

astonishment inches from her own and set in a sun-bronzed face so devastatingly attractive that she fleetingly wished she had met him under any circumstances but these. He was a man in his mid-thirties, about Daniel's age. Tousled hair the color of sand on a beach and slightly curling fell forward on his forehead; his disarray and his sleep-filled eyes revealed to her that he'd been acting in a half-conscious state, as though he'd thought she was someone else—perhaps a girl friend he was used to finding in his bed.

"You're drunk!" she finally spat at him. "And will you please release me!"

The look that flashed across his face, of intelligence and reserve, told her suddenly that this man was no more drunk than she was. But that made him potentially much more dangerous.

He moved away from her, and held her at arm's length, so that at least her hands were free. Instinctively, primitively, she struck out at him, until he gripped both her wrists in one hand, while with the other he forced her to face him.

"Who the hell are you, and to what do I owe your presence in my bedroom... in my bed, for that matter?" His deep voice was slow honey, and his eyes glittered dangerously, no longer gray blue but almost silver now in the lamplight. Their cool hard gaze, so self-possessed and in control, frightened her even more than had the abandon of his half sleep.

"I...I thought this was...42 Gordon Square, that the house was...empty."

"How did you get in?"

"I...have a key. My name is Ravenna Jones, and...." Suddenly she was lost for words as she stared into the close intimacy of his eyes, still only inches from hers as he leaned on the pillow beside her.

"And...?" he prompted, his sculptured lips distractingly near.

She closed her eyes in an effort to blot him out, feeling frightened again; the situation was unbelievable. She had to think fast. "I...I must have come to the wrong house," she mumbled, struggling against the pressure of his hands. "If you'll just let me—"

"But you have a key. Perhaps it *is* the right house. Perhaps...it's even the right bed," he added, his voice amused. He forced her to be still again by tightening his grip.

"What do you mean?"

He said nothing, but his eyes had darkened and strayed to her lips.

"If you don't let me go, I'll scream bloody murder," she ground out furiously.

He stared down at her, laughter leaping into his eyes. "I don't advise it, but go ahead."

She opened her mouth to yell, and in one sudden movement he had pulled her half on top of him and was kissing her hard and expertly. One arm pressed her waist and breasts against his chest, the other drew her head down to his. The whole move was so fast she'd had no time for thought. His tongue was stirring her senses with slumberous ease when she cruelly brought her teeth down on his lip and tasted blood.

He pulled her head back sharply, his hand tangled in her thick hair. "I deserved that, I suppose, but in return...." He leaned over her half-threateningly as he lifted her back against the pillows, holding her hands lightly in his own, their entwined fingers caught in the spread of her hair.

She stared up at him, forgetting to struggle as he murmured, "Damn it, but you're beautiful! I don't really care *who* you are." His eyes held hers, and the clean male scent of him was in her breath, stirring her, frightening her.

"Please," she begged, "please don't...."

His eyes softened, and he released her hands. She could hear her heart beating very loudly as they looked at each other for what seemed an eternity, until she felt herself hypnotized by the gray blue depths of his eyes. They seemed to gather her in, and she felt herself falling, drowning, all thought gone from her.

He bent and kissed her then very gently on the lips. When he looked at her again, desire was written in every line of his finely chiseled face.

"Don't..." she begged once more, but his mouth moved back to hers, sensuously tracing her lips, inviting them to open to him.

She didn't know if it was the darkness, her exhaustion or the strangeness of it all, but she seemed to hang suspended in time. Then in a dream her lips parted and his mouth was on hers, hard, sensual, demanding a response. She felt his arms meld her close to him, and threads of desire leaped in her limbs like fires flickering quietly awake. The pressure of his tongue twining with hers, invading her, filled her senses as he kissed her deeply, searingly.

The kiss seemed to go on forever, dissolving her rational mind, melting her will—until at some point, without meaning to, she began to kiss him back, tentatively at first, then with a growing fierceness, a feverishness—the intensity mounting between them until she heard him groan and knew that he had lowered his mouth to her throat, to the hollow between the soft fullness of her breasts.

He stopped, his lips pressed burningly against her flesh, and of their own volition her hands tangled in his curling hair. Some faint faraway voice in her head whispered disturbingly that this was impossible, could not happen, but the voice was like a leaf before a storm. No one had ever kissed her like this, not even Daniel... and for a hushed moment they lay like that, wonderingly.

Then he was molding her insistently to his body, lifting her against him, while her arms reached for the strong hard muscles of his back, his mouth hungrily seeking hers, and she was drowning, drowning....

A strange irritating sound penetrated her swirling senses. It came down a tunnel from far, far away.

In an instant the man froze and lifted his head. She opened her eyes and saw the sleepy eroticism melt from his gaze. A dry sardonic voice from another world shocked her into wakefulness. "It's the phone. It can't be for me. Perhaps it's for you?''

Her cheeks flaming, she tore herself from his arms and looked around her, reality crowding back to her. She had forgotten everything, even where she was, and the room rocked strangely into view again. Then she saw a telephone on a bedside table; it rang insistently, almost angrily.

Daniel. Daniel had said he would call her. *Please don't hang up,* she prayed. *Please don't hang up.* She scrambled for the receiver, falling across the bed in her eagerness and grabbing it off the hook with a gasp. One strap of her sheer nightgown had fallen down her arm, and she struggled to rearrange herself, curtaining her breasts by swinging her thick hair forward.

"Daniel!" she cried, her eyes glued on the man who watched her from the other side of the bed. She saw him flinch as if she'd struck him. Then he turned on his back and lay facing the ceiling as if she weren't there.

With deep relief she heard Daniel's voice at the New York end of the line. "Ravenna? What's wrong? You sound like you've been running."

"I . . . I ran for the phone," she said, aware of the mocking expression that crossed the man's face at this. She started to shake with fatigue and reaction, noticing with amazement that the hands on the bedside clock pointed to just before midnight; she'd thought it was much later.

"Well, how do you like the house? Was the flight all right?"

"The flight? The house?" Her voice rose, the sounds slowly shaping in her mind to form words, and she forced herself to speak more calmly. "I—I think the house is lovely, Daniel. And the flight was fine."

The man reached for a pack of cigarettes on the night table, lit one, then swung his legs out of the bed, his torso clearly naked. Afraid to see more, she turned her gaze primly to the opposite wall, feeling sick as the reality of the past half hour or so came to her. What if Daniel hadn't called? She sensed when the man moved across the room toward an upholstered armchair. Visible in the lamplight were his clothes, carelessly flung across it.

"Daniel, I—"

He interrupted her hurriedly, a note of guilt in his voice, "Look, Ravenna, I have more bad news. I have to tell you—"

Her voice exploded in anger as the man came into view, gray trousers now covering his long muscular legs and lean hips. But his chest was still bare, revealing the soft tangle of sandy hair she had felt her face press against so recently. His eyes collided with hers, their gray depths masked with sarcasm.

"Well, I have something to tell you, too! There's a man here, Daniel. Who is he? What's he doing in your house?"

There was silence at the other end of the line.

"Daniel. . .?" she said uncertainly.

"I never said it was my house," his voice came through in shocked surprise. "It belongs to the estate. What does he look like?'' This, in tones strangely unlike those of the Daniel she knew.

Ravenna unconsciously studied the man as she said slowly, ''Tall, lean, hair a sand blond, gray eyes....''

The eyes mocked her as she stumbled over her litany.

''He looks slightly like you, in fact,'' she almost snapped, nerves at breaking point, ''except he's not dark.''

''Damn.'' So softly did Daniel breathe this syllable that she was uncertain if she'd really heard it. Then he ground out, ''What's he doing back without telling me!''

''*Who* is back without telling you, Daniel,'' she asked, wanting to scream.

Again a pause. Then, ''Luke.''

''Luke?''

An eyebrow raised across from her, wearily almost. Then the man nodded as if acknowledging an introduction.

''My stepbrother,'' Daniel said.

''You mean your *brother*?''

''My *step*brother,'' he repeated, emphasizing the first part of the word.

''But you said he was in Africa!''

''Yes, so I did.''

Ravenna was silent, and her gaze, which had flown again to the man, dropped from his face as color spread across her own. So this was Luke Rathbourn! The thought was swept away by another: Luke would soon be her brother-in-law. The agony of her position hit her at once; he had been making love to her. In her exhaustion she had been tangled in some sort of sensual web he had woven around her. Now that she'd come to her senses she wanted never to see him again, and instead she would have to face him for the rest of her life. She wished suddenly she could drop through the floor.

"Did Annie tell him we were expected?" Daniel's voice cut through her thoughts.

"I don't know—"

Again Daniel interrupted her. "Put him on the phone, darling." It was a command, and wordlessly she held the receiver toward her silent companion.

"I don't want to talk to him," Luke said clearly in his deep voice, so clearly she knew he meant Daniel to hear. "As far as I'm concerned Daniel can go to hell...if they'll let him in, that is." He turned abruptly and picked up a shirt from the chair. Slowly, mechanically, he buttoned it, his face averted from hers.

"Daniel, he doesn't want to talk to you. What... what should I do?"

"What do you mean, what should you do?" Daniel's irritation at Luke's refusal crackled on the line. Then his voice softened, "Go upstairs to bed, Ravenna, and then drive down to Devon tomorrow. I won't be joining you as soon as I'd hoped. Wallingford needs me on the contract for a few more days."

A small cry escaped her at this.

"I'm sorry, darling, you know how I hate to do

it. But I can't leave Wallingford with this mess. It wouldn't be fair. Please be patient just a little longer.''

She closed her eyes. At least he thought they were still downstairs, not upstairs in the intimacy of the master bedroom.

"One thing, Ravenna. I'll tell you about Luke when I see you. Don't...ask him too many questions. I'm sure we'll be seeing him later at Rathbourn."

She heard his voice go on, explaining how she could rent a car near Piccadilly, road map included; how easy it would be to drive to Devon on the Bristol Road; how he would call ahead to Glynis and prepare her.... Her face must have registered her dismay at what she felt as Daniel's abandonment, for Luke was watching her closely now, drawing on his cigarette. His eyes were still, but she caught a glimpse of piercing intelligence and knew he was assessing her. She experienced an angry desire to ask him exactly what his thoughts were.

"Ravenna! Drive carefully and I'll call you at Rathbourn in a day or two. I love you, darling."

He was going to hang up. Desperately she clutched the phone. "Don't go, Daniel! I mean, I'm not sure of...of everything yet."

He sighed, and she remembered how much he had on his mind and how he must be as tired as she was. "Don't be silly, I'll be with you in no time at all. I promise, darling. Goodbye." But he paused before he hung up, and she knew he was waiting for her to say, "I love you." Somehow the words stuck in her throat with Luke in the room.

"Goodbye, Daniel," she managed in a low voice. She dropped the receiver into place and stared at it, chilled. Daniel was on the other side of the ocean when she most needed him, and she couldn't even tell him *why* she needed him.

When she looked up, she was surprised to see Luke's eyes still on her, his gaze speculative. "My charming stepbrother. I should have guessed." His voice and manner had become very cold.

"Guessed what?"

She was shocked at the scorn with which he bit off the next words. "Another of his women!"

In one motion she was on her feet, pulling the bedspread dramatically in front of her as his eyes flashed appreciation of the thin nightgown she wore. Her southern blood boiled, and she flung back her head, her red hair flying around her. "What exactly do you mean by that? For your information I am *engaged* to Daniel. We're going to be married at the end of August."

His intense reaction gave her some satisfaction after the slander of his remark against her and Daniel. His whole body jerked upright in the armchair with amazement, and he exclaimed, "Married?" before his face quickly became smoothed of all feeling.

"Yes...at the end...at the end of summer," she repeated, feeling wretchedly helpless again at the thought of Daniel so far away.

He stood then, moving toward the door and trail-

ing his coat jacket carelessly in his left hand. With
his fingers gripping the doorknob, he turned and
made a small ironic bow. "Forgive me—" his voice
came like Arctic frost "—but I'm not quite up to
welcoming you into the family. Perhaps I should
offer you my...condolences, instead."

"I'm not exactly thrilled to find you'll be my
brother-in-law!"

"Oh?" In two long strides he closed the space
between them. "And just what kind of relationship
would you prefer?" he asked softly.

His gaze, sardonic now, traveled over the bedspread she still clutched in front of her, as if he were
debating whether to tear it away. She blanched. He
couldn't, he wouldn't, dare touch her now.

"Leave me alone," she said flatly.

He leaned toward her for a moment, an inscru-
table expression in the shadowed pools of his eyes,
but made no move to touch her. For a frozen instant they stood there, and she was terrified of the
struggle she sensed in his immobility. Then he
stalked to the door and said with surprising bitterness, "For both our sakes, I suggest you lock this
tonight. I'll be sleeping in the room at the other end
of the hall, and I don't want to be tempted—beyond sanity—again."

He dragged the door closed so quickly she felt it
would be wrenched off its hinges, and she rushed to
lock it behind him. As she fumbled with the catch,
she heard his harsh intake of breath and knew that
only when the lock fell in place did he move down
the hall.

She leaned against the door as the memory of his kisses came at her like a blow, and hot shame enveloped her. Then she moved to the bed, exhaustion churning within her, mixed with bewilderment and anger. Anger at herself, at Daniel, at Luke, at the whole impossible situation. But she couldn't resolve things now. For now she wanted only the escape of sleep...or a good hard ride on Coyote. But Kentucky was thousands of miles away.

CHAPTER TWO

A SEA OF GOLD AND AMBER washed over Ravenna when she opened her eyes—the midmorning sunlight filtering through the brocaded drapes. The light transformed the intimate interior of the previous night into a bright, richly furnished room with sofa and matching chairs, antique bureau and writing desk—the carpet and fabrics all in the warm golden shades that echoed through the rooms below. Refreshed by a deep sleep, Ravenna took time to sit up, uncertain of her bearings.

Suddenly she remembered. A man named Luke, whom she knew next to nothing about, had held her in his arms, kissing her passionately; she could still feel the imprint of his body on hers as surely as if he had just left her. Her cheeks flamed as the sensations flooded back, sensations more intense than any man had yet aroused in her. But she was engaged to Daniel, and therefore had broken a trust. Yet it was Daniel who had sent her ahead to wait for him. If he'd let her stay with him in New York, none of this would have happened.

Anger replaced the wave of shame that burned within her. No, it had not been her fault; it had all been a ghastly mistake. Still, Luke's mysterious bitter treatment of her had made her feel to blame for the entire fiasco. It was grossly unfair.

She flung the bedcovers aside, wondering if he was still in the house. Chances were good, she told herself, that he would have left, not wanting to face her after the embarrassment of the previous night. Surely he'd have the sense to spare both their feelings?

A knock at the bedroom door made her momentarily stop breathing. "Miss?" a woman's soft voice called. "Miss? I've brought you some tea."

Hurriedly she rushed to the closet and rummaged inside for a robe, her hand alighting on a dark blue one that might be Luke's or Daniel's. She didn't care whose it was, since her own was still languishing in her case in the bathroom. She flung the garment on, then unlocked the door, aghast at having to do so. What would the woman think of her?

But the plump, middle-aged figure with the pleasantly plain face, holding a tea tray outside her door, didn't flick an eyelash as she said with a warm smile, "Sir Anthony thought you'd like to start with a cup of tea before coming downstairs. Oh, and my name is Annie, miss."

"How do you do," Ravenna said, wondering who on earth Sir Anthony was. Hadn't she had enough surprises?

"He said you wasn't to hurry down, either, seeing you had such a difficult night."

"That's very kind of him, Annie." Her voice was dry. Sir Anthony had to be Luke—although she had no idea why he'd suddenly acquired a title.

At the sound of her American accent, the woman looked at her curiously. Then she strode over to the drapes, reaching with short arms to pull them back from the filmy sheers beneath. "London's looking very lovely this morning," she said, then paused. "I hear Mr. Daniel was delayed. Is he still in New York?"

"Yes," Ravenna answered, sitting down in one of the armchairs to drink her delicious tea. "I'll be driving down to Rathbourn today, and he'll join me there later this week. By the way, Annie, had you told...Sir Anthony...that we were expected last night?"

"Why, no. He arrived after I left, unexpected like. No one was thinking he'd be back from Africa until the fall. I was that surprised to see him this morning!"

"But wouldn't the house have been prepared for Mr. Rathbourn and me when he arrived? Surely he'd guess someone was coming?"

"I don't know, miss. I just come in every week to clean, and I always leave a few lights on so the house won't get burglarized. He might think nothing of it. Was he surprised to see you?"

"Yes, he surely was." The understatement of the year. But at least that cleared up part of the misunderstanding. She must have given Luke quite a shock last night.

"Can I do anything for you before you leave for Devon?" Annie asked. "Any clothes to be ironed or the like?"

"Perhaps a skirt, thank you, Annie—the blue

one from my overnight case in the bathroom. Then I'll be on my way."

"Oh. . . you can't go that long way without a bite to eat! You'll be on the road more than five hours. I've made breakfast, and it's keeping warm downstairs."

At her anxious face Ravenna said hurriedly, "Oh, of course. That's very kind of you. I'll be down as soon as I dress."

Annie disappeared to iron the skirt, leaving her to drink her tea. Ravenna was surprised Luke had thought to send it up; she wouldn't have given him credit for a kind bone in his body. But at thoughts of his body she concentrated firmly on her tea.

By the time she'd finished it her skirt was ready, and Ravenna proceeded to dress, pairing the skirt with a white angora sweater, since the weather had been much fresher the previous night than what she was used to back home at the beginning of July. She applied her light makeup in the nearby bathroom, noting how her wide blue eyes still held a wary look after last night's confrontation.

Well, she would freeze Luke if she had to put up with even a moment of his presence this morning. He'd taken advantage of her situation the night before in the most ungallant way and deserved nothing less. At this she twisted, with unusual savagery, her long riotous curls into a tight chignon, pleased at the resulting look—sophisticated, almost mature really. It gave her courage.

Finally, taking a deep breath, she headed for the stairs. This had to be got over with sooner or later, for Luke was to be her brother-in-law. She was bound to see him more or less regularly during her married life, perhaps even in the two months before the wedding. She hoped it would be less.

The kitchen was at the back of the house, and as she pushed open the door leading to it, she saw that beyond the modern shelves and appliances, facing a wall of glass that overlooked a colorful flower garden and a patch of green lawn, was an alcove containing a round oak table and chairs. Beside these stood a sideboard laden with chafing dishes. In one of the chairs sat Luke, a newspaper hiding most of him from view. He lowered the paper as her heeled sandals on the slate floor announced her arrival.

"Good morning," he said, his face a perfect mask. "Did you sleep well?"

Ravenna took in the fact that there was no sarcasm in his question, that he was dressed in a black turtleneck and gray pants and that the face meeting her gaze was as shockingly handsome as she remembered. His sea-gray eyes faltered ever so slightly before she spoke, as if he in turn were not unaffected by the sight of her. Then the mask was back in place.

"Yes, I slept well," she said shortly.

He motioned her to one of the chairs. "Please join me. Annie has outdone herself with hot toast, eggs, kippers, bacon...."

"I'm not hungry. I'll just take a coffee upstairs." Abruptly she made a move backward as if to leave.

"Come, Miss Jones. We're a civilized people here

in England. There's no need to starve yourself because of the company—I'm considerably less dangerous in the morning." His eyebrows lifted. "Sit down."

This was issued as an order, and she stood there stubbornly a moment longer before she admitted to herself she was hungry. Finally she seated herself as far away from him as she could—which was not nearly far enough.

"May I help you to some eggs?" he asked very politely.

"Toast and coffee will be fine, thank you." She knew she was avoiding his eyes, hoping that the formality of his manner would continue and that he would make no mention of the previous night. It seemed the easiest solution.

He stood up and went over to the sideboard, and she took the opportunity to study his back. He was tall and broad shouldered, like Daniel—perhaps a bit taller—and, as she'd guessed earlier, about the same age. His sand-colored hair curled down into his collar, and the long lines of his muscled back which tapered to slim hips, were evident under the material of his knitted jersey. Memories of the feel of that body awoke in her hands at the sight of him, and she flushed, lowering her eyes quickly when he put a plate in front of her and poured her coffee from a silver pot.

"Cream?" he asked.

"I take it black." Nervousness made her voice higher than usual.

A silence followed as she ate her toast, each bite

seeming to echo in her ears. He buried himself in the paper again, doing nothing to make things easier between them. She found herself staring at the long brown fingers that held the *Times*.

With a sudden crackle of paper he put it aside and said calmly, "I'm sorry if I frightened you last night." His eyes looked directly into hers, and she saw that he meant it. The angry bitter man of the previous evening was gone, and this momentarily disarmed her.

But only for a moment. "Frightened me! You... you had no right!... You took advantage of a perfectly innocent mistake—"

"I don't apologize for the rest of it," he cut in, a coldness replacing the sincerity of his look. "What did you expect, waking me up like that? I suddenly found myself in bed with an attractive woman... and reacted normally. There was nothing more to it than that. You're not planning to do anything so outdated as accuse me of attempted rape, are you?"

"Mr. Rathbourn!" she said, grasping for dignity.

"Sir Anthony, if you must be formal. Sir Anthony Luke Rathbourn. We mustn't forget the baronetcy, minor title though it be." At this his eyebrows lifted sardonically. Confused, she bit back her retort.

"Look, Miss Jones. You were the one who presented yourself in my bed last night—quite an *unexpected* pleasure, I might add—and it would have been very inhospitable of me to throw you out." His eyes bored into hers. "And as for certain biological urges we all feel under such trying circumstances... I'm sure they're nothing new to a woman of your attractions." He turned back to his paper again, as if dismissing her.

A horrible urge to fling her coffee at him swept over her, she was so angry. She stood up, spluttering, "Why... you low-down..." but she caught herself and tempered this to "You... you're no gentleman. I don't care who you are. Daniel will—" She stopped as the paper was slowly lowered and several emotions flickered across his chiseled face in lightning sequence: surprise, annoyance, a mocking amusement.

"What exactly do you mean by that? That you intend to tell him how hotly you kissed me, how eagerly you returned my embraces? Do you think that's entirely wise?"

Her hand darted for her cup in a spasm of fury, and the next moment he was on his feet, gripping her wrist and turning her toward him with a rough grasp.

"Miss Jones—" his words glided like satin "—as I said last night, I don't advise it."

"You're hurting me," she whispered, afraid of the look in his eyes. His face made an infinitesimal move nearer to hers, and she felt the hot anger between them switch to a current that reminded her dangerously of the previous night's embraces. His hands—on her wrist and beneath her chin—burned into her, and she saw his eyes smolder and darken as his gaze fell to her lips. A breathless stirred moment hung between them—and then he swore under his breath, releasing her so quickly she stayed poised an instant longer, her head twisted awkwardly.

"I'm sorry," he breathed. A neutral expression slid over his features, all emotion erased as he sat down at his place again.

"That's two apologies in one morning," he added casually.

"Sir Anthony—"

"Luke," he interrupted. She was silent as he waited, both of them staring at each other.

"Luke, then," she finally said, trying to make her voice calm and reasonable, though his steady gaze distracted her so, that she went blank for a moment.

"Yes?" he said, smiling at her now.

"Can't we call a truce? I regret last night as much as you do. It should never have happened."

His smile deepened, his voice slightly choked, and she realized he was laughing at her. "I don't think my regret compares very well with yours. But a truce does seem in order." He took a sip of his coffee.

"Yes," she said. "After all, you're going to be my brother-in-law. Daniel—"

"*Step*brother-in-law," he corrected, emphasizing the first syllable as Daniel had done. "And I prefer not to discuss Daniel with you, Miss Jones."

"Oh, for heaven's sake!" she exclaimed. "Stop calling me 'Miss Jones.' My name is Ravenna."

"I preferred our introduction of last night," he murmured so mockingly that she blushed. **Again** the smile came to his lips, as if he enjoyed her distress.

"Please." She was determined to say everything on her mind now that they'd gone this far. "I want to forget last night. I'm engaged to Daniel, and what happened between us was owing to extreme exhaustion...."

Luke looked up skeptically as she continued. "And it was all a ridiculous mistake. Of course, you...you wouldn't...." She let her sentence trail off, unable to finish it. She was aware he was very quiet.

The pause lengthened. Then he said slowly, "Oh, naturally, Daniel will never know. Noblesse oblige and all that. Although if it was really as inconsequential as you say—"

"Daniel wouldn't understand!" she burst out.

"No, I don't think a fiancé would." His voice was very cold, again with that unwarranted undercurrent of bitterness. He stood up so quickly he jolted the table before turning his back to her and moving to a position by the glass doors leading to the garden. He lit a cigarette and was silent as she finished her toast.

Cautiously she regarded the forbidding set of those wide shoulders, feeling a sharp regret at their ridiculous sparring. But it was instinctive; he aroused a powerful irritation in her, one she'd never experienced. The fact that she couldn't read him easily didn't help—it only angered her at the same time that it intrigued her. Well, what choice did she have but to battle him? Their unfortunate beginning had seen to that...a beginning he was doing nothing to amend today.

And Daniel...why had he said Luke would be in Africa? Why wasn't he at her side now? Last night had been his fault in a way. *Coward*, she corrected herself. Blaming Daniel was just too convenient.

"What are you doing today?" Luke asked abruptly, turning from the window.

Her eyes flew to his in surprise. "I'm driving to Devon, to your family estate. Glynis is expecting me."

"Rathbourn? By yourself? Aren't you waiting for Daniel?"

"He asked me to go on ahead. He's...tied up in New York on unexpected business."

"And I suppose you've never driven on the left-hand side of the road?" he guessed, his words peculiarly hard, his eyes on the cigarette he was grinding into an ashtray.

"I've never been overseas before," she confessed, afraid to show she was nervous about the drive ahead.

Without a word he strode from the kitchen, and a moment later she heard him on the phone at the other end of the hall, his words indecipherable. His departure brought her back to thoughts of her own. She had to begin preparations for her long unnerving drive, which Annie had said would take five hours. That meant that at this rate she wouldn't arrive until nearly four in the afternoon. And first she had to find the car rental place near Piccadilly, wherever that was. A cabbie would take her, surely.

She was tidying the dishes into the sink—she supposed she could have left them for Annie—when Luke reappeared and said crisply, "We're leaving for Devon as soon as you're ready."

"We?" she gasped, almost dropping a saucer.

"Yes, we. I'll drive you down. Otherwise you'll never make it out of London." Calmly he lit another cigarette, as if he'd been speaking of the weather.

"I beg your pardon," she said frostily, collecting her wits, "but I insist on driving myself to Devon. and I'm quite capable of finding my way out of London."

He planted himself in front of her and took the saucer from her hand, placing it safely on the countertop. "Oh? Then tell me just exactly where you'll go when you leave Gordon Square?"

"I'll get a road map," she said stubbornly.

"You'll get your things...now. I'm driving you to Devon."

"No!" she almost shouted at him. "I won't let you drive me! I'm—" She stopped. Staring up at him, she was entirely conscious of his height, of his broad shoulders, his luminous eyes and chiseled sensuous mouth. He was standing quite close to her, and she found herself breathing with difficulty. But she could hardly tell him she was frightened of him, that five hours alone with him were five hours too many. "I'm perfectly capable..." she stumbled on.

"Perhaps. But I've already canceled two appointments so I can do this. I was going down tomorrow, and one day's difference won't matter." He looked at his watch. "I'll give you ten minutes to get ready."

Really! The nerve of the man! If he thought she was going to give in to this, he was very much mistaken. She stood there belligerently, her color high, her angry blue eyes locked with his lake-gray ones.

His mouth suddenly twitched. "Ravenna," he drawled as a silvery light rose in his eyes, a light she knew by now meant danger, "if you don't go upstairs and pack this instant...." He closed the small space between them in one swift step, and she moved backward almost as fast. With his eyes impelling her, she dragged her gaze from his and turned and stalked down the hall toward the stairs, fuming. All right! Ten minutes was more than enough time to pack, but he could wait. Yes, she'd make him wait twenty. The fact that this was largely an ineffectual gesture did not seem to matter.

THE DRIVE THROUGH LONDON was easier than she'd expected. Although Luke said he wasn't going to play tour guide, he made a point of going past Hyde Park on the Bayswater side; the park's fresh greenness spread for some miles before them. He also pointed out, with a surprising amount of knowledge, various churches and buildings. Ravenna's exasperation with him slowly dwindled as she was faced with the excitement of actually being in London. Finally, resigned to the long drive and tempted by the luxuriousness of the Lincoln Mark VI—one of the largest cars on the road, she noticed, for most Britishers drove compact models—she leaned back more comfortably against the seat, although every few moments found her upright and craning at the window. She'd felt the same thrill the previous day when the taxi had driven her in from Heathrow, but now Luke's comments gave life to what had been mere views of a very old city.

Later he grew silent, impatient to be out of the traffic and the uninspiring suburbs. He turned onto the A30, and eventually they were in pleasantly wooded countryside. They passed small neat fields separated by green hedges, which reminded her of toy farms after the spreading pastures of Kentucky, and the occasional town or village. The charming houses and cottages were so different from their American counterparts that she longed to stop and explore. But she could see Luke was anxious to get to Rathbourn, and she didn't dare suggest it. Besides, the less time with him, the better.

Finally he broke the silence. "Tell me about yourself."

She turned, surprised into a smile. At last a normal human question. "I'm from Kentucky, near Louisville," she said. "My family breeds race-horses—perhaps you've heard of the Elk Creek Stables?"

"I certainly have. We're interested in your Arabians. Did Daniel buy any?"

"No." She didn't explain what had distracted him from his original purpose but continued. "My father dabbles in local politics when he can tear himself away from his horses."

He grinned. "Somehow I guessed you weren't a

Yankee.'' He said this in such precise Oxford tones that she laughed, realizing her drawl, so normal to her ears, must sound as marked to him as his and Daniel's accent did to her.

"And. . .?" he added as she stopped.

Since he'd set himself the task of being charming, she might as well comply. After all, it would be a long drive, and words would help dispel the tension between them. "Well. . .I grew up there, on the farm, then went to New York University and studied art history. One of my sisters loves art, too, but she's the only real artist in the family, despite the fact that there are eight of us—four boys and four girls. I'm the second youngest. After my degree I returned to Louisville and taught my subject at the local college there the past year." She paused. "I've been planning to research and write a book on eighteenth-century buildings," she added, "and meant to come to England on a two-week research trip in August—but then I met Daniel."

The flash in his eyes told her this interested him. "Art history. And the book? Will you go on with it?"

"Sure. Marriage won't change my interests," she said with asperity.

He ignored her prickly tone. "Did you know there are some beautiful old Georgian manor houses in Devon?"

"Daniel told me about some, and I'd heard of others, of course. He said marrying him would be handy for my research!"

"You can start with Rathbourn itself," he told

her, skipping her mention of Daniel. "The hall was built in the eighteenth century from an earlier Tudor shell. The old kitchen, or part of it, actually dates from the fourteenth."

Impressed by this, she asked curiously, "Do you like old houses?"

He looked at her swiftly, as if puzzled. "Old houses are my business. I'm an architect. And I was born and bred at Rathbourn."

It was her turn to be surprised. Daniel's brother an architect? "I...I had no idea."

"I'm surprised Daniel hasn't filled you in on at least the bare outlines."

"Daniel, in fact, said only that you were in Africa, as I thought you might have guessed from my conversation last night." She spoke casually, concealing her discomfort at this reference to their first encounter.

His jaw tightened. "I suppose I really shouldn't be astonished at anything Daniel does—or doesn't do—these days."

"Do you design new houses?" she asked to change the subject; he'd already made it more than clear there was no love lost between him and Daniel.

"I have, but I prefer to restore old ones, strip then back to earlier periods, de-Victorianize them...." He turned to smile lazily at her. "A process I'd like to inflict on some young women I know."

"I'm sure you know lots of women who are anything but Victorian!" she returned acidly. The blush that comes so easily to redheads followed this, and she saw his mouth quirk at the corners. Damn all complacent men!

Calmly he went on. "I also will be teaching architecture again during the fall and winter terms at AA—that's Architects' Association School, in Bedford Square, conveniently close to Gordon Square."

She was taken aback, realizing that somehow she'd assumed Luke would be in business like Daniel, maybe something to do with gold mines in Africa, that sort of thing. Instead he shared in a different way her interest in houses and even, in part, the career of teaching. She stared out the window at the sun on the green hedgerows as she tried to absorb this new information.

"My professional name is Sir Anthony Rathbourn," Luke said now, his hands lightly guiding the huge car, eyes focused on the road. "Otherwise I avoid the title and go by Luke Rathbourn. Some people find it confusing, but it's often handy to have two personas."

Sir Anthony Rathbourn—where had she heard that name before? She tried not to stop breathing as something triggered in her brain. Then it came to her. Three years earlier, a term paper on English architecture, a required part of her art-history degree. She'd heard of him then, for Sir Anthony was quite a well-known figure in Great Britain in domestic architecture, with historical renovation his specialty. She'd pictured him as a much older man, even white-haired, a sort of brigadier type. Not this breathtaking specimen of manhood who sat so easily beside her. When she'd met Daniel, it had never occurred to her to associate the names...nor had Daniel given her any reason to. Funny, she would have thought he'd be proud of the connection.

She swallowed, unwilling to admit to Luke that she'd heard of one of his "personas." So he was well-known; she wasn't going to be intimidated by the fact, especially after all that had passed between them. Despite her stubborn refusal to acknowledge this, however, she couldn't quite prevent an alteration in her opinion of him. There was certainly more to this man than met the eye. And perhaps still more than Daniel hadn't thought to tell her.

Decisively she turned to Luke and said, "I want to ask you...a favor. Since Daniel isn't arriving in England for the next few days—and I'm sure he meant to fill me in on everything by now—I wonder if you would mind telling me some things about your family?" Again she blushed, feeling humiliated by her ignorance. "I'm going to be meeting your mother so soon—"

"Glynis is not my mother," he cut in. "She's Daniel's. But go ahead."

"You mean...."

The quizzical look on his face told her he was amazed at how little she knew, but he merely said, "I mean that Daniel and I are not blood relations in any way. We'd be half brothers if we were, not stepbrothers. Whereas Jerry is half brother to both of us, born after Glynis married my father."

"I see," she murmured, grateful for this clarification. She was remembering that Daniel had told her his father had died when he was seven and how, after Glynis had married Sir Richard two years later, he'd been adopted officially and become a Rathbourn. Not an easy time for him, he'd added curtly.

"Are you older than Daniel?" she asked curiously.

"I was ten when Glynis came to Rathbourn, and Daniel was nine. Jerry was born about six or seven years later."

Of course Luke had to be older if he'd inherited the title, she suddenly realized. And that probably meant Rathbourn was his, too. Dismayed, she thought how little Daniel had made clear to her, saying only that he managed the business side. Stupidly she'd thought this meant Rathbourn belonged to him or maybe to Glynis. Not that it mattered; she didn't really care where they lived. It was just that she wanted to be informed of it!

As if he were reading her mind, Luke said casually, glancing over at her, "My father left Rathbourn, the title and the real estate to me, and named Daniel agent and business manager in the will. Did he tell you that?"

"Well..." she hesitated. "I know he works for the estate. He did tell me that much." And so he had, including how Sir Richard had groomed him for the position from the time he was a teenager, later sending him to the London School of Economics rather than Cambridge because he had such a head for math and business.

"Daniel works for *me*," Luke corrected, "only we seldom put it that way, seeing as he's officially family and an heir. Certain investments were left to him and Jerry, of course—what's called a portion—and to Glynis, as was only fair. The really major investments support Rathbourn, though, a bloody expensive investment in itself. But my father was always very generous to Daniel. Not to mention Jerry, who's ungratefully trying to fail his course at the U of London right now. A thorn in the family's side is our dear Jerry."

Ravenna tried to disguise her confusion, listening to this calm recital. At the moment Jeremy didn't concern her, but Daniel did. Why had he given her such an unclear picture? Had it been to avoid mention of Luke? Unless, of course, he'd planned to fill her in on the flight over. Well, perhaps he would have.

Guiltily she remembered now that he'd told her not to ask Luke too many questions. She was doing just that.. but she had to know. "Do you live in the London town house, then? Last night you implied it was your house."

"Did I? What a charming memory you have for details." His lazy tones suggested he remembered other things, and Ravenna shifted uncomfortably in her seat. "Yes, it is my house," he continued, "part of the estate, the 'real' property left to me by my father. Old English families have always been reluctant to break up estates in any way, so I was landed with it all. Younger sons used to be stuck with the clergy, the navy or the army. I use the house when

I'm teaching, but I usually summer at Rathbourn. Naturally Glynis stays at Gordon Square when she comes to London. From time to time Daniel may have stayed there, too—I assume he gave you the key—when I was away. I've been gone all this past year.''

"Where were you in Africa?''

"Cairo, Algiers, Cape Town, Lake Victoria... everywhere.''

"A holiday?''

"Partly.'' His laconic reply told her the topic was off bounds for some reason, so she didn't press him.

Other questions clamored to be asked—about Glynis, about Rathbourn. But Ravenna contented herself for the time being with relaxing against the leather seat, her eyes half closed as she felt the effects of jet lag catch up to her again. There would be time enough to uncover all this once Daniel arrived. He probably had every intention of telling her about his family but, in the rush of their courtship and engagement and his business crisis in New York, he had forgotten to do so.

Drowsily she drifted, not quite asleep but pleasantly near it. She was thinking how the hard profile of Luke's face reminded her somewhat of Daniel's: the same straight English nose, the firm jaw, the facial planes that seemed chiseled, sculptured almost. Both men were striking, but Luke's face was less compromising in its lines and angles, more aristocratic, imperious.... Her thoughts floated on sleepily. His ebony lashes, incredibly long, distracted her as they brushed his cheeks from time to time. She watched his lips curl as he slowed down behind an uncertain motorist and muttered something under his breath. She suddenly flushed. In her dreamy state she'd been idly comparing the feel of those firm lips on hers with Daniel's.

"If you don't stop looking at me like that," his voice wedged her awake, "I won't answer for the consequences."

"I wasn't looking at you," she lied.

"No? Then why the charming blush? Redheads are notoriously bad liars." Although his eyes stayed on the road, she could tell by the slight smile on his lips that he was laughing at her again, and she bristled inwardly.

But she refused to be drawn by this, and they were silent until they ran through a small town named Andover. Then he said out of the blue, "The town house is Georgian, too, built in 1732, and there are some fine pieces of furniture in my third-floor study dating from Jacobean times. I'll show it to you sometime, if you like."

"I'd love to see it," she said uncertainly, unwilling to commit herself if it involved spending time with him.

"You shall," he promised. A moment later he added, "Perhaps you might like some advice on Georgian buildings?"

Before she could blurt out that she couldn't possibly impose on him, he quelled her with a brief look and went on, "I'd be glad to give you the run of both my libraries, the one at Rathbourn and the one in London. I have an extensive collection of books on eighteenth-century architecture and interiors that I use in my work—rather hard to come by all in one place, in fact. If you like, I could direct you to some little-known houses and some unusual period detail. Of course, you might prefer to go it alone, but the offer of the libraries is still there."

"Well, that's very generous..." she stalled.

"Unfortunately I wouldn't be around much to help you out, because of my London clients and a house I'm doing in Cornwall. But I think you could be trusted not to walk off with my collections. Interested?"

She was aware that his voice was very casual and his hands on the steering wheel rather tense. But he was offering her a gold mine. To have access to Luke's—no, Sir Anthony's—libraries, most likely superb collections, and possibly his advice on her book was wealth, indeed. Association with Luke, however minor, was another matter. But he'd been tactful enough to mention he'd seldom be around. She turned to him with a smile, her mind made up. "I can't possibly refuse such an offer. As long as you know that I prefer to work in solitude for the most part."

The long fingers on the steering wheel relaxed, unnoticed by her. He said lazily, "There's a room opposite my study, which you're welcome to use. As private as can be. Rathbourn has more rooms than we've ever known what to do with."

They left it at that, and Ravenna secretly crowed

at the opportunity. Having access to specialized collections would make all the difference. Perhaps she might even establish a distant professional relationship with. . . Sir Anthony. She knew beyond a doubt he was eminently qualified to help her, and the professional within her told her she'd be a fool to pass up this chance.

Luke might prove a likable brother-in-law, after all. On that thought she turned to study the rolling countryside. Every tree and hollow seemed to glow with a lush pastoral beauty. . . quite unlike the blue green haze of home.

THEY STOPPED FOR LUNCH in Honiton, a small town, Luke explained, that marked the beginnings of Devonshire. Hills rose steeply to either side of it, sweeping away green and soft, giving a breadth of view she hadn't expected. The town itself was pleasant, with a wide Roman road and a few houses from the Georgian period scattered among newer ones. They caught her eye here and there with the distinctive classicism she so much admired, inspired by the simplicity of Greek architecture. She was filled with a sense of antiquity in this region even more so than in London, a sense that England was a world she'd hardly dreamed existed but one that instinct told her she would love. She was glad, for leaving Kentucky had not been easy.

Given a choice, she insisted on having lunch at an old inn with timbered beams set in stucco, which beckoned from down a street that was hardly more than a lane. The inn's ivy-covered front and pots of flowers were as charming as a movie set from an old British film.

Luke laughed. "It's designed to capture the American tourist. Quite effective, isn't it?"

But there was nothing to criticize in her first taste of Devon cider, cornish pasties—meat enclosed in pastry—followed by fresh berries and the thick clotted cream Devon is famous for. Afterward Luke took her arm and led her to Marwood House, built in 1619 and now an antique shop, to stretch their legs before the drive to Salcombe. He was even patient while she bought an old piece of genuine Honiton lace after he'd told her that lace had been made in the area since medieval times.

"Daniel has no idea how much I'm going to love England!" she enthused as they returned to the car. She didn't see Luke's face as they settled into the Lincoln, but because he'd insisted on paying for lunch, she turned and smiled with genuine warmth. "Thank you, Luke, that was very kind of you." She swallowed her pride and added, "And I suppose I must admit it's also kind of you to drive me to Rathbourn."

His mouth was grim as he faced her. "It's not kindness," he said coldly. "I merely have no interest in seeing you get yourself killed trying to reach my ancestral home while Daniel dallies in New York. The roads are dangerous, as no one knows better than he does."

She turned away, the smile frozen on her face. What had she just said? Luke's profile had taken on a granite edge that shut her out. What a changeable moody man he was, impossible to predict.

For a while she simply stared out the window, and the silence between them grew. Depression settled on her, developing into an uneasiness. She couldn't help but wonder what was in store for her as Daniel's wife if Luke was anywhere in the picture. She wished wryly that she could pronounce a spell and send him back to Africa.

"Exeter's next," she heard him say, breaking the awkwardness. They were bypassing charming villages now with names like Gittisham and Clyst Honiton, but she saw little of them, because her thoughts preoccupied her. In a moment his voice penetrated once again, and she caught him glancing at her.

"Exeter is a cathedral town, which simply means it's famous for its Norman-Gothic church. It was originally a pagan Celtic settlement, then Roman and later Norman."

"Oh?" she said. Her knowledge of early English history was sketchy, and she was interested in what he was saying. Besides, she was glad to have the silence broken.

"Perhaps Daniel—" he stressed his stepbrother's name unpleasantly "—will show you around it sometime." She restrained from commenting on this, although her hackles rose.

They skirted the edge of the city, then turned south. Ravenna lay with her head resting on the back of the seat, her exhaustion suddenly as great as the previous night's. Luke became taciturn again, and she was thankful now; she didn't want to listen to his sarcasm and unfair innuendos against Daniel, and anxiety about her approaching meeting with Glynis filled her.

Once she was aware that he glanced toward her momentarily through lidded eyes, an indecipherable expression in their gray depths. But when she met his gaze, he immediately turned his attention to the road.

"We're almost there," he said.

The weather had swiftly changed in the past half hour, from brilliant sunshine with high scudding clouds to a misty darkening scene that was slightly ominous. Thus Ravenna first saw the long length of Salcombe Harbour as it started to rain. She could imagine it as beautiful, almost Italianate, in sunshine, with its soft, richly wooded hills, but at the moment it was lowering and storm ridden, soon blurred by a silver sheet of rain. By then Luke was concentrating entirely on his driving and Ravenna was sitting tensely beside him.

"You can relax," he said through gritted teeth, his voice sardonic. "I'm a very good driver."

"I didn't mean to—"

"You're sitting there as if ready to jump out the door at any moment."

She half smiled, admitting to herself this was true. "I'm afraid it's not your driving," she confessed. "It's...it's meeting Glynis." Only part of the truth, of course, but she wasn't about to confide in him that she was having fears about the entire line of Rathbourns.

He looked surprised. "Daniel certainly abandoned you to the wolves," he drawled.

"If you mean you, he sure did," she returned dryly.

A swift smile was his only acknowledgment, and then with a curse he turned to the twisting road again. The hills were steep as they headed in the direction of Bolt Head at the end of the harbor.

"Is she like Daniel?"

He said nothing at first, maneuvering another difficult turn on the old road. Then slowly, weighing his words, he replied, "Daniel is like her, yes, in some ways. In other ways not at all."

As noncommittal an answer as could be achieved, she thought skeptically.

Soon they turned aside from Bolt Head and passed a small village that gave way at once to wooded countryside southwest of Salcombe. They came to a gateway flanked by two old stone lions, weathered with age and moss, and Ravenna realized that for some time now a low stone fence had been bordering the roadway, barely visible under the tangle of bushes at the edge of the forest.

Luke pulled to the side of the road and stopped the car, although there was no gate to open. To her immense surprise he reached over and took one of her hands, holding it lightly. His eyes, now disconcertingly gray blue again, looked directly into hers with a concern she was unprepared for. "Are you really nervous?" he asked.

"You bet I am," she flippantly confessed, trying to laugh at herself. A heightened feeling came over her at his touch, and the electricity that had been so pleasantly absent between them for the drive sprang up again, as powerfully as ever. There had been moments in the day when she'd hoped they might become friends, but now, with the magnetism crackling in the short distance from his body to hers, the gray curtain of rain beating down outside the car and the road empty ahead and behind, confusion swelled inside her. It should be Daniel holding her hand, asking her this question in that tone, but it wasn't. Everything was strangely out of kilter—and had been from the moment she'd left New York.

Luke squeezed her hand in a comforting gesture and, before she realized what he meant to do, bent and kissed her lightly—a kiss that merely brushed her forehead, though his eyes hesitated near hers for a second. A brotherly kiss, of course. But she pulled her hand away instinctively and said aloud, "I wish Daniel were here!" All her longing for him filled her voice, mixed with panic at the meeting ahead.

She knew her mistake when Luke's hands came down fiercely on her shoulders, forcing her to face him.

"How long have you known him?" he grated out.

"Almost a month," she gasped. "Long enough to fall in love with him!"

"Not long enough for you to have any idea of what you're doing," he contradicted angrily. For an astonished moment she thought he was going to shake her, like a child who had done something irreparably stupid. Their eyes locked.

The spell broke when he said lightly, mockingly, thrusting her away from him, "Women!" and turned to start the car. His hand on the ignition key, he paused. Again so quickly she had no time to gather her defenses, he swore and turned back, pulling her firmly to him as his mouth came down on hers.

She was taken completely off guard as his tongue claimed hers, stirring her veins to unexpected fire. After the first startled moments her whole body began to battle him in panic, for there was nothing tentative about the kiss. It was aggressive, invasive even, and he was holding her so tightly against him she could hardly breathe. She could feel the steering wheel against her arm, and then her hair partially escaped its chignon as he pressed her back against the seat, his mouth fusing to hers. She felt herself tremble helplessly as a honeyed weakness betrayed her. Once again the taste of him was awakening some unknown depths in her—strange and frightening, mixed with fury...a fury that threatened to dissolve into something far sweeter, far more dangerous.

He lifted his lips for a moment—long enough for her to see a look of astonishment flash in his eyes, as if this were not what he'd meant to do—and then she was twisting her face away from his, clamping her mouth shut, closing her eyes.

"Don't fight me," he whispered. His voice was suddenly soft, tender almost, and her body stilled at the sound of it, as though it had reached a hidden part of her that didn't want to fight him.

Her cheek was crushed against his lips, her mouth buried in his sweater, and very carefully, very slowly, she heard him repeat, "Don't fight me, Ravenna." He held her then for a few moments, his body as still as hers, her breasts crushed between them, until, with infinite softness he trailed his mouth nearer her ear, his tongue finally searching the shell-like curves of it, sending shooting tremors through her limbs. Her very stillness became a torture.

Moving with ineffable care, Luke brushed his mouth sensuously back along her cheek, toward her mouth again, until against her will she turned to him, and his lips burned softly into hers. She was paralyzingly aware that his hands had slid up under her sweater, silkily moving on her bare back with the same deliberation, and that his lips slipped ever lower, trailing fire down her throat to the neck of her square-cut sweater, burning into the rise of her breasts until a smoldering awoke in her, teased and maddened by his slow exploration.

And then he was kissing her on the mouth again, swiftly, deeply, all hesitation gone, with a passion that was destroying her. There was a fierceness to the kiss, a fierceness he had made her crave. In the midst of it she felt herself dissolving, melting into him, the weight of his body pressing her heavily against the seat. Automatically she reached once again to tangle her fingers in his curling hair, drawing him more closely to her, into the dark cocoon of sweetness that swirled around her, and she almost cried aloud when his lips finally parted from hers, so at one did they seem. Her eyes flew open in distress.

"How can you tell me, Ravenna," he said huskily, his storm-gray eyes piercing hers, his mouth maddeningly near the parted lips that helplessly invited his again, "that you belong to Daniel?"

His words stunned her to awareness. For a moment she lay still, her eyes embraced by his but her body registering betrayal, her mind in turmoil. Then she sprang at him, intending to strike him across the face. He grabbed her hand at the last possible instant, his eyes shocked, and she recoiled in astonishment at her own violence. It had come from some deep primitive part of her never touched before.... She dragged her gaze from his, struggling to rearrange her sweater with one hand, the other still gripped by Luke.

"Don't ever try anything like that again, Luke," she finally breathed, still afraid of the expression in his eyes. Her action had obviously been the last thing he'd expected after her melting response to his kiss, and those eyes were no longer gentle.

But her terror was directed at herself, not Luke. What was happening to her? In a spell of madness she'd responded to him just as she had the previous night, and now she had no excuse of tiredness....

His eyes bored into hers as he reached into his pocket and took out the inevitable pack of cigarettes, releasing her to light one. She was shaking as she smoothed her skirt and rearranged her hair, delving into her purse for her makeup, not knowing what to say.

"Ravenna—"

At the sound of his voice, she panicked again, cutting him off before he could go on and using each word like a blow aimed at him in defense. "I want you to know something, Luke. Last night and today mean nothing. Absolutely nothing. A mere biological urge, as you so aptly described it. When we arrive at Rathbourn, apart from necessities such as meals, I hope never to see you again. I want nothing more to do with you, nothing whatsoever. When Daniel comes back...."

He stared at her, and after a moment his face shuttered. "When your beloved fiancé comes back, I'll probably be gone," he drawled.

The silence lengthened. She closed her eyes, willing her body not to lean toward him again. If he so much as reached to touch her.... When she dared look at him again, his lips curled mockingly, the same lips that had drunk so deeply of her own just moments earlier.

She heard him say coldly, ironically, "Until then, patience...my dear Miss Jones."

Sarcasm she could deal with; it meant that she was safe. Abruptly he reached for his keys and started the car, and she sank back against the seat in relief, her hands clenched tightly in her lap.

Neither of them spoke as the road wound on between the tall overreaching trees, until finally the forest gave way to parkland, long sweeping meadows with a few fine old beeches and chestnut trees and clusters of flowering shrubs. In the aftermath of rain, the scene looked otherworldly to her.

Just when she thought they'd never arrive, she saw the house. Around a bend, at the foot of a sweep of smooth green lawn, a rectangular two-story manor of silvery gray stone, startling in its simplicity. There were tall mullioned windows on each of the storys—nine above, and eight below divided by a central doorway. The hipped roof held six dormer windows and four plain chimney stacks; a wide Greek pediment over the central portion of the house dominated the entrance. Despite her distress, Ravenna registered that the total effect was of classical perfection, that the house's austerely symmetrical mass was satisfying in every detail. She gazed in stunned admiration, almost forgetting their quarrel.

Luke said coolly, as if nothing had happened, "Rathbourn Hall. An unknown architect designed it for Lady Anne Rathbourn in 1721." But she saw the hard line melt from his jaw and a light appear in his eyes. A light that said he had come home.

CHAPTER THREE

DESPITE HER RELIEF at their arrival, Ravenna couldn't have imagined a worse strain than the one under which she advanced to meet her future mother-in-law, Lady Glynis. Luke had left her anything but composed, though luckily there was little time to dwell on this. From a distance the house had looked deserted, a sleeping mass of stone, but as soon as the Lincoln pulled up on the circular gravel drive near the entrance, a gray-haired man in a butler's uniform hurried down the steps to assist them. He was obviously moved to see Luke, who spoke warmly to him and then introduced him as Peters. With a courtly nod at her, Peters turned to remove the luggage from the trunk—the boot, he called it—as two young hounds came racing across the lawns like ponies, making a great baying din and leaping to lick Luke's hands; both animals were furiously excited.

"Down, Albion! Gwydion!" Luke protested, and she found herself smiling despite herself; it was exactly like arriving home at Elk Creek, where animals were always underfoot, making an impossible racket.

The dogs quieted as they all entered the house

through wide oak doors that opened onto a huge central hall, at four-thirty already softly lit with wall sconces. On the dark wood paneling gleamed old oil paintings in ornate gilt frames, and Ravenna's eye went to an ancient painted coat of arms that took pride of place at the distant end of the hall over a huge fireplace. Rounded arches opened all along the hall onto spacious rooms, and to the right a staircase rose massively in two broad flights, leading to a balustraded gallery above.

Under one of the archways stood a tall slender woman in a tweed suit, a woman still beautiful in her late fifties, no matter that she was gray-haired. Hers was a beauty largely of bone structure, for her narrow face was delicate, almost exquisite. Her dark brown eyes were intelligent, and there was something of Daniel about her. "You must be Ravenna," she said, stretching out both hands as she approached, her face lit with genuine welcome.

Instantly Ravenna's fears slipped from her, as if they'd never been; one glance from those brown eyes told her she was going to like Glynis. "How do you do," she responded warmly, aware that Luke had moved to her side. Glynis kissed her on the cheek, then leaned up to kiss Luke, also. She was close enough for Ravenna to see little laugh lines around her eyes and to sense something earthy and pleasant about her, mixed with serenity.

"Luke, dear, welcome home. How like you to spring yourself unexpectedly on us! Daniel called to tell me the news, of course. It's a pity he's been delayed." She turned to Ravenna. "You must have been upset. I'm glad Luke could bring you instead."

"Yes, Luke has been. . . very kind," Ravenna replied with difficulty. Luke glanced at her and then away.

Glynis's face mildly registered this as she went on, "We've held back tea for you, although Jeremy swears he's starving—he came down on his motorcycle last weekend, Luke. But you'll want to freshen up first. You both look exhausted."

Ravenna flushed incontrollably, and her gaze flew to Luke's. There was a slight awkward pause.

"Ravenna's still suffering from jet lag," Luke explained abruptly. "And I suppose I am, too. I just arrived from Cairo via Paris yesterday evening."

"You could do with a drink." Glynis's tone was sensible. "Both of you." But first she offered to show Ravenna her room, while Luke turned to help Peters in with the last of the bags.

"I'll start with whiskey in the library, Peters," she heard him say quietly a few moments later as she and Glynis began to mount the stairs.

"Yes, sir." There was a touching deference in Peters's solemn voice, and she wondered what it felt like to come home to all this after an entire year abroad.

But she was occupied with her own experience as Glynis led her upstairs and across the gallery landing, then down a small hall to a white-and-gold room, large and airy, with four great windows that streamed with soft daylight. Window seats set in the thick walls looked over the terrace and gardens at the rear of the house to the woods beyond, and also southwest, where a cleft in some trees revealed a glimpse of blue.

"I didn't know we were this close to the sea," she said, crossing the room to peer out one of the windows.

A four-poster bed hung with brocaded silk that matched the window drapes enchanted her; opposite was a white marble fireplace over which hung a portrait in oils of a woman, a Berthe Morisot, she thought. There was also a white sectional sofa, a Queen Anne writing desk with matching chair and, here and there, white-pottery vases massed with pink roses. On the floor lay an Aubusson carpet in white, blue and gold. Ravenna thought of her apartment in Louisville and smiled; it would have fitted into this one palatial room.

"It's...exquisite, Glynis!" she exclaimed. "I'm going to love being here."

Glynis beamed. "I hope so. The colors are perfect for you—I hope you don't mind me saying so, but you really have the most magnificent hair and eyes. Daniel didn't do you justice when he called me, although he tried hard. Now, if he'd just said you burned like a Roman candle, he would have got closer to the truth!" She paused, then confided, "And I can't tell you how I'm looking forward to having another woman here at Rathbourn. The place has been overrun with males for years."

Ravenna laughed, thinking how her own mother loved it when her four brothers, all of them six-footers and as spirited as her father's horses, poured home for family gatherings and how she sighed with relief when the house emptied again, leaving only her and her husband.

Glynis was explaining that her bedroom was half of a suite. "Daniel's room is opposite—through the bathroom there."

"I suppose you and Luke met at the town house," she continued. "I was surprised to hear he was back so soon, although we've been communicating about Jeremy. His marks, that is. Luke wanted to have him down here to study this summer. I hope he made you comfortable at Gordon Square?"

"I did meet him there." Ravenna turned her face to the window again, ignoring Glynis's last query as if she hadn't heard it. She was trying to blot out the picture of how Luke had made her...comfortable. "I find him very different from Daniel," she added.

"Luke and Daniel are entirely unalike," Glynis agreed crisply, crossing to the white sofa and gesturing to the seat catercorner from her. Ravenna joined her. "Luke has the artistic temperament. He's intense like his father. Sir Richard painted all his life—when he wasn't sitting for parliament. But both Luke and Daniel are very stubborn men, I'm afraid...they have that in common!" She smiled. "I shouldn't be telling you this. I should let you discover all the family's quirks on your own."

"Luke said he was in Africa an entire year," Ravenna persisted, curiosity getting the better of her.

"Yes, he was." Glynis's beautiful eyes grew more sober. "I suppose Daniel explained why? It was very sad, really, Kristen's death. But of course Luke took an unreasonable view of it. Daniel was in no way to blame, and at the time Luke was utterly distraught—"

Ravenna looked so startled Glynis stopped short.

"Daniel hasn't told you about Kristen? Then I'm afraid I've put my foot in it, my dear. Never mind. Make him tell you, it will do him good to talk about it. I don't think he's quite got over it yet. Luke was very unfair to him. Still, I'm sure he feels differently now." Her eyes alighted on the mantel clock, and she started. "Do you mind if I leave you? We can talk again later, but I'd better go and ring for tea or Peters will stew about things getting cold." She paused, smiling. "Take your time coming down. It's not likely Jeremy will expire for want of food." Her eyes twinkled. "The library is at the far end of the great hall, on the left."

She was gone, and Ravenna sat gingerly back on the edge of the sofa, wondering about the story Glynis had begun to relate. Kristen? She was certain Daniel had never mentioned a Kristen. It was a Swedish name, wasn't it? She frowned, seeing a widening gulf filled with more and more questions. Daniel would be barraged, poor man, when he arrived!

An instant later someone who said his name was Garvey appeared with her bags and announced rather formally, "Madam has rung for Mary to unpack for you."

Unused to these luxuries, Ravenna tidied her hair and fled downstairs, wishing instead she could be alone just a little longer to collect herself before facing Luke again.

After two false tries she found the library by the sound of voices drifting from it. Through a small room whose walls were hung with antique muskets and swords she entered a long, book-lined room with French doors facing the terrace. Near one of these doors lounged Luke, drink in hand, looking considerably more at ease than when she'd left him, while Glynis presided over a low table laid with sandwiches, scones and cakes and flanked by a silver teapot. Evidently tea was even more comprehensive in England than she expected it to be. A fire crackled and spat comfortingly in the wood-paneled fireplace, around which deep armchairs were clustered invitingly.

"There you are," Glynis said, looking up. "We've hardly had to wait at all. Jeremy, this is Ravenna Jones, Daniel's fiancée."

From a leather wing chair facing the fire, a tall young man of eighteen or nineteen unfolded his lanky figure and turned to face her. "How d' you do," he said casually, and then his eyes widened at the sight of her in a way she was getting used to from the Rathbourn clan.

He crossed to meet her, hand outstretched, and

she thought he meant to shake hers, but she blushed as he took it instead and bent to kiss it with exaggerated, French-style courtesy.

"Rotten luck Daniel met you first," he murmured. "I'm pretty rusty at fighting duels." His eyes met hers—as brown as Daniel's and their expression, she thought impishly, a cross between a friendly cocker spaniel's and a rogue's. His hair was a darker blond than Luke's, his forehead rather too high and his nose long...but what he lacked in classic good looks she suspected he made up for in charm.

"Ahm very glad," she said, emphasizing her drawl wickedly. "Twenty men have dahyed for me in duels this year as it is, honey," and he bowed, clicking his heels together like a cossack as his eyes lit up with delight.

"Jerry is the ham in the family," Luke cut in dryly, grinding his cigarette in an ashtray. "Able to act his way through any situation...except school."

His brother threw him a hurt look and cleared his throat, asking what part of the south she hailed from.

"Kentucky." She sat down in the chair Luke offered her, and Glynis passed her the sandwich plate.

"Ah, yes, Kentucky," Jeremy sighed. "Famous for fast steeds and southern belles, right?"

"Right. I hope you can distinguish one from the other," she added with a laugh. His lopsided grin certainly was catching.

"Lord, yes. You're obviously a Thoroughbred," he parried, popping an olive into his mouth. "Why's Frère Daniel still in New York? If I were him, wild horses, so to speak, wouldn't drag me from your side. Though I don't suppose Uncle Luke here minded."

Ravenna was too surprised to bother about the aptness of this last remark. "Uncle?" she said. "But I thought you and Luke—"

"Are half brothers? We are," Luke said. "Jerry just likes to confuse an already complicated issue—pardon the pun—and make me feel the vast gulf between our ages, all of seventeen years. It's an old habit of his."

"Self-defense," Jeremy replied too blandly. "You make *me* feel like I'm still in nappies sometimes, so what's a chap to do?"

The signs of brotherly conflict—civilly suppressed, but just barely—were easy enough to read, and Ravenna wished she'd let Jeremy's remark go by. Too late now. But she was surprised at Jeremy's short-tempered reply. Was Luke that hard on him? She was interested, too, to see that the stubborn quality in his face and voice matched Luke's. All they needed now was Daniel to make a merry threesome....

Tactfully Glynis led them away from touchy ground by answering Jeremy's original question. "Daniel stayed in New York on business, as usual."

"Is he often away on business?" Ravenna asked with some misgiving.

"Lives out of a bloody suitcase—"

"Jeremy! Don't pay any attention to him, Ravenna. Daniel is home as often as not. With Jeremy in London most of the year, he has no idea when Daniel's here and when he's not."

Still oblivious to her feelings, Jeremy continued, "It was my impression—"

Glynis quelled him with a look, and he gulped, suddenly realizing his gaffe. But Luke said firmly, "Actually, Daniel *is* often away on business, flying between New York and London or Paris in order to keep the Rathbourn interests afloat. We've invested widely in the past five years in metals and commodities, and we own companies here and overseas. And besides France and the States, if his reports to me mean anything, he was also in Rome and Athens for several weeks last year, looking at investments in foreign films."

He had moved to sit in a deep chair by the fire, his long legs stretched before him, his gaze moodily on the flickering flames. Now he lifted his lashes to stare directly at her as he spoke, and Ravenna was forced to look at him while he did so, lest she appear rude. He smiled coolly, and anger flashed in her own eyes. Why, he was deliberately trying to upset her, to make her think she'd hardly ever see Daniel after they were married!

"I'm sure he's an excellent manager." She kept her voice steady.

"Yes, he is," Luke admitted easily, shifting his legs and shrugging.

Ravenna turned and smiled at Glynis, who

seemed to be disregarding the undertones of their dialogue. "I suppose you're wondering how Daniel and I met," she said quickly, and launched into a lengthy explanation of their first encounter, just to annoy Luke. She could see that he stayed against his will to hear the story, so she prolonged it, glad to see him uncomfortable for once. But suddenly she was ashamed of herself.

"Daniel never was a good rider," Luke said casually when she'd finished. "How's his back now?"

"His back? Why, it's still—" For a second she wondered how innocent this question was. "It's just *fine*," she stressed, looking him in the eye.

His dark brows drew together, and he lit another cigarette and stood up.

"Luke, darling, are you leaving us so soon?" Glynis asked. "You haven't told us about Africa." But she turned to butter a scone, while Jeremy talked to one of the hounds at his feet, his deep baritone mixing with the contented thumping of Albion's tail.

Luke took the opportunity to lean across to Ravenna's chair and say softly, "I want to talk to you. Come out on the terrace."

"No," she mouthed at him.

"Ravenna and I are taking a turn in the gardens," Luke announced to the others loudly. "I'd like to show her some of the grounds," and his hand on her back, although it looked innocent, actually propelled her from her chair. His other hand he placed in a friendly manner on her arm, but it was about as friendly as a warden's.

"It looks mighty chilly out," she protested.

"Nonsense, it's a fine Devon evening." He grinned. "You can borrow my jacket," he added, assisting her none too gently toward the French doors.

"Luke, I don't really think—" she began, trying to remain polite in front of Glynis.

"I'll join you." Jeremy's hearty tones drowned her out.

"I think not, Jerry. Another time," Luke said smoothly, and in another second they were outside on the terrace. She was half aware that Glynis threw one very curious look after them and that Jeremy had returned to Albion's side as Peters came in to clear away the tea things.

Luke said nothing until they were out of earshot of the house. He stopped then among some clipped ornamental bushes and turned her to face him. "You are the most presumptuous, infuriating, orneriest man I have ever met, Luke Rathbourn, and if you think you can treat me like this..." she burst out. "Why, down home they'd have shot you for a varmint!"

"What a quaint way you have of putting it," he said, taking off his jacket and placing it around her shoulders. Only then did he think to ask, "Are you cold?"

"No." She stopped short, aware she was shivering in the soft damp air. But it was mostly from anger.

She was about to demand they go back inside, when he said abruptly, "These are tea roses, im-

ported from China in the eighteen hundreds." He
pointed to a long bed of exquisite yellow roses.
"And those—"

"Luke! Why did you bring me out here? It
wasn't to look at the roses! I'm going back inside,"
she said fiercely, struggling to move away from the
arm that had slipped around her waist under his
jacket.

But he was silent, and she waited angrily for him
to speak, a soft breeze caressing her hair and face.
She could detect the sea on the air, but the musky
scent mixed with it was entirely male, made up of
cigarette smoke and the smell of Luke's skin as he
held her trapped beside him.

"So you've only been engaged to Daniel three
days," he finally said, his voice expressing satisfaction, his eyes still on the roses.

"I fail to see why that interests you in the
least!"

"On the contrary. I'm intrigued by the fact. It
throws light on a question that's been on my
mind."

"What question?" she asked, and immediately
wished she hadn't.

"I don't think we need to elaborate on it," he
said blandly. "I would say it's already been answered...twice."

"I don't know what you mean—and I don't care
to know," she added hurriedly, afraid to understand him. And she sure wasn't going to hang
around until she did. She turned suddenly to go
back to the house, but his arm at her waist tightened

perceptibly, dragging her toward him. He blocked her way, his eyes meeting hers.

"I think you do know what I mean. And I think we ought to...discuss...the implications."

"No," she said, her anger flaring. "I told you I have *nothing* to discuss with you, Luke." She struggled against his arm, face set and lips clenched.

He stood there unmoving, like a block of steel, for a moment longer, then said gently, "All right. We won't discuss it...now. I think you're very tired and muddled and should go straight to bed. Forget about dinner, in fact. I'll make your excuses to Glynis." His gray blue eyes flickered over her, their expression thoughtful. "You *are* exhausted," he added.

"And you're very fond of giving orders," she grumbled. "But the fact is you're right. I am tired and I'd love to skip dinner. Please do tell Glynis for me."

Abruptly he removed his arm. She lost her balance slightly, for without realizing it she'd been leaning into him. He reached to steady her, and when she stood there a moment longer, as if surprised, he leaned over her, and she froze. He was going to kiss her. The carved lips floated nearer, nearer....

Suddenly he laughed, a low infectious chuckle, and light as air, she felt him lift his jacket from her shoulders. That was all.

"Good night, Ravenna," he said, suppressing a smile, and turned to walk away.

It was only then she realized she'd closed her eyes.

"Damn!" she muttered, and stalked off indignantly toward the house, finding her way with some difficulty to the bedroom Glynis had shown her earlier.

She was relieved when the room's peace and quiet seeped into her, and some of her churning feelings subsided. She was about to crawl into bed, when she noticed Mary had left a window open to air the room. She walked over to it and opened the casements wider, breathing in the damp sweet smell of the gardens and the tang of the sea on the wind. The window seat invited her to curl up in it, and she did, staring out toward the green clump of forest, still illuminated by sunlight filtering down through ragged clouds.

How strange to think that she was actually in England, at Rathbourn. And without Daniel. The disorientation she felt surely accounted for her oddly intense encounters with Luke, and in a day or two, when she came into focus again, he would hardly affect her. Perhaps, too, it was his resemblance to Daniel that she reacted to...it was inevitable she missed him. If only he were with her.... She took a deep breath. That seemed to be her general refrain since the previous day—if only.

What was he doing at the moment? Talking to Wallingford about shares and Dow Jones averages and bear markets? Or better still, thinking of her, missing her fiercely, wishing he'd flown over with her. When did he intend to come to Rathbourn?

She leaned forward a bit, inhaling the fragrance of flowers beneath her on the terrace, the sweet headiness of honeysuckle and lily of the valley. It really was a magical place, like a storybook ancestor of all the ruined mansions she'd seen down home, holdovers from before the Civil War.

She started and pulled her head back farther into the window enclosure. Luke was standing at the end of the garden, resting one knee on a stone bench, smoking. Luckily he faced away from the house and couldn't have seen her telltale red hair at the window. Now why did he have to spoil her view? But she supposed he wanted to survey his domain, cast a lordly eye around the place again after being away so long. Sir Anthony Rathbourn....

Despite herself, she continued to stare in secret at him from the curtained alcove. The late-afternoon sunlight glinted silver in his sand-colored hair, and his wide shoulders strained the back of his jacket, which outlined, too, his long narrowing torso. His stance emphasized the lean muscles of one thigh and the curve of his slim hips. He was as still as a statue—a Greek statue, she thought absently. Suddenly he flung his cigarette butt in a wide arc and turned with abrupt swiftness. The statue had come alive. She jumped violently backward; he might have been in the room.

I'm tired, she thought. *I need to sleep. Luke was right....* She crossed the room and climbed into the high canopied bed, drifting off almost as soon as her head touched the pillow—only to leap up in astonishment moments later. A blast of raucous music had burst upon her ears.

Someone had turned a stereo up full blast in the room below. Jeremy, she guessed. So even enchanted manor houses had entered the age of high-tech. With a grin, because the music made her feel a little more at home, she got up and closed the window.

SHE CAME DOWN RATHER LATE for breakfast. Peters directed her to the small morning room, with its red-velvet walls covered with beautiful old portraits and hunting scenes. In its center stood a highly polished mahogany table and comfortable chairs. Glynis was lingering over coffee with the *Times*, but Luke and Jeremy were nowhere to be seen. Passing up the riches offered buffet-style on the sideboard, Ravenna took her usual toast and coffee and sat down.

Glynis was now going through some letters with a mild frown on her face. "Invitations," she explained. "Half the county wants to meet you already. We've been invited to tea at the Cunninghams, the Scott-Chadwicks, the St. John Nevinsons. I'll put them off as long as I decently can."

Ravenna smiled in total accord. "Goodness," she said, "I wouldn't know what to talk about!"

"Horses will do," Glynis said dryly. "You see, my dear, everyone's always breeding something— dogs or horses, a new species of dahlia, heaven knows what next. Then you can work your way around to how you met Daniel. All they want is some gossip to pass on—and mostly the chance to describe you to their friends. But let's wait until we're stuck with it. Oh, I forgot. Last night Daniel called after you were asleep," she added, folding her napkin.

"Daniel called? Did he say—"

Glynis smiled at her eagerness. "When he'd arrive? No, he didn't say exactly when. Just soon, and not to worry. He was glad to hear Luke brought you down here."

If only she'd stayed up last night! She might have cleared up a question or two...but just to hear his voice would have been worth it.

"Would you like me to show you the house when you've finished your coffee?" Glynis was saying.

"Oh...I'd love to see it if you can spare the time."

"I always have the time to show Rathbourn. Not that we've ever been open to the public like many old houses," she explained as they moved into the drawing room, "but every now and then someone writes and asks to see it, and we feel obliged. We're terribly proud of it, so we don't really mind."

They spent the next hour and more sweeping from room to room, from the small Red Parlour and the long picture gallery through several richly furnished drawing rooms, the gun room and the formal saloon—an English equivalent of the French salon—and back to the spacious library. By the time they'd penetrated to the old Tudor kitchen, Ravenna had confessed she was planning a book on old Georgian houses. Glynis was delighted and gave even more detailed attention to the Chippendale chairs, the Jacobean sideboards, the antique letter-box, until Ravenna laughed in protest. "It's like a museum tour," she said, "except Rathbourn is far lovelier than any museum."

And this was true. The tall windows that pierced each room let in streaming sunlight and a tantalizing view of the green mossy lawns on the south front, the spreading gardens with ornamental bushes, rose beds, stone walks and statues to the north. And from some of the windows a patch of blue sea was visible, wedged between the woods and sky. Outdoors and indoors mingled; this and the delicate greens, eggshell blues, peaches and soft yellows of the painted walls, decorated with swags of elaborate white plasterwork that led the eye to even more ornamental ceilings, gave the house an elegant airiness. Ravenna had been awed the previous night by its magnificence, but now, in the light of day, she saw how comfortable and warm it was despite its size. Only the vast entrance hall was gloomy, owing to its mahogany paneling. The rest of the house was meant to be lived in—and was.

As if to underline this fact, in every room were vases overflowing with flowers, mostly roses of every color, their fragrance steeping the house in sweetness.

"What wonderful flowers," Ravenna commented. "Do you arrange them yourself?"

Glynis's voice leaped with unexpected passion. "Not only do I arrange them, I grow them. My rose gardens are the best in the county." She couldn't disguise her pride. "If ever you can't find me, I'll be digging in the garden. I practically live on my knees out there!"

They were upstairs now, examining the bedrooms and sitting rooms that opened off the gallery surrounding the well of the two-story central hall. Ravenna fingered the rich chinoiserie wallpaper and bed hangings in Glynis's suite of rooms, pale cream silks figured with mandarins and stunted flowering trees—the original paper, Glynis said, from the seventeen hundreds. "Of course, Luke can tell you much more about the house itself in terms of architecture. He's terribly fond of the place."

Ravenna had happily forgotten about Luke as they explored the vast house, but when they entered a book-lined room with golden light and fresh air pouring in through its open windows, she was forced to remember him.

"This is his study," said Glynis, her hands sweeping toward the huge carved desk, which was strewn with papers and books; an architectural tome lay open at the drawings of some old building. "He's usually here. I wonder where he is?"

Tentatively Ravenna approached a drafting table in the corner of the room and examined the half-finished perspective drawing on it. She could smell cigarette smoke in the air, as if Luke had just left. Her eyes strayed to a doorway near the fireplace, and she wondered if it led to the small room he'd mentioned she might use for her own research.

But Glynis was explaining that she had to hurry
to a committee meeting in Plymouth—something to
do with local schools. She suggested that Ravenna
might like to walk along the cliffs until lunch.
"Unless you'd prefer to ride? But I really think it's
best you wait for Daniel or Luke to show you the
trails."

Although tempted to protest, Ravenna said nothing to this, and Glynis continued, "It's all National
Trust land, and there's a footpath right to Bolt
Tail—that's southwest of here," she added. "Very
scenic. I won't be here at lunch, but we're never formal except at dinners, Ravenna. Peters will look
after you. Forgive me for rushing off...can you
entertain yourself?" When Ravenna assured her she
could, she disappeared down the main stairs.

Meanwhile Ravenna traced her way back to her
room. She decided to change to forest-green cor-
duroy pants and a white-cotton blouse, and letting
her hair fall loose, she took her sketchbook and
some pencils from a drawer. She was longing to
escape into the late-morning sun, which flooded
gold across the lawns and terrace. The deep shadows of every plant and shrub threw the gold into
brilliant relief; Ravenna was glad that her first
Devon morning shone like a good omen.

Downstairs she sought out Peters, asking him to
wrap a sandwich and some fruit for her so she
wouldn't have to return for lunch. Then she slipped
into the library and studied the shelves. The
previous night, after the music had jarred her
awake, she'd made a firm resolve to start on her re-

search for her book the next day. It would give her
something practical to do while waiting for Daniel.
The floor-to-ceiling shelves held a wide selection of
books on architecture, not surprisingly, and she actually found a volume on eighteenth-century interiors. Luke's name was on the flyleaf.

She was about to step onto the terrace when she
heard a faint sound. Yes, someone was whistling an
air from Handel's *Messiah* with no little skill. The
next moment Jeremy, who seemed to have eclectic
tastes in music, poked his head around the doorjamb and called down the long length of the library,
"Off on a jaunt?"

"Yes, and I'd love company," she responded,
smiling at him. He was wearing white pants and
shirt and a black neckerchief and was carrying sun-
glasses. He looked the height of sartorial splendor
for July. But he was also, she now noticed, incon-
gruously shod in cowboy boots.

"Um. . . depends where you're headed," he replied.

"I thought I'd sneak off to the stables and ad-
mire the horseflesh, then take the coastal path on
foot. Glynis says I'm to wait to be shown the horse
trails. Me, who grew up in a Kentucky bluegrass
saddle!"

He grinned. "Well, she's right, you know. Easy
to get lost around here. I've done it once myself."

"Really?"

"Yes, and didn't crawl home until midnight.
Bloody awful out there in the pitch dark, with the
cliffs at your feet and those great looming trees

hulking down at you. But let's see. I can escort you as far as the stables—that's probably safe at this hour.''

''Safe?''

''I'm avoiding Uncle Luke,'' he said matter-of-factly. ''Our paths cross at my peril. Y' see, he's playing the heavy this summer. Came home early, he told me, all the way from darkest Africa to make certain I swot up for my third year at university. That's why I'm stuck here under house arrest. I'd give anything to be up in London.'' He sighed. ''Ruining my lovelife for one, he is. But don't tell him that...in fact, I'm afraid I'm going to have to swear you to secrecy all round. D' you mind?''

Ravenna had to laugh at his comically stricken look of complicity. ''As long as it's not in blood.''

''Oh, I don't think we have to go that far. But the truth is, I'm supposed to be sweating over French and German lit right now...Luke thinks the family pride's at stake. I was slated to go to Cambridge like all the other respectable Rathbourns have since the War of the Roses, but I talked him into letting me go to London—he won't let me forget it. Says if I'm going to break with tradition I have to do more than scrape through, or else I'll have to cut out my acting classes. I said, 'Academia be damned'...but Luke holds the purse strings. Get the picture?''

''Why did you want to go to University of London? I thought everybody would give their eyeteeth to go to Cambridge or Oxford. Better than Harvard back home.''

He swept her out onto the terrace with a laugh.

"Theater, my dear Miss Jones. London is the capital of the theatrical world nonpareil. I had to be there, university or no. I'd go as a busker if I had to—" at her faint look of incomprehension he explained "—A street musician. Except I can't sing or play worth a damn. But I can act," he said firmly. She suspected he could.

"Like to help me give him the slip?" he asked, peering through the library door. Then he looked up and down the terrace in the manner of a Victorian villain and gave a rollicking stage wink.

She chuckled. So someone else wanted to avoid the lord of the manor! She knew she shouldn't, but she heard herself saying, "Sure. What do I do?"

"Stroll with me toward the stables, and then if Luke asks, pretend you never saw me. I'm going to walk my motorcycle up the lane and then head out."

She waited for him to say where to, but he didn't. She thought it the better part of valor not to ask; her brother Jamie, whom Jeremy most reminded her of, had once told her it was often safer not to know his whereabouts, because then she could tell no tales.

A few minutes later, after admiring Jeremy's monstrous gleaming Harley Davidson, which he handled with as much pride as a Rolls, she parted with him at the garages. He directed her to the stables before he left. "O'Reilly will show you about. And remember, if Luke asks—"

"I haven't seen you since yesterday's tea. You owe me one, Jeremy," she laughed.

"Righto." Quietly he wheeled his motorcycle onto the rear driveway toward the tall overhanging trees.

The red-brick stables were like stables the world over, smelling richly of horses, well-cared-for leather, saddle soap, oats, hay and bran. Although the Rathbourn buildings were as spotless as those at Elk Creek, they were considerably smaller and of another age, gleaming with brass horse plates from days gone by. But the stables' rich complex smell, so pleasing to Ravenna, was overlaid suddenly with the odor of Kevin O'Reilly's cigar as the short, agile, monkey-faced man with the tweed cap on his dark hair approached her. He would not have been out of place at a Kentucky racetrack.

It didn't take long for them to discover their mutual love of horses. Not much was said, but the look in Ravenna's eye when she came face to face with the Rathbourn hunters was enough for O'Reilly. And when she told him that she came from the Elk Creek breeding farm, his manner was almost deferential. Almost. Kevin O'Reilly was never exactly deferential.

"Well, there's Jessie, as would suit you, miss. A high-sperrited craiture as loves good handling. Lady G. won't ride her anymore." He stopped before a bay mare and stroked her forehead. They went on past a silvery mare with a slow watchful eye. "And Silvanity, she's a tricky mavoureen—wants curbing." Next was a handsome chestnut stallion called Lloyd George, and in the last stall was a great nervous black beast, nostrils flaring at the sight of Ravenna and ears laid back.

Like all but Lloyd George, whom she recognized as an Anglo-Arab, he was an English Thoroughbred. "He's magnificent," she murmured.

"Napoleon here, that's Sir Anthony's horse. He wouldn't be lettin' you ride him, miss. Very particular he is about that horse.... We've two ponies, too," he continued, "little fellers, Shetlands. Grazin' in the park right now." He paused, his eyes curious. "So you grew up in Kentucky. Me brother Liam went out there in '68."

She would have liked to settle down on one of the benches and talk to this slight, soft-spoken man with the gift of the gab. Her father had always said the Irish had a way with horses no other people had, except perhaps the Indians. And since Elk Creek and Louisville had more Irish than Indians these days, there had always been several employed in the Elk Creek stables. She was almost made homesick by the sight of him—but he wouldn't stop talking long enough for her to feel it.

"Mr. Daniel was sartain he could get us some Arabians from yer father...you say he didn't? I'll have to be after talking to him about it," and he shook his head darkly. "I've had me heart set on it."

"Oh, but he brought me back, instead," she said with a smile.

O'Reilly brightened. "Aw, he's got some sense, that lad. And would y'be Irish yerself? From the looks of you...." His eyes fell on her bright red hair.

"There's one not very far back," she confessed. "My mother's father, a Devlin from Waterford."

"Ah, the Devlins. A wild bunch, that clan. I remember a man named Tommy Devlin up Wexford way who was the very devil of a man with horses...."

And it was only with the greatest of reluctance that she tore herself away, promising herself she would ride Jessie the first chance she got. She patted the mare's nose in passing and whispered a word into her delicately poised ear.

"She'll be waitin' for you, Miss Ravenna."

Still clutching her sketchbook, Luke's volume and Peters's neatly bagged lunch, she headed for the woods through the garden side of the house. Albion and Gwydion appeared from nowhere and loped companionably beside her.

She heard the sea before she saw it, a fierce crash of breakers against the rocky shore, the pounding relentless waves of the English Channel. When she finally reached the footpath, a bare ribbon snaking among the gorse, she saw it first as a spume of white spray and next as boiling white water where it heaved and churned against the jagged rocks far beneath her. And then the flat distance of it, spreading blue and jade green to a soft horizon. The clouds above were white as down and lazily scattered across the sapphire sky. It was at this place, with the iron-colored coast at her feet, the hammering waves, the far-flung distant blue of water and sky before her and the thick gorse scratching at her legs, that she fell in love with Devon irrevocably. Rathbourn had begun to inspire the feeling, as had the charming villages on the drive down; this one swift sight of the sea merely completed the process.

She followed the rough path for several miles, reveling in the space and freedom. Then she flung herself down on a patch of grass to watch the gulls wheel and cry and to stare up at the white clouds banking overhead in whimsical patterns. She'd intended to sketch, but instead she dozed dreamily for a while, waking with fresh determination to outline her book.

She didn't want to attempt an overview of her subject, she decided, chewing on her pencil. That had been done many times, much better than she could ever hope to do it. No, she would write something more personal, indulging her love of particular houses and sharing her excitement about their beauty and history. She would weave some colorful social history throughout to give a feeling of the times. . . a tapestry of the eighteenth century, she thought, beginning to visualize her project more clearly.

Flipping through Luke's book, she was surprised to see how many old houses were available for visiting right there in Devon. Daniel had been correct; staying at Rathbourn *would* be good for her research, an unexpected bonus.

Saltram House, just outside Plymouth, would be first on her list. The famous designer Robert Adam had done several key rooms there in the latter half of the seventeen hundreds.

So absorbed and interested was she in her plans that the darkening sky didn't come to her attention until the first drops of rain fell on her open page. She looked up in surprise. The downy clouds she'd admired earlier were thickly massed and inky gray with rain that threatened to spill at any moment. And she hadn't even thought to bring a sweater!

She remembered how yesterday the golden weather had changed to sheets of rain, and shivered. She'd come a long way from Rathbourn by a narrow footpath that wound near steep cliffs plumeting to rocks and the sea. The prospect of returning in a downpour was unnerving.

Gathering up her things, she called the dogs. But they were nowhere in sight. Probably gone home long ago, she thought, realizing she hadn't seen them since she'd dozed off earlier. Hurriedly she dashed down to the path, but as the worsening rain changed it to mud, it threatened to become slippery, so she turned back toward the woods. At first the giant beeches and chestnuts offered some shelter, but not for long. It was soon pouring. Ravenna's hair was in her eyes and Luke's book was getting wet. She held the volume against her, then slipped it between the pages of her sketchbook. Then she stopped suddenly in consternation. She was completely surrounded by tall cathedrallike trees. Which way to Rathbourn? She no longer knew.

Great! Her first day on the family estate, and they'd have to send out a search party for her! Except that no one would think of doing so. Glynis was in Plymouth at a meeting, Luke probably safe and warm in his study and not giving her a thought, and Jeremy? As far away as Exeter or Torquay for all she knew. She'd arrive home looking like a drowned rat hours from now, perhaps not until nightfall—at this dispiriting thought she remembered Jeremy's own gloomy tale of being lost—and if she was lucky, she could creep off to her room without being seen.

After half an hour of slogging along through wet leaf mold and dodging branches that seemed to slash at her with dripping spikes, she was thoroughly soaked and miserable. Her blouse was plastered to her skin, and she was becoming chilled to the bone. She'd found a sort of path and was sticking to it, hoping it would lead eventually to the road that went past Rathbourn. It had to lead *somewhere*, in any case. Ravenna knew she'd got turned around when she'd left the footpath.

Then she heard another sound, louder than the steady drumming of the rain...the sound of horses' hooves, a sound she couldn't mistake after growing up with it. She turned and jumped sideways off the path as a man mounted on a tall black stallion cantered into sight. A gray slicker protected him from the rain. It was Luke on Napoleon.

Luke's eyes were relieved when he recognized her. Aware that she looked a sopping mess and feeling very foolish, she turned to trudge on. He reined his horse in and dismounted beside her.

"Ravenna! Damn it, it's pouring rain. You'll

probably catch pneumonia as it is. I'm used to our weather, but obviously it's caught you unprepared. I'll take you back on Napoleon.''

She stopped and looked up at him. Despite the downpour she said clearly, ''No, thank you, Luke. I prefer pneumonia.''

He swore, then reached for her, but at the look in her eyes he stopped himself. He schooled his voice to be reasonable. ''Ravenna. You are three miles from Rathbourn. You're just lucky Peters told me where you were headed, or you'd be lost all day. Come back with me.''

Before she could answer, he took off his slicker and slipped it over her shoulders, then lifted her in one easy motion onto the waiting horse, astride the front of the saddle.

Napoleon stepped skittishly sideways, and she felt a wild urge to spur him on and leave Luke standing there. But he grasped the reins, swung himself up behind her, and it was too late. It would be inhuman to leave him to freeze, anyway—even if she did hate him.

But when he put one arm firmly around her waist and his other grazed her thigh where he held the reins, despair again settled over her. Fate kept throwing them together, as if it wanted something to happen between them. She gritted her teeth as he held her tightly.

''I'm going to canter. Are you comfortable?'' he asked in her ear.

''No,'' she replied perversely.

When he settled her more closely against him, she

bit her lip in anger but had the sense to say nothing
this time.

The smooth motion of the horse pressed her even
more intimately to his chest; her head was tucked
beside his chin, his mouth in her hair, but he made
no move to take advantage of the fact. Once he
murmured, "You're shivering," and she felt his
embrace grow more tender.

"I'm not," she protested, her teeth chattering.

He said nothing to this, and the silence grew.
When the hot flowing current began to melt her
again, she felt no sense of shock; from the moment
his arms had gone around her she'd expected it. She
sighed. There was no doubt she and Luke had a
fatal attraction for each other; she had to admit it.
It wasn't due to tiredness or jet lag or culture shock.
It was pure physical chemistry, more intense than
she'd ever encountered. But it had nothing to do
with love—Daniel was the man she loved—and she
would quell the attraction with every ounce of her
will.

His arms had tightened almost imperceptibly
around her, holding her so closely that she was
nestled against his hard chest, with the lightweight
slicker barely separating them. The rain splashed
down continuously and monotonously. She could
smell the rich damp earth, the acrid bark of trees,
the horse beneath her and the rubber slicker. Mixed
with these was another more disturbing fragrance—
the male scent of Luke, the scent of sweat and to-
bacco and virility.

She didn't know when, on the long ride through

the woods, the rocking canter, a feeling she had loved from the time she was a child, relaxed her so completely that she no longer fought the current that joined her and Luke, that made her feel as if they were one being melded on the horse. His breath was sweet in her hair and tender, and her thoughts were suspended. Held like this—without passion, without violence; simply closely and protectively—feeling the warmth and strength of his body, she was swept by a sense of peace, of belonging, a feeling she did not examine but sank into with relief. This was how Daniel had never held her.

With a start she realized what she was thinking and tried to pull away, but Luke gripped her firmly. "Relax," he said into her hair, "we're almost there." And she allowed herself to sink back again, not questioning anything, almost as if she trusted him.

With the rain pattering around them, dripping from every branch and leaf, she lost all sense of time, of century. She could almost imagine them riding thus long ago, back to a Rathbourn newly built, crowded with servants and county visitors, moving to the rhythms of another, slower age. She would be wrapped in a long wool cloak, and Luke would have lace at his cuffs and throat, a pistol tucked at his waist like a highwayman, perhaps. She smiled at the thought.

Stirred by her fantasies and clasped closely in his arms, she emerged with him from the woods into the park at Rathbourn. She looked up to see how the woods and meadows and soft cushioning hills to the left and right sheltered the manor house in a setting of green—emerald of the lawns, black green of the trees and a lighter lime of some flowering shrubs. Like a jewel it sat there among them, palely beautiful, private, composed. Yes, she could imagine the centuries stretching quietly into the past.

It was only after their swift canter under the trees that they saw the car parked in the drive by the entrance to the house—a gray Mercedes. It had been hidden by the mist of rain until they were almost upon it.

Luke's arms tightened suddenly, possessively, making her gasp. And then she saw Daniel unfold his long length from the car. Daniel!

Mounted high on the powerful Napoleon, both of them looked down on him in shock, as if he'd stepped from another world. And in his three-piece suit, hastily throwing a Burberry over his shoulders, Daniel did seem to breathe of New York still.

The two men stared at each other, the air electric with tension. "Hello, Ravenna," Daniel finally said, a strangely abrupt quality darkening his voice. "Luke."

Dismayed, Ravenna tried to dismount but in the encumbering slicker could not. Luke's arms still held her as he stared down at his stepbrother, but she pulled forward, hearing him say very casually, "Hello, Daniel. Ravenna got lost in the rain. Foolish girl, she's no idea of our changeable weather."

"You need a drink and a hot bath at once," he

whispered in her ear. "Doctor's orders." Then he began to lift her from the horse. But some strands of her long hair, curled even more tightly by the rain, tangled in the buttons of his shirt. Ravenna's agony was prolonged as he settled her on the horse again while he loosened her hair. It seemed to take hours. Then she was on the ground, and Luke, with one hard brief glance at Daniel, reined Napoleon in the direction of the stables.

"Hello, Daniel," she said, smiling brightly at him. She knew that with her cheeks burning, her hair a tangle of wet curls, the unshapely slicker falling to her ankles, she looked entirely unlike the fashionable picture she was usually careful to present to him.

There was only the slightest of pauses before he came forward and kissed her. His voice was tight with some emotion he strove to suppress as he explained, "I came straight down. I wanted to surprise you. Wallingford and I finished the basics yesterday, but I've brought someone along to type up the contract this week."

At a loss for words, Ravenna stared at him as he turned back to the car. Only then did she see that a woman was still sitting in the front seat, as if reluctant to come out in the rain. She was dark haired and slight; Ravenna could make out a small oval face through the rain-obscured windshield.

Daniel opened the passenger door. "You'll have to make a dash for it, Fern, I'm afraid I can't get any closer to the steps."

The woman said something Ravenna didn't catch

and, a moment later, with a flurried movement, ran into the house, her slight form hunched against the downpour.

Daniel and Ravenna followed, dripping copiously onto the beautifully waxed floors. Glynis met them in the hallway. She was the only completely dry one of the lot. At the sight of Daniel she hurried forward to embrace him with obvious affection.

An instant later Daniel drew Ravenna to his side, wrapping his arm in hers. "Darling, I want you to meet my secretary, Fern Anderson. A compatriot of yours."

Secretary? Daniel had a secretary? Ravenna just barely concealed her surprise, for it was the first she'd heard of it. The woman looked very young, with a sweet face and a shining cap of black hair. She was dressed simply and professionally in a green pleated suit and white blouse. She surveyed Ravenna with unconcealed interest.

"How do you do," she breathed in a low voice. Then her dark eyes fell unmistakably to Ravenna's slicker, from which rivulets were running onto the floor.

Glynis took one horrified look at her, following Fern's gaze. "Ravenna, you go right upstairs and change at once. You'll catch a chill if you don't. Perhaps Daniel could bring you some brandy."

"Of course," he said, carefully removing his trench coat and folding it over his arm.

"And then we'll fight this rotten weather with an extra long tea. Fern, why don't you come and sit by the fire with me,'' Glynis added, placing her hand on her arm as if they were well acquainted, ''and tell me the latest news from New York.'' She led her off to the library.

Ravenna gratefully handed the slicker to Peters—who, she was fast learning, knew when to appear and when not to. Then, with a meaningful look at Daniel, she cast her eyes toward the stairs.

But he made no move to follow her, saying instead in a low voice, ''Go along, darling. I'll talk to you when I've brought up your drink.''

Briefly she wondered if he was angry, and her eyes dropped uncertainly from his as she turned to the stairs. Daniel had at last arrived—at one of the most inopportune moments possible—to find her clasped in Luke's arms. And then a savage thought occurred to her. If she were really honest, she'd have to face the fact that since she'd come to England, *opportune* moments had been few and far between.

CHAPTER FOUR

WHEN RAVENNA EMERGED from a hurried bath twenty minutes later, tying her soft velour robe around her and pulling her hair from the collar so that it fell down her back, she stopped on the threshold of her room. Daniel, his back to her, was seated on the sofa, a tray with a brandy on it before him on the coffee table. He himself was well started on a glass of bourbon. She sensed he needed it, noting how tensely he held his shoulders in the cashmere pullover he'd exchanged his suit jacket for. Was it her imagination, or did he really look different from what she remembered— still as darkly handsome but somehow removed? And was it only days since she'd last seen that back departing from her in the airport? It felt like months.

"Hello, darling," she said softly. He started. "Thanks for bringing up the brandy." She crossed to sit beside him, taking a sip of the swirling liquid at the bottom of her glass. Its fiery warmth banished the last remnants of the chill she'd been fighting off.

Silently he removed the glass from her hand, set it down and kissed her. A moment later his eyes flew open, as if he felt a change in her response. "Are you angry I didn't come with you?"

"No. I think...'dismayed' is the word, not 'angry,'" she said slowly. "I know you couldn't help it. Did your business with Wallingford go all right?"

"Yes, we've got the company sewn up, I hope." His dark eyes gleamed. "But it was crucial I stay. Otherwise we might have lost it. A move at the right time...." He paused, taking her hand, and she felt how excited he was about his triumph. "But I'm sorry it worked out that we flew over separately. I missed you, darling."

She leaned closer, burying her face and damp hair in his shoulder. "Oh, Daniel," she whispered, "I'm glad about the company, but how I wish you'd come with me."

When he lifted her head to look at her, she held his gaze unsteadily. "Is anything wrong, Ravenna? You had no trouble getting down, did you? Glynis told me Luke brought you."

She made her voice light. "Oh, no trouble. Yes, Luke drove me down. He was worried about my driving on the left-hand side of the road."

"Oh, lord! I didn't think of that!" He struck his forehead in mock horror. "I'm sorry, darling. Sometimes I get so wrapped up. I'm embarrassingly single-minded when it comes to my work. Am I forgiven?"

She laughed, but it sounded forced. "I'll get used to it. And...and of course I forgive you. But you won't always be called away places, will you?"

"No," he promised, squeezing her hand. "Although it's a bit like being a doctor, I suppose. There are always crises I have to see to. Never mind, we'll work that out. Tell me how you get along with Glynis."

"Glynis? I like her very much, and I think she likes me. She's not at all fearsome. Jeremy, as you said, is completely charming and is already putting me in his pocket. And Luke—"

She stopped, uncertain what to say. He picked up his drink and fiddled with it in his hand. "I rather gathered you were on...friendly terms...with Luke."

"Oh, no!" Had her denial come too quickly? "I merely got caught in the rain, and he insisted on bringing me back to Rathbourn, that's all. I was lost and would have been for hours if he hadn't come looking for me on Napoleon." She removed her hand from his in consternation. "In fact, I'm afraid I don't like him all that much," she insisted, looking him in the eye. "He's a bit...unnerving." It was the truth, after all. Except *totally* unnerving was more like it.

Daniel seemed to find nothing odd in this as he said, "I was very upset to hear he drove you down, despite what I told Glynis. I don't want you associating with Luke."

Her eyebrows raised. "Why, Daniel, honey, that's very imperious of you. What do you two have against each other?" Whatever it was, they certainly had one thing in common: ordering her around.

"So he has been talking to you." His face clouded.

"No, not about you. In fact, I have no idea why you don't like each other."

He looked away from her for a moment, then said gruffly after a swallow of bourbon, "Well, it's a long story."

"Is it...about Kristen?"

His head came up rather too sharply. "Did he tell you about that?"

"Glynis mentioned someone named Kristen. She thought you would have told me about her, but when she found you hadn't, she left it hanging. Will you, Daniel?" she asked, drawing his hand back into hers. "I've collected a pile of questions since I've come here."

"Well, I'm glad it was Glynis. Luke's version is so distorted...."

"*What's* distorted, Daniel?" Although Ravenna's voice was gentle, she couldn't quell her impatience. She was sick to death of hints and innuendos from both Luke and Daniel.

He stood up—she noticed he was still stiff from his riding accident—and slowly moved toward the windows to stare out at the gardens, hands behind his back. Silhouetted by the light, his face away from her, he was a commanding presence in the elegant room. Yet he seemed to be nerving himself for some ordeal.

"I didn't plan to tell you just yet," he finally said. "But since Luke's back...." He launched into it then, quickly, unwillingly. "It happened a year ago, just before Luke went to Africa. Kristen was his fiancée—a Swedish girl, very pretty, lighthearted. She was staying down here for the summer with him, and he was called up to London for an architects' meeting—something to do with an association he belongs to. They'd been invited to a party, he and Kristen, in Exeter—old Cambridge friends of his. I knew them slightly.'' He swallowed, then said more slowly, "She was disappointed when Luke left. She asked me to take her to the party instead because she was eager to dance. She...loved that kind of thing.''

He continued, subdued now. "We were driving back at three in the morning across Dartmoor. It was very dark and misty, and it was a long empty road—the moors are unnerving even in daylight. I remember her saying something quite silly...about trolls and little people—she'd thought she'd seen a light moving on the tors. We'd been drinking a bit, too. I turned to reply, there was a tremendous ringing impact...and the next thing I knew I woke up in Exeter Hospital with a splitting headache.''

"What happened?" Ravenna asked in a hushed voice.

"I'd hit a van—a small black van with one man in it—as it swung around a corner. A patch of mist had rolled in and obscured it. The fellow was unhurt, like me...but Kristen was killed...outright.'' He shuddered and, hands tightly jammed into his pockets, paced back to the sofa, where he sat down again.

"Oh, Daniel!" Ravenna took both his hands in hers. "How awful for you!"

"It was bad enough, but then Luke...." He

stopped. His voice lowered. "Luke hadn't heard about it in London. Glynis was unable to contact him that morning because he was on the road, and Kristen's name was withheld on the newscast until they could reach her father. When Luke got to Rathbourn, I had just returned from the hospital. We told him about Kristen...and he...." Daniel stared at his hands as if he were reliving the scene. "He slugged me so hard I thought I'd end up back in Exeter again. I think he wanted to kill me."

"Why?"

"He thought I was responsible, because I'd taken Kristen to the party without his knowledge and because I'd had a couple of drinks...that my driving was at fault." He leaned his head wearily against the back of the sofa, eyes closed. "It wasn't a pretty time. Luckily Luke went to Africa—but first he said some of the bitterest things I ever hope to hear."

"Why Africa?" she queried softly, imagining Luke's response when he heard his fiancée had died, the response of a man in deep shock, a man very much in love....

"Kristen's mother lives in Cape Town. Her father's in London—they're officially separated. Luke felt he had to go and see the mother in person because she's an invalid and couldn't fly up for the funeral. He has friends in South Africa, too, in other cities. That's why he stayed so long, seeing the continent. Took a year off from teaching. I suppose it rather ripped him apart."

"But he blamed you!"

"Yes." His dark eyes turned to her, a measure of anguish in their depths. "Ravenna, I swear I had no more than two or three drinks that night, not enough to make a difference. It was just that it was so dark, and the van came out of nowhere. I didn't even know what hit me. One of those freak accidents you hear about."

"I believe you, darling," she said, distressed at the look in his eyes. So this was what had come between him and Luke!

"Surely it was clear that it was an accident. Was there an investigation?"

"Yes, of course. But Luke flew to Africa before the final results. Not that it would have made a difference," he said gloomily. "I've had nothing but business communications with him since. And when he wouldn't speak to me on the phone the other night, I knew he still felt the same. It makes it damned hard."

"How do you mean?"

"I hoped not to see him at Rathbourn this summer, that he'd stay in Africa until late fall. I don't like having him around, not with this hanging between us." His voice slowed. "Well, unfortunately Luke and I never were the best of friends. I shouldn't be surprised he feels like this."

"That happens between brothers sometimes," she said, aware she was out of her depth. Her own four brothers, to the contrary, were all on good terms, despite minor disagreements. She moved closer to him, still concerned at the bitter undertone to his words. Luke's attitude had cut him deeply.

"Luke has always had a temper," he said. "When we were kids, we were always coming to blows over stupid things. It was really too bad."

"That's normal, honey, among children."

"Well, yes and no. Luke's rather violent. His reaction to Kristen's death was out of proportion. Even Glynis will tell you that."

But Ravenna was remembering the swift translation of Luke's thoughts into action in regards to her. In other circumstances might this not come out as violence? There was about him something of the lean pantherlike wildness of an animal... but an intelligent animal, she corrected. He wasn't a man whose body overrode his mind. It was more that it did exactly what he asked it to. For a brief disloyal moment she wondered what Luke's version of the story was.

"If he was very much in love with Kristen, it would have been a terrible shock to him," she said aloud, thinking again with a sudden tightening of her heart how upset Luke must have felt. Surely his response had been understandable.

"Let's not talk about him anymore, darling. Let's talk about us," Daniel said abruptly, twining her hands in his. His lips sank against hers, but all she felt was his distress communicating itself to her. She had to force herself to relax when his hand went to her back and his mouth lowered to the open vee of her dressing gown.

A knock at the door startled them apart.

"I'll get it, Daniel," she murmured with a guilty sense of relief.

"Madam wanted you to know that tea is ready in the library," Mary said at the door.

"Tea be damned," Daniel called. "Tell her we'll be down for dinner."

Mary left, and Ravenna crossed once more to the sofa. But the romantic mood Daniel had tried to inspire had been quashed. There was more to say, though. Might as well get it over with.

"I was very surprised to meet Luke at the town house," she began. "I think you could at least have told me about him."

"Told you what?" he asked, irritated at her return to the subject of Luke.

"Well, that he's Sir Anthony, for one. An architect for another. That he owns Rathbourn. That you work for him." She swirled her brandy in her glass.

"I didn't think it mattered. You're marrying me, not Luke."

Hearing it stated so baldly, she almost spilled some of her brandy. His voice was cool but with an edge of jealousy she suddenly felt went back years.

"Daniel, all I meant is that I want to know about your family. . . so as not to be caught at a disadvantage."

"Luke seems to have filled you in quite nicely."

"I would have preferred to hear it from you."

"Ravenna—" she noted a weariness in his voice "—I have to warn you about something. I don't always remember to do the usual things—and our engagement happened so fast. I only flew down to your father's farm to buy two Arabians, remember? It's slightly disconcerting to an old bachelor like me to come home with a fiancée, instead." He grinned then, so engagingly that she had to smile. The smile rose slowly to her eyes. This was the Daniel she'd left behind in New York.

"I don't want to quarrel when you look so beautiful," he added, running his fingers through her tangled curls. Once more his eyes darkened, and he drew her to his chest. "If I wasn't so tired...."

"You do look tired," she whispered, suddenly angry at herself for making him go over the upsetting details of Kristen's death. She ought to have waited a day or two at least. But all she said was, "Wallingford must be a monster. Why don't you lie down before dinner?"

"You're right, I've hardly slept the past two days. You sound almost wifely," he teased. "But first I ought to run down and see that Fern has everything straight."

He stood up, and she followed him to the door. Just as he was about to leave she said casually, "I didn't know you had a private secretary, Daniel."

"Fern? Oh, yes, I hired her temporarily in New York to do some emergency work for me several years back. She proved so indispensable I kept her on. A good sort once you get to know her."

"She looks so...so young."

He laughed. "I think that's cultivated, darling. She was twenty-five when she first came to me—that must be four years ago now. She's got one of these faces that never change." He spoke absently, his thoughts elsewhere. But he took her in his arms and kissed her deeply before he left, and she held him eagerly.

Everything would come out all right, now that Daniel was there, she thought. Luke meant nothing to her, had only been toying with her for selfish reasons. As he must have done with other women before Kristen, perhaps after... stirring their senses until they were putty in his hands. Her response had been a tribute to his experience and skill, nothing more.

Daniel suddenly broke from her, his eyes inquiring. "What are you thinking about?"

"Thinking about? Why, nothing, I guess...."

"You've changed," he said, looking at her lips. "Something's changed in you."

"No, I haven't! It's just the strangeness of being here... when you were in New York."

He held her at arm's length, studying her, then murmured in echo to her thoughts, "Ravenna, we've had a rough start, but it's going to be all right, now that I'm here. I promise you."

She smiled, and her blue eyes met his. "Of course it will be." And she repeated the words to herself as he left.

THERE WAS NOTHING REMARKABLE about her first dinner at Rathbourn, except that she almost immediately put her foot in her mouth.

Just after Garvey, who filled in as footman at meals, and Peters handed around the soup course, she heard Luke's deep voice asking Jeremy how he managed to look so chipper after a day with the books, when he'd gone up to study that morning like a condemned man going to the wall.

With a loud clatter Ravenna dropped her silver soup spoon. Almost simultaneously Jeremy, seated directly opposite her, kicked her on the ankle. She knew what it meant: shut up. "Ow!" she exclaimed. Everyone turned to look at her. "I mean, *how* do you do it?" she amended. The slight acknowledgment in Jeremy's eyes told her it was a fast recovery.

"Good clean living," he blazoned. "No wine, women or song all the bloody day long." He looked so blithely morose that everyone, including her, burst out laughing.

To her relief, Jeremy determinedly steered the conversation to Luke's Africa trip, and she relaxed. Damn his plots, she'd almost given him away. But now she leaned back to study the three men: she couldn't resist, so interesting was it to see them together for the first time.

All were handsome virile men, but Daniel was dark, the other two fair—although Daniel's skin was pale compared to Luke's healthy bronze and Jeremy's sunburned glow. Too much work, she figured. In the States she'd thought Daniel easygoing and relaxed, but the past few days had allowed quite another side of him to emerge. He could be totally wrapped up in business for one thing, with everything else receding—including her! She knew he loved his work, but it was disconcerting at this early stage in their relationship to feel so excluded. After all, it wasn't as if they'd been married ten years. She believed in a degree of independence after marriage, but she'd have to encourage him to take more time for just plain living—and loving, she suspected.

For a moment her eyes lifted appreciatively to take in the dinner scene, which reminded her of the setting for a play. The candlelight flickered and pooled in the cut crystal and fine old china, struck pale fire from the long strands of pearls Glynis wore with her dark red crêpe-de-chine dress, picked out the gold threads in Fern's exotic caftan—that was a surprise—and cast soft shadows on everyone's faces. Ravenna smiled to herself, glad she had dressed so elaborately, especially after her ignominious return from her cliffside walk, soaked to the skin. The blue green sheath, a shimmer of silk that was completely shoulderless, became her—or so the glittering eyes of both Luke and Daniel had told her when she'd entered the dining room on the dot of eight. And Jeremy's, too, as his lips formed a silent wolf whistle. Even Fern had looked startled, as if she'd thought that underneath the ungainly slicker might have lurked something less shapely.

"It's a country of raw undirected power," Luke was saying, and in the pause that followed she felt his eyes caress her bared shoulders, then lift to her dusky red hair. His voice went on, and she survived a feeling of blankness to recall, *the three brothers. I was comparing the three of them.*

She forced herself to focus on Jeremy. He played

the clown, but she sensed a purposeful young man under that sparkling exterior, a young man determined to get what he wanted from life. Such an innocent look in those brown eyes as he asked Luke if the natives were friendly in Zaire. She couldn't guess his thoughts, but ten to one they weren't on the natives of Zaire. Still, she detected a grudging admiration in the gaze that rested on Luke.

Luke himself. He sat at the head of the table, opposite Glynis and to Ravenna's immediate right. For the first time he was dressed formally, in a beautifully tailored gray suit that made him seem more formidable than in the turtlenecks and pants he'd worn previously. His long fingers, resting beside his plate as Garvey served him some roast beef, drummed softly, and she realized there was a restless quality to him even at Rathbourn, something tautened and coiled. He had an animal's ability to be at ease, yet ready to spring into action, an intense quality Daniel didn't possess, thank heavens. It threatened her. Suddenly she pictured that elegant hand in a fist slamming against Daniel's jaw...and she thought of Kristen.

"A penny for your thoughts, Ravenna," Luke murmured, his eyes burning aquamarine in the golden light of the tapers.

"I'm afraid they're...not for sale," she replied with a guilty start, fingering the stem of her wineglass. Lord, couldn't she think faster than that? She sounded provocative.

From beside Jeremy, Fern gazed at her, disconcerting Ravenna still further. Fern's expression was demure, but the stressed difference between her childlike face and the exotically embroidered caftan was oddly sophisticated. Although Fern's gaze fell to her plate immediately, Ravenna had the sudden impression she was listening to every word.

"What I mean is, they're hardly worth a penny. Perhaps a guinea," Ravenna rallied.

"A pearl of great price." Luke's words were dry, and yet his eyes smiled as they flicked over the single chained pearl that nestled at the cleft of her breasts. For a moment she felt his gaze burn against her skin.

"Have you had a chance to visit our stables yet?" Jeremy threw in, obscurely aware she needed rescuing. She almost kicked him in return; he knew perfectly well she'd been there that morning, though she'd never know it from his face or voice. A very good actor, Jeremy.

"Why, yes, I had a talk with O'Reilly this morning. He says I'm free to ride Jessie...if you don't object, Luke." She turned sweetly to him, only the faintest edge to her voice.

"Jessie? She's a mettlesome horse."

"You're forgetting Ravenna grew up on a horse-breeding farm, Luke," Daniel cut in firmly from her left. It was the first time he'd directly addressed his stepbrother since they'd sat down, and Luke made no sign he'd heard. "It was her horse, Coyote, that threw me," Daniel explained. "As mettlesome as they come."

"When I was a kid I lived to ride," she said hastily. "I'm really used to horseflesh. The more 'high-sperrited,' as O'Reilly says, the better."

Luke's mouth quirked. "Well, then, you can start with Jessie, but we'll have to see about getting you a firebrand. I like to see a woman meet her match."

Ravenna turned uncomfortably from the challenge in his eyes, cursing the swift flush that leaped to her cheeks. Luke was too fond of implication.

"Do you ride, Fern?" she asked quickly.

"Me?. No, I hardly saw a horse until I came to Rathbourn. Where I grew up in upper New York State, we rode around in rusted-out old cars." She grinned.

"You know I've offered dozens of times to teach you to ride," Daniel said impatiently.

Not a very businesslike offer, Ravenna thought in surprise.

Fern smiled at him, a slow smile that lit up her face to a gamine prettiness. "And I've had the sense to say no dozens of times. I'm terrified of horses," she confessed to Ravenna. "A coward of the first water."

"Nonsense," Daniel insisted. "Not everybody has to ride in this world. I was never very good at it myself."

Talk turned to the idiosyncrasies of the Rathbourn horses. Glynis led the discussion, determined to prove that Jessie was worse than they thought and liable to bolt on Ravenna if she wasn't prepared. Daniel's hand slipped discreetly to Ravenna's and stayed entwined with it, resting on her thigh while dessert, a delicately flavored *crème caramel*, was brought in. Eventually the conversation petered to an end, and Glynis suggested coffee and liqueurs in the library.

This, like the great hall earlier, was now dimly lit by wall sconces, and outside the French doors—the curtains were still drawn back—dusk was darkening to nightfall. A fire had been started by Garvey, for even in summer Rathbourn needed fires against the west-country damp. It burned brightly in the book-lined room, and everyone gravitated toward the long Victorian sofa and old leather wing chairs that faced a low table, near enough to the blaze to catch its romantic flickering light, yet far enough away to be comfortable. Daniel seated himself on the sofa beside Fern, with Glynis opposite. Luke chose to sit somewhat shrouded in darkness, only the firelight catching the gold red gleam of brandy in his glass, while Jeremy stood whistling softly by one of the French doors. Ravenna joined him briefly.

"Thanks for the bruised ankle," she whispered.

"Sorry—a survival reflex," he said unrepentantly. "Gratitude and all that for keeping my little trip to yourself. Luke could be damned stuffy about it if he knew."

"Jeremy, I don't want to be put in a position where I have to lie to Luke. Luckily your whereabouts didn't come up today, but—"

"Righto," he chirped, moving to pour himself a liqueur when Daniel stood up to offer Ravenna a Cointreau. When Jeremy sat down, she followed suit, aware that his lighthearted reply had been a sight too agreeable. She mustn't get involved in his plots, she resolved. Instinct told her they would thicken quickly. And goodness knew exactly what was involved. Taking sides in family disputes was not her idea of a good beginning at Rathbourn.

"Have you recovered from your walk?" Luke asked her as she settled into one of the spacious chairs.

"Yes, of course."

"Next time go prepared. I think you've got the idea of our weather by now—highly unpredictable."

The weather was not the only thing that was unpredictable.

"Where exactly did you go today?" Daniel cut in, obviously irked by their tête-à-tête.

"West along the cliffs for a few miles—it was very beautiful. And so sunny I didn't even think to take a sweater."

"Luke seemed to have everything well in hand." Daniel's voice was smoothed of expression, but Ravenna saw his dark eyes settle on his stepbrother. The two men held each other's gaze, and Ravenna felt their cold anger flash. Was she the cause of it? No, surely it went much deeper than that. To Kristen and the past. To things she couldn't heal between them.

"Luke always does have things in hand," Glynis said in her warm peacemaking voice. "It's certainly good to have you home. We must plan to go over repairs to the grounds and outbuildings, Luke. Garvey had drawn up a list for your return—it's a mile long, of course."

"Certainly. Perhaps tomorrow. And Daniel," he said coolly, "we might take some time to go over the books this week."

Daniel gave a curt nod, then launched into the story of how he and Wallingford had won the bid for the shares he'd wanted against their cutthroat competitor, Jayson and Wharton. The story was not without its drama, and everyone listened more or less attentively, except for Jeremy, who stared into the fire with a preoccupied air. Thinking of his sins, Ravenna wondered? Not a chance...more likely some girl he'd left behind in London.

Luke rose to light a cigar and lean against the mantel, and Ravenna's thoughts sifted again to the surface, pleasantly mellowed by the sharp-sweet Cointreau and the snapping fire.

She was content to listen to Daniel talk, to watch him gesturing with his hands from time to time. It occurred to her that he was much more animated when talking of business and New York—that that city was his true setting because it galvanized him to action, excited him as this quiet old manor house did not. The sleepy power emanating from Rathbourn Hall didn't find its echoes in him as it did in Luke. She wondered idly if they would live at Rathbourn—it seemed Daniel had always kept his rooms there. They would have to be there periodically because of the agentship, anyway.

Aware, and not for the first time, that Luke was supremely at home in this setting—the master of the house—she wondered how he would feel about having them stay at Rathbourn after the wedding. She doubted he'd want it, despite the convenience of having Daniel at hand businesswise. And certainly she would prefer to live elsewhere, although she already loved the old house. It was just that it contained...Luke. But as her feelings for him faded—and how long could purely sexual flames last when a deeper love was at hand, after all—it might become possible. She liked Glynis; she could happily live with Glynis. No, it wouldn't be so difficult to live at Rathbourn once Luke was in London, she decided, watching Daniel's fine-boned face light up as he described this latest of his business coups. Hearing him, she realized he approached his work with all the challenge of an exciting game of chess and wished once again she could share in it.

Her eyes moved to the fire, and even though she didn't look directly at Luke, she knew exactly how the shadows fell on the sculptured planes of his jaw and how dark were the pools of his eyes as he nonchalantly leaned his long frame against the mantel. Why did he have to do everything with such natural grace? She wished she could find a way to erase her constant impression of him, and as Daniel continued on, she impatiently rose and crossed to the French doors to look out at the night. A full moon broke through the clouds, casting its unearthly glitter on the trees and gardens. She almost fancied the old statues along the paths stirring to life.

When she turned back to face the room, dreamily wishing she could escape into the velvet night, Luke's gaze moved deliberately to capture hers. He merely lifted his lashes and looked at her, and a sleepy but powerful current leaped across the long space between them with an easy naturalness, silently riveting her. With a slight knowing smile, barely visible in the dark light, he lowered his eyes to the red curve of her lips, then, caressingly it seemed, to the pearl that touched the cleft of her breasts.

If they had been alone in the room, she knew he would have moved toward her. As it was, he stood perfectly still, and she froze in turn, hypnotized, vaguely hearing Glynis say, "But, Daniel, you mean your competitors actually plotted to outbid you at the moment they thought you were en route to England? How dreadfully piratical." Their voices were muted, distant.

Luke's lips might actually have burned against her flesh in place of the softly glowing pearl, so piercing was his look. Her own lips parted slightly; her eyes hung shamelessly on the aquiline face across the room, bewitched, caught in the current that isolated them from the others. For a second she swayed almost imperceptibly toward him, like a plant drawn to the sun, and as if she'd given him permission, his gaze swept with a raking intensity over her slender bared shoulders and then to the full swell of her breasts, which lifted the milky pearl with each slow breath. They dropped to her waist, and with a gasp she knew he was mentally undressing her.

The careless male power in every line of that lean hard body facing her said he had the right to do so. If the blue green silk of her dress, faintly lustrous in the firelight, had slipped sensuously to the floor like a shed skin, she would not have been surprised, for his eyes, glittering silver with the same sleepy eroticism she'd seen in their depths when she'd lain in his arms that first night, seemed to strip her naked for his pleasure.

Slowly, like a memory of his hands, she felt his eyes slide to the curve of her hip, linger at her thighs, then slip to her calves, her feet, his gaze like midnight silk. A hot fire suffused her. She stood there transfixed, enduring his scrutiny not as an insult but as an exquisite and beautiful pleasure, feeling as if he were touching her softly all over, divesting her of all that stood between them. She waited for his eyes to meet her own, her body going up in flames. When they lifted to hers, his storm gray and darkly aroused, a sobering shock triggered through her, a cold realization of the liberty he'd just wantonly taken. As if he owned her! A rush of quiet fury leaped in her. She refused to let him look away, challenging him. But the fury in her eyes did not lessen his enjoyment...to the contrary!

It had all happened silently, swiftly, unnoticed by the others. Luke stood apart from the circle, his face partly shadowed, and she was far enough away herself to be disregarded for the moment. But how long had they stood there? Moments? Hours?

With a violent thrust backward she shattered the spell. She walked quickly to the sofa and sank down beside Daniel on the side opposite Fern, twining her hand tightly in his and leaning her cheek against his shoulder. When he put his hand possessively on her knee, glancing at her in surprise while Glynis was talking, she didn't look up. But she knew Luke wanted to kill. She knew it as surely as if he'd exploded with murderous rage, and yet not a word passed between them.

Despite her triumph she felt shaken—and it wasn't fear or rage, she knew, that shook her. She kept her gaze away from Luke's, focusing on Glynis's graceful hands folded in her lap, listening to the conversation but understanding not a word of it. A feeling of bewilderment gripped her; how could any man make her tremble merely by looking at her across a room?

"Are you cold, Ravenna?" Daniel asked, feeling her shiver.

"No, darling. I'm...I'm not cold. Just glad to have you back."

When she glanced up a moment later, Luke was gone. He'd left silently, without a good-night to anyone. The room felt strangely empty, but it was possible once more to breathe.

"Africa hasn't helped Luke's manners any," Daniel commented as everyone simultaneously noted his absence. And he leaned across Ravenna to light Glynis's cigarette.

SHE SPENT THE NIGHT tossing and turning, plumping up her pillow and then slamming it against the mattress in disgust. Nothing helped. She didn't know how long she lay in the dark, seeing Luke's eyes,

then his lips, his face, his body. In growing panic
she tried to superimpose upon them Daniel's face,
Daniel's lips...to see the eyes as brown and not
gray blue, the hair as black and not a silvery sand.
She would not let him affect her this way; she would
not. But she could only think that somewhere on
the same floor, in the room behind his study, Luke
lay sleeping—no, surely he, too, saw a face in the
dark. She didn't think he slept.

In the weak light of dawn she fell into a troubled
sleep, awaking too soon afterward and slipping
wearily down to breakfast.

For one terrible moment she thought the man behind the newspaper was Luke, but then Daniel
lowered it and said, "Good morning, darling." He
gave every sign of having had a peaceful untroubled
sleep. And why not, when last night he'd kissed her
chastely at her door, his face drawn with fatigue
from his late nights with Wallingford and the
change in hours from New York to London. She
suspected, too, that his back still bothered him.

After breakfast they walked to the cliffs. Ravenna was feeling very subdued and unsure of herself
but determined to spend every moment of the day
with Daniel in order to exorcise Luke. She had to
prove to herself that his power over her was il-
lusory, that her growing passion for him did not exist...could not engulf her in the flicker of an eye,
as it had at every encounter up to that moment.

The sea was no less spectacular than earlier that
week, and Daniel was in an easy mood. Once he
stopped to slip a buttercup behind her ear, and she

smiled with painful tenderness at him. But at some
point, as they meandered down the gorse-bordered
path, her despair lifted. After all, what was she so
upset about? Luke had merely looked at her across
a room... so why should her world fall apart? With
Daniel beside her, smiling and content just to be
with her, her fears vanished. As Daniel had said, it
was he she was marrying. She wouldn't have to con-
tend with her fears of Luke... of being consumed
by his fierceness, his wild passions, his unpredic-
tability.

At this she remembered with a jolt that it was
Daniel who had left her in the lurch a few days
earlier and that was what had precipitated the whole
chain of events. But it was just one of those... what
was it Daniel had called it? Freak accidents. The
kind of thing one couldn't blame anyone for—or
shouldn't. She shivered. These were the things that
changed people's lives.

"Darling, we won't live at Rathbourn, will we?
We'll go to London?"

Daniel swung her hand in his, his dark eyes smiling, the sun glinting gold and onyx in their depths.
"We can stay at Rathbourn from time to time, but
we'll want our own home, of course."

"Yes, I'd much prefer that."

"But why the rush? Don't you like staying at the
hall?"

"Um... it's a bit isolated, don't you think?"

"I thought you liked the country—particularly if
there are horses." He looked surprised and drew
her closer to his side.

She looked away from him, out over the blue expanse of sea. Was it cowardly of her to want to flee Rathbourn? It wasn't like her to run away. But then, Luke wasn't like any man she'd ever met back home, either, and her fear of having her orderly world swept away on a tidal wave of inexplicable passion was too great.

But she only murmured that she was, of course, eager to try Jessie, and then she suggested they stroll back through the woods. A short time later, hands entwined and Ravenna feeling a little more at peace, they reached the gardens, with their stylized topiary bushes, sculptured box pyramids and hedges and long rectangular beds of roses, which sweetened the air as they walked by.

The terrace, of a silvery gray stone that matched the house, had three broad steps leading up to it and a low stone balustrade separating it from the garden. Garlanded stone urns marked the corners, and as they passed one of them, Ravenna noticed someone standing behind the French doors, watching their approach.

A moment later Fern stepped out to meet them, once more dressed in a businesslike suit and blouse, this time gray and white, her face expressing little but the relationship of dutiful employee to employer. For an instant her eyes fell to their clasped hands. Then she said in a flat voice, "Mr. Wallingford called half an hour ago. Peters passed the call to me. He asks you to phone back as soon as possible."

Daniel looked annoyed, and the faint line between his brows deepened.

"Curse Wallingford," he muttered, but nevertheless turned to touch his lips to Ravenna's. "It looks as if we're fated to be interrupted, darling. I'll join you shortly."

Our morning together will be spoiled, she thought unhappily as he stepped into the house.

Fern made no move to follow him but stood motionless, looking at Ravenna. She appeared so tentative that Ravenna smiled. Then Fern walked casually over to the balustrade. "What a lovely morning! I'm so glad for a chance to breathe some real air again," she said.

"The air does seem to sparkle, doesn't it, almost like diamonds," Ravenna agreed. "It must be the moisture from the sea."

"Which part of the South are you from?" Fern asked, dropping her hands lightly onto the ledge and shifting so that she half sat, half leaned on the stone rail facing Ravenna.

"Kentucky, near Louisville. And you? Oh, I'm sorry. You already mentioned New York State."

Fern didn't seem offended but ran her finger across the stone surface, making a small grating sound.

"Do you have family back in the States?"

"I don't have a family," Fern replied quickly. "I grew up in an institution until I was fourteen. Then I stayed with a foster family for a while."

"Oh... I didn't know, I mean...."

"It's all right. I don't think of it much. You can't miss what you didn't have."

Ravenna would have liked to change the subject

but was uncertain how to do so without it being immediately obvious. Fern seemed such a sensitive sort, despite her offhandedness. She was fiddling with a ring on her finger, a plain band that Ravenna suddenly realized was a wedding ring.

Fern's eyes followed her gaze, and she laughed pleasantly. "You're wondering if I'm married, aren't you?" Before Ravenna could reply, she explained, "I divorced my husband seven years ago...I'm older than I look. Anderson's my married name." Her small dark eyes glanced penetratingly at Ravenna, then turned toward the gardens. "I always think Rathbourn is like an enchanted kingdom, a place in a fairy tale," she mused. "Do you like it here?"

"Yes, I find it very beautiful." How many years had Fern come here? She spoke as if she'd known it a long time. Uncomfortably Ravenna stood beside her, too curious to leave and yet not sure how to continue their conversation. But she wanted to like her; it would be unfortunate to dislike someone working so closely with Daniel.

"What do you think of Luke?" Fern asked, turning suddenly to face her. The question caught Ravenna completely off guard.

"Luke? I—I think he's, why, I don't know what to think. I've just met him."

Fern gave a small indecipherable smile. "He usually has quite an effect on women."

"Is that right?" Ravenna asked dryly.

Fern looked at her speculatively. "I find Luke interesting. You know...because of Rathbourn. It's not like anything I grew up with. And you?"

"Oh, Elk Creek was very down home, so to speak. This is all new to me, too," Ravenna confided, thinking that after all Fern was sincere and rather talkative under her enigmatic exterior. And they were both Americans. They should be allies in this strange new world.

"It's the first time I've seen him since the accident," Fern continued. "Since the day Kristen died. Do you know about that?"

"Daniel told me about it," Ravenna answered a little stiffly.

When Fern, probably aware of her hesitation, became silent, Ravenna felt her curiosity grow. Against her better judgment she began to wish the woman would go on. "I'm sure it was awful for Daniel," she felt compelled to say.

Fern slowly lifted her gaze once more to meet Ravenna's, a certain relish in her voice. " 'Awful' is an understatement. I saw the whole thing. I mean, I saw what happened when Luke heard the news. He went berserk."

Ravenna's eyebrows raised.

"Oh, well." Fern began to tug at a small weed that twined its way up the stone wall. "You know what they say—when the blood gets too blue...." She stood up as if she were going to leave.

A queasy feeling washed through Ravenna, but she heard herself ask, "What was Kristen like?"

Fern looked at her assessingly. "Blond, beautiful, Swedish, very sexy. The kind that drives men mad. Not that I'd know," she added coolly, her gaze flicking over Ravenna's own sunlit face and dazzling hair.

Ravenna diplomatically kept herself from examining Fern's slightly sallow complexion and fairly ordinary features. The woman was rather sweet, but somehow lackluster—the kind men glance at unseeingly. No light rose in men's eyes when Fern walked into rooms, she guessed.

But she'd known women far less attractive who nevertheless compelled men's gazes. Perhaps it was the stilled quality to Fern—it made her too sexless. But her comment suggested a hidden bitterness masked by self-pity, that ate at her.

Fern's startling smile suddenly swept these thoughts aside, and for an instant Ravenna saw a fleeting beauty in her, like a lamp that had been lit in a dark room. So her fires were merely banked. By what? Her marriage? Her childhood?

Fern laughed deprecatingly at herself. "Don't mind me," she said. "We can't all be blond and Swedish. Kristen was Luke's student before they became engaged," she added after a moment. "Personally, I think it's kind of tacky when a teacher gets involved with a student. But I guess it's hard to resist all those susceptible, dewy-eyed types." Again the cynicism. "Luke has a reputation for flings, from what Daniel tells me."

This was gossip, and Ravenna was shamelessly listening to it. She should leave... But Daniel certainly told his secretary a lot.

"I understood he loved her. That he found her death very hard." There, at least she'd stood up for Luke.

"Loved her? Well, they were sleeping together,

of course. And he almost killed Daniel." Fern's face grew thoughtful. "You're a romantic, aren't you," she continued with a strange look. "You really believe in all that stuff."

"Love? Of course I do. Don't . . . you?"

Fern's eyes darkened scornfully. "You forget, I've already been married." At the shocked look on Ravenna's face she added, "Well, it's different for you. You're marrying Daniel. Things will work out for you."

"Yes, of course," Ravenna murmured awkwardly.

"Some men aren't the marrying kind," she explained as if to a child. "Like my husband." Her voice lowered. "I don't know why Luke got engaged to Kristen. He's not the marrying kind, either. Men like that . . . they simply lift their little finger and women come running. Marriage never changes them." Her face was bitter.

As if she were suddenly aware she'd revealed a lot, Fern dropped her gaze. "Forget I said that. Me and my big mouth." Again the charming melting smile. "I'd better get back to my typing. Daniel may be kind, but he doesn't like slackers! The slave driver!" She laughed. "Talk to you again," and she slipped across the terrace into the library.

Ravenna took a deep breath, wondering what to make of Fern's strange mixture of jaded worldliness and childlike charm. Their talk had left her feeling churned up, but Ravenna admitted she deserved it. She could have tactfully refused to discuss Luke and Kristen, she supposed. Could have talked about . . . what? What did she and Fern have in common, after all? Well, there was Daniel. The absurdity of this struck her as, still uneasy, she went in to lunch.

She almost walked into Peters as she rounded a doorway. He told her madam had asked that lunch be served on the lawn under the chestnut trees, to take advantage of the splendid weather. He directed her to the right exit, and Ravenna's train of thought was broken.

It was while they were handing around the sandwiches that Glynis told her Luke had left Rathbourn. "He was gone before any one was up," she said. "I do think it odd. He said only last night we might discuss the estate with Garvey today. It's not like him to go away without attending to things."

"Perhaps he was called to London by a client," Ravenna suggested glibly, thinking that to the contrary she knew exactly why he'd left—after their encounter of the previous night. But her heart soared. Luke had gone! She was shocked at the amount of relief she felt . . . as if she'd been given an unexpected reprieve. And then, as Glynis went on, she was angry that even his absence could affect her so.

"Oh, no. He told Peters exactly where he was going. He's in Cornwall, working on a house near Fowey," Glynis was saying. "Something he started more than two years ago, I believe. But you'd think it could have waited a few days." Her large soft eyes were thoughtful.

"Luke doesn't live in the same world as everyone else," Daniel volunteered. "And he seldom takes other people into account."

Ravenna's and Glynis's eyes met. They both looked slightly startled, as if each were thinking Daniel might be describing himself. But they went on to talk of other things, and Ravenna was soon happily aware that Daniel's mood had lightened almost as much as hers with the news of Luke's departure.

All through lunch he was full of good humor, reminding her once again of the man she'd fallen in love with in Kentucky. His eyes rested on her with a certain unmistakable intensity when Glynis left them, but his expression changed as she attempted unsuccessfully to hide a yawn. Her sleepless night was catching up with her.

"You're tired," he accused mildly.

"Oh, not really. Just very relaxed. It must be the change of climate." She fumbled for words and willed herself wide awake.

He leaned over her and took her hand in his. "I was thinking we might drive into Salcombe for dinner, but—"

"Oh, let's, Daniel. I'd love to see it."

So it was that half an hour later Salcombe lay before them, a pleasant town of narrow irregular streets winding up from the waterfront. It basked in sunshine at the end of its long silver harbor, in sharp contrast to her first rainy view of it on the drive to Rathbourn. Its waters were now alive with boats, small and large, scudding about in this yachtsman's paradise.

They parked near the docks and spent a while strolling alongside the boats, watching fish being unloaded, sails being furled, nets sorted, all the intriguing tackle of men who spend their days on the sea. When they tired of this, Daniel led her in the direction of an old seafood house for a quiet romantic dinner.

On their way, as they were crossing a busy corner, Ravenna said in a surprised voice, "There's Jeremy!"

"Jeremy?" Daniel turned to follow her gesture as she waved at a young man who had turned his back.

But she added in a disappointed voice, "He's gone inside that building. Should we go after him?"

"It couldn't have been Jeremy, darling. He's holed up at Rathbourn. I saw him loaded down with books this afternoon—said Peters was sending up his meals."

Knowing this was small guarantee, Ravenna said only, "Well, I didn't see him clearly. Perhaps you're right."

But as they reached the curb, she looked back. Salcombe Playhouse, the signboard swinging above the building's entrance read in a flourish of stylized script beside a red-painted griffin. Suddenly she was certain it had been Jeremy. So that's where he disappeared to. Luke would be less than pleased if he found out. But she could hardly tell Luke her suspicions—it would be like spying on Jeremy. No, as far as she was concerned, it was none of her business. She would just let events take their course, and the two brothers work things out themselves.

After a delicious dinner of fresh lobster, they drove back in the dark along the shadowy lane to Rathbourn. Once again Ravenna felt awe when the house loomed silver in the darkness, a solid mass of pale stone that did seem like something from a fairy tale, as Fern had said. But this time Ravenna was feeling more at peace. Her day with Daniel had restored her perspective; she was certain now that everything would come out all right, as he had promised. And Luke was gone...she was safe from him. She breathed deeply of the fresh summer's night as they silently mounted the steps to the house. A faint chirping of night insects and the wind in the leaves came to her, reminding her of peaceful nights on the farm, under the same moon that shone down on them at Rathbourn.

Although convinced she would fall asleep the instant she reached her bed—how could she not, after the cool air, the wine, the good food and her sleeplessness of the previous night—she was still tempted to ask Daniel to stay with her. She didn't admit it was to erase all thoughts of Luke. It was just that...she needed to be close to her fiancé.

He read this in her eyes, and his lips lingered hungrily on hers, but he finally said, "You're too tired, Ravenna. Tomorrow, darling."

She was touched by his concern, she supposed, and his patience. But when she saw him turn in at the door next to his bedroom, the one that housed his office, a small ignoble doubt nagged at her. Was it really concern for her? Or just that he wanted to work?

She did fall asleep almost at once, too tired to worry and grateful that her mind cast up no tormenting images. Only she would have liked, she thought as she drifted off, to have slept in Daniel's arms....

When did she feel the arms go about her? Perhaps it was midnight, for it was very dark beneath the hangings of her four-poster bed. The arms enfolded her slowly, gently, and she murmured in her sleep as lips softly touched her hair and face, and a hand slid down her back, caressing her through the satiny folds of her nightgown. The other hand tangled in her hair. The covers moved, and someone lay beside her in the bed, shifting her carefully into his arms. A feeling of warmth spread within her, and she nestled close, stirring in her sleep. She would have sunk more deeply into dreams, but a pair of lips touched her throat; she was being held a little too tightly.

Then she knew. These were not the right arms. She mustn't give in to them. She mustn't.... Gray blue eyes flashed in her dreams; she was back in Luke's arms at the town house, struggling to be free.

"No," she murmured, "you mustn't. Please...." And her hands pressed sleepily at the shoulders and arms of the man who held her.

"It's all right, darling, ssshhh, it's all right. Go back to sleep. I'll be close beside you...."

But it wasn't all right. These were not the right arms.

"Don't, Luke, don't!" she cried, pushing wildly against him.

Her own voice wakened her.

Daniel stared down at her, and even in the dark she could sense that his face was flushed with a cold shocked anger. He was only inches away—she could feel the medical tape still binding his sore back—but in a second he thrust her roughly from him, back into the pillows. Then he swung out of the bed and threw his dressing gown about him.

"Daniel! You startled me!"

"Did I?" His voice was deadly. "I don't think it's the first time you've been startled...is it, Ravenna?"

His eyes dragged over her, darkly accusing. Then he turned on his heel and disappeared through the adjoining bathroom to his room.

She was too stunned even to think of following him.

CHAPTER FIVE

IN THE MORNING her mind was made up. She had no choice but to tell Daniel the truth—or a version of it—if she was to mend the breach. Perhaps she could tell him she'd arrived at the town house in the dark and walked into Luke in the drawing room, without knowing who he was. That on impulse he'd taken her in his arms and kissed her... frightened her. That she'd been dreaming of this incident when Daniel had come to her bed. It sounded very implausible, but real life was often implausible.

Would he believe her? Well, she'd take her chances. It wasn't the whole truth, but there was no way she could tell him what had really happened. This much would be upsetting enough.

It would do nothing to help the already damaged relations between the stepbrothers, she realized. But her choice was clear. This, or risk losing Daniel.

She decided all this while pacing up and down her bedroom in the morning after a miraculously sound sleep. So tired had she been that not even that bizarre midnight scene had kept her awake long. She was glad, for her rested mind was now crystal clear.

Steeling herself with a last brave look in the venetian mirror in her dressing alcove, she crossed the bathroom to tap at Daniel's door. No answer. Well, it wasn't surprising. At eight-thirty in the morning he'd likely gone to breakfast. She gathered her courage and marched downstairs. If she was lucky, she might catch him alone in the morning room.

But only Glynis was there. She glanced up as Ravenna entered. "Good morning, my dear. You look very rested." She put down her coffee and made a face. "You've just missed them, you know. I told Daniel I thought it a terrible shame, leaving you alone again."

Leaving her alone again? "Oh," Ravenna said cautiously, going to the sideboard to choose her breakfast. She kept her back to Glynis, her voice normal. "Well, these things happen," she ventured. But *what* had happened?

"Daniel said you were being very understanding. Frankly I would have put my foot down—that man's been married to business for too long. But I suppose Wallingford's the real villain."

Ravenna gripped the edge of the sideboard. He had gone to New York *again*? Without talking to her? For a moment she felt faint and quickly moved to sit down on one of the straight-backed chairs near Glynis, her face a chalky white.

"Ravenna! I knew it—he's been insensitive, and of course you feel dreadful. Imagine! Rushing off like that!" Quickly the Englishwoman stood up and poured her a hot coffee. "Here, drink this."

The hot liquid brought back the blood to Ravenna's face, and she gulped it down gratefully, scrambling to gather her defenses. "I'm. . . I'm all right, Glynis. It's just that, well, I hated to tell him how much I would miss him," she lied.

"Of course you will, but not to worry. They'll be back soon. Daniel hates New York in the hot weather. And I didn't believe him for a moment when he said you didn't mind, the ass. How people can be so blind. . . ." She patted her arm awkwardly.

Ravenna, feeling a fool, managed a weak smile and began to chew automatically on her toast. It tasted like cardboard. So Fern had gone, too. But why had he rushed away without giving her a chance to explain? Why? It was so unfair, so infuriating. . . .

She grasped at straws. Maybe Daniel really had been urgently called to New York. Maybe something had gone wrong at the last minute with the shares he was bidding on. She simply couldn't believe he would leave Rathbourn willingly, condemning her by his silent departure. Perhaps she could ask Peters if a call had come through. . . . She dared not ask Glynis, who obviously thought Daniel had told her everything. Including when he would return, she supposed.

"Well, we're down to three now—you, me and Jeremy. My sons are uncommonly hard on their mother—rushing off at the least notice." Glynis sighed ruefully, and Ravenna realized she'd been selfishly thinking merely of herself. For of course, Luke had left only yesterday, and now Daniel.

But it wasn't Lady Glynis who had made them go.

Ravenna spent a depressing morning walking in the gardens, unable to work or think. Finally she gravitated to the stables, where she asked O'Reilly to saddle up Jessie for her. She still hadn't been shown the trails, but no matter. She felt compelled to ride... just to *do* something.

"Now, miss, if you head down the rear drive, you'll hit a trail in the woods, branchin' off to the left. Stick to the left again when you come to a forkin' of the ways, and you'll come out all right... 'bout opposite the house on t'other side." O'Reilly waved her off, smacking Jessie's flanks lightly as she passed.

The ride restored her. Jessie *was* spirited, and the familiar lighthearted Ravenna partially emerged again. She'd had too much simple, down-home happiness in her Kentucky childhood to believe that life could fall to pieces because of one misunderstanding.

Anyway, Daniel ought to have more faith in her. She'd done nothing deliberate to betray him—circumstances had merely connived against her. It was easy to forget her worries on the wooded trail, with the sun sifting golden through the network of branches high above. Flushed and almost happy again, long hair flying in the wind, she reached the end of the woods, and Rathbourn came in sight. A fast gallop across the parkland meadow brought her to the lawns and house and the red-brick stables. No, nothing was irresolvable, not if she could help it.

Determined not to brood, she spent the afternoon

and early evening systematically going over the shelves in the library, looking for books that could help her with her project. There was row upon row of handsome, leather-bound volumes from the expansive days when books had been privately bound. She handled these with delight, smelling the covers and fingering the soft vellum pages and old marbled endpapers. But eventually she got around to her original purpose and collected a sizable pile of large and small texts on Georgian Palladianism as well as the neoclassical period, when Robert Adam had been working.

She stacked these unceremoniously on the faded but still beautiful Persian carpet. Then she hunted up Garvey in the servants' hall. He was younger and stronger than the gray-haired Peters and was delighted to help her cart them to the little room upstairs off Luke's study. After all, she needed a place to work, and Luke was in Cornwall. When—if—Luke came back, she'd move everything into her bedroom. A vision of that lovely room strewn with papers and books made her grimace; she hoped Luke would stay away. But this was the least of her reasons.

"You and Mr. Jeremy make a pair, miss," Garvey said, struggling with the last of the heavy books.

The elusive Jeremy, whom she hadn't seen since yesterday in Salcombe. Garvey assured her he was working as usual. "Won't even come down to tea. Says I'm to set his sandwich outside the door and leave him to his suffering. Never seen him hit the books like this before. Goes up like clockwork right after lunch and not a hair on his head do we see till dinner. Unnatural, don't you think?''

At least he had his escape route down to a system.

THE NEXT MORNING Ravenna started on her book in earnest. Daniel hadn't called yet—as if uncertain what to say—and she resigned herself to work and wait, fighting off a deepening depression. The small study, she was glad to see, was perfect for her needs, with its old fruitwood desk lined with cubbyholes, its capacious bookshelves and an additional table beneath the tall windows, long and broad enough for her to spread out her research books on. There was also a reading chair upholstered in dark brown wool and an old footstool beside a good lamp. Luke seemed to use the room as a holdall for the overflow from his main study, she noticed; the filing cabinet behind the door was overstuffed and untidy, and one whole wall was jammed with books and the architectural magazines he subscribed to by the dozen. Still, when she cleared the desk and table there was ample room to begin.

She read for three hours, tentatively choosing ten buildings for her book, three of them in London. Then she began skimming the books and putting slips in any relevant chapters. Few weren't relevant, it seemed, and she foresaw long hours of reading.

She was deeply absorbed for a while, till suddenly a wave of despair again hit her. Daniel! She wasn't made for intrigues or waiting for solutions. If something didn't happen soon, she'd fly to New York herself. And beard him in Wallingford's den? The thought made her smile.

"Oh, hell!" she exclaimed aloud, knowing her concentration was ruined. Sweeping the books aside, she almost ran out through Luke's study and down the gallery and the stairs. As she came around the curved banister at the foot of them, she dashed straight into Jeremy. He reached out both arms to steady her.

"Whoa! Where's the fire?"

"Oh, Jeremy! I was just going out."

"Funny thing, I was just going out, too. Amazing coincidence. Like to join me for a ride?"

"On your motorcycle?"

"Lord, no! On Rathbourn's handsome nags."

Minutes later they were trotting through the estate woods mounted on Lloyd George and Jessie, moving in single file along the same trail Ravenna had taken yesterday. But when they got to the fork, Jeremy led her to the right instead of the left.

"Where are we heading?"

"Through the woods to the fields near the coastal path. A good long ride. Up to it?"

"You bet."

They rode in pleasant silence for a while, enjoying the sun and soft, sea-moist air, with Gwydion and Albion running ahead, stopping to sniff at tree roots and mark the trail in their own inimitable way. Ravenna's long hair was several times in danger of tangling in the tree branches, and she wished she'd tied it back, until Jeremy looked around, then stopped to hand her a neck scarf from his pocket.

"That'll do it," he said. "Scarlett. I think I'll call you Scarlett, Scarlett. That O'Hara woman."

"She had dark hair and green eyes."

"Never could figure out why she was called Scarlett. Suits you a damn sight better."

She smiled as they took up their reins again. Jeremy began to whistle and continued for a while, until suddenly he said, his tone coolly matter-of-fact, "So you spotted me in Salcombe."

"Jeremy! It *was* you!"

"You mean you weren't sure?"

"Mmm . . . pretty sure."

"Well, are you going to turn king's evidence?"

"You know perfectly well I'm not. It's between you and Luke. And you and your flabby conscience."

Jeremy moaned, smiting his breast with the flat of his hand. " 'A challenge, on my life.' "

"Do you go to Salcombe every afternoon?"

" 'Thou hast most kindly hit it.' "

"Pardon?"

"We're rehearsing *Romeo and Juliet* six days a week."

"Jeremy! You mean that every single afternoon—"

"I cannot tell a lie."

Hmmph, she thought, *you and George Washington*.

"This is my one day off. And I also can't bear to face Goethe and Rimbaud."

"Have you considered that you might fail your next year, Jeremy? Have you even thought of it?"

"Then I'll apply to RADA—the Royal Academy of Dramatic Arts. That's where I wanted to go, anyway. Luke strong-armed me into a university degree...if I ever get that far."

"Surely he was thinking of your future."

"Blast Luke! What does he know about my future? I'm almost twenty years old and all I've got under my belt is one summer of repertory touring Ireland and now this summer-stock company. Gielgud made his debut at the Old Vic when he was seventeen and played Romeo, at the Regent, when he was twenty. And all I've done is walk-ons and a gravedigger in a light comedy and now Mercutio at Salcombe Playhouse. Nobody's even heard of Salcombe Playhouse! Mind you, I'm partial to Mercutio—it's a good part—but I'm getting on in years, and let's face it, Ravenna, Luke has no heart. He won't listen to a word I say. With all my money tied up in trust until next year, he's got me—"

"Hog-tied?"

Jeremy chuckled. "Ravenna, you're a sight for sore ears," he misquoted glibly. But she was thinking that despite his sad tale, with his expensive Harley Davidson and beautiful clothes, Jeremy hardly struck her as deprived.

"Say, do you ever think of acting? I've noticed you've got natural timing," he was saying now.

"No," she confessed with a gulp. Natural timing? It was her timing that had been getting her in hot water ever since she'd come to England. Luckily Jeremy, ahead of her on Lloyd George, couldn't see her face. She redirected the conversation. "What are you studying at U of L?"

"English literature and history. French and German lit are just minors. It's interesting, I suppose, but it's not what I really want. Y' know, nothing works unless you're going for what you really want in life."

This was true, she thought, as they rode agreeably onward, passing an old thatched cottage under the trees, whitewashed and quaint, which Jeremy said had been used for hunting purposes years ago and was still kept up. Then minutes later they came to the fields, where they dismounted by a fallen tree at the edge of the woods and let the horses graze. It was a stunningly beautiful day, and the heather, a sea of purple spreading before them under a turquoise sky, smelled strong on the wind.

"You remind me of someone, you know, Scarlett." Jeremy, looking strangely like Luke, was leaning against a tree and smoking. Ravenna sat nearby on the ground. "Name of Angela Heyward. She's hot right now in London at the Globe. Friend of mine," he said casually. "American."

She smiled curiously. Was this who Jeremy pined for in London?"

"Where's she from?"

"LA, land of the celluloids. But she's a stage actress, well-known over here. I mean, known in certain circles." His tone hinted that he, too, moved in these circles, and his offhandedness made it clear to Ravenna's discerning eye that Angela Heyward was

more important to him than his words suggested.
But if she was well-known, surely she must be older
than Jeremy?

"Angela's coming in to Salcombe to see me open
in *Romeo and Juliet*. Thinks I might be the coming
thing, y' see." He laughed deprecatingly. "Like to
tag along and meet her?"

"In Salcombe, you mean? Why not bring her to
Rathbourn?"

"Wouldn't work," he answered hurriedly. "She
said she'd like to visit Rathbourn, but not yet. No,
what I had in mind was your taking in the play, then
coming backstage afterward. Maybe a late dinner
for the three of us. D' you like Shakespeare?"

"Yes, but Jeremy—I don't really think I want to
get mixed up in this. You're supposed to be studying every day, and Luke and Glynis have no
idea...."

He blew a few smoke rings in the air before answering. "Look at it this way, Ravenna. All I'm
asking you to do is see me act. Daniel and Luke
have never come along to one of my plays. I could
use some family support." He was looking straight
at her. So it was his work he wanted her to see as
much as or more than Angela Heyward. His appeal
was so sincere that her hesitation melted like ice in
the blazing sun. If Jeremy wanted to act, why
shouldn't he act? And he deserved an audience if he
was so serious about it. What right did Luke have to
try to arrange his half brother's life, anyway? That
autocratic so-and-so.

"The one thing I can't understand, Scarlett—"

his voice was rough "—is this. Luke loves his work. It's his heart and soul, architecture. Why can't he let me have mine? Y' know, when I was a kid, Luke could do no wrong. Worshipped him, I did. Used to cut out every clipping on him—he was always being written up, the famous Sir Anthony—and paste them in a big scrapbook. Big-brother Luke. I wanted to be like him when I grew up. But now I don't understand him. As soon as dad died, he changed—seemed to take everything so much more seriously. Especially my bloody future!"

"I suspect he feels responsible for you."

"*I'm* responsible for my future, not Luke! If he would only come to see me act, he'd know he can't stop me. He shouldn't even try."

"I'm sure he will see you act one day," she said, distressed at the conflict in Jeremy's face. How unfeeling of Luke never to go to his plays; didn't he care about what was important to his brother?

"But you'll come, won't you? Thursday after next?"

There was no way out of it now. "Yes . . . yes, of course. Perhaps Daniel—"

"Daniel will tell Luke," he said quickly. "Better not bring him."

"But I thought you said—"

"I'd like Luke to see my work when the time is ripe," Jeremy explained, "but if he cottons on to the Salcombe thing too soon, it'll cost me my summer. Scarlett, he'd hit the bloody rafters. All those stale sandwiches eaten in vain . . . ugh!"

"I beg your pardon?"

"Oh, Garvey brings 'em up everyday at teatime. The mice nibble them till I get in. Then I take over so Mary won't do some detecting in the wastebasket. Live-in help are the devil on a life of crime."

She fixed a mocking eye on him. " 'O what a tangled web we weave/When first we practice to deceive,' " she quoted, and suddenly stopped short. Jeremy wasn't the only one weaving tangled snarling webs these days, was he? She was getting pretty good at it herself.

Nevertheless her ride with Jeremy helped take her mind off her own problems, and it "Put the roses in yer cheeks," as O'Reilly told her when they got back.

"Mr. Daniel on the telephone for you, Miss Ravenna," Peters said after lunch as she crossed the great hall toward the stairs. She stopped dead, then turned and said she would take it upstairs in her room.

"Darling!" she exclaimed, safely ensconced on her sofa. "How...how are you?"

"Very well." He didn't sound it. "And you?"

"I'm perfectly fine. But, Daniel—"

"I just called to see that you're all right. Look, if you don't mind, I prefer to discuss the other night when I get back. I'm in Wallingford's office right now...and it's hard to talk."

She had no idea if he'd listen, but she plunged ahead. "I simply wanted to say, Daniel, that there's really nothing to explain. I was just having a bad

dream...for some silly reason I was dreaming of
Luke. I...didn't think it very fair of you to rush
off like that.''

He was silent a moment, and she held her breath.
Did he believe her? She *had* been dreaming of Luke.
Then he said uncertainly, ''I suppose I frightened
you, coming in when you were asleep.''

''You did startle me.''

He had the grace to apologize. ''I'd been working
in my office...came in on impulse. You looked so
beautiful lying there. It was selfish of me, I admit,
but I didn't plan to wake you. Look, Ravenna, I expect to be back soon—we'll talk more then. I had to
rush back here on short notice because Wallingford
called. We're having more trouble with Jayson and
Wharton, and now I have to go over the money
market with him—we're considering trading in the
Japanese yen and the Swiss franc. Well, don't let
me bore you with the details. Fern says to say
hello.''

''The details don't bore me, Daniel,'' she said
quietly. ''I *want* to know about your work.''

He sounded surprised. ''Fern said...oh, never
mind. Well, then, I'll be glad to explain more about
it some time. Not now.'' Then softly he added,
''Ravenna...perhaps I was a bit hasty, leaving like
that.''

''A bit hasty!'' Her mouth dropped at his euphe-
mism for ''wildly unpredictable.''

''Yes, I think so, honey,'' she breathed.

''I told Glynis you knew about it, too...when of
course you didn't.''

"So I gathered." When he came back, she would tell him how upset she'd been at his mishandling of this.

"You're really all right—no problems at Rathbourn?"

"No. . . but I miss you, Daniel." And she did.

He paused. Then his voice deepened, as if he, too, hated to be separated. "I'll be back in a day or two, darling. Say hello to Glynis for me." He rang off, and Ravenna put down the receiver with the beginnings of relief. At least they'd made a start at getting things back to normal—if any engagement could be normal with both parties on opposite sides of the Atlantic.

Staring at the phone, still lost in thought, she suddenly wondered what Fern had said.

THURSDAY DAWNED a brilliant day, and she and Glynis spent the morning shopping in Salcombe. Ravenna was unable to resist the beautiful wool sweaters found everywhere for sale in Britain and added another handknit Fair Isle and a fisherman's cableknit to her already more than adequate sweater stock. A knee-high pair of riding boots in ox-blood leather caught her eye and helped empty her wallet for the day. With a laugh she told Glynis they'd better skedaddle—and received a polite request for a translation.

"Have you planned your trousseau?" Glynis asked as they drove back to Rathbourn.

"Daniel promised me we'd spend a few days shopping in London sometime before we fly home—to Kentucky, that is, and then a day or two in New York. And I'm wearing my grandmother's wedding dress, so that's taken care of." The beautiful full-skirted satin dress with handmade lace trimming the bodice and skirt had been carefully preserved through three generations in her family. Faithful to family tradition, it had been worn by each of her sisters, except for the still single Ginia. With a few tucks at the waist it would fit Ravenna perfectly.

"My dressmaker is making me up some things, too," she explained. "A little old Hungarian lady, Mrs. Cserepy, who designs and sews like a New York couturiere. My sisters and I keep her strictly to ourselves—we're afraid half the U.S. would flock to her doorstep. She does the most wonderful French lingerie and basics such as wool suits and coats. And I get most of my evening wear from her."

"What about your wedding plans?" Glynis wanted to know. "Isn't it awkward, with you here and the wedding taking place on the farm? Who's arranging it all?"

"The whole thing would be impossible except that my mother loves to do such things. She's having the invitations printed for us—that reminds me, I have to send her the list! And the rest will be very small and simple, at our parish church, with Ginia as bridesmaid and Alix and Melissa—my married sisters—as matrons of honor. The reception will be on the farm. Mom's been through it all twice before. Says she's an old hand. We'll be back just in time for the rehearsal. You're coming with us, aren't you?'' She turned to Glynis. ''We'd really love to have you there.''

Glynis smiled. ''I wouldn't miss it for the world.''

Ravenna had made it a habit to ride Jessie every morning now, but the shopping trip had prolonged itself to lunchtime, and after lunch she debated whether to head for the stables or go up to Luke's study as usual. With a mental apology to Jessie, she opted for the latter and strode upstairs to work, patting herself on the back for such discipline. Still, her research was so truly absorbing that an hour flew by, ending with her curled up in the brown armchair over a book on historic Saltram House.

At two she stood up and yawned, then wandered into the larger study to stretch her legs. She really ought to examine the books in there, she thought, glancing around at the solid masculine room hung with small landscapes painted by Sir Richard. But first she strolled over to the drafting table and studied the floor plans and watercolor renderings of what was obviously a private home. Had Luke designed it? Perhaps it was the place in Cornwall. Idly she noticed how much more modern than Rathbourn it was; it reminded her of sketches she'd seen of houses by Frank Lloyd Wright. Surely not Luke's taste!

After a desultory study of the framed degrees, the photos of several renovations—all historical in character—and a picture of Luke in an informal classroom setting, she considered the bookshelves. There were probably as many or more books there on eighteenth-century architecture as in the larger but less specialized library downstairs. Why hadn't she thought of looking there earlier? Because, she supposed, it meant a lot more reading!

She climbed the tall A-shaped ladder—an antique—that was sitting by the shelves and sat on the top rung to pull down a large volume entitled, *Houses under the Four Georges*. Something beside it slipped and almost fell, but she reached out and caught it. A photo in a heavy gold frame.

Kristen. She was certain it was Kristen. A beautiful laughing girl of obviously Swedish origin, hanging on Luke's arm, while he smiled down at her. The perfect couple, handsome and fair, both bursting with vitality. Fern had told the truth: Kristen had been very beautiful, with a faintly exotic piquant face and silvery blond hair. Ravenna could imagine the children she and Luke would have had—exquisitely blond and blue-eyed.

She stared at the photo as if doing so would reveal Kristen to her, feeling the faint sadness of knowing that this beautiful woman had died before she'd barely lived. The picture had an unreal quality about it. It seemed misted with time—although it must have been taken only the previous summer.

"Hello, Ravenna."

Her stomach lurching wildly, Ravenna dropped the photo. Luke deftly caught it, glanced at it briefly and then placed it back on one of the shelves. She gaped at him, her heart suddenly gone awry and hammering too loudly. He was very life-size in riding breeches and fisherman's sweater—exactly like the sweater she'd just bought in Salcombe, she noted—his carved lips curving to a slow smile. Where had he appeared from? She hadn't heard even a rustle behind her.

"Cat got your tongue?"

"You're back," she said stupidly.

"Of course I'm back. I live here," he mocked.

"Well, I meant . . . ."

"Yes?"

"It's just that you left so suddenly. I thought—"

Her eyes gave her away. "That I left because of you?" he asked in seeming surprise. Then he laughed outright. "It astonishes me, Ravenna, how much power you women attribute to yourselves. No, I had a sudden whim to go to Cornwall, that's all."

Was he lying? Her cheeks flamed in embarrassment as his gray blue eyes rested steadily on her face. She felt an itch to slap its perfection but had the sense to realize that any urge for physical contact with Luke was suspect. The last time she'd tried that—without success—had been in the car outside Rathbourn, and she had few illusions as to the feelings behind it. Her eyes fell on the photo Luke had replaced on the shelf, and with an effort she said the only thing that came to mind. "She's very beautiful."

"Kristen?" His face closed, the expression unreadable. "She was." He added nothing more but moved to sit on the edge of his desk.

Perched on top of the ladder, Ravenna began to feel rather silly as he watched her, his eyes as cool and gray as morning mist, his hair slightly silvered from the sun, his face more tanned than when he'd left. He must have been working outdoors. And now he'd been riding, she could see. Had probably returned while they were in Salcombe, since he hadn't appeared for lunch, and gone directly to the stables.

"When did you get back?" she asked, coming carefully down the ladder. She paused halfway—perhaps it would be safer to stay up there, she suddenly thought.

"A couple of hours ago." His eyes flicked over her; he folded his arms across his chest and said sternly, "Finding you in my quarters is becoming a habit."

She lifted her chin. "I wasn't snooping. I was just looking for some books on the Georges. You said I could use—"

He laughed, and she saw that his sternness was a pretense. Then he stood up and crossed the main study to glance into the little room. "Don't protest so much, Ravenna. It gives you away. You look quite nicely settled in."

"I'll be glad to move everything to my bedroom," she said coolly.

"Whatever for?" He looked genuinely surprised. "I meant it when I said you could have this room for yourself." His eyes narrowed with sudden amusement. "Of course, you won't get much work done if you're afraid to come down off the ladder...."

She descended with as much dignity as she could muster after that, his eyes on her every move.

"That's better," he pronounced. Slowly he sat down in the swivel chair behind his desk, lifting one foot, encased in a tall riding boot, to rest on top of the paper-strewn surface. This lordly gesture irritated her enormously.

"Instead of standing there like a self-righteous Orphan Annie, why don't you sit down and talk to me," he continued with a charming grin, reminding her exactly of Jeremy in that moment. Charm did run in the Rathbourn family, all right. "Catch me up on the excitements of home."

"What excitements?" Her irritation escaped into her voice, but she seated herself on the sofa opposite him.

"Well, how's your book coming, for one?" he asked, ignoring her sharpness.

"Very well, thank you. And how was your work in Cornwall?" she inquired with studied politeness. Why was he being so pleasant? Was it possible she'd misread that whole scene on Sunday night? It *had* been very dark in the library.

"Glynis mentioned Cornwall?"

She nodded.

"It's going well—as well as can be expected when I've been away from it for a year. Everything's got to be set up again... workmen's schedules, the lot."

"I really ought to be getting back to work on my book," she said abruptly, even rudely.

"Of course." Luke's reply was swift, and he was still smiling openly as he played with a ruler on the desk. "That's exactly what I was about to suggest."

"You were?"

"In the form of a field trip. How about I take you over to Saltram House this afternoon? It's as purely Georgian as you'll get and ought to go into your book."

Of course it was going into her book. She didn't need his advice to decide that. But still she cast around for a good excuse to say no to several hours of his undiluted company. His gray eyes pinned hers, amused and cool...but, no, not dangerous. This Luke was pleasant, almost too pleasant.

"I really have a lot more reading to do today before I can even think of looking at houses," she murmured, getting up and moving to the door of the smaller study.

Luke said casually, "Well, suit yourself, but Glynis and I are going over to see it today. She wants to make inquiries about having some local school children go through it with her next week—one of her projects. I'll tell her you can't make it." He stood up with a disinterested air.

She stopped on the threshold and turned back to him. "Glynis is coming? Well, perhaps...I wouldn't want to disappoint her. She might like to have my company—we had such a nice morning together." Great—a way to see Saltram House with an architect, and safely chaperoned by Glynis!

Luke smiled and swung his foot off the desk. His voice hearty, he said, "Fine, then. We'll leave just as soon as I change. Oh," he added, "and bring your notebook. You'll need it."

AN HOUR LATER Saltram House, a magnificent old manor built of warm yellow stone and about five times the size of Rathbourn, stood before them. Set deep in its emerald lawns, with the soft blue hills beyond and the sky hanging above it misted to a faint lilac, it overlooked the wide sweep of the River Plym and in the distance the old city of Plymouth, from whose docks the Mayflower itself had set sail for America in 1620.

Ravenna already had the idea of using this lovely old house as the major focus in her book, and it wasn't long before this became a resolve. The outside views themselves were spectacular, and one glance inside made her glad she'd also taken the time to change before Luke had ushered them out to the car. Even now her paisley-silk shirtwaist barely did justice to Saltram's majesty.

Luke was welcomed at the manor house by the woman in charge, a dark-haired, petite lady in her mid-thirties. "What a delight to see you back from Africa, Sir Anthony. Certainly you must feel free to take Lady Glynis and Miss Jones around the house. You won't need our assistance, I suppose?"

"No, thanks. We'll be taking our time, as Miss Jones is researching a book. Do you mind?" He smiled easily, and Ravenna saw the woman warm visibly under his gaze.

"Not in the least. Perhaps you might join us for tea in the Red Velvet Drawing Room when you're finished."

Luke said they would, and they moved away through the Entrance Hall into the even more imposing Staircase Hall.

"You're known here," Ravenna remarked.

"I did a TV production on Saltram a while back—portrait of the times, that sort of thing," he told her. "I'm quite familiar with the house. Now, Glynis—" he turned to her "—can you bear it if I go into detail for Ravenna's sake? It won't bore you?"

"Go ahead, Luke. I'll use the material myself when I bring the school children here."

The rest of the afternoon flew by as they explored the house and grounds, with Luke expounding on every aspect for Ravenna's sake. She could see how he must captivate his students, for something of Luke the professor came through, as did the touted warmth, authority and energy so much mentioned by the press. He delved into the history of the materials used, the craftsmanship, the artists employed, the background of the architecture. Occasionally he threw in sidelights on the times, the events happening in London and on the continent—for Saltram had been well-known in the days of that famous man of letters, Dr. Johnson, and his sidekick, Boswell. Luke mentioned David Garrick, the actor; painters as different as Sir Joshua Reynolds and William Blake; the designers Chippendale, Sheraton and Hepplewhite. England had been a world power then, and the American colonies were just being settled. A context grew for Ravenna from his words, wrapping the house in history.

Luke in turn seemed to take pleasure in her continual delight in everything. A subtle shifting in their relationship occurred as she opened toward him in this new sharing of interests. Gone were her guarded looks and careful manners, to be replaced by a more normal state for her, one of enthusiasm and enjoyment. Luke himself was relaxed, and when he occasionally took her arm or touched her shoulder to direct her attention to something, he did it naturally, caught up in what he was showing her.

Some of the lower rooms had been renovated by Robert Adam, one of the greatest neoclassical architects and designers, and it was largely these for which Saltram was justly famed. Ravenna found them breathtaking—the blue-and-white Eating Room, which had once been a library, and the so-called Great Room, an enormous blue-and-gold drawing room of palatial dimensions. These were in Adam's exquisitely airy, light, elegant style—his own interpretation of the Palladian style from the continent.

As the afternoon wore on, they visited the greenhouses, the kitchen gardens, the arched wine cellars, the Orangery—a small, Palladian-style garden building designed for the wintering of exotic shrubs such as orange trees—and the stable block, with its lovely clock tower and bell. The deer park, too, its entrance guarded by stone stags. The gleaming River Plym flowed in the background, and the wooded hills climbed nearby. Using up three rolls of film, Ravenna found, was no problem at all.

"Bloody American tourist," Luke teased, and she stuck her tongue out at him.

In the ride back to Rathbourn, after a sumptuous tea with the manageress during which Glynis discussed her coming visit, Ravenna suddenly realized how completely at ease she was feeling with Luke. She had actually enjoyed every moment of their outing. He'd been just as charming as Jeremy, so she'd found herself relating to him with the same camaraderie, as if all her fears had dissolved.

"Oh, my feet," Glynis groaned from the back seat. "I feel like I've walked miles."

"You have," Luke confirmed. "About four, I should think. Tired, Ravenna?" His gray eyes glanced at her and then returned to the road.

"Not really. I found it marvelous—a great help for my book, thank you. I have a sense of having just stepped back into the past—kind of awesome, if you know what I mean."

"Yes, I think I do. I frequently feel that way myself in my restoration work."

The peacefulness lasted as they neared Rathbourn. Ravenna reflected that not once had Luke looked at her meaningfully or spoken mockingly; the intensity between them had diminished to point zero. *Thank heavens,* she thought.

"I would have liked to have taken you both to dinner in Plymouth," Luke was saying, "but I hate to leave poor old Jerry to dine alone after a heroic day hitting the books. I know how he hates it."

"You know, Luke," Glynis said, "I'm worried about him. I can't understand this new phase. He ought to be groaning his way around Rathbourn, violins sobbing in the background. But he's not. It's out of character. Do you suppose something's up?"

"Like what?" Luke asked.

"Maybe he's in love," Glynis suggested.

"Jerry's always just in or out of love. It's nothing to worry about."

Ravenna, herself only three years older than Jeremy, was silently indignant. Didn't he think being in love at nineteen was just as heartfelt as at any age?

"I rather think he might still be interested in that Mrs. Heyward, the woman he was crazy about last year."

"The American divorcée? I thought that was over before I left for Africa."

"So did I," said Glynis. "I think it was a very one-sided kind of friendship. But he's never mentioned anyone else since then, and I thought—"

"Dammit, he can't still be mooning over her. She's some twenty years older than he is!"

Ravenna stirred nervously in the front seat of the Mercedes, feeling guilty for knowing what she knew.

"Well, Jeremy is Jeremy," Glynis said calmly. "I never could tell him anything."

"Forgive us, Ravenna," Luke turned to her, "it's just that we worry about the old chap."

"I gather," she said dryly.

He looked at her sharply. "You disapprove of so much brotherly concern?"

"Well, since you ask, Jeremy's hardly a child anymore. Can't he make up his own mind?"

"He *is* in line for Rathbourn and the baronetcy. It makes one rather careful of the Mrs. Heywards of this world. She's an actress, you know."

"You make it sound like she's a Martian," Ravenna said stiffly. Goodness, did Luke actually think like that? It was out of a Victorian novel. Scheming actress chases young baronet-to-be. No wonder Jeremy felt trapped.

"Let's just suppose I suddenly popped off—"

"Luke!" said Glynis. "You're simply bursting with health."

"All right, all right." He sighed. "It's unlikely, I know, that Jerry will ever have to worry about being saddled with Rathbourn. I stand confronted. But I can't help feeling responsible for him."

"Luke, dear, perhaps Ravenna's right," Glynis said from the back seat. "Certainly your father could never tell you anything at nineteen, if I remember. What was the name of that Italian woman you liked at Cambridge—the one with the eyebrows?"

"Never mind, Glynis," he laughed. "You both have a point. Deliver me from my past." But Ravenna was not convinced Luke had really heard her.

Dinner was pleasant, with Jeremy as guileless as ever and Luke quizzing Ravenna on her book. Despite Daniel's absence she was feeling happy, still filled with the richness of Saltram. Even Luke's questions uncovered new concepts and ideas, giving her exciting directions to explore in her research. She was grateful for his help and finally confessed, "I found your talk inspiring today. And Saltram was wonderful."

"Good." He sounded pleased. "After dinner I'll show you another book you must read...it will open your eyes to the undercurrents of the eighteenth century, the inner workings of things, so to speak."

True to his word, he led her to his study after coffee with Glynis and Jeremy. The whole day was swimming in Ravenna's head by now, a haze of beautiful rooms, stretching emerald vistas—and something else. Luke's easy smile, his good-natured attitude—these were proof they could be friends, not enemies. When Daniel returned he'd see how foolish his suspicions had been.

"I almost think I loved those old bricked stables best. But on second thought I prefer Rathbourn's. They're cozier..." she was saying as she crossed to the bookshelves, turning with a smile.

He stood leaning against the closed door—the only exit—his eyes glittering. The soft easiness of him had gone; he was all steel and raw male power now, and with an incontrollable tremor she saw the Luke who'd faced her across the library on Sunday night.

"Forget Saltram," he said coolly. "We're going to have a little talk."

CHAPTER SIX

"TALK? ABOUT WHAT?" she finally managed, swallowing to ease her suddenly dry throat.

"About us. The talk we've been needing to have since London. Or don't you agree?"

"You know perfectly well—"

"I know perfectly well you've been running from your feelings since the moment I laid eyes on you."

"May I remind you, Luke—" her blue eyes were icy "—that I'm engaged to Daniel?"

"You've been reminding me at every opportunity! Do you think I'm likely to forget?" He spoke harshly, digging into his pocket for a cigarette, the steel in his voice edged with anger. An image of his response in the library, when she'd gone to Daniel, leaped before her. Yes, he'd been enraged. She hadn't dreamed it.

Pulling herself up to her full height, she said with cold insistence, "It's a fact that I am engaged to Daniel."

"Things have changed."

"Nothing's changed," she flung at him.

"Yes, it has. *We've* met." His words had such a ring to them she could think of no reply. He made it sound like destiny, or fate. But it wasn't like that. There was Daniel to consider.

"What are you afraid of, Ravenna?" he asked softly, moving a step nearer.

She pressed back against the shelves instinctively as he did so. He was right; she *was* afraid. Afraid of what? Something told her that her fear went deeper than hurting Daniel, much deeper, to the core of her. . . .

But she brushed this thought away, saying quickly, "Do you think, Luke, that two people get engaged merely to fling their agreement to the winds less than two weeks later? Merely because. . . ." She paused.

"Because what?" he challenged.

Her face flamed, and her eyes fell. Then she raised them and looked straight at him. "Because you and I have an attraction to each other that is purely physical, a sexual urge. . . ."

"So that's how you see it?"

"Well, isn't it?" she cried. "You think you have only to lift your little finger—" ruthlessly she paraphrased Fern "—and I'll come running! It's not like that, Luke! *I'm* not like that. I love Daniel, and I have a commitment to him."

"Spare me," he ground out, his face darkening at her little speech. His eyes swept her, and she saw his hands flex. Had she angered him that much? A tiny shiver crept up her spine. Suddenly Fern's words that day on the terrace flashed back. "When the blood gets too blue. . . ." She told herself not to be ridiculous.

"Don't you realize what I'm saying?" she questioned a little wildly. "You should understand. You were engaged to Kristen."

"Leave Kristen out of it," he growled.

"Why? Because you loved her? Don't you know that that's how I love Daniel? I don't love you, Luke. I don't love you, and I don't want you."

Her mistake was that she'd kept on going. In two strides he crossed over to her and lifted his arms, pinning her in their enclosure by leaning his hands against the shelves behind her head. She was unable to move without touching him, and she knew she touched him at her peril.

For one horrible second she had thought he was going to strike her. But he only stared at her, his gray eyes flashing. Then his mouth descended on hers.

The kiss was intoxicating, without a shred of mercy. She wanted to fight him, or else remain totally aloof. But as soon as their lips touched, her body betrayed her, flaming wildly for him, every fiber in her yearning to feel the hard length of him against her. For that moment she was his, and he knew it. Yet only his mouth had taken hers, the rest of their bodies hardly touched. It was like a whisper, a promise of what could be unleashed between them.

With incredible self-control she prevented herself from reaching out to him, keeping her arms pressed back against the shelves. But she couldn't hide her hungry response, the slight arching of her body toward his, the tautening of her breasts so visibly beneath the thin silk of her dress.

When he finally lifted his mouth, his eyes glittered. "You don't want me? You're lying, Ravenna," he murmured huskily. "But your body doesn't lie...."

Desperately she ducked under his arm and found herself free of him. Ahead was a door, the only door she could safely reach in time, and she flung it open, then slammed it behind her. She stood breathing in the darkness, fumbling to find a lock.

But before she located one, the door pushed open and Luke stood beside her, tall and immovable. "I didn't think you'd choose the bedroom for our talk, but if you insist..." he said dryly.

Horrified, Ravenna turned to see the shadow of a bed in the deep luxurious room they'd entered. Night poured in through the windows, a molten darkness.

"Please be reasonable, Luke," she whispered, whirling to face him.

"I am being reasonable," he countered. "You're the unreasonable one. You're the one who won't face up to how you feel."

"Stop saying that!" she almost shouted. "It's not true. It's not!"

She dived for an armchair in the corner of the room, intending to put it between them. Her foot in its high-heeled shoe came up against the edge of a soft rug, almost silver in the darkness, and she felt herself falling. Luke reached too quickly and too far to save her, and both of them tumbled to the floor.

She lay on some kind of fur, she realized with a

shock, thick as wolfskin, deep and silvery, with
Luke lying half on top of her. It couldn't have been
worse than if he'd choreographed every step. Both
of them stared into each other's eyes, his gray and
tender suddenly, smiling down at her in amusement, his anger gone; her own face mirroring every
silklike thread of desire racing in her limbs as his
hips molded to hers and the hot fires rose within
her. His eyes compelling hers, he lowered his mouth
slowly this time, kissing her gently, thoroughly, seductively... she knew he was waiting for her arms
to go around him.

A great longing for him washed through her, neu-
tralized by a sense of despair. What would happen
if she gave in to this: an affair with Luke, Daniel's
brother, a loveless affair hurting Daniel to the core?
"No, Luke," she whispered. But she heard how
weakly she protested.

The thick fur beneath them, like a field of moonlight, breathed of a faint animal fragrance akin to
Luke's as he lay beside her now, simply watching
her and waiting. He didn't make a move as she lay
against him, his mouth near hers, his eyes dark with
arousal, the whole length of his body warming hers.
She found herself thinking she could lie there
forever in a strange suspended state of peace, gazing back at him.

His eyes seemed to tell her, *this is what you want,
Ravenna. Me... my arms about you.* He was willing her to admit it, she knew. But she couldn't. She
wanted only to stay with him like this, not moving,
in the safety of a stilled present. Not going into a

future from which there could be no return...a future filled with unknown storms that would leave inevitable havoc in their wake.

"Ravenna," he breathed, and she lay spellbound as his free hand began to trace slow patterns on her hip, rising in a tantalizing trail across her waist and up toward the buttons of her dress, soon sliding the silken fabric aside to reveal the swell of her breasts. The sensuous movements of his exploring hands tortured her. Her eyes still caught by his, she felt him pull her lacy bra aside and heard the swift intake of his breath as he lowered his eyes to travel over her exposed breasts, their nipples tautening at his gaze. And she trembled, feeling completely helpless as he looked down at her. Then, with a smile at her softly parted lips, he lowered his own—not to hers, but to the small pulse beating at her throat, then slowly, to a rose-tipped nipple. His lips met her flesh so gently that shivers shot through her while he caressed her, pleasuring her with indescribably tender skill, his mouth an instrument of an exquisite torture she never wanted to end.

A small cry escaped her. Finally, inevitably, the storms were loosed at whatever cost; she drew him closer to her, and her restraint exploded. In a flash they were kissing wildly—their mouths met as if starved for each other, their bodies strained together, and when in one impatient motion Luke undid the rest of her dress by sending the buttons flying and lifted her possessively in his arms, Ravenna knew it was too late to stop. Nothing would keep them apart. And she didn't want anything to do so as the dark silk of the fur rug became the dark silk of his skin. . . .

She couldn't tell whose lips, whose hair, whose eager reaching hands were whose, as she helped him undo his shirt, felt him slide her dress above the satin of her thighs. And then they were swaying together on the rug as a great wave of desire swallowed them both, swept them in a relentless rhythm toward the inevitable lovemaking.

But as they sank downward once again, wrapped blindly, ecstatically, in each other's arms, they must have shifted to one side. For one brief instant Luke's face hung over hers, clearly outlined, and then an explosion of pain burst in Ravenna's head, followed by a sinking blackness. The harsh blackness of pain, not the velvet sables of pleasure.

There was a blankness, an utter empty calm.

SHE AWOKE lying on something very comfortable—a bed—still in semidarkness. Her head swam with pain and dizziness, and her eyes widened with uncertainty. Then she pulled back in amazement from the hands that gently wiped her temple with a cloth. Luke knelt beside her.

"Where am I?" She heard herself whisper the classic line.

"In my bed," said Luke's quiet voice, filled with a deep relief. "Don't panic," he added softly as her eyes expressed exactly that. "I'm not there with you, Ravenna. You hit your head against the glass night table."

Hit her head? But how? Had she fallen? How had she even come to be in his bedroom?

"Don't you remember?" he asked in concern.

"No," she said, trying again to move away from his ministering hands.

"It's probably only temporary," he explained slowly, carefully, his voice gentle. "I mean, the loss of memory. You've got a small scratch—skin on the head bleeds like blazes, but it's really not much." He paused. "You gave me quite a scare."

"I—I thought we were talking in your study," she began.

"You came in here and I followed...you actually don't remember any of it?"

She shook her head, suddenly aware of the sensuous tangle of gold hair revealed by his shirt, which was unbuttoned to the waist as if he'd been in the process of removing it. A moment later her hand moved to her own open bodice, and she pulled the parted silk together in mortification.

"We were about to make love," he said, following her gaze and smiling wryly. "But it looks as if we'll have to wait a while."

"I don't believe you," she whispered, staring up at him. "You...you're lying."

For a moment he said nothing, his eyes locked in hers. "It's true," he murmured at last, his eyes narrowing. "I rather thought you wanted to." Again he was the mocking Luke.

She started to move farther away from him, but he reached to stop her. "Don't," he said more coolly. "You've nothing to be afraid of, Ravenna. I think you might have a slight concussion, though. You're in a bit of shock. I think perhaps I should drive you into Salcombe Hospital.''

She shook her head slightly. "No! I'm sure I'm all right."

"Then you should sleep here tonight...I'll sleep in the study. That way I can check on you periodically."

Sleep in his bed, in his bedroom? He must be crazy!

The fear in her eyes was too much for him. In a voice filled with sudden bitterness he asked, "Are you really so frightened of me as all that?"

She didn't answer, her eyes miserably caught in his. They stared at each other, the tension between them vibrating in the air, a breeze stirring the curtains at the windows and the whole scene eerily limned in moonlight. Luke's skin and hair shone silver, and his eyes were dark pools looking down at her with an inexplicable bewilderment in them.... Once more she felt herself falling into them against all laws of gravity, falling upward toward their bottomless depths, and some of the rich sweetness of their encounter on the rug almost returned to her. But before she could grasp it, Luke's voice came harshly from above her, and she realized he'd stood up beside the bed.

"In that case, I won't touch you. That's what you want to hear, isn't it?" His words were low and grating. "I think I'm beginning to understand you, Ravenna. You like to remain in control of the situation. It's safer that way, more predictable. And so

Daniel's tepid love suits you fine—Daniel, who runs off to New York at the drop of a hat, leaving you alone.''

"Luke!" He had gone too far.

"Isn't that it, Ravenna? Daniel's a safe haven, saving you from facing who you really are—a tempestuous firebrand whose needs are as great as mine!"

A hot fury filled her, and she spat at him, "I hate you, Luke Rathbourn."

"No," he mocked, his voice still harsh. "I don't think you do, Ravenna. But you can call it hate if you like." He turned his back on her and walked to the window.

"I'll go now," she said dully, sitting up and smoothing her dress mechanically.

He said nothing.

Holding the silk together, she stood up unsteadily, but Luke made no effort to help her, despite his concern of moments earlier. She still felt dazed, and as she crossed the room, he didn't even turn his head. "One thing, Luke, you need to understand," she said as coolly as she could from the doorway, "I could never love a man...like you...even if I didn't love Daniel." As she spoke the words, she willed them to be true.

He turned quietly on his heel. "I see," he said. "But then, we weren't talking of love—were we?"

She swung the heavy bedroom door behind her as she left, making it crash against the doorjamb.

THE NEXT DAY dawned cold and gray, with rain

sweeping in over the headlands in pallid sheets. Ravenna heard the gulls coming inland as she lay in bed, unable to move. Their piercing cries were as chilling as her thoughts.

When she'd awoken, she had remembered, despite a throbbing headache, the past night's sequence of events—her flight to Luke's bedroom, the fall, their passionate embraces. Luke had not lied.

"What are you afraid of," he'd asked her. And now she knew. Their least encounter rocked her to her foundations. It was as if the person she'd known herself to be was annihilated in his presence and an unknown woman emerged—ignited to a holocaust by the curve of his lips, the touch of his hand, the sight of one lean thigh. She was afraid of being consumed in her own fires.

But even as she faced that truth she knew she wanted him.

Now, in the cold light of day, she considered her alternatives: to stay and try to reestablish her love for Daniel against all odds; to leave Rathbourn, or, though this was hardly an alternative, to have an affair with Luke. Finally she admitted to herself that so great was the spell Luke cast she would have said yes to him...in any other circumstance. As it was she couldn't consider it. It would be too deliberately cruel to Daniel, like flinging his love in his face. He didn't deserve that.

Instead she'd blindly struck out at Luke, wanting to hurt him as he was hurting her. But if she apologized, wouldn't it be tantamount to an invitation to resume where they'd left off?

Her other alternative, to leave, meant running away without giving Daniel a chance. Tempting...but cowardly. For surely he'd return in a day or two? To leave before she even saw him again—when his presence might have the power to heal her longing for Luke—that she could not do. No, her only hope was to stay at Rathbourn and search for a solution.

Finally she forced herself to get up, dress and go downstairs to breakfast. If she didn't move immediately, she would never find the courage to face the world, she knew. And somehow she did manage to grind through the day.

DANIEL PHONED twice in the three days after the visit to Saltram. The first call came through on the afternoon following Ravenna's fight with Luke, when she'd hardly yet had time to collect herself. In a bleak state of mind, she'd been in her bedroom, sorting through the books she'd carted from Luke's study and stacked on the floor. She'd been wondering where would be a reasonable space to spread out her papers. Her elegant writing desk was not much use.

Daniel spoke as if he'd almost forgotten why he'd rushed off to New York four days earlier, leaving her bereft. Had he really thought their last call had settled the matter? Or had he become entirely absorbed in his work again?

"I miss you, darling," he ended.

But by now she was beginning to believe Daniel would always be saying that, missing her from somewhere faraway...seldom at her side, as Luke had pointed out. Would it become a refrain after they married?

"Yes, Daniel, of course," she said. "Please come home soon." There was nothing else to say.

In the second call he explained that he'd planned to be home the next day but Fern's foster mother had had an emergency operation, and he wanted to drive Fern up to see her in Syracuse for a few days. They should arrive at Rathbourn the following Saturday.

"But, Daniel—"

"It's the least I can do, Ravenna. Fern's been with me a long time."

This was hard to bear when Ravenna herself needed him so much. And it did seem somewhat above and beyond the call of duty. Couldn't he have simply paid her plane fare? After all, Fern was his secretary...while she was his fiancée. One would almost think it was the other way around. But Ravenna was so disappointed she couldn't think of what to say. It was Sunday—she had a whole week to wait. Didn't Daniel realize how preposterous this was?

One thing cheered her: he had news of Elk Creek. He'd flown out for an afternoon, and everyone was well, her mother full of the wedding plans. She was anxious to receive their list of guests, he said, and Ravenna's heart sank, remembering that she'd mailed it a few days earlier. Well, her relationship with Daniel just had to work out, because the die was cast.

Not surprisingly the week dragged by, made harder by the fact that although she lived in the same house as Luke, it was hardly the same planet. He spoke to her only at meals, and then with such studied politeness it was like a slap in the face. On all other occasions, she suspected, he took steps to avoid her. She'd first become aware of this when she'd gone to the small study to remove her things the day after their angry encounter. He'd been conspicuously absent, although she could see from the architectural drawings spread over his drafting table that he'd resumed work. To her amazement he'd left a large book with her others—the one on the eighteenth century he'd promised her when he'd lured her to his study. She was pragmatic enough to take it with her; likely it would be as valuable as he'd said.

As usual she rode Jessie in the mornings; O'Reilly mentioned that Luke rode Napoleon in the afternoons. Once she determined to ride after dinner in the dusk and had walked out to the stables, hoping to escape unnoticed into the woods. Luke had been there in the stone courtyard, grooming Napoleon. When she'd approached, he'd stared at her across the gleaming back of the hunter—with such a cool assessing look that she'd retreated to the house, shaken. From then on she stuck to the mornings.

Burying herself in her work helped, but in the

midst of a quiet read she would suddenly catch herself thinking of him. What was it Luke had implied? That she was running from herself? Perhaps—but it was he who wouldn't face up to facts: the fact that she would *not* have an affair with him. And if she'd ever been tempted to imagine he offered her anything else, his parting shot had put paid to that.

Or her thoughts would wander as she looked up from her notes to gaze out over the gardens—what if she had met Luke first? A useless speculation; they had met second.

Once she heard again his deep voice saying, with stubborn finality, "*We've* met." The arrogance of the man! As if the world would remake itself because of this. As if *she* would remake her world for him! And she had stood up blindly, scattering her papers about her.

Finally she had to force herself not to think, so exhausted was it making her. It took energy enough just to face Luke once or sometimes twice a day at meals, to have to sit stiffly in the same room with him, trying not to indicate by word or manner to the others that it was torture. Luke, too, seemed to be feeling the strain. She thought he looked tired, although most often he seemed merely bored.

Was it her imagination, or did Glynis leap in too quickly to cover awkward gaps left in the conversation? Ravenna began to worry that she guessed something was amiss—Glynis knew Luke very well, and she herself had never been good at hiding her feelings. Ravenna was thankful that Jeremy was

just the same, still humorous and comfortable to be
with, a godsend when they dined. Still, his secret rehearsals were taking their toll—once or twice he had
a worn preoccupied air about him, and Ravenna
caught the others noticing this. How long would it
be before Jeremy met his Waterloo? Crossing Luke
was no small matter.

The unbearable fact was that she was still
haunted by him. Despite his coolness it was sheer
pain to sit near Luke at dinner, aware of every fiber
in his well-knit body, remembering the hard
strength of it against her, and then to see his eyes
turn briefly to her, cold as a winter sea, and hear
him ask, "Ravenna, how is your work going?" in a
voice that said he didn't really care to know.

In her loneliness she took to chatting with O'Reilly after her morning rides.

"There ain't never been another horse created
like the Arabian," he declared. "Now you take
these English Thoroughbreds here, beautiful craitures though they be—" and they were off on a
pleasant hour comparing the breeds, discussing
American and English horsemanship, the Kentucky
Derby and his favorite homemade remedies for
saddle sores and swamp fever. With O'Reilly she re-
captured some of the simplicity of Elk Creek again,
if only for that hour. He and Jessie were her daily
tonic.

"Luke's in Cornwall for a couple of days,"
Glynis told her on Tuesday. At first Ravenna was
grateful, but she soon found it made little difference to her, so seldom did she see him anymore.

Dinners were less of an ordeal, however, and it took away her fear of running into him unexpectedly in the halls or on the grounds of Rathbourn. Jeremy seemed to breathe easier, too, although she saw him about as often as she did Luke. He had no time for rides these days; every moment was taken up with rehearsals for *Romeo and Juliet*.

Then she found a new and absorbing way to pass the hours: digging in the garden when the weather cleared, with Glynis. They worked in silence for the most part, Gwydion and Albion nosing the earth nearby or rushing about after the squirrels. Sometimes Glynis, preparing a new bed, was in the mood for recollection, and she'd talk about earlier days at Rathbourn and Luke's and Daniel's growing-up years. Perhaps it was Ravenna's imagination, but she seemed to dwell on Luke as much as Daniel, and Ravenna found this irritating. She didn't want to hear about Luke, however fond Glynis was of her stepson. Or so she told herself; the fact was, she listened avidly.

Often they worked at some distance from each other, calling across the rose beds from time to time, while Ravenna pulled out weeds by hand and felt the sun grow hot on her skin. Glynis had her hands in the dirt, too, unabashedly kneeling there in old overalls and a squashed hat. "Me and the Queen Mother," she'd laughed when Ravenna had come upon her the first time by accident in the corner of her beloved China teas. "I mean, the Queen Mother loves to garden, too. Sometimes even the servants don't recognize her, they say. But I doubt she wears this kind of getup!'' She'd brushed at the grass-stained knees of her outfit with a smile.

And Ravenna did have to laugh when Peters, in his black suit and with his impeccable manners intact, picked his way fastidiously through the garden to inform "madam" that "cook is having trouble finding last year's pear preserves, the ones madam herself prepared and so carefully labeled," while Glynis knelt there, every inch the lady even in her overalls.

The gardening, her rides on Jessie and the work on her book got Ravenna through to Thursday, which was Jeremy's opening night. Since Daniel wasn't back yet—and Jeremy had forbidden her to bring him, anyway—she arranged to borrow Glynis's little blue Renault for the trip to Salcombe.

"What should I tell her?" she asked Jeremy as he left at noon on his motorcycle.

"You'll think of something," he replied jauntily, and with a wave of his hand was off.

My life of crime—not to mention Jeremy's—is well underway, she thought grimly while she lied to Glynis that she needed a quiet night out at the movies alone.

"You mean the cinema? Well, why not? I won't wait up, if you don't mind. Jeremy's off somewhere tonight, too. Have a good time, dear. You've been looking tired these past few days."

Glynis's concern made Ravenna wince, but she *had* promised Jeremy.

She arrived in Salcombe near dusk, parked the car on a side street and walked to the theater. She had some trouble finding it again, despite Jeremy's careful instructions, and arrived in the nick of time. In fact, the lights were already lowering as she slipped into her seat near the back of the crowded audience. Well, she was glad to see that Salcombe had avid theatergoers. And somewhere in that stirring mass of humanity, which looked strangely uniform in the dark, was Angela Heyward, she supposed. Their introduction would have to wait until after the play, however.

The poignant drama of *Romeo and Juliet* was an ambitious project for a summer-stock company— the theater had been rented just for the season, she remembered Jeremy saying—but the director presented the play intelligently and authoritatively. From the opening lines, "Two households, both alike in dignity/In fair Verona where we lay our scene," she was caught up in the swift sad story of the star-crossed lovers. Both the leads were good; the dark young man who portrayed Romeo aptly conveyed the impetuousness of an Italian youth, despite his Oxford accent, while Juliet was spontaneous and charming, with a depth to her characterization that entirely moved the audience.

Jeremy didn't appear until the fourth scene, and when he did, she was startled to realize it was him. No longer the affable stubborn young man she was beginning to know, but Shakespeare's Mercutio— hot-blooded, quick-witted, weaving his fantasies in the air. Something in Mercutio's inspired swagger and brilliant invention suited Jeremy; he breathed life easily into the character, so that the audience instinctively responded. During the long Queen Mab speech even Ravenna forgot his identity as the opening words fell upon her ears: "She is the fairies' midwife, and she comes/In shape no bigger than an agate stone." One of Shakespeare's most imaginative monologues, delivered by one of his most charming characters—and Jeremy made the most of it. From beginning to end one could have heard the proverbial pin drop. Yes, he had them in the palm of his hand...through the witty taunting of Juliet's ancient nurse, on to the final fatal duel with Tybalt, "the Prince of Cats." In the middle of Jeremy's scenes Ravenna surfaced only once to the real world, to think, *if only Luke could see this!*

There was a brief fifteen-minute intermission, and afterward the play came swiftly to its tragic end. Mercutio expired in Act III, but the play was well cast and held her riveted throughout. When the houselights came up, Ravenna blinked in disorientation.

Jeremy received an extra loud volley of applause when he appeared, making his bows with an aplomb worthy of a London stage, she thought. Yes, he was good. Could become very, very good, given the training.

Getting backstage was difficult, for the crowd thinned slowly and the old theater was a warren of halls and tiny rooms. But she finally found Jeremy by the sound of his voice. He was noisily illustrating his dueling technique to a short attractive blond who was leaning against the wall, smoking a cigarette in a jeweled holder.

" 'Ah, the immortal *passado*! The *punto reverso*! The hay!' " he quoted, lunging forward, then executing a quick backhanded stroke with his rapier and thrusting home into the wall, a sight too near the folded arms of the unconcerned blond.

"I thought you told me your dueling technique was rusty!" Ravenna remarked as she joined them.

"Tybalt got me in the end, didn't he?" Jeremy said, pretending he was about to blubber. "Though if that fool of a Romeo hadn't come between us. . . . Did y' like the play? Oh, Angela, meet Ravenna. My brother's fiancée."

"How do you do," Ravenna said, startled to realize that this lovely woman, whom Luke had said was about forty, was Angela Heyward. She looked twenty-eight at a glance.

Angela turned a dazzling smile in her direction and in a deep voice said, "Marvelous, wasn't he? Absolutely bloody marvelous."

"He certainly was," Ravenna agreed, responding with a smile. "I really enjoyed the play, Jeremy, especially you," she added.

"I did rather break a leg, didn't I? But I had a devil of a time before I came on. . . couldn't find my damned rapier."

"Never mind, Jeremy. You've got what it takes," Angela soothed. "You simply have to talk to that brother of yours and get into RADA—don't you think so, darling?" She turned her large hazel eyes on Ravenna. "You're American, aren't you? Kentucky? Right the first time. I'm an Ohio girl myself, would you believe. You must come and see me in London at the Globe—we're doing a domestic comedy. Jerry's longing to get up to London to see it."

"Oh, well, perhaps..." Ravenna replied uncertainly.

"Maybe in the fall, Angela. Luke's got me glued to Rathbourn. If he guessed I was doing this Salcombe gig—well, talk about the Prince of Cats! I've told Glynis I'm working nights at the Salcombe library for the next few weeks."

Angela blew a desultory smoke ring. "I'd like to get my hands on this critter, believe me. We've got to get you into a course of study, love, before you're over the hill. You're being wasted at that university. It's an absolute crime."

"Let's say we drop it and have a good feed somewhere," Jeremy cheerfully suggested. "Hungry, Scarlett?"

Ravenna suddenly realized she hadn't eaten since tea. "Yes, famished. Where to?"

As Jeremy hustled them along the narrow halls, a pretty, dark-haired girl called after him from one of the dressing rooms, "There you are, Jeremy! You're partying with us, aren't you? Oh, excuse me, didn't see your company!"

But Ravenna caught her disappointed look and recognized the girl who'd played Juliet so well.

"You're welcome to bring them," she added as an afterthought.

"No, we'll pass...we're on our way to eat. Tell the cast I'll be along tomorrow," Jeremy called after her. "Great stuff tonight, Carole." But he'd already turned back to Angela with a devoted look he couldn't quite conceal.

Ravenna wondered exactly what his relationship with Angela was. Were they going together, despite the vast difference in their ages? Then Luke's remarks about Jeremy's being next in line for Rathbourn came back to her, and she had to smile. There was something about Angela suggesting that if she'd wanted an eighteenth-century manor house, she'd have managed to marry into several of them long ago. No, Ravenna instinctively felt that, under her theatrical veneer, Angela was trustworthy. A shrewd but warm woman who had carved her own road in life. Luke had no right to prejudge people like that. And after all, if Jeremy was dating an older woman, wasn't that Jeremy's business?

The cool night air was unexpectedly sweet as they exited through a stage door into a lane behind the theater. Jeremy went down the dark steps first, followed by Ravenna, who was saying, "I thought the way you moved on stage—" She stopped short, almost bumping into Jeremy's tall back when he halted abruptly on the sidewalk.

" 'But I'll be hanged, sir,' " he quoted softly from Act III.

Not ten feet away, Luke leaned nonchalantly against the gray Mercedes, smoking. The faint light of an old streetlamp carved his profile in the dark. At their appearance he tossed the cigarette away in a burning arc. "Well, Jerry," he said clearly, his voice cold steel. "Rather unwise of you, don't you think, to leave tonight's program lying around in the library?''

Jeremy turned slightly aside, as if to signal to the others, and Ravenna came fully into view.

She saw Luke freeze in astonishment. She stepped unthinkingly backward, but just as quickly he strode over to her and gripped her arm.

"What the hell are you doing here," he hissed, as if they were alone. He'd obviously expected only Jeremy.

"Jeremy invited me," she began angrily, and then stopped, afraid she'd damned him by admitting as much. Her eyes challenged Luke's, and she set her mouth in a stubborn line.

His voice chillingly calm, he ordered, "Get into the car, both of you," as if they were two erring teenagers. Neither Jeremy nor Ravenna moved, however, in this moment of disaster, and Ravenna waited for Jeremy to say something—anything.

"Ahem!" The sound behind them startled them all.

"Why, aren't you *the* Sir Anthony Rathbourn?" Angela purred, stepping out of the shadows of the deep doorway. "I hope you don't mind, but I couldn't help recognizing you from your pictures. My name is Angela Heyward, Mrs. Angela Heyward," and she extended her hand in a hearty American manner, her face literally beaming with warmth. Gone was the blond siren Ravenna had glimpsed in her earlier. Angela the Ohio girl had stepped guilelessly into the street...and Ravenna realized she was watching a quick-change artist in action.

If the situation hadn't already looked so black, Ravenna might have burst out laughing. Luke stood there, completely nonplussed. For a moment he stared at Angela, then he nodded and extended his hand, which Angela pumped up and down like an enthusiastic tourist.

"How do you do," he finally managed in a stiff formal voice.

"Angela's a friend of mine," Jeremy explained suddenly, his words slightly strangled in quality, whether from laughter or sheer nerves, Ravenna couldn't tell. "Came all the way down from London to see the play tonight. Sir Anthony is my brother, Angela, but in the family he just goes by Luke."

It was Angela's turn to look slightly confused, for Jeremy had obviously not explained his relationship with the well-known architect. She managed to cloak her confusion immediately, however. "Well, I've heard so much about you," she murmured ambiguously, still smiling.

Luke glanced from her to Jeremy and back again, and Ravenna could sense that under his impeccable manners he was still very angry. "Am I to assume you're coming with us, then?" His voice was ironic.

Angela turned to Jeremy, and Ravenna saw his brief evocative signal for help. Amazing what he could convey simply by widening those brown eyes.

"Of course I am," she said cheerfully. "In that case, where are we off to? We were planning on dinner, Sir Anthony, er, I mean Luke. Perhaps you'll join us?'' She didn't wait for an answer but rushed on with, ''Good acting always makes me hungry. Did you see the play?''

''Enough of it to know Jerry was in it,'' Luke admitted a little less coldly as he opened the car door first for Ravenna and then for Angela.

''And surely you thought he was simply too marvelous? If you didn't, I'm afraid we'll have to question your taste. But then I'm sure there's no need—you must have thought Mercutio well played.'' She spoke firmly but gaily, turning the full battery of her well-made-up eyes on him, her smile saying there wasn't the slightest doubt in her mind that Luke would agree. Ravenna let out a long quiet breath and leaned back against the front seat. Angela's presence of mind was saving Jeremy's skin, and she could have kissed her for it.

''Oh, the Renault!'' Ravenna suddenly exclaimed. ''I left Glynis's car parked—''

''Never mind,'' Luke interrupted. ''Garvey will pick it up in the morning. As for Mercutio—yes, well played,'' he admitted reluctantly.

''And Ravenna, darling,'' Angela went on, seeking more ammunition, ''what did you think?''

Given her cue, Ravenna expanded on the excellence of Jeremy's acting until Luke half turned as he spun the steering wheel of the car to get them out of the tight parking space. She was relieved to hear mere exasperation in his voice instead of the cold calmness she so much dreaded. Some of his natural charm even returned as he said, ''Looks like I'm outnumbered by your fans, Jerry. You and I will discuss this matter later—for now we might as well find a place to have dinner.''

Although Jeremy's tone of voice suggested this could be his last meal before the execution, he directed them to his favorite restaurant—a quiet, intimate ''ye-olde-fashioned'' place that came by its age honestly.

The owner led them to a dark corner, to a table with banquette seating on one side and two chairs on the other. Ravenna found herself crammed in rather tightly beside Luke, whose nearness was as inflammatory as ever. His thigh brushed against hers once as they sat, and he didn't move it away; she felt it burning into hers, and, as usual, her whole body began to melt.

''What will you have, Ravenna?'' Luke asked— apparently for the second time.

''Pardon?'' she answered, lifting her eyes to meet his faintly amused ones. She suddenly realized he was speaking to her.

Angela, across from her, looked at her indulgently and then in her well-modulated voice asked Jeremy to order her a filet mignon, rare. ''And a martini first, darling. Very dry.'' She'd dropped her ingenue role to play herself again.

Somehow, by discussing Shakespeare, theater staging and Mercutio's character, they got to the end of the meal. Luke had the grace to set aside his quarrel with Jeremy, and the strain lessened as Angela did her stint at peacemaking, her natural high spirits smoothing over the situation. Diamond cigarette holder very much in evidence, along with her humor, she poured charm everywhere, like balm—but especially on Luke. She was wise enough to concentrate on stories of her own career rather than focusing on Jeremy, although she did manage to underline that she thought him very talented and deserving of the schooling to develop himself.

Luke said nothing to her opinion, merely smoked and listened with that calm air Ravenna knew to be deceptive. Jeremy, by the looks of him, had no doubts about how his brother really felt. Angela had a one-woman show on her hands, although Ravenna tried to keep up her end as well as she could—increasingly difficult to do with Luke sitting so near to her. Although he hardly glanced at her, she felt as if he were as aware of her as she of him, and he acted as if her position close at his side were exactly where she belonged. His arm, reaching along the back of the banquette, lightly touched her hair, and that alone was intimate. The unsettling flames burned between them again. Or at least she felt them. Perhaps he didn't; he seemed so self-possessed.

It was nearly midnight when Luke pointed out they must be getting back to Rathbourn. It was then that Jeremy, anticipating trouble on the drive home—for Luke had insisted he leave his motorcycle in Salcombe until the next day—made a move Ravenna thought worthy of Luke himself.

"What say Angela spends the night at Rathbourn, Luke?" he said. "We've that extra bedroom set up on the second floor."

Jeremy spoke confidently, turning to smile at Angela, who leaped in with, "Why, Jerry, what a lovely offer! The hotels here are charming, of course, but I must confess I'd intended to drive on to Exeter...if it wasn't so late."

Naturally Luke had to extend hospitality to Mrs. Heyward, and he did so with an ironic glance at his brother, like someone acknowledging a good chess move. A moment later they left the restaurant. Angela walked back with Jeremy to get her car, leaving Ravenna to drive home with Luke.

"A nice piece of work," Luke muttered to Ravenna as soon as they were alone. "And I'm not referring to the damned play. How long have you been mixed up in this?"

"Never mind that," she said. "I think Jeremy has every right to pursue his talents. And you're not being very supportive of him." All her resolve to stay out of the family quarrel disappeared on the wind.

"Oh?" His tone was again dangerous. "Perhaps you'd like to explain that comment."

By the time they'd reached Rathbourn they were engaged in a full-fledged argument. The few minutes' grace in the great hall, when Jeremy came in on their tail, escorting Angela, was only an interlude. Jeremy ushered his guest off to the extra bedroom, and a few moments later Ravenna and Luke in turn mounted the stairs, Ravenna still reasoning—or so she thought—with Luke. But by this time her Irish ancestry, mixed with her Southern blood, was flying all its flags.

"You're being pigheaded, Luke! Jeremy is nineteen—almost in his twenties. And you're acting like a nineteenth-century father, trying to impose your will on him—ridiculous! You're only alienating him, treating him like a child. That isn't the way to bring up anyone!"

"Oh? And I suppose you're an expert on child rearing?"

"Well, I did have seven brothers and sisters. You can't help but develop an understanding—"

"That I haven't developed?"

They stood at the junction of the hallways near her bedroom, their voices raised, totally oblivious of everything but their argument.

"Yes! I mean, no, you obviously haven't developed anything of the sort! If you ever have children of your own—"

"If I do, what makes you suppose it will be any of your concern?" He stood there, arms folded, looking down at her with half-closed eyes.

Suddenly she became aware he was staring at her lips.

He seemed to realize this in the same instant and recollected himself enough to say, "If I had had any idea you were involved in one of Jerry's irresponsible schemes, I would have—"

"You'd have what?" she challenged hotly, hands on hips.

"I always think," a heavily ironic voice came from behind Luke, "that when it comes to raising children, only having your own proves the utter inadequacy of any theory."

This stopped them both dead. Glynis, in slippers and a flowered-silk dressing gown, her hair carefully gathered in a rather absurd sleeping net, had come up behind Luke. Obviously she'd been in bed, if not already asleep. "Don't you think your... conversation... would best be continued downstairs? Perhaps in the library?" she went on as they stared in surprise at her. She raised both eyebrows expressively before turning back toward her room. Neither of them saw her smile.

Brought to her senses, Ravenna barely had time to realize that the great hall was acting as an echo chamber for their voices and to wonder what Glynis had implied by "having children of your own" before Luke took her arm and steered her toward the stairs again. Their week-long silence might never have been.

"Good idea," he muttered. "We're going to get this settled now, tonight." And his tone left no room for disagreement, though so intent was Ravenna on making her point about Jeremy that she wasn't about to stop, either.

"Jeremy ought to be at RADA," she whispered heatedly as they crossed the open hall.

Luke said nothing more until he'd sat her down in a wing chair near the banked fire in the library and put a glass of brandy in her hand.

"All right," he started slowly, settling in the chair opposite her after pouring himself a whiskey and soda, "let's try to discuss this like two adults. Tell me why you think I've messed things up with Jerry."

She swallowed a drop of the potent brandy and took a deep breath, suddenly amazed to find herself in the middle of this unexpected argument. But she was being asked to present Jeremy's case...and perhaps he was finally going to listen. "Jeremy wants to be an actor," she began. "Naturally, therefore, he wants to study acting. So why insist he get his English degree, instead?"

"Not instead—first."

"You mean—"

"I mean I'm perfectly aware that Jerry wants to act and that he's talented—very talented. But there's no harm in his getting his degree beforehand."

"But you've never encouraged his talents!"

"He told you that? Blast Jerry!" he exclaimed, echoing Jeremy's own sentiments toward him. "He has a way of taking things and twisting them to his own ends, Ravenna...something to do with his damned imaginative powers, I suppose. Obviously he's convinced you I'm the villain in the story."

"Well, aren't you?" she asked indignantly.

Unexpectedly Luke said nothing but only studied her, his gray eyes cool and direct. She began to feel very self-conscious sitting opposite him in her old-fashioned, white-cotton dress, her tiredness and the brandy combining to make her feel dangerously relaxed. Her flashing confrontation melted, to be replaced by waves of more familiar feelings, and she had to force herself to continue looking at him as he said seriously, "Jerry will never succeed at anything if he doesn't learn to succeed now in the simple matter of passing his year. Glynis and I have discussed this at length and decided he needs to stick it out. *Then* we'll back all his efforts to get into the theater world. Not before—not while he's shirking classes to go to rehearsals all year and skipping his studies to take in live theater almost every night—a pattern he seems to have blithely continued here in Devon quite underhandedly.''

"I don't suppose it's occurred to you that Jeremy sees it differently," she declared, hurriedly collecting her thoughts again. She must have been crazy to come downstairs with Luke after her last experience alone with him. What had she been thinking of?

Luke raised his dark brows. "I'm surprised you champion him like this. Can't you understand, as a teacher yourself, the need for a broader education than RADA supplies? Jerry needs an academic base."

"But you've never even been to see him act! Not when he did repertory last summer or anytime this year!"

"You forget," he said ironically, "that I've been in Africa. Jerry joined the repertory company after I left. I suppose he neglected to mention that? I used to call his very plausible arguments 'jerry-built,' and with good reason."

She had the grace to blush. Of course. Luke had been away, and Jeremy had spoken to her as if this were not the case. For a second she wavered. But even if Luke wasn't the villain Jeremy had painted, the problem still remained.

"Luke," she said less heatedly, an appeal in her

voice, "try to understand. He's fighting for something very important to him against what he sees as unfair odds. Haven't you ever wanted something utterly crucial to you that it seemed you could never have?"

He looked at her, obviously startled, for a long moment. Finally, leaning back in his chair and closing his eyes he said quietly, "Yes. Yes, I have."

She froze. He still grieved for Kristen, she imagined. Why had she stupidly blundered into this? "I'm sorry," she murmured just as quietly. "I meant something like Jeremy's acting."

He opened his eyes and smiled mockingly at her. "Of course." A moment later he added in a normal voice, "As a matter of fact, my father wanted me to go into politics. But that's got nothing to do with Jerry. I don't disapprove of his ambitions, only of how he handles them."

"And you and your father?" she asked, ignoring his latter remark.

He smiled suddenly, his gray eyes gleaming pewter in the faint light. "I stubbornly went my own way."

"Remind you of anyone?" she asked softly.

He looked fully at her, then dug out a pack of cigarettes and lit one. "All right," he admitted with a slight grin. "You've won your point. But I did take a masters at Cambridge before I moved on to more specialized studies in architecture. I still want Jerry to finish his last year. That means giving up the Salcombe run."

"But he can't do that! Not now that it's opened!"

"He must have an understudy," Luke said dryly.

She stared at him, appalled. If Luke pulled Jeremy out of the play.... "Don't you realize what that would do to him, Luke? And he'd probably never speak to you again."

Drawing on his cigarette, he gazed at her, then stood up and paced the length of the room. When he sat down again, he said wearily, raking his fingers through his hair, "Maybe I'm not cut out to be a father figure."

His words were sardonic, but she suddenly felt for him.

"Jerry was fourteen when our father died...I just stepped into the role without thinking about it. Daniel was traveling a lot even then and never had the time."

This was the first occasion on which Daniel's name had come up so easily between them, but neither of them seemed to notice.

Cautiously, feeling the brandy swim in her head, she said, "I'm sure you've been very important to Jeremy. It's just that you seem to have forgotten what it feels like to be nineteen...."

Why did her eyes have to catch in his, their gray blue depths quietly holding hers? That familiar sensation of drowning.... She forced them from his, but her gaze fell to his sculptured lips, and she felt a hot blush slowly stain her cheeks. Luke, staring now at the gleaming cigarette in his hand, missed this.

"He used to trail around after me when he was a kid. We were inseparable—to my annoyance sometimes,'' he was saying musingly. ''For a few years he even wanted to be an architect when he grew up, just because I am. Well, perhaps you're right. Maybe I've become too hard on him.''

Silently, closing her eyes against the sight of him, she stretched back in her chair as if suddenly exhausted. The truth was, she felt she couldn't bear to look at Luke a moment longer... that curling silver blond hair, that chiseled face and broad shoulders, the cigarette between those lips... lips she could taste so well in unbidden memory.

His deep voice came reassuringly, calmingly to her. ''You make a good champion for the defense, Ravenna. I don't think I'll take him off the Salcombe run—if he'll promise to spend time studying every day.''

''Thank you,'' she whispered after a pause, eyes still closed.

They sat there a while longer in silence, peacefully, with Luke seemingly lost in thought. She didn't know it, but he was smiling at her as he smoked.

She opened her eyes. *It's now or never,* she decided, and with a certain courage suddenly leaned over to him and offered him her hand. ''Truce, Luke?'' she said, smiling.

He looked at her a long second, surprised, his gray blue eyes searching hers, while her offered hand hung in the air. Both knew she wasn't referring to the trouble over Jeremy. Then he said softly, his eyes challenging hers, ''No, Ravenna. No truce. You asked for one earlier, remember?''

That morning at the town house—and the night before it—came rushing back.

"We're not made for truces." He waited before adding slowly, "Let's call it what it is—a stalemate."

Her hand fell back in embarrassment.

"And," he said, exhaling smoke from his cigarette, his eyes grave, "you had better go to bed now. If you intend to go alone, that is." His gaze fell deliberately and sensuously to her lips, then to her throat and the soft swell of her breasts, which rose under the embroidered bodice of her dress with every breath. His thoughts were unmistakable.

It took a moment for his words to sink in. When they did, she got up hurriedly so he wouldn't see the leaping response in her eyes.

"Good night, Luke," she said uncertainly.

"Good night, Ravenna." He made no move to follow her but sat staring at the fire.

CHAPTER SEVEN

CONSIDERING THEIR WEEK OF SILENCE, Ravenna was somewhat surprised to find herself in London on Friday, facing Luke over a hearty English lunch with a man named John Hadley. In a sense it was a side effect of the trip to Salcombe, for it came about at breakfast, through Angela.

For once everyone had been present at the same time, with Glynis taking Angela's presence in her stride and, with habitual graciousness, making her feel at home. When Angela announced she had to make an early start for London, Jeremy had looked disappointed, and Ravenna herself felt sorry she had to rush away.

"Thursdays and Sundays are my only reprieve. . . the play must go on," Angela laughed.

It was when she'd said her goodbyes that Garvey had come in with the bad news: her Volvo wouldn't start; he thought it was the engine.

Angela panicked. "I simply have to be in town tonight, and I was hoping like mad to make it by one. Can it be fixed in time?"

Garvey said it was most unlikely and suggested she take a train from Exeter, about an hour's drive away.

"Could you drive her there, Garvey?" Glynis interposed. "I know it's officially your day off, but...."

Regretfully he explained he had a dentist's appointment on the dot of nine in the opposite direction—Plymouth—and plans to go in to Salcombe afterward with Peters to drop Jeremy off and pick up the abandoned Renault.

Glynis looked bewildered at this.

"Jerry could run her up to Exeter and still be back in time for his...." Luke paused, and Ravenna realized he hadn't yet broken the news of Jeremy's double life to Glynis. "For whatever he's up to this afternoon."

He frowned thoughtfully and, before Jeremy could agree to this, declared, "Or perhaps I could propose another alternative. I'd be willing to make the trip to London myself...if Ravenna is interested in lunching with my publisher."

She looked up from the morning papers, completely startled. "You mean, to talk to him about my book?" she asked, catching her breath.

His eyes met hers across the table. "Yes," he said. "Although you'd need some kind of outline to show him."

"What a lovely idea, Luke," Glynis said enthusiastically, as if she hadn't caught them arguing at the top of the stairs the previous night.

"Well, it's very rough yet." Ravenna hesitated, the wheels of her mind turning rather ineffectively at this early hour. Could she trust this proposal of Luke's to be just what it appeared to be?

Yellow caution lights were flashing in her mind.
"Well?"

There was a world of challenge in that one word.
Suddenly, looking at him, she thought of Daniel's
loitering in the States because of Fern, making her
wait for him. And something in Luke's eyes told her
he wouldn't make this generous offer twice.

"All right," she said, throwing caution to the
winds. "I'm game."

Luke had Peters put a call through to John
Hadley's home—it was still too early for him to
be at his office—and five minutes later it was settled. They were lunching with him at one-thirty,
which meant they had to leave at once. But Angela
and Luke were patient for another ten minutes
while Ravenna rushed to her room to change her
casual slacks and sweater for a neat wool-flannel
suit in crisp navy, with a white-silk blouse and pat-
terned scarf. She scooped up her notes to sort in the
car.

At the bottom of the stairs she found herself momentarily alone with Luke and bluntly, in a low
voice, asked, "Why are you doing this?"

He half smiled, his gray eyes mocking her suspicions. "I said I'd help you. I see no reason to go
back on my word just because we happen to dis-
agree on almost everything else." She stared at him
uncertainly, and he added, "It's just a business
lunch, Ravenna. We'll drive back afterward and be
home in time for dinner." He turned away as Angela appeared along with Jeremy, who lingered until they were out the door.

Well, she'd have to be satisfied with that, she supposed. That Luke was difficult to understand was nothing new to her, but he *had* said once that he wanted to help her with her book. And she couldn't deny she was glad he wanted to keep his word.

JOHN HADLEY was a pleasant gregarious man with iron-gray hair and a neatly trimmed mustache. His company's specialty was art and architectural books of the highest quality.

"Thought we'd lost you to Africa for good," he said to Luke just after one-thirty, beaming at him as they shook hands in the White Hart Public House. It took only minutes for him and Ravenna to warm to each other over the very English meal—"Ethnic," Luke called it with a grimace—of shepherd's pie and scotch eggs, washed down with Double Diamond ale.

John wanted to hear about Luke's trip before moving on to the specifics of Ravenna's book, and she let her mind and eye wander a bit over the dark-paneled walls of the Victorian pub with its turn-of-the-century ambience, enjoying the red-velvet seating and the mahogany tables, the gleaming brass fixtures and rows of well-polished glasses behind the immaculate bar. The English pub was an institution, she knew, like the cafés of Paris, although totally different in fact and spirit. She was delighted that John Hadley liked to conduct business over lunches there.

And when it was time to discuss her book, despite

an initial nervousness she managed to present her special viewpoint on the ten buildings she'd chosen and to give some argument about why the book would have appeal. Luke once or twice asked the right question or made a helpful comment calculated to reveal her plans further, and John seemed impressed.

"Bring me a finished outline and a few chapters in the fall," he said with a smile at the end of the meal. "We'll give you an answer on it within the month—sooner if we can. My editors' desks are usually piled high with work, so be patient if it takes longer—the fall's our busiest time. But I like your idea. It's got merit—bringing in the social background like that. I can't promise, of course, until we've actually seen some of it. Still, if the theme is well developed I can practically guarantee our interest."

"Oh, I quite understand it must come up to your standards," Ravenna said eagerly, thrilled to think that her book would at least be in the hands of a publisher—and one whose list she'd always admired. Because of Luke she wouldn't be just a signature at the bottom of a covering letter but a face with a name attached to it...matter, indeed, for gratitude.

Luke was smiling across at her, pleased at her excitement, and when John turned to the waiter for the check, he unexpectedly winked at her. She smiled back happily.

"Well, it's been good to see you, John," Luke said finally, rising to leave.

"Always delighted, Sir Anthony. We must think about another book project for you soon. Something on Africa? It would be unwise to lose sight of your public, you know."

"I'll be getting back to writing sometime this year," Luke informed him cheerfully.

As Luke turned to Ravenna, a young messenger who'd been searching the room impatiently for a few minutes saw them and hurried over to their table—a blond youth of seventeen or so, dressed in a courier's uniform. "Mr. Hadley's party?" he asked in an East London accent.

"Tracked me down, eh?" John muttered good-naturedly. "Can't escape my minions for a second. Which one of them is it this time?"

"For Sir Anthony and the lady," the boy said to Hadley's surprise.

Luke took the envelope and opened it. Two tickets slid into his palm, and Ravenna saw that they were for *Walk Softly*, Angela's play. Her eyes flew to Luke's, who looked just as startled as she felt. But he simply tipped the boy and deposited the tickets in his breast pocket with a, "Thank you." On Oxford Street they shook hands with the publisher and said their goodbyes.

John Hadley bent over to kiss Ravenna's cheek when she took his hand, and he whispered, "Hang onto him, my dear—he's a good man."

Whatever gave him that idea, she thought in astonishment. But she managed to smile in reply before he moved off in the direction of Tottenham Court Road.

Alone with Luke, she blushed slightly, hoping he hadn't heard.

"There's a note with the tickets," was all Luke said, handing it to her to read.

Addressed to them both, it simply stated: "I wanted to say thank you—see you backstage tonight. Angela."

Again Ravenna's eyes touched Luke's, distressed. "This makes it very awkward. We can hardly not show up when she's gone to such trouble. Unless we could call her and explain."

Luke glanced at his watch. "Good idea. Tell her we planned to be back at Rathbourn tonight. She obviously thought differently."

Only then did it fully dawn on her. If they went to the play, it would mean staying over in London. Luke would hardly want to drive back in the small hours of the morning.

"Unless you don't mind staying at the town house," he said slowly. "That's always a possibility."

She looked away from those sea-gray eyes and hedged. "It really would be better if we got back this evening, don't you think?" The thought of a night alone with him after all that had passed between them was more than unnerving—it was impossible. Only Angela's, then John Hadley's, presence that day had taken the edge off her being with Luke; left alone with him the power of their attraction would.... Well, she had no intention of finding out what it would do. "Besides, I'm expecting Daniel tomorrow," she added.

"In that case. . ." he said abruptly.

They walked to a nearby phone booth, and Ravenna, amid the noise of busy Oxford Street, volunteered to make the call. Angela's number was in the phone book, but when Luke deposited a coin and she dialed, she listened to the phone echo in the empty flat.

"There's no answer."

"Maybe she's gone early to the Globe. Try there."

But the ticket seller who answered had no idea where Angela was, and since it took so long even to make clear who it was they were trying to reach, it seemed pointless to leave a message.

Luke put his hand in his pocket and pulled out the inevitable pack, smiling at her. "Well," he suggested, eyes intent on lighting his cigarette, "why don't I show you a bit of London, then? You can call her again in the next hour. What's your pleasure?"

"St. Paul's," she said with a startled laugh, taking only a second to adjust to this new plan.

And so they drove to the old section of London known as the City and spent a desultory hour in the monumental cathedral of St. Paul's, admiring its splendid classical dome and then, far beneath it, the beautiful choir stalls carved by Grinling Gibbons, master carver of the late sixteen hundreds. They inspected statues and monuments in the transepts, and in the crypt, the tombs of Nelson and Wellington and finally that of Sir Christopher Wren himself, the architect of the massive church that entombed him. The original cathedral, Luke explained, had been almost totally destroyed in the Great Fire of London in 1666, and Wren had been hired by the king to design a new version.

When they tired of so much stately splendor, Luke took her to see a much smaller Wren masterpiece, the Church of St. Stephen Walbrook, which was within easy walking distance. It was another domed church, wonderfully coffered and molded, with a peculiarly sensuous soft lighting and coloring and an Italian-influenced design. Luke would have insisted on yet another, for the area held several fine Wren churches and he was obviously a fan, but Ravenna judged it was time to try Angela again.

This attempt was as fruitless as the last, and when, after half an hour's coffee at a small café they tried again without result, Luke said, "If we're leaving for Devon, it should be now, before the traffic becomes impossible. It's three-thirty."

Mildly put, but nevertheless an ultimatum. And Ravenna found herself in a quandary. On the one hand, she didn't want to stay over. But for Jeremy's sake she felt he had a lot to be grateful for where Angela was concerned and hated to ignore her kind gesture. Naturally she couldn't expect Luke to see it in the same light. She couldn't say to him, "Because Angela helped out in a crisis I don't want to disappoint her now." All she could do was insist they accept her invitation. "I think we should stay for the play, Luke. It would be rude not to show up when she's expecting us."

"That means spending the night here." His voice was more than ironic. It held considerable surprise at her decision.

"I'm sure we can be back in good time tomorrow, probably early enough for me to meet Daniel," she said, invoking her fiancé's name like an amulet. A very useful amulet, she acknowledged ruefully.

"That's not the point. I don't think we should stay. Shall I be more specific?" he said clearly, gray eyes probing hers.

For a moment she faltered. Had she gone mad—spending a night alone with Luke, in the very place in which they had met so stormily? Then she declared, "We can't let Angela down." Her voice and face were stubborn. *Let him think what he likes,* she thought, biting her lip in annoyance. So it meant a night in London together. She was tempting fate, but she was tired of being afraid, tired of running. She would face whatever happened when she came to it.

Luke looked at her long and thoughtfully.

"Do WE HAVE TIME to order coffee?" he asked.

Seated at a very private table in Luke's London club, they had just finished a sumptuous meal of arctic char, followed by brandied pears. The head waiter had expressed great satisfaction at seeing Sir Anthony back from his year abroad and had led them to Luke's favorite corner. Unlike the comfortable but merrier atmosphere of the White Hart, this was an exclusive Piccadilly establishment, discreetly elegant; its muted plushness quietly breathed luxury.

"I think we do," Ravenna said, smiling across at him. The meal had been delicious, and Luke's pleasant but slightly reserved air had done much to calm her anxieties about her decision to stay in London with him. They'd talked of her book, and she had gracefully thanked him for her introduction to John Hadley. Then the conversation had turned to the city's architecture, until Luke made London seem like a paradise of hidden and not-so-hidden delights. She wished she could visit them all with him, thinking now that she could easily listen to him forever. Daniel, unfortunately, didn't share her love of the old and the beautiful. "Someday I'd like to see your own work," she said suddenly, and he'd promised her she would.

It was over coffee that their talk turned to more personal things. Luke's curiosity about her life was gratifying; he wanted to know about her childhood, what she liked, what she had done, what she wanted to do. Without seeming to, he managed to extract a surprising amount of information, until with a laugh of protest she insisted he talk about himself, hiding the fact that Glynis had already enlightened her on some aspects of his childhood.

But like her, he proved better at recounting the more distant past than the recent. He said nothing of the one subject she still wished she could broach: Kristen.

Conscious only of her own enjoyment as they ate and talked, Ravenna had nevertheless been subliminally aware for some time now of the tall beautiful woman a short distance away across the room, eating at a table with a distinguished-looking, gray-haired man. The woman had come in after them and was so stunning that the eyes of many had been drawn to her, except for those persons who, like Luke, had their backs toward her. A thick mane of curling blue black hair fell almost to her waist, and in the heart-shaped face that turned to study Ravenna once or twice, under dark dramatic brows, burned the most astonishing catlike eyes Ravenna had ever seen—a clear jasper green in color. The woman was wearing a suit of raw silk, in royal blue—obviously a designer creation—with a single strand of large pearls and chunky pearl earrings that set off her beautifully made-up face—not an English face, but a face such as one might meet in Greece or Rome. Vaguely aware of her admiration for the total effect, Ravenna felt an uneasiness when that green gaze fell on her. . . a flash of ice.

Ravenna was riveted when she saw the stranger, after staring in their direction two or three times, finally rise and move slowly, sinuously, across the room toward them, unseen by Luke. Her slender hand with long painted nails, a huge emerald on one finger, reached caressingly for his shoulder just as he was checking his watch.

"Luke." The single word was low and fluting, like a thrush's.

He glanced upward, and a lazy smile crossed his face, warm yet ironic. "Melina! What are you doing here?"

"I might ask you the same thing. You didn't tell me you'd be in town today."

"How did you even know I was back? I've only been here—"

"Two weeks today, darling. The grapevine is as healthy as ever. How naughty of you not to call me." But the voice with its faint foreign accent did not accuse...it seduced.

"Culture shock," Luke laughed. "From Africa to London is a big jump...I decided to take a little time before plunging in again." And he turned to introduce Ravenna, whom the woman had pointedly ignored.

Now her unusual eyes coolly skimmed Ravenna's flaming hair and glowing youthful face. She barely acknowledged Ravenna's, "How do you do?" when Luke said, "Ravenna Jones, Melina Arnold-Grant." He didn't elaborate, and Ravenna knew the woman was assessing her relationship with Luke...just as she was hers with him. She didn't think either of them got very far.

While she listened—it felt more like eavesdropping—Luke and Melina quickly moved through a host of names as she brought him up to date on all the year's changes, completely excluding Ravenna in the process. Then she murmured, her eyes intimate, "Luke, you simply must come down to Kettering soon for the weekend...for old time's sake. I won't take no for an answer."

Luke, Ravenna thought, didn't look the least inclined to say no. "I'll be in touch with you in the next few days," he replied easily, as if that settled it.

Melina practically cooed her pleasure, murmuring suggestively, "You know where to reach me, darling." And then she bent and kissed him softly, her green eyes melting into his until Ravenna looked away in embarrassment. Luke was enjoying it a little too much for her comfort.

Finally, with a glance at her casually abandoned companion, Melina said she must leave, that Eric was waiting. She nodded coolly but triumphantly in Ravenna's direction. The parting dramatic wave of her beautiful hand—the one with the emerald—was splendidly choreographed, Ravenna thought, watching her glide back to her own table.

"We'll be late now if we don't hurry," Luke said when she'd gone, and signed for the bill, ushering Ravenna out. But she saw him glance a warm farewell in the direction of Melina Arnold-Grant.

"Who was that?" she asked casually on their way to the car.

He paused, then said with a smile, "An old... friend."

"English?"

"Half Greek, half Hungarian. A singer with a really beautiful contralto voice and what could mildly be called a fascinating temperament. Used to be married to someone in the cabinet before I knew her. The man with her is her impresario." His eyes lighted on her challengingly, as if he guessed her thoughts, and she busied herself looking for a nonexistent object in her purse while they pulled away from the curb.

Exactly what part had Melina played in his life—before Kristen. . . even during? It was far more likely they'd been lovers than friends. At any rate, it was a part the singer seemed only too eager to take up again, now that Luke was back in London. And Luke? Was he eager, too?

Ravenna was gripped by an all-too-certain pang of. . . she supposed she had to call it by its rightful name—jealousy. But of course Luke would have a past, she reasoned. "For old time's sake," Melina had huskily murmured. If it was old, her voice and eyes suggested it was hardly dead! Well, Luke was thirty-six; Kristen couldn't have been the only woman in his life. There must have been dozens. . . most of them, she imagined, still gladly at his beck and call. Only did they have to look the way this Melina did? Ravenna made a face to herself, resolving not to be childish. She had no reason to be jealous. It was just, she explained inwardly, that Melina what's-her-name was definitely not the kind of woman she would choose for Luke. . . after all, Ravenna was going to be his sister-in-law. She left it vague as to exactly what her choice would be.

The Globe was situated on Shaftesbury Avenue in Soho, in the heart of London's theater section, with the Apollo Theater, Queen's and the Lyric within easy distance. Luckily they found a parking space and succeeded in being on time, hurrying in at the last minute with a few other latecomers. The play itself turned out to be hilarious. Angela starred as a kooky young woman pursued by a married man, convinced he was the reincarnation of the tempestuous Italian lover and poet Gabriele D'Annunzio, a man with a taste for the bizarre. The comedy scenes might have been a bit clichéd, but the actors made them unfailingly funny, and Angela proved a wonderful character actress. Sitting in the dark, caught up in the play's spell, Ravenna was reminded of the previous night's experience of *Romeo and Juliet*.

But there was this difference: Luke sat close beside her, and she was utterly, overwhelmingly, aware of him. Although he made no move to touch her—it seemed he hadn't forgotten his promise of a week ago—she felt an intimacy weave itself naturally around both of them, and her longings for him were stirred in the darkness at every glimpse of his shadowed profile. Once or twice she whispered innocuous comments on the plot to him merely to break the spell the silence laid. His replies were brief—he seemed entirely focused on the play. But from time to time she felt him look at her, once long and penetratingly, as if weighing something in his mind.

Wine was served at intermission in the lobby—a pleasant touch she wasn't accustomed to back home—and then the second half of the play wound on to its end. It had been a long day, and both of them acknowledged they wanted their visit backstage to be brief.

Angela's dressing room, they discovered, con-

tained all the messy paraphernalia of a resident star:
wigs, jars of makeup, a dressing table and cos-
tumes, large glittering mirrors and reviews of this
and other plays—some framed, some simply tacked
to the walls. A few well-used chairs and ashtrays indicated Angela was used to visitors. Still wearing
the glamorous black dress and startling makeup
from her last scene, she shooed some fans and a
fellow star out of the room as Luke and Ravenna
entered, embracing them both in her expansive
style, as if they were old friends.

Ravenna took the earliest opportunity to whisper
in her ear, "Thank you for saving Jeremy," and
earned a swift, humor-filled glance.

She turned from studying the glittery chaos of the
room to find Angela pouring champagne into three
glass goblets and saying, as she raised her glass to
theirs, "To the wedding."

Ravenna choked. The wedding? What wedding?

"When is it?" she heard Angela's deep enthusiastic voice go on. "I confess to a simple-hearted
pleasure in weddings—if it's in town, I'd love to
come to the church part. Or are you having it done
up proper? I always think churches make it real,
you know—my first marriage was at the city hall in
Cleveland and never did take. But you haven't told
me when it is."

She stopped long enough for them to get a word
in edgewise, but before Ravenna could explain her
mistake, Luke said coolly, outrageously, looking
right at her, "We haven't decided exactly when yet.
Ravenna can't make up her mind."

She had been about to swallow a mouthful of champagne and, unable to believe her ears, really did start to choke as it went down the wrong way.

Luke patted her on the back in apparent concern and hustled her over to the sink, running a glass of water and holding it to her lips before she'd recovered enough to say anything.

"Obviously Jerry has misinformed her," he said very softly between her coughs. "Why spoil it for her? Besides, I want to get out of here without going into long explanations so we can get to Gordon Square before midnight. Say our goodbyes, and let's leave."

He was right—explanations would be lengthy, so after a few more minutes she did as he directed. Angela kissed her heartily and wished her well, thanking them for coming to see her. Their visit had obviously mattered to her, and Ravenna, despite her dismay at Luke's comment, was glad they'd decided to come to the play.

"Keep in touch," Angela said as they left. "And give my love to Jerry."

Ravenna promised they would. A moment later, hurrying alongside Luke in the narrow backstage halls, she furiously whispered, "How dare you tell her we hadn't decided—"

"She'll hear from Jerry soon enough," he interrupted. She couldn't see his expression as he added, "Don't take it so tragically. I'm not about to propose." His mocking tones sobered her, and neither of them said much more on the way to Gordon Square, which wasn't far from Shaftesbury Avenue, but on the other side of Oxford Street, in Bloomsbury.

Realizing that most of the day had been surprisingly pleasant, dissolving the cold anger of the previous painful week so unexpectedly, she shrugged off her annoyance, determined not to make a mountain out of a molehill. But as they drew nearer to the town house, a rush of anxiety suddenly invaded her. And her awareness of Luke gathered intensity in the darkness. She felt it was the same for him. But despite her brave plans to confront her fears, she felt tired and knew that Luke was, too; she would excuse herself at once and go to bed. And this time she would make no mistake about which bed she got into. . . alone.

Moments later they stood on the steps of number forty-two as Luke turned the key in the lock, his tall presence vividly beside her. She remembered standing there once before, alone, fresh from New York. It seemed a thousand years ago.

With a sense of déjà vu she saw that the house glowed just as peacefully now as it had then, the living-room lamps gleaming exactly as before. She sensed Luke's pleasure at the sight.

"Annie must have been by recently," he said as he opened the door. "It's—" How he intended to finish the sentence she never knew. He stopped abruptly, stepping closer to her in a protective gesture. . . but it was too late.

Down the short hall from the entranceway was a small elegant sitting room, and in it she could see Daniel, as darkly handsome as ever, seated in an armchair. Fern was perched cozily on the arm with a drink in her hand, laughing down at him. She looked anything but naive at that moment, despite the fact that she still affected a very simple suit and blouse—a blouse whose top buttons were provocatively undone.

Daniel saw them in the same instant and leaped to his feet. "Luke!" he exclaimed. "Ravenna!" He looked stricken. "What are you doing here?"

"I was just going to ask you that," Luke countered, one hand placed on Ravenna's shoulder as if to steady her.

In a voice that struggled to be casual, Daniel explained, "We just came in from Heathrow. I called here and no one was using the premises—I thought you were at Rathbourn." This last phrase was almost accusing. He added, "I have a key...got rather in the habit of using it when you were away—and it's unthinkable to drive to Devon at this hour."

"Exactly our sentiments," Luke murmured with a look of distaste at Daniel.

At that moment Ravenna found her voice. "We've been up to see Luke's publisher, John Hadley," she explained as if by rote. "Luke's been kind enough to introduce me to him for...my book." Her voice shook slightly.

Daniel returned Luke's look in spades, his dark eyes suddenly glacial. "I see." For a moment she was afraid the two men might come to blows.

But the force of English etiquette was very strong; Daniel moved first, toward the sofa, and

simply sat down. She had no idea if he believed her
or not—likely their untimely appearance had just
confirmed his suspicions of a liaison between her
and Luke. But at that moment she didn't care what
he thought...the sight of him with Fern had
shocked her beyond all expectation. Fern and
Daniel? Was something going on between them?

Fern remained coolly seated on the arm of the
chair while greetings were exchanged, sipping her
drink, her sleek cap of hair shading her eyes. Other
than nodding hello, she seemed unconcerned with
who thought what and took a neutral position in the
background. Yet Ravenna was reminded of how
small animals freeze to stillness at the slightest
alarm...an attempt at camouflage.

"Well, if you don't mind I think I'll toddle off,"
Fern said after a minute in a perfectly normal voice,
suddenly reminding them of her presence. "It's
been a long day." And after making a great play of
stubbing out her cigarette in a nearby ashtray, she
sauntered down the hall toward the stairs without
the least uncertainty as to her direction.

Ravenna, watching Daniel glance sharply after
her, still stood frozen beside Luke. The thought of
making an exit exactly like Fern's held its appeal,
but she knew she couldn't run. Luke's hand still
gripped her shoulder, strong and comforting, and
as Daniel turned to pour himself another drink, she
heard Luke's deep voice say close to her ear, "Do
you want me to stay?"

His eyes touched hers as she shook her head,
"No, but thank you." For a second she thought an-

grily, why did their time of quiet togetherness have to end like this? Briefly she stared at him, regret in her eyes, and for an instant the gray blue depths of his pierced into her, until they seemed her only world. The moment broke apart, and she remembered where they were only when he released her shoulder from his warm grasp and made toward the hall door.

"I'll say good-night, also," he said.

Daniel looked up sharply from the liquor cabinet. "I'm afraid I've laid my bags out in your room. I'll move them."

"Don't bother." Luke's voice was brusque. "I'll sleep in my third-floor study."

Ravenna moved to sit down as Luke left, feeling utterly bereft in his absence. There was a Louis XV bergère near the sofa, covered in peach velvet, and she lowered herself onto it as if she were made of glass.

"Can I mix you a drink?" Daniel asked uncertainly.

"No. . . no, thank you."

Slowly he moved to sit near her on the sofa facing her, and they stared at each other like strangers. Her eyes took him in—dressed in a perfectly tailored, pin-striped suit, his wavy hair brushed back from his forehead, his pale skin slightly flushed from the drinks—or was it embarrassment at being found with Fern? She looked away from him, still unable to think of anything to say. The swishing of his swizzle stick in his drink, the clinking of the ice cubes, grated on her ears.

Finally he spoke. "I suppose you've been seeing a lot of Luke in my absence." His voice was bleak.

"Actually, very little." Her blue eyes rose to meet his.

"He was in Cornwall when I left."

"He came back last week."

"I thought you told me you didn't like him," he accused.

"Luke's been very kind to me about my book!"

"I'm sure." His tone was so suggestive that her temper burst—her head flew up and her eyes flashed. "You've been gone eleven days, Daniel. I can hardly be expected to sit moping at Rathbourn while you...while you...." She felt she couldn't go on without exploding.

"Yes?" he goaded.

"While you escort Fern around New York, then take her to Syracuse!"

"I had a lot of business to settle with Wallingford, and then Fern's fostermother had a kidney operation."

She stopped. She could well imagine that he saw accompanying Fern home as a charitable work—and perhaps that's all it was. But she couldn't hold back her anger any longer. "You seemed quite startled when we arrived," she said, her expression saying bluntly what she'd thought.

It was Daniel's turn to be defensive, and running his hand through his dark hair, he growled, "Don't be ridiculous. There's nothing but friendship between me and Fern. And of course I leaped up guiltily. This is Luke's house, and I was caught making myself at home...naturally I was startled." He paused, changing tactics. "You and he are the last two people I expected to see tonight—*together*, that is," he added with emphasis. "Rather a habit of yours, isn't it?"

Both of them had spoken in low rushed voices, anxious not to have their words carry. She stood up at this last insinuation, wearied of all the attacks and counterattacks. Daniel had come back, and everything was supposed to be all right. Instead they were quarreling bitterly. "I think we'd better leave this until Rathbourn," she said, her voice heavy. She saw his shoulders slump with weariness at this, as her own defenses weakened. "I can't argue anymore, Daniel. I'm going to bed."

Suddenly, farcically, she realized she had no idea *where* she was going to sleep. Fern must have taken the only extra bedroom, and Daniel had Luke's. She looked around helplessly, feeling the wine from the dinner and the theater, mixed with Angela's champagne, swim woozily in her head.

"Darling...." Daniel's voice was sudden velvet. "Can't we forget this nonsense and—"

"No, we can't forget it," she said sharply. If he thought that all of this could be smoothed over and forgotten simply by taking her in his arms...!

"All right," he said coolly. "Take Luke's room, then. I'll sleep on one of the sofas down here. There are some blankets in the linen closet." He didn't look at her.

"Thank you," she said, too angry to feel more than a perfunctory gratitude.

"And don't worry that I'll bother you this time."
He threw the words at her so quietly that she turned
in one movement and fled upstairs, unable to bear it
anymore. She wanted only to be alone.

Lying in Luke's bedroom shortly afterward, she
stared into the darkness, shocked at the turmoil rag-
ing inside her. She'd expected things to improve on
Daniel's return; instead the sight of him with Fern
and her own ill-timed arrival with Luke had thrown
everything into utter confusion. Why did nothing
go right for her and Daniel? Put another way, her
rather lovely day had been spoiled by the return of
her fiancé. How bitterly ironic!

For a moment she was tempted to regret her stubborn decision to see Angela's play. If she'd refused,
none of this would have happened. But the fateful-
ness that had plagued her and Daniel's relationship
from the beginning would have hounded her until
another absurd situation arose. No, it wasn't a simple question of whether or not they had returned to
Rathbourn that evening. She sighed and turned on
her side, wishing she could sleep away her confusion.

An image suddenly rose up to shock her: Luke's
arms going around her so unexpectedly her first
night in England, in this very bed. His lips meeting
hers, the naked nearness of him in her arms. Luke,
who had dominated her thoughts—and feelings—
since the moment she'd set foot in England. If
they'd spent the night alone as planned, what would
have happened? Would they have been able to stay
apart?

She closed her eyes, envisioning his face, remembering how she'd opened her eyes to see him looking down at her in the lamplight. At the memory such a fire of longing for him swept through her that she clenched her fists in frustration.

And she had the nerve to accuse Daniel, at least in her thoughts, of a possible involvement with Fern!

She hadn't deliberately let things grow between her and Luke; they'd grown despite all her efforts to stamp out the feelings and deny their very existence for fear of being swallowed up. She had fought him like the proverbial tigress... for this and for the sake of her engagement to a man she suddenly felt she hardly knew.

Again she saw Fern laughing down at Daniel, poised seductively on the arm of his chair; Daniel's surprise at seeing them, his bluff covering over of the situation. Could she believe his denial? She measured the distance in her heart between what she felt for him now and what she'd felt for him in those carefree days at Elk Creek, when he'd convalesced at her parents' home, showing a side of himself she'd rarely glimpsed since then. They had rushed into the engagement, she now saw, before they'd had time really to know each other. Their summer together had been meant to fill that gap, not widen it. And she had to face the fact that it *was* widening—it was almost a yawning fissure by now. Perhaps she and Daniel just weren't right for each other after all.

Her "love" for Daniel—was it now only a handy shield to protect her from the storming passions Luke so easily aroused? All her energies had focused on Luke since coming to England, on keeping him at bay....

She stared at the ceiling, gripped by thoughts of him. Luke, whom she'd begun slowly to know better than Daniel. It was he who'd been at her side when Daniel had left her alone; who'd wanted to drive her to Devon, to help her with her book, to share her interests...protect her even from the hurt of seeing her fiancé with Fern....

Daniel had implied that Luke was violent, unpredictable, and Fern had said with quiet poison that his blood was too blue. But next to the reality of the man himself this all seemed nonsense, woven from Daniel's quarrel with him over Kristen. Echoed by Fern.

It was Fern who was the enigma, Ravenna admitted. That slight pale face held too many surprises. It was hard to imagine her involved with Daniel... unless she was pursuing him without his awareness. Daniel was so devoted to his work he just might not realize what was happening.

Finally she did sleep, having arrived nowhere, found no real answers. A stalemate, Luke had said. Yes—all around it was the right word.

DRESSED in her navy skirt and white blouse again, she applied her light makeup in the bathroom the next morning, finger-combing her thick mane of hair so that it fell full and curling. She'd just returned to the bedroom to make the bed when there was a soft knock at the door. It was Daniel, wanting something from one of his suitcases.

"I hope you slept well," he said reproachfully, searching through his bags.

Ravenna was about to answer, when she turned and through the open doorway saw that Luke had just come down the stairs from the third floor, dressed in gray flannel trousers and a fisherman's sweater. She stared at him, suddenly feeling incredibly awkward.

"Good morning," they both said at once.

His eyes questioned her, then flew past her to the rumpled bed behind her, its sheets flung sensuously aside as if she'd just left it, and then to Daniel, rummaging in his bag. When they returned to Ravenna, the concern had gone out of them. For a frozen moment he stared at her, then nodded coldly, like a stranger, and walked downstairs.

She turned, saw the unmade bed and read his thoughts. He believed she and Daniel had made up and then slept together! She blanched and sank down on the edge of the rumpled spread. It was suddenly irrevocably clear to her that this was the last thing on earth she wanted him to think... that whatever she felt for Daniel paled beside the urgency of letting Luke Rathbourn know she hadn't slept with her fiancé!

"Ravenna, do you suppose we might have coffee up here and discuss this sensibly?" Daniel said softly a moment later.

Discuss what sensibly? What was he talking

about? Looking in bewilderment at his strained face—evidence that he, too, had slept little—she understood he was referring to their argument of the previous night.

"I'd prefer to wait until we're more comfortable at Rathbourn. Surely...L-Luke—" she stumbled over his name "—will want to make an early start." When he moved toward her as if he might touch her, she actually found herself leaning away from him, feeling trapped.

Daniel said sharply, "You still think—"

"I don't think anything," she answered hurriedly. "I merely want to get...home. Please understand, Daniel." An absurd plea when she hardly understood herself.

"All right," he sighed. "But I want you to know—"

"Please."

He stopped and merely looked at her, then crossed the bedroom and went downstairs without another word. In a moment she followed, uncertain of everything around her. She had only one need: to talk to Luke.

The thought conjured him up; she almost bumped into him in the hall.

"Excuse me," he murmured, his gray eyes preoccupied. And he walked past her into the kitchen as if she weren't there.

The morning dissolved into the long tense drive to Rathbourn. Luke had insisted on Daniel's and Fern's coming back with them, of course. Fern alternated between bursts of chattiness and outright silence. Daniel spoke of business and New York and seemed determined to put a good face on things, giving the impression that everything had been resolved between Ravenna and him. She by contrast was as silent as Luke, if not more so, reflecting with a certain bitterness that the two men were like the two sides of a vise, helplessly crushing her between them, yet each pretending to care. The trip to her was no more than a vague dream of flashing highways, green hills, small towns—a backdrop to her confusion.

Sitting in the rear of the Mercedes behind Daniel, she found herself too aware, even with her eyes closed, of one person only: Luke. The back of his broad shoulders, the hair curling at the nape of his bronzed neck, his long fingers guiding the wheel. But he'd retreated inside himself, and when their eyes met briefly once in the mirror, he looked away immediately.

Except for a few gas refills, Luke drove nonstop to Rathbourn. They arrived just after two, and Ravenna immediately excused herself and went to her room, saying she had a headache. It happened to be a handy truth.

The relief of being alone was enormous, and she sat quietly in her window seat overlooking the gardens. Unsympathetic to the chaos within her, the afternoon shone a pure faultless blue, hazed with gold; the roses below bloomed red and pink and white, tempting her to go out. But she sat there for a while longer, unable to think, wishing only to be emptied of feeling.

Presently she got up, wandered around the room and finally lay down on the bed. She awoke with dismay at seven-thirty—almost dinnertime. Damn, she'd slept through tea. But when she got up and bathed, instead of changing into a dress, she put on her jeans and sweater, still determined to go out and walk. She simply could not face Daniel yet, let alone Luke. She'd barely faced herself.

Her escape was not made easily, though. Crossing the great hall, she was startled to meet Luke, just emerging from the library. Spontaneously she reached out and laid her hand on his arm as he made to pass her. "Luke!" she breathed. Had she but known it, the face she lifted to him glowed with warmth, and her eyes under their heavy lashes were starred with emotion.

He stopped and raised his black eyebrows in inquiry.

"I'd. . .I'd like to talk to you," she said with no clear idea of how to begin.

"I'm very busy," he answered wearily, staring at her hand as if he wanted her to remove it.

Instead her fingers gripped his arm anxiously as his voice penetrated, and she whispered urgently, "Please, Luke! It's important."

His eyes cut into hers. "The truth is, Ravenna, I don't want to talk to you. There's really nothing important left to say between us that hasn't been said." He paused. "And perhaps I should remind you, you're engaged to Daniel. Remember?" He shook his arm free and strode toward the stairs.

Peters came into the hall at that moment and

found her staring after Luke. "Is there anything wrong, miss?" he asked in concern, looking at her white face.

His voice brought her back to reality. "Wrong? Oh, no, Peters, nothing at all." But as he continued to stand there, she remembered to add, "Please tell Lady Glynis I won't be coming down to dinner. I have a headache and need to rest."

"Certainly, miss."

She waited until he'd gone, then slipped out the front door and around past the stables, heading blindly toward the cliff path.

CHAPTER EIGHT

How LONG OR HOW FAR she walked, trying to shake the numbed response she felt to Luke's words, she didn't know. But after a time her blankness gave way to the realization that her eyes were drinking in the coastline with unconscious pleasure, tracing the deep jagged cuts worn away by the sea. The heaving path of the boiling water lifting upward to crash against the cliffs, to churn into crevices, to splash into rocky pools and then be sucked backward into the hungry sea, helped to tranquilize her. She watched, too, the long shadows cast by every twig and branch deepen to dusk, the forest and water empty of color and finally a full moon rise. Night-fall made no difference to her; she wanted only to walk, as she had always walked or ridden when upset—hearing this time the wild soothing tumult below the cliffs. She was glad the moon marked her path.

She discovered the small beach unexpectedly, with a sudden thrill. A rim of sand below her, it spread invitingly in a gentle beckoning curve, and the long glassy breakers washing up on it gave the sea the illusion of being tamed for once, compared to the shooting spray and thunderous impact of wave against rock. An overwhelming urge to walk barefoot along its edge overtook Ravenna as she gazed at it. Why not? If she could find a way to climb down...for most of the shoreline was inaccessible in this area, she'd been told.

Searching carefully, she found a break in the gorse about thirty yards farther along and a steep trail leading downward, rigged with a makeshift banister of rope. Obviously people used the beach for bathing, then. It must be safe. But thank heavens for the rope—without it she doubted that she'd try to reach the bottom, for the cliffs were as mountainous there as everywhere, though a bit more gently canted. Most of the rock facings fell sheer to the sea about sixty feet below.

Scraping and sliding, she finally reached the base and stood in awe on the sand, which on three sides was surrounded by a citadel of towering black rock. The sea lying before her was strangely flat and intimate from this perspective. Without the breakfront of the rocks to dash against, it flowed long and sibilant, and the moon shone so eerily that in places the waves ran with silver and purple lights. It was so incredibly beautiful that Ravenna walked enchanted along the margin of the water, letting the salt foam wash over her bare feet, careless that her jeans were getting soaked. And for the first time since the previous day her mind began to clear... her dull headache stopped its pounding.

Her misery, she had to admit, was inescapably tangled up with Luke. Luke—intense, passionate, so infuriatingly arrogant—who had thrown her feelings into wild confusion from the moment she'd met him.....

Ravenna rounded an outcrop of rock and was glad to see that the beach ran farther, stretching a good half mile or so ahead with a much wider slope of glittering sand. She followed along it, still conscious of peace in the beauty of the night and of the strange silvery light reflecting on the waves rolling in. Finally, higher up where the sands were dry, she sat down and wrapped her arms about her knees, staring out at the channel.

She'd hidden from herself long enough, she had to admit. Just as she'd clung to her so-called love of Daniel. To go on with either would be foolish and dishonest.

If Luke hadn't entered the picture, she wouldn't be in this predicament—caught between two men. Yet he had, firmly and inescapably. She had to deal with the fact—and with him. So far she'd done everything but.

Watching the waves, she wondered if she'd been missed at dinner. She could imagine the Rathbourns sitting there as usual in the candlelight, Glynis presiding, Luke taciturn, Daniel talking to Fern. Was Fern secretly glad Ravenna was absent? Likely. And Daniel? She'd thought she had heard him look in on her this afternoon when she was dozing but was glad he hadn't awakened her. What she had to say to him could wait...just a little longer. Because she had to be very, very sure of what she should do, and she wasn't yet.....

As if the sea could counsel her, she gazed out at

the murmuring rushing waves. They were casting a spell on her, she mused. *And* reminding her foolishly of Luke. He, too, was a spellcaster—one glance from his eyes and she'd been entranced. And suddenly she knew for a fact that if she stayed at Rathbourn, stayed even in England, she would never be free of him. She would always be helplessly caught in whatever spell he cared to weave around her, binding her to him. . . .

That meant she had only one choice left to her: to break her engagement and go home to Kentucky. Why hadn't she seen it earlier? She would simply tell Daniel the truth—that she couldn't marry him. No matter what she felt for Luke, that much at least was finally clear.

Feeling sad but somehow relieved, she got up off the sand. It was time to go back—past time. She'd been sitting there perhaps an hour, she judged from her telltale stiffness. And her jeans were mighty chilly. It might even be as late as midnight, for with such a bright moon it was easy to be deceived. She had a long walk ahead of her. . .and then in the morning, the awful task of speaking to Daniel.

The empty stretch of beach unnerved her a little now, although she'd given no thought to it earlier. She'd been so totally wrapped up in her worries. . . .

It took ten minutes or so to reach the barrier of rock leading to the smaller arm of beach where the path was. But when she got to the outcrop, dimly aware that it looked different, she rounded it in astonishment. The quiet rim of sand was nowhere to be seen.

Instead the waves crashed against the cliff edge as wildly as they had along the rocky coast earlier. And with a feeling of bewilderment she suddenly realized that the tide had come in. How utterly stupid of her not to remember the tide!

For a minute she stood there at a complete loss. Her eyes told her that her route to the cliff path was impassable, and with a slight tremor of fear she prayed there was another way to get up . . . along the stretch of beach she'd just traveled. But when she turned back, she saw that even the sands behind her had narrowed ominously and that the rock she was standing on was being washed by waves. Quickly she headed back along the way she'd come, close to the cliffs, her eyes roving over them intently. Curse her thoughtlessness! But how was she to think of tides when she'd been brought up in landlocked Kentucky?

Her gaze continually raked the rocks, no longer admiring the funny little caverns, crevices and ledges, the knife-edged jags hewn by the waves. Now she measured them with cold despair, searching only for a foothold that would offer escape. But they were as impregnable here as elsewhere, shooting fifty, sixty, sometimes seventy feet straight up. And then with a sickening feeling she saw what she'd missed earlier—the high-water mark, green with seaweed, ten feet up the cliffs. No matter that she could swim a dozen pool lengths. Unless she could get above that mark the churning powerful waves would sweep her out to sea.

She was furiously angry at herself. How could

she have got herself into such a dangerous predicament? It was then she began to shout, yelling herself hoarse, hoping someone had been as foolish as she'd been and was walking the cliff path at night. But her cries echoed long and emptily, and after a time she faced the fact that instead of carrying inland, they were being lost in the roar of the waves.

If only she hadn't told Peters she wouldn't be at dinner! Even now someone would have gone up to her room, would have discovered she was gone.... But, no. They would be considerate, even Daniel, leaving her alone to sleep off her headache....

Grimly she searched the beach from end to end, with a growing desperation. Only when she'd reached the farthermost point did she see it—an almost invisible path twisting up the rocks. Hardly a path, just a few precarious holds a mountain goat might find useful. But Ravenna's heart leaped anyway. It gave her a chance! And with the breakers pounding closer as the wind came up, who was she to argue?

She had hoisted herself up only seven feet of the chill, slithery cliff when she fell—backward, to the beach. She lay there, luckily unhurt but filled with disgust, until the cold shower of an encroaching wave brought her back to her senses. It was urgent she get out of there immediately. No matter how she felt.

The twenty-minute climb was a nightmare—long moments of clinging to tiny outcrops, wedging her hands into hairbreadth crevices, feeling one foot scrape the side of the cliff helplessly until it found a ledge, searching for the next handhold. Once she looked down by mistake and saw the angry waters licking below like some hungry animal, and dizziness overcame her. She buried her face against the rock, willing herself to be calm. So this was the sea she'd thought so beautiful, was it? Ready to sweep her to her death as if she were a branch or a leaf... sweep her utterly away. Just like her feelings for Luke were always doing.

With a sudden shock of longing she thought of Luke, and then she let the vision of his face draw her on. From that moment nothing mattered but that she see him again—one more time at least before she went home to Elk Creek. Nothing in the world existed but her need to see him.

She had to make it. She *had* to... and so, at last, she ultimately did. With a final wrenching gasp, after what seemed hours of climbing, she heaved herself up the last few feet, feeling the hard surface of the cliff face tear at her sweater, feeling the ungiving rock... and then the soft sweet wonder of the grass. Breathing a prayer of profound thanks, she collapsed there, staring in shock at the close dark sky. How beautiful it was, though thickened with clouds now, hiding the moon. How beautiful!

For a long time she lay there, thinking of Luke but unable to move. She felt exhausted, from the struggle she'd gone through and the fear she'd just faced. It was only when—true to form—the sky began to drizzle that she decided she had to get up and start back to Rathbourn.

But when Ravenna stood up, her ankle buckled

under her, shooting with pain. She must have wrenched it somewhere during the climb and never noticed, for now she could hardly bear any weight on it. Cursing, she tried it gingerly. How she'd ever manage to get home she didn't know.

That was when she remembered the cottage she and Jeremy had ridden by—somewhere near there, on the bridle path. It was much closer than Rathbourn; maybe she could make it there. At least it had a roof. Jeremy had told her it was never locked.... Yes, she would head for the cottage, for she had a sudden overwhelming need to get out of her spray-soaked clothes and lie down and sleep. When had she last eaten? At breakfast... and that had been only a coffee. After all she'd been through, no wonder she felt like a breeze could knock her down.

Slowly she experimented on her foot and found she was able to take short, half-hopping steps as long as she placed a minimum of pressure on her ankle. A stout branch she'd unearthed from the gorse helped her make better progress.

She found the cottage more quickly than she'd dared to hope—a long low shadow among the trees, thatched and whitewashed, a small rectangle that held perhaps two rooms. But in the rain and the dark she decided her senses were fooling her. She was certain she smelled woodsmoke. Yet Jeremy had told her the cottage was empty and seldom used. Suppose a tramp had taken up temporary quarters in it? Well, he would just have to share his fire, then, because after her agonizing trek she was certainly going in! And so weak and dizzy did she feel when she reached the low doorstep that she didn't stop to think but simply put her hand out and turned the knob.

The door swung inward. Its ancient creaking had the effect of a gun report on the man sitting before the embers of a fire. He leaped to his feet, his face registering in a second such concern that she thought every moment of agony on the cliff had been worth it. Through the fog that enveloped her she grasped at a question: what was Luke doing there? It seemed like some kind of miracle! He'd almost reached her when, to her disgust, she felt the room go black. How corny, she thought, and then she slid to the floor in a dead faint.

She came to cradled in his arms in a chair near the fire. Her first thought was, *of course he's here. I love him, that's why. It's as simple as that.* . . . The truth she'd kept at bay so long had finally broken through.

Her second was of the strength of his arms, protecting her. But when she tried to speak, he said, "Don't try to talk, you can tell me later," his voice exceedingly gentle as he tipped a glass of whiskey to her lips. She choked as it burned down her throat, but its hot glow on her chilled bones a second later was bliss. She stared up at him. In her dizziness his eyes above her swam with tenderness, until she thought she was dreaming.

"The tides. . . the cliffs—" Again she tried to speak, her voice a husky gasp, but he hushed her, and she drifted off, conscious only of his arms.

Later she half awoke to find herself lying on something. His fingers were lightly examining her swollen ankle, then tugging gently at her salt-caked jeans. Feverishly she drifted off again.

In the middle of the night she awakened fully. She was stretched out close to the fire on a bed he'd drawn up and was wrapped in his arms. She could smell the musky fragrance of him, so male and heady as he lay there, his eyes closed in sleep, and all her senses luxuriated in the sudden richness of him. Wearing nothing but a blanket, nestled very close to him...she wondered if her feeling of being kissed over and over had been a memory or a dream.

As she stirred, his arms closed around her and his eyes opened. "Go back to sleep," he ordered.

She moved weakly in his arms, and he took it for a protest, murmuring gently, his voice reassuringly gruff, "Trust me, Ravenna. For once just trust me."

She smiled at him, her eyes telling him she did trust him—because she loved him. Him, not Daniel. This arrogant tender man who from one moment to the next commanded her emotions in a thousand ways. This was what her helpless surrender meant, had meant from the moment they'd met. But when she tried to say this she couldn't shape the words, so dazed were her senses by the firm hard length of him—this time as he lay fully clothed beside her.

Still looking concerned, he smiled back at her, repeating, "Trust me. Now go back to sleep."

But sleep was her least desire. As he closed his

eyes again, she hungrily drank in the sculptured lines of his face beside her, his carved lips, so near her own. Once more she saw the angry waves below and the image of his face beckoning her upward through fear to safety, to this embrace.

Her fears of drowning in the sea had washed away all fears of drowning in the emotions that raged between them. Nothing mattered but her wanting him.

She moved her arm and reached to touch those lips with one finger, following their curve slowly, sensuously, her stroke feather soft with meaning.

Luke's eyes opened again, and this time she glimpsed astonishment in them.

"Luke," she whispered huskily, moving against him, her finger tracing his jaw, feeling the faint bristle of unshaven skin, then moving lower, pulling down his collar to feel the cords of his neck, down to the tangled matted hair of his chest. His wool turtleneck was in the way, so she slipped her fingers along the rough fabric, tucking them into the waistband of his trousers. She wanted her message to be unmistakable.

The astonishment in his eyes gave way; they burned now with a slow hot light. "Your ankle. Your blasted ankle," he whispered in her hair.

"It doesn't matter. My ankle doesn't matter."

His eyes, smoky with desire now, swept her into a cloudy fire as their gazes hung on each other's. "Are you sure, Ravenna?" he asked, his voice as husky as hers.

"Yes, Luke. Please...." And it was she who finally pulled his head down to hers so that their lips met.

His kiss was like a breaking storm. The vehemence of their passion, so long denied, carried them away, wave after wave of it pounding like a fiery sea. Ravenna felt as if he were drawing everything out of her into him. Then he tore his lips from hers, only to slip the blanket from her shoulders to her waist and bury his mouth hungrily against her breasts. Her senses swirled with a liquid fire. When one of his hands slid caressingly to her inner thigh, the other to the curve of her hip, her lips parted in a moan and her own hands began to clench and tangle in the thick curls of his hair. She heard herself murmuring his name again and again, and her own was a silken caress on his lips, deeply tender. Once he stopped and lifted his head to gaze down at her, and she was falling into his eyes, deep gray pools that told her she was his. She couldn't believe she'd ever thought he didn't care when his whole self was telling her he did.

And then he was drawing the blanket away so that, still caught in the spell of those eyes, she lay naked before him. He moved slightly away from her so he could see her completely. She watched the lowered lashes of his plundering gaze.

When she drew him down to her again, his lips began slowly to trace the path his eyes had taken, ravishing her, arousing flames that ripped through her like wildfire. Her desire mounted steadily to a white-hot intensity, until she thought she would go crazy with it.... And it was only then that he finally stood up and shed the barrier of his clothes. For one brief moment he stood over her—gloriously male, naked and beautiful; her eyes drank him in with shameless delight.

Then he was with her again, in ecstatic exploration, easing himself into her until she moaned with joy. Slowly, breathlessly, they began the sweet struggle of love—to wrest every ounce of pleasure from their heated union, to give unreservedly to each other. Their fire crested, leaped and raged... until the final arching burst of joy swept them in each other's arms into a floating golden peace.

"LUKE," SHE WHISPERED some time later, saying his name like a god's as she lay spent in his arms, his lips pressed to her temple. The word was filled with love.

How long they stayed there, arms and legs tangled, she didn't know or care. Finally Luke nuzzled her ear and wrapped his fingers in one luxuriant curl. Then his mouth trailed across her cheek and caressed her lips apart. He was kissing her again, long and pleasurably, with a slow honeyed sweetness. She savored the sleepy feel of his mouth on hers, the warm musky scent of his skin pressed against hers.

He shifted onto his elbow, and when she opened her eyes, she saw him looking down at her, the expression in his eyes so tender that she trusted him completely. She reached to trail her fingers along his matted chest, and his gaze darkened once more with desire. But he simply drew her into the crook of his arm and, bending his other arm beneath his head, turned on his back and lay staring at the ceiling.

It didn't occur to her to question him about his thoughts, so sweet was the drowsy silence that stretched between them. And soon, exhausted, she slept.

IN THE MORNING, waking to the smell of fresh coffee, Ravenna stretched pleasurably. She was uncertain where she was but knew that she felt wonderful. Then she came to with a jolt and sat upright, gathering the blanket around her.

Luke faced her across the small gas stove he'd lit on a table, where the coffee bubbled in an old percolator. He was in his usual turtleneck and pants, the latter tucked into high riding boots. The sun streamed in around them through the cottage's large leaded windows.

Gazing at him, she remembered with a blush how wildly, how beautifully, they'd made love the previous night. And she had been the one to initiate it! She, who'd wanted to go home to Kentucky and escape the Rathbourns forever. Now her love for Luke was the only thing that mattered.

She'd almost been swept out into the channel, she remembered suddenly. She'd been so frightened....

It was a shadow of that fear that Luke saw when he looked up at her. And his own watchful expression hardened. "Breakfast is almost ready," he said quietly.

His eyes, she decided, had more power than any sea tide to sweep her utterly away. Her own filled with love for him until he added, "While we eat you can tell me what happened last night."

She felt herself flame as the blood rushed to her face. "You know what happened. We made... love." She hadn't meant to hesitate before that final word. She'd been so sure she loved him, that he loved her, but he was acting so remote....

Luke's eyes flashed, but he said only, "I meant before we made...love." Was he mimicking her hesitation? "What happened to you on the cliffs?"

Reluctantly, between hungry mouthfuls of the warmed-up stew he handed her, she told him how she'd found herself trapped on the diminishing beach, shuddering as she saw it once again.

"You little idiot!" he said softly when she stopped. "You could have been drowned!"

It was true; she could have been.

"Promise me you'll never do anything so hare-brained again."

His choice of words was hardly tactful, but she supposed she deserved it. Nevertheless, looking up from her stew, she said perversely, "I don't see why I should promise anything of the sort."

"You'll promise me, or...." He moved a little closer to the bed, and she saw that he was upset, as if the danger she'd been in had been a personal threat to him.

"Or what?" she whispered, unaware of how she tempted him. For she was hugging the blanket to her, her hair tangled sensuously about her in curling fires. She watched as his eyes traveled over her appreciatively—as if the blanket weren't there—and she thought again of their passionate night... and of how her limbs still burned for him.

His words jolted her back to reality. "Your clothes are in the next room—I'll get them for you."

When he brought them he merely lay them on the bed near her. But his eyes seemed to penetrate the skimpy blanket, which revealed a naked shoulder, one slender curving thigh and a bare knee. He was more moved by what had happened between them than he was pretending to be, she realized intuitively. Yet she must've been mistaken; he *didn't* love her as she loved him. She pulled the gaping edges of the blanket together, trying to cover herself. Why was he acting this way, as if...as if the previous night hadn't mattered in the least. "I can't dress in here," she said hurriedly. Quickly she slipped off the bed, but when she put her weight on the wrong foot, she gasped with pain.

In a flash Luke's eyes filled with concern. He picked her up in his arms, then moved to sit in the chair beside the fire, capturing her against him. When he buried his lips in her hair, her doubts again fled like storm clouds blown away in the wind. He loved her. Surely he loved her! And as his mouth came down on hers, she surrendered to his arms, willing him to lift her to the bed a few feet away, knowing he would.

She could feel desire surging within them both, all-consuming, as earlier. Yet it threatened to be greater now, now that the waiting fires had once been lit.

First she would tell him she loved him—that there was nothing left between her and Daniel. She wanted him to know so that doubt would never again come between them. With an effort of will she lifted her mouth from his. "Luke, about the night before last at the town house...."

The eyes that met hers were suddenly shuttered, "Ah, yes." She felt his arms about her slacken. "Your dashing...fiancé. I was wondering when you'd remember him."

Fiancé? She started and drew back from him. Could he still possibly imagine—after they had made love so passionately, been as one body—that she still intended to marry Daniel? What in blazes did he think of her? Or perhaps the scenario *was* for a brief affair. Perhaps he thought he had another Melina at his beck and call.

"Daniel..." she began again less certainly, yet still resolved to tell Luke she loved him. But at the sight of his carved face she stopped. Did he want to hear it?

"That reminds me," he cut in, his voice cool as he scooped her off his lap. "There are some things I have to see about at Rathbourn. Would you mind terribly getting into some clothes."

The words of love died on her lips. His business at Rathbourn was more important than the two of them, than their love? The previous night, after their passion had been spent and he'd become so thoughtful—had he been thinking of it then, too?

She turned away, gripped by pain. She shouldn't
have been so forward, so honest, so seductive! The
previous night had been a mistake, a terrible mistake.

At least she hadn't been fool enough to express
her love to him. And staring into the cottage fire,
she was suddenly certain how unwelcome a confession this would be to a man who knew no ties,
whose passions were freely indulged in.

"I really want to get back now. Do you mind?"
His eyes as they fell on her were preoccupied. Compared to the searing passion in them moments earlier, they might have been a stranger's eyes. The
travesty of this stirred her at last to movement, and
she straightened, pulling the blanket around her
carefully, as if he had no right to look at her.

There was no need. He'd already turned away to
cross the room, opening the cottage door. She
heard the click of his lighter and felt the morning air
and sun pour in while she pulled on her jeans, and
her thoughts tumbled about her in despair.

She looked up as he stepped inside the door and
crossed to douse the fire he'd lit earlier, and for an
instant their eyes locked. Had she seen a flash of
tenderness in them when he saw her standing so unhappily in the center of the room, leaning on the
edge of the table as she tested out her ankle?

His words told her she'd been mistaken. "Don't
look so hopeless," he said gravely. "It was bound
to happen between us sooner or later."

Of course. No words of love had passed *his* lips—
not once. Hardly a small detail, but she'd missed it

in her eagerness to voice her own feelings. Sobered, she wiped her vulnerability from her face.

"Yes," she said, struggling to make her voice sound casual. "It had to happen once. These things are inevitable in certain...cases."

She was unprepared for the leap of anger in his face, and their eyes battled until she turned quickly away, unable to bear it. Then, without warning, he strode to her side and scooped her up in his arms.

Her astonishment left her speechless for one gasp. "Put me down," she grated a second later. How dared he touch her after...after.... "Put me down!" she warned icily.

"You can't walk on that blasted ankle, and you know it!"

"Well, I won't let you carry me! I—I don't even want you to touch me!" In her dismay at the fire his arms evoked, her voice faltered on the final words.

Before she could say more, he pulled her more tightly against him, and she felt an unleashed emotion prickle along her spine. "Ravenna," he said in a low dangerous growl, "I am carrying you back to Rathbourn, like it or not."

She tried to kick, but after one jolting stab of pain, she sank against him, her face white.

"You deserved that," he said grimly as he opened the door. And for the next half hour she had to endure the silent thundercloud of his anger as he strode with her all the way to Rathbourn, her breasts and face pressed against him. She thought she'd never hated him so much.

SOUNDING TRUMPETS, Ravenna thought in disgust, couldn't have created a less discreet entrance than the one Luke contrived simply by carrying her in his arms through the front door at 11:00 A.M. Fern and Jeremy, sitting at the foot of the stairs in the middle of the great hall, leaped to their feet when Luke swung the door to with a crash.

"Good lord!" Jeremy breathed. "What happened to Scarlett!"

"Caught by the tides, the idiot," Luke growled, and made to push past them.

Ravenna felt her face flame with mortification.

"Daniel's just discovered your bed wasn't slept in. He's been out of his mind," Jeremy volunteered helpfully to her before they could move. He looked unnerved by the closed expression on Luke's face and turned questioningly to Ravenna. She tried to smile. "No damages, I hope? Peters said you must have hoodwinked him last night."

"Excuse us, Jerry," Luke said impatiently, but Fern blocked their way on the step by standing directly in front of him.

"Sir Galahad to the rescue? Or...Sir Lancelot?" she asked in a cool drawl. "I can never get my knights-in-shining-armor straight. My, you do look healthy, Ravenna, for someone caught out all night on the shore. I assume it was all night?"

Sir Lancelot, Ravenna clearly remembered, was the one who'd seduced Guinevere, King Arthur's wife. "Of course I'm healthy," she snapped, though in truth her ankle was hurting like hell.... The second of Fern's remarks she was careful to ignore. And when Luke started resolutely up the stairs, she spluttered at him, "I can manage the stairs myself . . . you may put me down!"

"You will *not* manage," he said tightly, and Jeremy and Fern stared after them, realizing he was furious. Jeremy rolled his eyes at Fern.

"But I thought you'd gone to the cottage," Fern called at Luke's back insistently. "Glynis said—" She stopped.

"Maybe they spent the night there," Jeremy supplied unthinkingly when Luke didn't answer, and then blushed. "I mean. . . ."

Fern looked after them speculatively, her mouth curving to a slow thoughtful smile.

But Ravenna saw only the figure who'd come to the top of the stairs: Daniel. His face looked pinched and strained as Luke advanced with her clasped stubbornly in his arms. She could have cheerfully clobbered Sir Anthony Rathbourn at that moment.

"I'm all right, Daniel," she said, noticing he really did look sick with worry. But his eyes were stony as they flew from hers to Luke's. He was ready to kill, as well, she thought.

Luke faced him at the top of the stairs, and their eyes dueled. "Your . . . fiancée," Luke ground out coldly, as if presenting her to him, and for one instant Ravenna was certain he was going to drop her at Daniel's feet like a sack of potatoes. The hatred of the two men crackled above her almost visibly.

And then Daniel said a peculiar chilling thing. "I

never thought you'd go this far to get back at me, Luke.''

Pressed as she was against the hard sinews of Luke's torso, she felt him start. Daniel's words had been unexpected...and he'd spoken as if Ravenna for that moment did not exist.

Luke turned away blackly when she said again in measured tones, "Let me down, Luke...if you please." He ignored this and moved down the gallery, to push the door to her bedroom open with one foot. Daniel paused, nonplussed, then followed quickly behind.

She expected Luke to drop her unceremoniously on her bed, but he laid her down with surprising gentleness. She realized then how careful he'd been of her ankle all the way back, despite their anger. But her body, suddenly, devastatingly, registered loss...as soon as the touch of his hands left her. Her body, not her mind. She glared up at him where he leaned less than a foot away under the canopy of her bed and saw him likewise gripped by the inescapable magnetism that linked them both for many instants longer than was necessary. In spite of himself, his stormy eyes told her that given the slightest excuse, he would drag her to his bed again—and punish her with his body. On a spasm of anguish she tore her eyes from his but got no farther than his mouth. His sensitive sensual mouth.... If only he cared! If only it hurt him to leave her alone with Daniel. She wanted it to hurt him, wanted to see him rage with jealousy. But of course he didn't care...at least not in the way she wanted him to.

Still staring down at her, he said to Daniel, who was behind him, "This has nothing to do with Kristen, Daniel."

It happened so quickly that Ravenna jacknifed upward on the bed in a vain effort to stop them. Luke had no sooner straightened and turned, when Daniel's fist flashed toward him, hard and deadly, blocked by Luke at the last moment in an upward motion. Daniel had seen the signals flying between them, and his drawing-room manners had melted away. Now he stood there seething, breathing in short gasps heavy with unsatisfied rage. Any second, she was sure, they would come to further blows. Two men, one woman, she thought—an ancient primitive rivalry. Then she gasped. She'd made the mistake of leaning on her swollen ankle.

Luke's hands, strong and steady, reached back to lower her again to the bed, his eyes telling her not to move. Then he drawled, as if it were unimportant to him, "How dramatic of you, Daniel. But there's a difference this time. Ravenna's...alive." He paused, and she remembered Kristen. "I was about to explain that Ravenna fell and hurt herself on the cliffs last night—and almost drowned."

Daniel sank into a nearby chair. "The cliffs?" He looked bewildered. "How...how did you find her?"

If Luke chose to crush her, all he had to do was hint to Daniel what had happened at the cottage.

"I didn't. She found me," she heard him say, her whole body one tight unexhaled breath of tension.

"At the old cottage. I walked over there last night, remember... so as not to have the pleasure of your company... and decided to stay over. One of those fortuitous coincidences, I guess. Ravenna showed up this morning about an hour ago. She headed there because it was closer than the manor."

She resumed breathing. *Thank you, Luke. Thank you.* It was a small reprieve, but one she needed. Although, strangely, she felt no guilt about their lovemaking, she wanted to tell Daniel about her decision to break the engagement without this added complication.

Luke didn't see how her body relaxed as he stood there a few feet from the bed, blocking her view of Daniel—blocking, too, Daniel's view of her very expressive face. For the first time it struck her that his action might be deliberate.

"I hurt my ankle, Daniel," she explained hurriedly. "I... couldn't get back up the cliffs. You see, I'd found my way down to this little beach a couple of miles from here. I never thought of the tides." Remembering how terrified she'd been when she'd realized she was trapped, she blanched, beginning to relive her experience again.

In one step Luke was back beside her, his face masked with exasperation. "Never mind," he said quickly, "it was a fool of a thing to do. I'll have Peters call our doctor—I want that ankle looked at."

And abruptly her fear faded, distracted by this thought. She watched him leave, and then she was alone with Daniel.

Lying there, she shivered, sorely tempted to stare steadily at the silk canopy above her. Face to face with Daniel, where should she begin?

"Are you really...all right?" Daniel asked softly, drawing his chair up to the bed. "Darling?"

Somehow she found the strength to turn and look at him, her eyes swimming with unexpected tears.

"Yes, I'm fine. Just...just my ankle." She wanted to say outright that she had to go home to Kentucky—that everything was over between them, but she couldn't think how to begin. "Daniel, I..." she attempted.

"Try not to be so upset," he murmured, patting her hand awkwardly, and then they both turned as Glynis rushed into the room, forgetting to knock.

"My poor darling! Dr. Warren is on his way— Luke just got him on the phone," she said. "But how could you have gone out last night without telling any of us!" And the whole story had to start over again.

In the end Ravenna had a splitting headache. Then thankfully Glynis rang for Mary, asked Daniel to wait downstairs for the doctor and insisted Ravenna get undressed and under some warm blankets.

"You're in a bit of shock, my dear, I can see. And no wonder," Glynis said as Mary helped Ravenna pull off her jeans.

Ravenna groaned as she flexed her ankle, hating the fuss they were making over her. But at least one good thing came of it: it distracted her from her aching heart. She refused to say broken. Luke wasn't going to do that to her; he wasn't worth it.

The doctor arrived half an hour later, a cheerful portly man sporting a golfing cap. Carrying an old-fashioned black bag, he was exactly her image of the kindly country doctor, even to the cap. He told her he'd been snatched from the middle of a golf game. Then he examined her foot carefully, announcing that it was unbroken but badly sprained. And then he began an examination of the rest of her.

"But I'm perfectly fine!" she protested. "It's just my ankle."

"Sir Anthony insisted," he explained. "And you never know after a fall like that."

Inwardly she fumed as her Kentucky Irish temper kindled once again. Sir Anthony was always insisting. And such scruples hadn't stopped him the previous night! Just wait till she was on her feet again. Why, she'd show that insufferable varmint....

"Your blood pressure does seem a mite high now," the doctor said after he'd slid the inflatable tube around her arm.

That rotten, no-good.... "What did you say?" she asked.

"Ah, it's nothing. You're a healthy lass, I can see." And he proceeded to tape her ankle, advising her to stay off it as much as possible for a week.

Great. So much for her plans to rush off to Kentucky.

"And no more going to the cliffs at night," he cautioned in fatherly tones. "The sea is not to be made light of in these parts. We've had many a drowning here, and it's well you know it.''

"All right,'' she murmured meekly, and his stern expression dissolved in a smile as he said goodbye.

She slept much of that afternoon, awaking only once to see Daniel sitting faithfully on the chair beside her bed. Or she supposed it was faithful—perhaps he was merely reasserting his territorial rights.

But he'd dozed off himself, and for the moment he looked so devoted, so vulnerable sitting there that she thought guiltily of what she had to tell him.

Almost immediately she slept again, more exhausted than she'd known. It was late when she awoke next, and by this time Daniel had gone.

The night alone was the hardest part. Every time she tried to rearrange herself more comfortably, she thought of the one comfort she was without: Luke's arms. And the warm length of his body pressed close to hers, the beating of his heart joined with her own, the touch of his eyes...his hands. She tried to stop her thoughts, for she knew if she let them drift on, they would arrive at that morning's tumultuous ending and that she'd be faced with the grief she hadn't really acknowledged. *Let the numbness stay,* she prayed, *until I'm gone from Rathbourn.*

But inevitably the whole scene reeled back to torment her, in every sensuous exquisite detail, followed by Luke's crushing withdrawal from her arms. He had loved her, she'd believed, for that brief time when his body told her she was his. Until he'd tired of her. "It was bound to happen between us sooner or later...." She heard it again, each casual word a blow, and wanted to tear him apart inch by inch. But even that pleasure was denied her.

So she lay awake, inventing tortures for him... tortures that had a strange way of ending differently than she'd planned.

CHAPTER NINE

ON MONDAY MORNING, just dressing and making it over to the window seat constituted a major challenge. Once there, Ravenna realized she'd forgotten the book she'd intended to read—a novel from the library downstairs. She had to go all the way back across the room to get it, then hobble to the window again; this frustrating beginning did nothing to sweeten her mood. But finally she curled up, determined to hole up all day and forget the world. Any world that held Luke deserved to be forgotten.

The first knock came just as she'd finished the first paragraph on page one. It was Jeremy, trailing an old pair of crutches he'd used when he'd gone skiing two winters ago in Wales. "Thought you might like them," he said. "Broke my leg coming down a mountain with an unpronounceable name. When I got back to London, my theater pals victimized me with their wit, I can tell you, while I hopped about in plaster."

She had to smile, remembering the traditional "break a leg" said for good luck to an actor or actress about to go onstage. Sort of an ancient attempt to ward off evil by naming it first, she supposed. He grinned at her, the same old lovable Jeremy, and her day began to brighten a few watts.

"I was able to divide my friends into those who just thought it and those who said it, if you know what I mean. The strong and the weak."

"How's the play?" she asked on a reluctant chuckle.

"Terrific. Got my best review yet—two whole lines in Salcombe's main rag. 'Mercutio splendidly and wittily played by the "mercurial" Jeremy Rathbourn.' Well, it's a start."

His face clouded just as hers began to light up. "Luke buttonholed me yesterday, though. What a rotten mood he's in lately. Treated me to two whole hours of a bloody ridiculous harangue on school," he grumbled. "The usual, but I've never seen him so black. I couldn't believe it when he finally said I could stay in the play as long as I slaved two hours a morning over the books. I was waiting for him to clap me in the cellar, judging from the look on his lovely mug. Kept repeating himself, too, as if his mind had turned to mush. Not like old Luke."

He plunked down on the window seat beside her as her mouth fell open. She had a hard time imagining Luke anything but incisive. She'd wished she'd been there to see it. But at least he'd kept his promise to let Jeremy stay in the play.

"Oh, well, as long as he doesn't get the wind up about Angela. What d'ya think of her?" he asked eagerly.

"I thought she was, oh—" she reached for a suitable word "—wonderful. And by the way, she sent

you her love when we were in London. She had a
courier deliver tickets to us at lunch. That's why we
stayed over. The play was hilarious.''

He smiled in satisfaction. "Good old Angela.
Nice of her to think of that. But I know you went to
see her—I've been on the phone to her. . . about the
best I can do while I'm stuck here at Rathbourn and
she's in London. Had to thank her for that fancy
footwork with Uncle Luke on opening night. I
thought he'd make 'worms' meat of me', y' know.
Funny thing, though. She mentioned you and Luke
were getting married. I couldn't believe my ears.''

Ravenna gulped, remembering the champagne.
Of course—Angela had mixed Luke and Daniel up.
Or had Angela known how she felt about Luke even
before she herself did? And John Hadley, too, had
said something odd.... Was she as transparent as
that? She felt herself blushing in annoyance.

"When I told her it was you and brother Daniel
getting hooked, she wouldn't buy it. Said she was
never—quote, *never*—mistaken.'' He paused, his
large brown eyes woeful, while she thought, *there's
always a first time, Angela.*

Jeremy sighed. "Scarlett, sometimes I can't
understand you women. Even Angela. Especially
Angela. I kind of had her pegged for the sensible
sort.''

Sensible? Women, Jeremy would learn someday,
had their own kind of sense. *Not that it does us any
good,* Ravenna inwardly complained.

"It's so damned inconvenient,'' Jeremy muttered
blackly. "Being trapped here at Rathbourn!''

For a moment he looked so troubled she was tempted to forget her own cares and encourage him to confide in her, just as her younger brother Jamie often had in his darker crises.

But he leaped up too quickly, insisting in a lighter voice that she try out his crutches. He hoisted her to her feet and tucked them under her unwilling arms. They were about a foot too high, and her feet dangled above the carpet. Jeremy burst out laughing.

He calmed down enough to say, "Hmmn. Well, you could do with a pair of elevator shoes, but let's see. Say, you know you'd look great even in a straitjacket, Scarlett."

She made a face at him and suggested he help her down.

"Not to worry. I'll take 'em to Garvey and get him to saw off the bottoms for you. Fix you up in no time. But poor old Jessie's going to miss you. Have you thought of that?"

No, she realized, surprised at herself. She hadn't given it a single thought. Ordinarily she'd be pining to get back to the stables. . . but she wasn't. Instead she was mooning around indoors, thinking, *poor old Ravenna*. But even riding Jessie as an incitement to a fast recovery held no appeal.

He left, carting off the crutches, and she watched him go with a sharp miserable pang, realizing suddenly how she was going to miss Jeremy—in some ways more than anyone else there at Rathbourn. He'd become like another brother to her.

The second knock followed shortly after the first. Daniel came in this time, and as she struggled to her

feet, the lighthearted mood Jeremy had almost succeeded in inspiring disappeared entirely. The first
thing he said was, "I can easily carry you downstairs if you want to join us for meals or anything.
You don't have to lock yourself away in your
room."

Oh, but she wanted to. "No, no thank you. Maybe another time," she demurred. Her reaction surprised her, because it was almost entirely physical:
the image of his arms around her after Luke's....
She sank once again onto the window seat.

When the third knock came—it was Garvey,
wheeling in a cart with a sumptuous breakfast she
couldn't possibly eat—she thought wearily that she
knew what it was to take up residence in Grand
Central Station. But she smiled when he quipped
good-naturedly, "Room service...no tipping
allowed." Peters, she knew, wouldn't have been
caught dead saying that kind of thing.

"I'm really not even hungry yet—" she began.

"Nonsense," Daniel cut in. "I've noticed you've
been losing weight. If you aren't careful, your wedding dress won't fit." And he proceeded to help
Garvey place the tray on the marble coffee table.
When Garvey left, Daniel came over and offered
her his arm.

Well, now is as good a time as any, she thought
with a despondent heart, letting him assist her to the
sofa. "Daniel...about the wedding." She watched
as his hands paused in midair over the lid of her hot
meal.

He turned to her slowly. "Yes. What about it? I

understand from your mother everything is going according to plan." His voice was level, but the brown eyes that faced her faltered slightly. Then he smiled. "You aren't worrying about foolish things like that encounter in London, are you, Ravenna? You know I wouldn't want—"

"Daniel." The insistence of her tone stopped him. "We have to talk. I—I want to go home."

"But you *are* at home, Ravenna. England is your home now."

She took his hand in hers. This was going to be as hard as she'd thought. "You see, Daniel—"

"You mean, move up the wedding date?" he interrupted her hurriedly. "Is that it? You want us to go back for an earlier wedding? As a matter of fact, I've been meaning to talk to you about exactly that."

"No, Daniel." He was deliberately misunderstanding her. "That isn't what I mean. What I'm trying to tell you—"

His hands gripping her shoulders startled her and told her he knew exactly what was coming.

"But I don't want you to tell me," he muttered. "I won't let you go back home—without me." He put his finger to her mouth to hush her when she opened it to speak again, and they stared miserably at each other.

"Please, Daniel," she finally said. "Please listen to me. It's not working out. You know it as well as I do. I want to go home to Kentucky. . . for good. I'm sorry." She'd finally got it out.

Daniel stared at her incredulously, then dropped

his hands from her shoulders and walked to the window. He took up a position facing the gardens and, keeping his eyes averted, said quietly and quickly, "Ravenna, please don't act rashly. It's just that you're still angry at me for flying off to New York without even talking to you. It was rotten of me, I know. But you don't understand how I felt. Seeing you with Luke on the horse that day I arrived...hearing you say his name in your sleep...I really thought the worst. I know now I should have trusted you, but instead I acted like a hurt schoolboy."

Great. Now that it was too late he'd decided to trust her. Send in the clowns.

"Afterward, in New York, I could have kicked myself for it. And then Fern's mother getting ill... I wanted to rush back here, but I felt I couldn't because Fern was so upset. She asked me to stay. But if you think that she and I— What you implied in London simply isn't true. Fern, well, it's a fact she *is* rather fond of me, but our relationship is strictly business. And Fern knows that. I've made it quite clear." He wheeled and returned to her. "I promise, darling, things will go all right now. Just give me another chance."

She lifted her deep blue eyes to him, staring in surprise and aware of two things: first, what this lengthy humble speech had cost him, and second, that he'd promised once before that things would be all right—the night he'd come to England. She'd believed him then, although time had proven otherwise. But on this occasion she read the situation correctly: things would never be all right, no matter what he said or did. Only Luke could make it so—and that would never happen.

"I...I can't go through with it, Daniel. I can't marry you," she repeated simply.

Suddenly Daniel turned on her and uttered one dangerous word. "Why?"

She stalled for time, pouring herself a coffee from the small urn on her tray. If Luke's name came up again between them—he'd brushed so lightly over it just a moment ago—their talk would become very bitter. And immediately she was sure she couldn't bear to drag Luke into it. What had happened between them was theirs...or rather hers; Luke wanted no part of it. "We became engaged too quickly," she said at last.

In one fast movement Daniel leaned in front of her, dragging at her wrist in a way that reminded her unhappily of Luke. For someone who'd declared his stepbrother violent, Daniel had been acting very surprisingly lately. "Why?" he repeated.

"I've already told you, it's not working out!" she cried angrily, shaking her arm free.

"Have you?" He looked down at her for a second, then moved away again, turning his back to her.

His voice when it came held a new note, a casual suggestive note that unnerved her, with each word slowly stressed. But at first she hardly followed him, so abrupt was the switch. "Funny...Luke's always been the playboy in the family. His engagement to Kristen was his one aberration. She took a fancy to me last summer, too. You know these beautiful, free-thinking Swedish women...."

He paused, and her stomach clenched to a tight hard ball. Why was he implying something had happened between him and Kristen? Then she knew.

"Luke wouldn't hesitate to get back at me by—"

"What are you talking about?" she burst out before he could continue, her face seeping color.

"I'm not sure," he said slowly, looking at her now.

"I think you should go now, Daniel." She heard how cold her voice sounded. Was he actually implying that if Luke had made love to her, it was only to revenge himself because of Kristen? She wouldn't believe it.

Daniel still stood there stubbornly, his face reflecting both shame and determination. "No, I'm not going. Not until you promise me one thing, Ravenna. Stay one more week at Rathbourn." His voice and eyes softened appealingly. "Just one more week. You owe me that—owe it to yourself, too. Then you can go home if you insist, though I don't think you should make any final decision until you've thought things through at Elk Creek. Promise me."

She looked at him, feeling like a subtle blackmail had just been perpetrated. But seeing the suppressed pain in his face, she said wearily, "All right, Daniel. One week. I'll stay for just one more week. But only because I haven't much choice," and she pointed to her bandaged ankle. "Then I'll go home.

I suppose I ought to agree to think it over—but please don't expect me to change my mind."

"Thank you," Daniel murmured. He stood there for a moment, looking rather lost. But there was nothing more for them to say, and with a curt nod in her direction, he finally left.

WHEN GLYNIS POKED HER HEAD IN an hour after Daniel had gone, chiding Ravenna on hiding herself away, Ravenna finally agreed to come out of isolation—not that she'd had any—and join everybody for lunch. This, Glynis announced, was to be another summery picnic out under the chestnut trees to the southwest of the house.

Ravenna's decision had a lot to do with a casual remark Glynis let drop that Luke had gone away somewhere again and that she never had a full contingent of her sons these days. Jeremy, too, would be absent, she'd added. He was in Salcombe brushing up on a scene. Luke had told her all about the play, and she was anxious to see it that night. Just that...no recriminations against her youngest son, reprobate though he was. Yes, it was Luke who played the heavy.

"I'll send Daniel and Garvey to help you down the stairs," Glynis told her with a warm smile when Ravenna reluctantly agreed to emerge. And so Ravenna was carried between them, seated on the crossed and clasped arms of the two men...so much less romantic than Luke's style, she thought with gratitude.

But sitting under the spreading branches of the

beautiful trees, with luncheon spread on a damask-covered table, she sharply regretted that she'd come. Daniel's attentiveness made her aware how unwise her promise had been, and with his every word and action she felt herself tied to it. First he went into the house to bring a cushion for her back. Then he asked Peters to bring out a hassock for her foot.

"Really, Daniel, please don't bother!" she said, a hint of sharpness in her voice.

"It's no bother, darling, really," he assured her, his endearment setting her teeth on edge. It wasn't fair when he knew how she felt. But she supposed he wanted to keep up appearances.

Fern had greeted her sweetly and now helped herself to another glass of wine, her ears ever alert, Ravenna sensed. Glynis was chatting with gusto about her favorite topics: rose bugs, Japanese beetles, blackspot and cankers, and Ravenna nodded at what she hoped were appropriate times. It was hard to be enthusiastic at the moment about the blights of others, especially roses.

"I really think you should move into the shade," Daniel said at Ravenna's shoulder. "Let me move your chair a bit."

"No, Daniel, I like sitting in the sun."

"Perhaps I should go in and find you a hat."

"No! Please! I'm perfectly all right."

Fern glanced at her, hearing the sharp whisper, and even Glynis looked at them oddly. Ravenna blushed, and Daniel assumed a nonchalant expression. Still, he was miffed, she could tell, his eyes saying clearly to her, *I was only trying to be helpful.* Didn't he know it was a form of torture, considering how things stood?

A moment later Peters came over to announce that Ravenna's crutches had been "adjusted" and that he thought Garvey wouldn't mind if Daniel fetched them now...Garvey being himself indisposed. He was, ahem, under the engine of the Mercedes, covered in grease, but he wished to discuss the shortcomings, so to speak—Peters coughed nervously at his unexpected pun—of the new cut-down version with him.

Daniel left with alacrity, and Ravenna knew it gave him a perverse pleasure to be able to wait on her against her will.

She almost sighed with relief when he'd gone. But when Glynis left, as well, for a school meeting, she suddenly felt deserted. There she was, alone with Fern, the last person on earth whose company she would deliberately choose—no, the second last.

The skirmish began mildly enough. Fern sat there smoking, staring up through the branches of the tree at the sky. Then she turned her dark appraising eyes to Ravenna and inquired, "How's your ankle doing?" A neutral enough question.

"Oh...really much better. I'll be fine in a week, Dr. Warren said." *And in Kentucky,* she thought to herself.

The leaves rustling above them filled the next long pause.

Then Ravenna asked, "How's your foster mother?"

"As well as can be expected. She's had a kidney transplant, and they're waiting to see if it takes. Their prognosis is tentatively good." Fern's face was wary.

"I hope very much that she's well."

"Naturally, so do I. She's my only kin."

Ravenna would have liked to reassure her. But Fern's expression was so bleak she decided it would be better to change the subject. She remembered that Daniel had said Fern was very upset about the operation.

At first glance Fern's composure seemed real enough, aside from the usual restive quality in her gaze—a quality Ravenna found unsettling. Then she noticed one of Fern's hands, the one not holding her cigarette. It rested on the arm of the graceful old wicker chair. But "rest" was not the right word; "gripped" was more like it. The whitened knuckles of that small hand struck Ravenna forcibly, telling her what Fern's face and voice did not: that she was much more ill at ease than she let on. But, why? Daniel had said there was nothing between him and Fern, and Ravenna believed him.

"What did you tell Daniel in New York that made him think I wasn't interested in his work?" Ravenna finally asked, wanting to clear that matter up.

Fern looked at her in surprise, her eyes widening. Then she said, "Why, do you mean to say you are?"

Ravenna felt flustered. To avert question with question was a neat tactic, one she herself was hardly up to today. Why had she bothered, anyway—when none of it mattered anymore. "I think a wife is always interested in her husband's work," she generalized, knowing how inappropriate a statement this was.

"Think again." Fern blew a smoke ring at the sky and said conversationally, "My husband was in computer programming. Used to tell me all about the courses he gave and bored me to tears."

There was nothing to say to this, for of course thousands of wives must feel as she did. And to be really honest, Ravenna herself had no fundamental interest in Daniel's work. She'd tried dutifully to drum some up and never quite succeeded. Perhaps if he'd been willing to share it with her. . . . But the fact was crystal clear, now that she knew she would never marry him: investments, contracts, business details, the Japanese yen—all that Daniel loved—could sink into the Pacific, and she'd hardly know it.

"Whereas I—" Fern paused to stub out her cigarette butt "—have a *natural* interest in Daniel's work."

Ravenna shifted uncomfortably. So the battle lines were being drawn, were they? "I beg your pardon?"

"Just what I said. I have a natural interest in Daniel's work. . .working so *closely* with him all these years as I have. I believe we've been together four years now. A long time. Almost as long as. . . my marriage," she added.

Ravenna found her cheeks reddening at this clear

territorial inference. Considering her own supposed
engagement to Daniel, it was an outrageous thing
for Fern to say. It was amazing how adept the
woman was at riling her. There had been that disturbing conversation of two weeks earlier...about
Kristen. She felt her temper rise, and bit her lip.

Then she suddenly heard, "You know, you
needn't pretend with me. I'm not as blind as..
poor Daniel."

Ravenna turned to stare at Fern, not believing her
ears.

"There's something going on between you and
Luke, isn't there?" Fern's eyes met hers coolly.

"My dear Miss Anderson," she snapped, "inter-
fering in people's lives seems to be a hobby of
yours!"

Fern backed off as Ravenna's eyes flashed fire.
She said more slowly, "Of course, it's none of my
business who's involved with whom. But I don't
like to see Daniel made a fool of."

"No one is making a fool of Daniel!" Ravenna
ground out furiously. Heavens, did the woman really see it like that? Was that, too, how Daniel saw it?
But whatever Fern believed, she was right about one
thing: it was none of her business.

"On the other hand," Fern went on doggedly,
her own eyes veiled, "you and Daniel really aren't
very suited."

"And I suppose you and he are? Is *that* what
you're thinking, Miss Anderson?" Ravenna
paused, hating their conversation. *Oh, let them do
what they like! It doesn't concern me anymore!*

Why pretend it did? She would even be glad to think that Daniel had someone else. But she couldn't stop herself. "Why don't you say what's on your mind?"

Under Ravenna's gaze, Fern's control snapped and the real woman broke through the cool facade. She turned to Ravenna with sudden ferocity, intense emotion in her voice at last. "You and Daniel *are* different . . . too different to make it work," she cried. "I knew it the moment I laid eyes on you!" She brushed back her hair and stood up, her feelings finally written on her anguished face. "Look, I can see what you're thinking. But there's nothing between me and Daniel, nothing! There never has been. I'll be honest with you. I damn well wish there was! Daniel and I would be happy together, because we *are* suited. But do you think he even notices me with *you* around? Do you think a foster kid from a hick town in New York State—with a failed marriage and no family to speak of—can compete with glamor girls like you and Kristen?"

Ravenna looked at her in amazement. Fern actually felt that way? Relief washed over Ravenna; Fern was not cold and unfeeling after all. She was even choking back tears as she rushed on, "Yes, before you it was Kristen! Luke's Kristen . . . with Daniel. So don't think you'll be the last!"

Kristen again. But her words hardly sank in as Ravenna reached a hand toward her, wanting to calm her. Fern didn't see this gesture of concern. She had already spun around to run across the lawns, knocking blindly into Daniel, who had belatedly appeared with the sawn-off crutches. She rushed past him without even apologizing.

"What did you say to upset Fern?" he barked, waving the crutches. "I really think she was crying. I've never seen her so upset...I don't think she even noticed me!"

Ravenna stared from him to Fern's retreating back, suddenly insightful. So Fern was not just attracted to Daniel, she was in love with him. No wonder she'd acted so strangely toward her, his supposed fiancée. She must feel tortured by Ravenna's very presence. And Daniel himself—he hadn't asked what had happened between them just then or what Fern had said to her, but what *she'd* said to upset Fern. She looked back at him, wondering if he realized that his secretary had taken first place in his concern. Perhaps it was more than concern. But, worn out by the intense encounter she'd just been through, she couldn't go on with her thoughts. All she said was, "I think I'd like to go inside now, Daniel. If you don't mind."

THAT WAS THE NIGHT she booked a flight home— for the following Saturday. She needed something private to hang onto. Still, if things had gone on as they'd begun, she doubted she could have lasted the week, even though her ankle kept her at Rathbourn. Luckily the next few days were pleasantly low-key—a welcome respite from the madness of the weekend. She forced herself to spend Monday evening quietly absorbed in research for her book, the first time she'd been back to it since her lunch with

Luke and John Hadley. With a stab of disappointment, however, she realized now that her return
home would mean she was without the very helpful
resource of Luke's library...and also that she'd
have no access to the buildings themselves. Her
emotions were messing up more than one situation!
Still, there was nothing for it but to leave. She could
always visit Britain later for a two-week research
trip, as she'd originally planned.

For a moment she considered not leaving but instead renting a flat in London somewhere near the
British Museum so she could continue to work and
visit Palladian London. In particular, Spencer
House, a mansion overlooking Green Park, and a
lovely old town house in Mayfair—reputedly now
used as a gambling club—designed by William
Kent. Both these houses she hoped to feature in her
book.

Immediately she knew it wouldn't work. It
wasn't so much the possibility of running into Luke
once he was back teaching in the fall, for such a
coincidence was unlikely; it was just that the constant fear—and hope—of doing so would haunt
her.

No, she had to go back to Elk Creek. To Coyote,
whom she missed; to her mother's warm common
sense; her father's single-minded but lovable devo-
tion to his stables; to those rolling green hills with
the white fences...all these as familiar as a well-
worn glove. When she closed her eyes, she could
picture it all. Home. She had to get home.

But she was grateful that she was getting pretty

skilled at hobbling around on Jeremy's renovated crutches and soon could even manage to hop down the stairs by hanging onto the banisters. By Saturday she'd be back on her own two feet, she fervently hoped.

The next morning she determined to visit Jessie— somewhat guiltily. She found O'Reilly feeding and watering the horses with the help of his sister's son, who'd come in from Salcombe for the day.

"Now, Kevin, mind you don't slop those oats on me clean floors," O'Reilly warned just as she entered his spotless realms.

"Ah, Miss Ravenna. Decided to pay us a call at last, did you? This here's Kevin, me sister's child and me namesake." He indicated the sturdy eight-year-old, whose mop of carrot-red hair kept falling in his eyes. His pixieish face was an ocean of freckles.

"Hello, Kevin."

"Pleased ter meet y', miss," he said shyly, busying himself with the feedbag of oats.

"Jessie's been mopin' all week," O'Reilly complained. "Kevin had to take her out on the trails himself. She's thinking you deserted her for good, she is. You'd better tell her different."

But she *was* going to desert her for good, and Ravenna almost wished she hadn't come by. The horse took an apple snitched from the kitchen from her hand and chewed it as solemnly as if she already knew the truth. Ravenna whispered in her ear that she'd return once more, would even get in one more ride if she was lucky.

"Want to see how I feed Lloyd George?" Kevin interrupted her morose thoughts, his shyness melting away after a swift study of her. And she stayed awhile, delighted to find that on acquaintance Kevin was a natural-born spellbinder, rather on the lines of his Irish uncle.

When, a short time later, Daniel asked her to spend the rest of the day with him, visiting the ancient cairns of Dartmoor, she steeled herself and refused. There didn't seem much point in spending time with him, fostering false hopes.

But he didn't leave at once. They were on the terrace near the library doors when he added softly, "About Kristen...." He cleared his throat. "I want you to know, Ravenna, that nothing actually *happened* between us, nothing at all. Kristen was very flirtatious—but it was only habit. She...she really did love Luke. I only said what I did to make you jealous—and I'm not very proud of myself."

She listened patiently, leaning on her crutches, her eyes averted. Finally she said, "Thank you, Daniel, for telling me the truth." And she knew it was the truth this time. Kristen had loved Luke, and Luke still grieved for her. He wasn't free to love.

As she made a move to go inside, Daniel stopped her. "Did it?" he asked quietly.

"Did it what?"

"Make you jealous?"

"No, Daniel," she admitted after the slightest hesitation. At least not in the way he'd planned.

He left after this awkward admission, looking very discouraged, and sadly she hobbled upstairs to try to work on her book again. On the stairs she asked herself if she was surprised he'd lied to her— or at least implied something quite untrue. But when she put herself in his position, she couldn't find it in her heart to blame him.

Daniel disappeared after dinner, following a whispered conference with Peters. Another call from New York? Fern made a graceful exit a few moments later, probably to join him, Ravenna decided. Since their embattled encounter the previous day Fern had retreated into herself again, giving nothing away. Still, Ravenna suspected that the disappearance of both Daniel and Fern boded only business and that Daniel had an understandable nervousness about admitting this to her. Not that it mattered.

So, with Jeremy onstage in Salcombe, she was left to drink her coffee with Glynis in the firelit library, which was fast becoming her favorite room at Rathbourn. She watched the flickering shadows falling across Glynis's face, stretching to the rich leather of the bound books and the dark, nineteenth-century oils—portraits of former Rathbourns, not a few of whom reminded her of Luke.

Glynis had reached for a piece of unfinished needlework as soon as she'd sat down—an evening habit of hers. Ravenna liked sitting with her but was herself content to stare at the fire, slipping into reverie. . .slipping this evening, if truth be told, almost into sleep. For she didn't want to think, talk, or be other than completely relaxed.

"Daniel's looking rather. . .tired. . .these days, don't you agree?" Glynis's voice reached her.

"Tired? Oh...perhaps he is." Ravenna started guiltily. How like Glynis to miss very little where her sons were concerned. She supposed Daniel had said nothing yet about her desire to go home.

"How's your ankle today?" Glynis's needle went in and out, like one of the three Fates.

"Not so bad. I can hop around pretty well on it now."

"I remember spraining mine badly, oh, years ago. I had to get around on crutches for a week or two myself. I believe it was when I was going with Harold Moreton, come to think of it. I must have been only twenty-six or so, not much older than you." She stopped to choose a different colored thread.

Ravenna smiled dutifully. "Harold Moreton?" she prompted, wishing instead that she'd gone upstairs to her room. But she could at least pretend to listen.

"The man I almost married. I mean, after Daniel's father died. Of course I wanted very much for Daniel to have a father again. Harold was the obvious choice."

"But you married Sir Richard."

Glynis smiled, her eyes on her work. "That's the end of the story. The beginning was very different." And she said thoughtfully, "Harold Moreton was a good steady man—the kind who looks fated for a happy marriage."

"So why didn't you marry him?" Ravenna asked, her curiosity beginning to be aroused. Daniel was a good man, wasn't he? Though not exactly *steady* in any but a financial way.

"He courted me—we used to call it courting in those distant days—for two years. My husband had left me a small country house in Sussex—it's sold now—and Harold would drive in from town every Sunday in time for dinner. He'd begun as a friend of Eddie's and, when Eddie died, just continued coming. I had no idea he was interested in me for the longest time. Harold wasn't the romantic type," she said dryly.

"And?"

But Glynis was in no hurry. "After a few months of that, he asked me out—to a local play. A year later he asked me to marry him. I liked him very much, you know. I even fancied I was in love with him for a while, perhaps because I was lonely. I liked his kindness and humor. And he wanted so much to marry me—which can be rather persuasive. He and Daniel got on well, too. Oh, I was on the point of saying yes."

Ravenna sat up straighter, fiddling with a cushion at her back.

"You see, dear, I didn't really expect romance. I thought it had gone out of my life with Eddie. And Harold so nicely met all my expectations of a nice respectable husband." Her eyes flashed to Ravenna's, then back to her embroidery.

"But you met Sir Richard?"

"At a garden party, of all places. He'd come because he wanted to talk local politics with some of the husbands—he was a member of parliament even then. Harold introduced us."

"Love at first sight?"

"Heavens, no! I thought he was the most arrogant, pigheaded—and handsomest—man I'd ever met! We started arguing immediately, about, of all things, how to bring up children." She paused, glancing again at Ravenna with an enigmatic look. "You see, he had Luke, and his wife had died some years earlier, when Luke was hardly seven. A worse blow for a small intense child, I always think, than the death of a father, as in Daniel's case. I rather think that's why Luke—" she held up her needlework at arm's length "—is so sensitive sometimes. And then there I came, stealing away even his father. He was very wary of me at first—a proud independent boy whom you would think needed nothing at all. But inside I knew he felt differently. He and Daniel took all those early insecurities out on each other, I'm afraid. But I'm getting ahead of myself."

Glynis seemed suddenly as fascinated with the fire as Ravenna had been. Ravenna meanwhile felt her eyes begin to smart—and not with smoke. Could within Luke be buried that little boy Glynis had described so clearly? Under that very assured and infuriating exterior of his, could he be as vulnerable as she herself was? The picture Glynis painted somehow rang true, and a host of small things Luke had said and done came back to her... sensitive thoughtful things, such as his gentleness with her ankle and his kindness over her book. Had she misjudged him?

She bit her lip suddenly. So what if she had, if he didn't love her? And he'd proved that he didn't—when that was all that mattered.

"Daniel... told me they fought a lot as children. That Luke was... violent." Ravenna was careful to use the past tense.

"Luke, violent? Nonsense," Glynis laughed. "Daniel always gave as good as he got, as I remember it. Of course he was rather jealous of Luke... Sir Richard was very close to his son. And then there was the title and the estate...." Glynis sighed. "But he'd have been hopeless in Luke's shoes—no feeling for the place at all," she said realistically. "Where was I? Oh, yes, the garden party. Sir Richard and I argued fully two hours... over by the hydrangeas... until Harold meekly returned to collect me. I think both Richard and I were astonished to find so much time had passed. I remember how he looked at me when we said goodbye...." Here Glynis's voice slowed. "I had an unnerving sensation of having known him for years.

"I didn't really expect to see him again. It was obvious I was with Harold, and then Richard usually moved in different circles from me—more county, you know, and Devon at that. But just a week later he called, asking my advice on roses. I'd mentioned in the course of our conversation how I adored gardening... a lifesaver when Eddie died. And it gave me a sense of myself, working with growing things. He wanted me to look at his imported Damasks. Said I had to come immediately, or they'd all die!"

Glynis chuckled. "Of course there was nothing wrong with his roses, as he well knew. They just happened to be the most beautiful I'd ever seen. He had varieties of all kinds, Teas from China, French roses, American—well, you know what's in the garden. While I oohed and aahed, he proceeded quite calmly and unexpectedly to sweep me off my feet. And I simply never looked back. Told him later I'd married him for his gardens,'' she said with a chuckle. But when she picked up her needlework again—long since dropped in her lap—her face was wreathed in smiles.

"What happened to Harold Moreton?'' Ravenna asked after a long pause. Something seemed to have caught in her throat.

"Harold? Oh, he married someone else. A perfectly nice young woman from the town...I forget her name. They've been very happy, I understand. Much happier than he and I would have been. He sends a card at Christmas.''

But when Glynis turned and looked straight at her, Ravenna was caught completely off guard. Those dark eyes were softly lit with compassion, and she was instantly certain that sharp-eyed Glynis knew more than she let on.

"My dear,'' she said, "may I give you a word of advice? If I've learned anything at all in life, it's this. Always follow your heart. I suspect the price we pay when we don't is just too high.'' She stood up rather awkwardly and swooped to kiss Ravenna on the cheek. "And now I must say good-night. Shall I ring for Garvey to help you up the stairs?''

Ravenna stared up at her, still astonished, and mumbled, "No...no, I think I can manage, thanks, Glynis.'' And she sat there a long while after Glynis had left, her eyes swimming with tears. That long rambling story had been deliberately staged... support coming to her from the most unexpected quarter—Daniel's mother! And until that moment she'd had no idea how deeply she needed it.

But Glynis was also Luke's mother, by marriage to his father...who sounded so exactly like Luke....

A spasm of grief shot through Ravenna. In her case things were completely different. Though she longed to take Glynis's advice—how she longed to—there was nothing she could do when Luke didn't want her. Or wanted her only in his bed—and not in his heart.

CHAPTER TEN

ALTHOUGH THERE WERE MOMENTS when she cursed her decision to stay on at Rathbourn for one more week, Ravenna gritted her teeth and determined to get through the seven days with a minimum of fuss and at least some remnant of dignity. That meant going through the ordinary everyday motions as if nothing had happened. And so on Wednesday, a lovely soft day with a sea breeze riffling the red poppies that grew wild along the edge of the woods, she could think of no good reason to refuse when Jeremy invited her to join him for a ride. It was his day off, and he seemed determined to cheer her up. But at first she'd raised her eyebrows—didn't he realize she couldn't mount Jessie with her sore ankle?

"Just up the lane on my motorcy'," he explained. "Do you good, Scarlett. Won't hurt your ankle a bit."

Daniel seemed about to protest, but Glynis beat him to it. "Jeremy! What if she falls off?"

"You never worry about yours truly falling off," he grinned.

"Oh, don't I, my lad! Well, drive slowly if you must. We don't want any more accidents. Do you have an extra helmet?"

"For a ride up the lane?"

At Glynis's firm look he relented. "Helmets for two coming up."

"I don't really think you should, darling," Daniel finally got in as he buttered a scone.

That did it. "Don't be silly, why not? Jeremy, I'm ready when you are." And she aimed her brightest smile at the youngest Rathbourn. After all, these might be the last few hours they would spend together.

Glynis's and Jeremy's idea of "slow" had little in common, she found out, as she tightened her grip around his waist while they zoomed up the long winding lane on the powerful bike. None of her brothers had ever owned a motorcycle, what with all the horses and cars available at Elk Creek, so this was a new experience; she found herself beginning to enjoy it, despite her despair over Luke. A part of her, at least, still functioned.

Moments later Jeremy began to ham things up with a series of imitations, ending with Snoopy as the Red Baron. He had her choking with laughter—and rather grateful, too, that Glynis had insisted on helmets, for his shenanigans did nothing to help their balance. With his scarf twitched back in her face like a flier's, he sat upright now, his face a mask of doggy fantasy.

Back at the garages again, Jeremy swerved for a second trip. But halfway up the drive an enormous, dark blue sedan—the Lincoln Mark VI—appeared suddenly, just as they were taking a long curve.

Luckily the two vehicles were far enough apart for both to stop.

It was Luke who leaned out the window, the sun striking his sand-blond hair to gold. Ravenna froze as he said mildly, "Rather than killing me, why don't you two give me an official escort back to the house?" He directed this comment at Jeremy, but his eyes were on her as she sat there in blue jeans, sweater and helmet, her red hair spraying over her back, looking for all the world like a teenager, she supposed. She hid her face behind Jeremy, angry that her heart was racing. *Oh, no, you don't, Luke Rathbourn. Not this time.*

Because the narrow lane didn't provide much choice, Jeremy turned in good spirits, driving at a stately processional pace Luke had not intended, she realized with a ghost of a smile. From the Red Baron to a royal escort. Well, well. She could tell Jeremy enjoyed this fantasy quite as much as the others, curving slowly from side to side as if clearing a path through crowded streets.

All very well, but the hot aim of those piercing gray eyes fixed on her back was too much.

"Can't you speed up a bit," she urged Jeremy.

"Aw, let him sweat, Scarlett. Think of Salcombe."

So Jeremy was getting a bit of his own back. But she wished he'd do it when she wasn't in the line of fire! Her agony ended as he finally accelerated just before the garages, and they were inside before the Lincoln could enter. Jeremy helped her off the monstrous bike, and as he reached to outfit her with the crutches leaning nearby, she threw her arms around his neck in an enthusiastic bear hug, planting a big kiss on one cheek.

"Thanks, Jeremy. I'll remember today," she said softly.

He was, she knew by the surprised flicker in his pleased eyes, about to ask her why she wanted to remember it, when they both realized Luke had slid the Lincoln in beside the Mercedes and opened his door. Damn! She'd meant to move faster than that.

"Hullo." His deep voice jarred her as he emerged, looking very casual—and far too attractive—in gabardine pants and an open-collared shirt. But he avoided her eyes, she noticed, as if he were no more pleased at running into her this way than she was. "I hope you two enjoyed your little spin. I don't imagine, Jerry, you school yourself to that pace too often."

"Pace?" he said innocently. "Oh, you mean the speed. Thought it sort of a special occasion, don't you know. Arrival of big brother and all that. Lord of the manor." And before Luke could reply, he strolled off rather too nonchalantly, leaving Ravenna to follow.

Luke stared at him, his brow knit, and then reluctantly fell in beside her as she started toward the house. *Don't talk to me,* she willed.

"You seem to hand your kisses out rather indiscriminately around here," he drawled as if to spite her.

Why this man had the ability to infuriate her at the drop of a hat she didn't know, but have it he did—in spades. She rounded on him with a spontaneous, "*You*...you are one of the most ridiculously jealous men I have ever met!" As soon as the words were out of her mouth, she stared at him in astonishment. Of course it was true! Luke *was* jealous. Jealous of Daniel. Jealous of Jeremy....

His eyes connected disturbingly with hers, destroying the path of her thoughts. "Oh, is that what you call it?"

"Yes!"

"Are you implying, by any means, that I have nothing to be jealous of?"

"Yes!"

Now she'd put her foot in it. He spun her around, almost knocking her off balance, and the touch of his hands on her shoulders sent dizzying signals to all her nerves.

"Would you care to explain yourself?" He looked as if he were trying to read her mind.

"I would not," she flared stubbornly. "I most certainly would not!" Explanations were the last thing he deserved after the way he'd treated her. She dropped her eyes from his, finding herself facing his open collar and the burnished hairs revealed there...and memories of his body sprang back. She blushed, uncertain where to look. With relief she felt his hands drop from her shoulders, but her attempt to stomp away, hampered by the crutches, was decidedly ineffective. She felt more like a loping kangaroo.

In one stride he caught up, and she saw his mouth quirk as if he wanted to laugh at her. "All right, then don't.'' But she caught the hint of a smile, the first one since.... She refused to remember when. There was a look of something else dawning in his face, too—amazement? Some of his reserve vanished, but this was not desirable. Not at all.

They continued in silence across the terrace, through the French doors and into the smoking-and-billiards room.

"Of course you're dying to know where I've been—I can tell."

"I am not the least interested in where you've been!" But her ears perked up. Had he been visiting the waiting Melina? Or someone else equally distracting?

"Good. Then I won't tell you. Although you'd be very interested to know."

She swung into the dining room, inwardly fuming. Couldn't he see that his company was not wanted? Did she have to spell it out for him? She turned at the dining-room door and said with deadly sweetness, "Why don't you go ahead, Luke? I think I'll just sit here for a while."

"Are you tired?" he asked skeptically.

"No, but if you don't mind, I prefer—"

"Oh, but I do mind, Ravenna. Things are not going to be quite that easy, you know." He moved disturbingly nearer to her, his voice serious, and for a moment they stared at each other, the tension between them electric. Then she backed away a step— and almost stumbled against a chair. His hands reached to steady her, and his eyes touched hers with a question. Something quickened within them both.

But an instant later he removed his hands, and his voice was casual as he asked, not looking at her, "Why don't you join me for a drink in the library? I have something to tell you."

"Well, the fact is I intended to do some work."

"I have news about a favorite project of yours— Jerry."

"You have?" The question escaped her.

"Yes. So come and sit down." He steered her deftly through the door, slipping the crutches from beneath her arms and resting them against the wall. "Where did you get these damned things, anyway? Here, lean on my arm."

Bereft of her crutches, she really had no choice, although the sudden contact with the heat of his arm sent panic signals winging through her.

"They were Jeremy's," she grumbled, busy trying to ignore her emotions. "He went to...to a great deal of trouble to have them cut down for me."

"Ah, yes. Jerry's erstwhile flight down a mountain. I remember it well. He persuaded the nurses at the hospital that he'd really been mountain climbing. Thought it a more romantic way to go, I suppose." He smiled down at her, while his gray eyes examined her face as if looking for changes.

Distressed, she glanced away, concentrating fiercely on the other end of the library. "What about Jeremy," she asked hurriedly. Her body had the most maddening way of demanding to be close to him, she realized as their thighs brushed, this slight contact alone making her knees buckle.

Luke was the first to move away—very quickly, as if reluctant to ignite those well-remembered fires. She was glad his arm still supported her—even if he was the reason she needed it. But he didn't answer her question. Surely he'd heard it?

She was more than relieved when Glynis came in a second later. Then Ravenna glimpsed Daniel, standing uncertainly in the doorway before he decided to enter, his face a battleground of emotions at the sight of her standing close to Luke. But he said nothing as he resolutely strode over to them. She wished he hadn't come in.

"Here you are, Ravenna," Glynis said. "And you're back, Luke. Were you in London or Cornwall this time?"

Luke assisted Ravenna into one of the wing chairs and said, "Both. London since yesterday noon. I had to see a client. Hello, Daniel," he drawled, for the first time seeing him there.

Daniel muttered an answer, looking deeply frustrated.

With Glynis here, he can hardly repeat his stunt of last Sunday, Ravenna thought gratefully.

"I was also checking out RADA," Luke added.

"RADA?" Both Glynis and Ravenna spoke simultaneously, looking up in surprise, while Daniel sat down possessively next to Ravenna.

"Yes. I was checking the entrance requirements—two three-minute auditions and an interview with the registrar and the principal. Jerry won't need any specific academic requirements, but he'll have them under his belt when he passes next year, anyway. By the way, where is he?''

"He's gone upstairs," Glynis supplied. "Just a few minutes ago. But what possessed you to check out RADA this week, Luke?''

He looked a bit as if he'd been put on the spot, and Ravenna suddenly suspected he'd done it to please her—not Jeremy. A peace offering? Or a guilty conscience.

"I just thought it time to consider it—with Jerry doing so well in Salcombe," he added hurriedly. "After all, he has only a year left at university. Might motivate him to pass.''

Glynis smiled. "My friend Iris Beecham and I went to see him Monday night in *Romeo and Juliet*. I thought he was brilliant. But then I *am* his mother. What did you think, Ravenna?''

"I thought he was brilliant.''

"There! What did I tell you? I'm glad you're finally seeing the light, Luke.''

Luke's eyebrows rose as Glynis firmly moved herself to the opposite camp. He grimaced. "Well, I guess it's clear by now what it means to him. If he's prepared to deceive us all—Ravenna excepted—we may as well get behind him. Otherwise he'll continue to ride roughshod over us without compunction.''

"You can hardly blame him!" Ravenna flared protectively. "No one's paid him much attention.''

Luke smiled indulgently at her. "Ah, to be young and ruthless again.''

"What's all this about *Romeo and Juliet* and Jeremy and RADA?" Daniel burst forth.

"While you linger in New York—" Luke faced him squarely, his eyes coldly ironic "—your brother is on his way to becoming the next Sir Laurence Olivier."

"I think it's Gielgud," Ravenna corrected. "That's his hero."

"Ravenna is Jerry's confidante," Luke explained dryly to Daniel. "She infiltrated the ranks very quickly, considering how long the rest of us have been kept in the dark. It must be her... charm."

Glynis snorted. "I knew something was up when he sailed upstairs everyday to study, meek as a lamb. I knew it! But I thought he was in love and sneaking off secretly to meet someone."

Ravenna ducked her head, thinking of Angela, and Luke said, "Speaking of which, have you seen this?" He drew a folded *Guardian* from the inside of his jacket and handed it to Glynis, indicating a boxed item on the page it was folded to.

" 'Angela Heyward,' " she read, " 'well-known stage actress presently appearing in Howard Bennett's *Walk Softly*, at the Globe, to marry famous racing-car driver Gilles Lamont, winner of last year's Grand Prix. See page 18.' " She turned to page eighteen and opened to a large photo of Angela on the arm of a handsome Frenchman with a chiseled Roman profile, leaning over a Ferrari at a racetrack. Neither of them looked as if they'd been aware of being photographed.

"Who's Angela Heyward," Daniel asked in annoyance.

"An actress, dear," Glynis said, passing the paper to Ravenna. "But do you really suppose he'll mind, Luke? Perhaps they were just good friends... though Jeremy did seem awfully fond of her that day she was here."

"I don't really know. But it takes a load off my mind." Luke finally folded his length into a chair, stretching his long legs in front of him.

Someone must have summoned Peters, for he appeared with a tray and offered Luke a drink.

"Thanks, Peters. Just what I needed," Luke said.

"Angela's a perfectly nice woman," Ravenna protested as she shook her head at Peters. So Luke was pleased Angela was out of Jeremy's reach. The estate was safe!

Luke turned to her, his eyes ironic. "A perfectly nice forty-one-year-old, yes. I have nothing against her, Ravenna. In fact, I like her, but she's simply too old for Jerry. And he's at the age when he'll leap before he looks. I know Jerry a lot better than you do... believe it or not."

There he was, arranging other people's lives again! And pretending it was for their own good.

"Surely Jeremy had no serious plans..." Glynis began.

"Oh, well." Luke sipped his drink. "I'm just glad he won't have the chance. No reason *he* should make a mistake just because...."

His eyes were on Ravenna as she dared him to

finish the sentence. When he didn't, she stood up to leave, fed up with his heartlessness—and forgetting once again her blasted ankle. She sat down on a gasp.

Daniel sprang unnecessarily to her side. "Are you all right, Ravenna? Perhaps you ought to let me help you upstairs."

"I'm fine," she muttered. "Please sit down, Daniel."

Luke, watching their interaction, smiled and took out a cigarette as Daniel leaned toward Ravenna's chair.

"I thought we might go in to Plymouth for lunch." Daniel's face was stubborn—and his motive transparent as a plastic bag.

Ravenna could feel how really desperate he was to remove her from Luke's presence. He needn't bother, she thought, as she refused to move an inch from her chair; she had no intention of subjecting herself to Luke much longer, anyway. She might as well go with Daniel this one time, since he knew she would be leaving England in a few days. "All right, Daniel. What time?"

Luke's hand froze in the middle of lighting his cigarette, and his eyes skimmed the top of her head. Then he threw the match into the open fireplace.

"In a few minutes?"

"Half an hour? I'd like to change first." She looked down at her blue jeans.

"Fine," he said, beaming at her. "I'll meet you in the hall." And he got up to leave, a look of relief on his face, now that he knew she'd be spending most of the day with him. She almost wished she'd said no, but it was too late.

"Daniel *finally* taking a holiday?" Luke asked darkly as soon as he'd gone, his eyes resting on his empty whiskey glass.

Ravenna didn't answer, and Glynis shifted uncomfortably.

"About Jeremy," Glynis finally said.

"Yes, what about him?"

"Perhaps we should tell him about Mrs. Heyward?"

Luke looked startled. "No, that's the last thing I'd do, Glynis. Let him find out himself. If Angela's as nice a woman as she seemed, she'll tell him. And maybe it's just some rumor the press got hold of. There's always that possibility."

"Hmmm. Well, perhaps you know best." She stood up and moved to the French doors, looking out at the gardens. "If any crises happen, you know where to find me," and she left them alone, with Ravenna trying quickly to think of an exit line herself.

Luke glanced at her. "It doesn't take half an hour to change," he grumbled as she opened her mouth.

She closed it. All right, she'd let him have it. "You're being rotten about Jeremy and Angela, Luke. He has feelings, you know. Not like *some* people."

He turned slowly and looked at her, obviously as ready to square off as she was. "Of course Jeremy has feelings. If you think I like to see him hurt . . . "

His face changed as he watched her, and his words rang heavily with sarcasm, "As for *my* feelings, which you're so obliquely refering to—well, perhaps it's just that I don't have much faith left in matters of the heart."

The nerve of him! Matters of the heart! What had happened between them had nothing to do with *his* heart; it was hers that had been mangled.

"I doubt you have much experience...in matters of the heart, that is. Now if you'll excuse me—"

"Oh? I don't have much experience in that line, do I? How interesting. How very, very interesting of *you* to remark on that."

"Excuse me," she repeated, irked because his legs stretched effectively to bar her exit.

He didn't move them. And as he leaned back in his chair, glass in hand, he watched her with a lazy unreadable look, a look that masked what—fury?

"And so you're rushing off to Plymouth with Daniel."

She stared down at him. What right did he have even to speak to her about it?

"Is there any reason why I shouldn't?" she grated.

He looked her up and down, as if measuring the distance between her and his lap, and for a moment she knew she was in danger of being pulled into his arms. The leap of longing in her for him almost betrayed her. But the angry glitter in his eyes suddenly dulled, and he said flatly, looking away, "No reason. No reason that I know of."

Then he moved his legs, careful not to touch her,

and she made her way past him as best she could, limping slightly as she went down the length of the room, this time without the support of his arm. Her whole world seemed to crumble behind her as her anger ebbed. If only there was a reason, she thought, tears silently blinding her now. If only Luke would give her the one reason that mattered.

THE CALL CAME Thursday night. Peters handed the phone to Ravenna as she came downstairs to return a book to the main library. "Someone asking for Mr. Jeremy...but he's out, miss. Perhaps you could help them. They seem somewhat perturbed."

Ravenna crossed the small drawing room and took the phone Peters indicated in the saloon, a room she'd seldom entered because it was used only on very formal occasions and mostly in days gone by. "Hello?"

"Oh, hello? Is that Lady Glynis? This is Carole McKenna speaking, from Salcombe Playhouse. We're looking for Jeremy. I'm afraid it's terribly urgent."

"Somewhat perturbed" was an understatement, she thought, hearing the note of panic in Carole's voice. "Juliet?" she said without thinking. Wasn't Carole the girl who'd played Juliet?

The voice on the line laughed nervously. "Well, yes, but actually it's Carole. So you know about the play. We were afraid it was still under wraps. But, Lady Glynis—"

"It's not Lady Glynis, Carole. I'm Ravenna

Jones. I'm. . .staying with the Rathbourns. You say Jeremy hasn't shown up there?"

"That's right, Miss Jones. And he's due onstage in a few minutes. We're tearing our hair out here, especially Jason, our director. Is Jeremy there? Has something happened to him? It's not like him to be late."

Ravenna tried to get a word in edgewise. "Just a minute, Carole. What time is it? Almost eight-thirty? Perhaps he's just been held up. Maybe he got a flat tire or something." As she said this, her mind had gory visions of Jeremy sprawled in the dark across the road, his motorcycle in a ditch, and she had to take a deep breath before she could go on. She was trying hard to remember when she'd last seen him. Yes, it had been in the garage the previous day, when Luke had driven up in the Lincoln. He hadn't appeared at dinner when she and Daniel returned from Plymouth. Nor had she seen him that day. "Can you ring me back in just a few minutes, Carole?" Ravenna finally said. "We'll check things out here. Try not to panic."

Peters materialized, hovering near the door. "He left at five, miss. And I just checked his room again. I think he went into Salcombe, as usual. He told me he often eats an early dinner there before the play."

Granted, but if he'd skipped appearing onstage, something really serious was up. She knew he wouldn't do that without the strongest of reasons—illness, or maybe an act of God.

Or Angela's engagement? It was just possible

that this could have affected him deeply enough to make him lose his sense of perspective.

"Did he seem at all upset?" Ravenna asked.

"Preoccupied I would say, miss."

"Did you talk to him before he left?"

"No, miss. He rushed right past me—I don't think he saw me. About five o'clock, just as I said."

"Did he . . . happen to be carrying a newspaper?"

"Yes. Yes, he was, miss. Crushed in his hands."

Why, oh why had they been stupid enough to leave that blasted newspaper lying about!

The phone rang again, and Ravenna snatched it up before Peters could even lift his arm. "Carole? Has he shown up?"

"No. John Bermondsey will have to go on—his understudy. He's scared, but he thinks he can scrape through. It's his big chance, after all. Jason is furious at Jeremy. But, Miss Jones—"

"Ravenna, please."

"Ravenna. If anything's happened to Jeremy, I . . . I would like to know personally. Could you ask for Carole McKenna when you call?"

Ravenna was surprised at the intensity of this request, then suddenly remembered Carole's expression when she'd seen Jeremy with Angela that night in the theater.

"I'm sure he's all right, Carole." Ravenna's voice was calm, but she wasn't at all sure. "We'll let you know when we find him."

"I have to go on now. *Please* call. If I'm not here—" and she gave her another number before she hung up.

Ravenna stared numbly at Peters, who looked just as worried. "Shall I get Sir Anthony, miss?"

"Yes, Peters. At once."

Three minutes later Luke was at her side, and at the sight of her face he made her sit down in the nearest chair. "What's happened?" he demanded, hands on her shoulders.

She began to breathe again, feeling his strength flow into her. "Jeremy's gone. He's not at Salcombe, even though he's supposed to be onstage now. Carole McKenna just called—she's Juliet in the play. Luke, I think it's serious. Jeremy wouldn't miss a show."

He looked at her—she could see his mind churning—then turned to the butler. "Have you seen him today, Peters?"

"Yes, sir. He left at five, just as I was saying to Miss Ravenna. Had a newspaper crushed in his hand like this..." he repeated in his excitement, demonstrating for them.

"Damn! Angela's engagement." Luke immediately connected the two events, as well, and strode to the phone. "Directory of Enquiries for London, please. I'd like the number of Angela Heyward, operator...." While he waited, Ravenna said hurriedly, "But she's at the Globe, Luke!"

He shook his head, jotting down the number the operator had given him. "No, it's her day off—Thursdays," he said after he'd dialed.

Angela herself answered. "Jerry? Why, no, Luke. He's not here. Funny you should ask, though. I've been thinking of calling him all day. Is anything wrong?'' His tense tone had finally sunk in.

"No, or we hope not. It's just that he's supposed to be appearing in *Romeo and Juliet* right now, and he's nowhere to be found. It's not like him. Forgive me if this seems like prying, Angela, but we think he's seen that bit in yesterday's *Guardian* about your being engaged to Gilles Lamont. Would he be upset enough to come to see you in London?''

Angela paused. "Curse the Press!" she expostulated. "I haven't seen the *Guardian*, but there was a journalist lurking around the racetrack that time in Dijon. You know, I had a premonition I needed to reach Jerry today. This is the last way I wanted him to hear.''

"Would he come to see you?''

"Yes. Yes, I think he would, straight off. If he's not at Salcombe where he's supposed to be.... But Gilles is here. There are liable to be fireworks.''

"Can you handle it?''

Angela laughed. "I can handle a whole lot of things, love, but have you ever seen Jerry mad? I don't know where he gets that temper, but—let's just say I'm not looking forward to it if Jerry shows up.''

Luke glanced at Ravenna, who was leaning close to him, trying to hear both sides of the conversation.

"Angela, I'm going into Salcombe. If Jerry hasn't shown up at the theater yet, I'll call you again. It'll mean he's probably headed straight to you. He left here at five, so he'll get in about...ten-thirty. If so, you can expect me later—after midnight. Do me a favor and keep him there, please. I suggest you send Gilles out somewhere and give Jerry more than a few drinks.'' He rang off and called for Peters, who was only five feet behind him.

''Have Garvey check for the Harley, Peters. If it's gone, he can bring the Lincoln around to the front for me immediately. Oh...and he'd better throw a few horse blankets in the back and some flares, just in case.''

Ravenna shuddered. So Luke hadn't ruled out the possibility of an accident on the road! She grabbed his arm as he turned to leave. ''Luke! What if he's lying in a ditch somewhere....''

At the look in her eyes, he took her face between his hands. ''I don't think he is, Ravenna,'' he comforted her. ''Much more likely he's doing hell-for-leather on the road to London.''

''And abandoned the play?''

''Yes.''

''Is that what you'd do?'' she asked, seeing the look in his eyes that said he was mentally tracking his brother down.

''Yes, at nineteen I would. Jerry's just young enough to take Angela's...betrayal very much to heart. I know him. Under that clownish exterior....'' He didn't finish. ''Look, Ravenna, I want you to tell Glynis as gently as possible where I've gone, and—''

''No! I'm coming with you,'' she burst out, surprising both of them. If anything had happened to Jeremy, she was going to be there.

"No, you aren't. I won't get into London until two-thirty in the morning—one-thirty, if I can help it."

"I'm coming with you, anyway. You'll need someone to keep you awake on that long drive. Besides, I know Angela better than you do." This was hardly the truth, but she felt a lot more sympathy for her.

He stared at her and, at the stubborn light in her eyes, finally gave way. "All right. But if you're coming, you're not bringing those damned crutches," was all he said.

"But I need them!"

"You're not bringing them. Peters, please bring Miss Jones her coat. And get Lady Glynis for me."

Ravenna blinked at this sudden formality in him, but just then Garvey came in with the news that yes, Mr. Jeremy's motorcycle was gone and had been since just after teatime; he'd seen him leave himself. The Lincoln was waiting with blankets and everything and did Sir Anthony want him to come along just in case something had happened to Mr. Jeremy?

"No, thanks, Garvey. I think he'll turn up all right, safe and sound. We think he's just gone to London unexpectedly."

"Will he resent our following him?" Ravenna asked, suddenly imagining Jeremy's hurt pride as they stormed into Angela's. It would hardly be dignified.

"I'd rather risk that," Luke said, "than Angela's having to referee Gilles and him, or his wandering around London all night—most likely drunk. He doesn't have a key to the town house.''

There was no time to debate this. Luke quickly outlined the situation to Glynis, who swiftly approved, and then he headed for the door. When he looked back, Ravenna was just testing her sore foot—it *was* getting better. Luke cursed and returned, scooping her up in his arms. She bit her lip in embarrassment but wisely said nothing. Luke in a hurry was not to be argued with.

It was only when he placed her in the front seat of the car that he thought to ask, ''What about Daniel? Don't you want to tell him where you've gone?'' For once he wasn't being sarcastic.

''Glynis will tell him,'' she replied simply, looking him in the eye. And that was that.

Neither of them spoke as the huge car purred smoothly down the lane into the darkness of a velvet summer's night.

THEIR STOP IN SALCOMBE was brief. No one had seen Jeremy during the play or earlier, the director told them, and he was ready to wring his neck...unless, of course, Jeremy had a damn good reason. Here Luke cut him off to go phone Angela again, confirming that she was to expect them. Then began the long drive through the night, a drive made far easier now, because no grisly sight of an overturned motorcycle had met them on the way to Salcombe. If Jeremy had made it this far, it was just as Luke said. He'd gone to London. Ravenna was beginning to believe he *did* know Jeremy.

After declaring she was coming along to help Luke stay awake, she disgraced herself by falling asleep just past Honiton. Awaking later to a delicious sensation of comfort, she found herself nestled against Luke's shoulder. Embarrassed, she sat up quickly. "You should have woken me."

"Why? I like driving at night. And you looked so content." There was a faint smile on his face.

Her ramrod straightness lasted another ten miles. When she next awoke, it was much later and they were in London. Luke was just pulling up in Gordon Square. She heard him call her name softly and felt his hand under her chin. When she opened her eyes for a few seconds, she didn't know where she was...except that she was with Luke and that his gray blue eyes were unexpectedly tender. But they changed as she looked at him, their tenderness receding like a dream.

"Where are we?"

"In London, at Gordon Square. It's one forty-five, and—" he opened his door and came around to hers "—we're going inside. Or rather, you are."

Leaning on his arm, she watched as he unlocked the door. *Jeremy,* she remembered, *we came here to find Jeremy*. "But where's Jeremy?" she asked, yawning.

"He's at Angela's. I called her again when we reached Salisbury. I'm going there now, but you—" he helped her inside the living room "—are going to bed. Can you manage the stairs?"

"Yes, but Luke...I want to help you!"

"In the state you're in you're better off here. But

don't worry. Jerry's all right. Angela told me he's just distraught. And I know exactly what he needs. I'll be back soon—but don't wait up for us.'' His eyes willed her to obey as he closed the door behind him, leaving her alone.

It was then that she finally woke up.

An hour later she was no nearer to sleep, although it was nearly 3:00 A.M. There was no sign of Luke and Jeremy yet. Couldn't Luke have at least called her? She'd gone to the bedroom at the end of the hall—the one opposite Luke's—and turned on the lamp to read, lying on top of the spread. She was determined to wait up for them, despite Luke's order not to do so. After all, she'd come all that way, and there she was, stranded helplessly at the town house when all the action was elsewhere. Maybe they would want coffee when they arrived or...something. Finally she gave up and ran a hot bath, tired of listening for the door. She even decided to wash her hair, so wide awake was she by then, with a ridiculous spurt of energy and no outlet. She had to do something to keep from worrying. For what on earth could be keeping them? Surely it didn't take that long to get to Angela's Mayfair flat and back!

She had just toweled herself dry and wrapped a dark blue velour robe around her—one of Luke's, which was several sizes too large—when she heard a sound. She started. Was that really someone's deep baritone voice singing...an old Beatles' song? Followed by the front door slamming loudly.

They were home, she realized on a note of pure

relief. And of course she was going down. Checking that she was decent, she wrapped her hair turban-style in a dry towel, picked up the hem of the robe and took a few cautious steps toward the stairs.

"Luke? Jeremy?"

"Hey...Juuuude," the baritone continued. She clutched her robe tighter. Surely it was them. No one else would have a key. Slowly, soundlessly, she inched down the stairs and peered into the hall. The sounds were coming from the living room. She tip-toed toward it and peeked around the doorway.

"Saaaay...s'a woman here, Luke," Jeremy slurred as she looked straight at him. He stood half supported by Luke, his hair tumbled and his cheeks flushed, and even at this distance she could tell his breath was heavily laced with liquor. Angela had done her job too well...helped along by Luke, she guessed. The two brothers looked oddly alike at this moment, arm in arm, though Luke had the advantage of appearing none the worse for wear. He arched his eyebrows in greeting.

"Ahh...s'not a woman, s'only Scarlett," Jeremy breathed with amazed relief as she stood frozen there, her own relief at the sight of him safe and sound changing to indignation. He was drunker than a skunk, as her brothers used to say. And Luke looked as if he'd had a few, too. So that's what they'd been doing while she fretted at Gordon Square, waiting!

"I'm glad you found him, Luke," she said crisp-ly. "And I can see you did know *exactly* what he needed!" She turned to Jeremy. "We were very worried about you. Couldn't you at least have told someone where you were going?"

"Me? Worried about me? Ah, Scarlett, s'wunnerful of you t' think of me and all that, but I'm all right. Luke's lookin' after me, y'see. Scarlett's wunnerful, isn't she, Luke? Not like the rest of 'em. Le's have a drink to her." He made a swipe at a lamp, almost knocking it off the table, and Ravenna leaped to rescue it as he sank onto the sofa. "Women!" he suddenly snarled, as if he'd had enough of them.

Luke had gone to the liquor cabinet to pour himself a whiskey, turning back again as Jeremy finished, and she wondered for a second how many drinks he'd had himself. It was hard to tell, for he showed no sign of being anywhere near Jeremy's state. But when he came toward her, the arm that he laid on her shoulders was rather too heavy, convincing her that he'd shared at least some of Jeremy's sorrow drowning.

"Luke!" she protested, not liking the look in his eye.

"Luke!" he mocked. "No, Jerry, Scarlett's not wonderful, not by a long shot. She's like them all...a woman...sweet, seductive, soft as silk, and the devil take them!" He dragged her closer, laughing softly.

"Take your hands off me!" she hissed as Jeremy droned on, paying no attention as Luke drew her to him.

"Angela and that fellow...whatsisname, Luke, that Frenchie fellow...I could have punched him out if...if you ..." Here he lay down on the velvet-covered sofa, cowboy boots and all. "I could have laid him out neat if you hadn't...." He dozed off in the middle of the sentence and then suddenly awoke. "G'night, Luke. G'night, Scarlett. S'wunnerful to see you here, Scarlett. But why'd you...." He fell dead asleep.

"He's asleep," Luke said unnecessarily, his arm still gripping her. But he left her side to pull off his brother's boots and then went to a closet and took out a blanket with which to cover Jeremy.

"Yes," she said dryly, "I noticed. The two of you are a disgrace, and I'm going to bed. Good night, Luke." She moved as quickly as she could down the hall—but not quickly enough. He got to the stairs before she did, lightly, as if the drinks had not affected him after all. She remembered he was English and that the English have often an infuriating ability to handle liquor.

But when he merely disappeared into his bedroom and collapsed on the bed, as instantly asleep to all appearances as Jeremy, she softened as she stared at him from the doorway of her own room. Still, she hesitated fully a minute before she walked slowly down the hall and up to his door. He'd flung one arm to the side as he lay there, and his face was stilled, peaceful. Of course he must be exhausted by that long drive and then the strain of worrying over Jeremy.... Gathering courage when he didn't move, she went in and carefully removed his shoes.

It was a new sensation to see him helpless before her, abandoned in sleep, and it gave her a curious satisfaction. For the first time he was at her mercy. The tables had turned, hadn't they?

But the least she could do was make him comfortable for the night. He hadn't let her help with Jeremy, but this time he couldn't say anything about it. She bent to undo his shirt collar, her hands lingering longer than was necessary as she undid the buttons. Then she stood uncertainly, watching his chest rise and fall rhythmically. The memory of their lovemaking at the cottage came flooding back all of a sudden, until she bit her lip. His hair had tumbled down on his forehead, and she reached to brush it back, seeing how his face had smoothed of all scorn and remoteness. He looked, yes, he looked *undangerous*, she thought, pleased to arrive at a word. And beautiful in sleep.

But was he really asleep? Silently she bent nearer, studying his face for the least sign of movement, afraid even now that he was bluffing. But the deep regular breaths came evenly, reassuring her, until the urge was irresistible. Suddenly she bent to touch her lips to his very lightly. It would be the last time, after all, before she flew home. The last time ever. How soft and warm they felt, yielding even. If only.... She sighed and began to straighten up. She'd go to the other bedroom now.

But in a flash he'd grabbed her and she was lying on top of him, pressed to his chest, her face inches above his. Slowly he opened his eyes and smiled at her wickedly, like a cat who has captured a mouse. "Don't stop now," he drawled. "I'm just beginning to enjoy it."

Damn him! He was no more asleep than she was! Her blush reached to the roots of her hair.

In one lazy swipe he pulled the towel away that had bound her tresses, so that they poured over him, damp and sweet and utterly sensuous. Then he shifted her, his smile broadening, so that she was completely on top of him, her whole length resting on his as he lay on his back beneath her, their hips and thighs meeting and her lips hanging ripely above his. Her body was fusing into his, and she knew he could read in her eyes her melting surrender. He slid his hands to her hips, molding them more tightly to him, smoothing them like the softest silk.

"Go on," he said sleepily, "kiss me. That's what you want to do, isn't it, Ravenna?"

The curve of her lips did not deny this, but she whispered only, "You are very, very deceitful," the catch in her throat betraying her as his hands wreaked their havoc.

"And you. . . are very, very beautiful."

Both were smiling, caught in a spell, as she sank deeper and deeper into him. His hands traveled in insistent waves from her shoulders to her hips, lifting her hair in handfuls, letting it drop in scarlet waves over them both. Finally he tangled one fist in her locks and drew her face down to his to kiss her slowly, luxuriously. That he tasted of whiskey, there was no mistaking, but so mixed was this taste with the honeyed sensations spiraling in dizzying leaps from her loins to her throat, from the tips of her bare feet to what felt like every fiber of her hair, that it bothered her not at all.

He turned, shifting her so that she lay beneath him now, and her rush of helplessness was more than sweet. She felt his lips trail to her throat and then lower, nuzzling aside the top of her robe, while his hands still swept up and down it, making it a second skin.

"Luke," she whispered, willing him to go on.

"Yes?" he asked, stopping. "What is it?"

The lazy knowing look of those eyes dismayed her. She said only, "You...you smell like whiskey."

"And you—" he lowered his mouth to her shoulder, where the robe had slipped away "—smell like...cinnamon. Do you have anything on under...my robe?" he murmured, reaching to explore beneath it.

"No," she gasped.

"That's good." His voice a sleepy drawl, he moved to undo her belt, and then he pulled the blue velour away. For a heady second his mouth hung above the silken tips of her breasts. Then his head pressed heavily against their swelling softness, and he didn't move.

She waited...and waited longer as the moments stretched. "Luke?" Again, more loudly, "Luke!"

He didn't answer. And the rhythmic motion of his breathing told her he was asleep...sound asleep! Just like Jeremy.

Slowly she eased to his side, wondering wryly what she was going to do now. Thoughts of escape held no appeal, and when his arms pulled her drowsily closer, she told herself it was impossible.

Her hands went to his hair, stroking it tenderly. Why not stay... and have the bliss of sleeping in his embrace this one last night? Happily the iron grip of those arms—as if even in sleep they feared her evasion—gave her no other choice.

IN THE MORNING, as she lay listening to his heart beat in rhythm with hers while he slept in her arms, she couldn't find it in her to regret her action. Maybe later, but not now.

But soon she had only one thought. Some inner protective alarm told her to ease out of those arms before he awoke. And slowly, very slowly, she managed it, till finally she was on the other side of the bed.... At last, her heart beating wildly, she took one final look from the door of the room.

Luke lay sprawled in sleep, his face hidden by one arm, as the first faint light of morning gave color to the curtains. Every step away from him was like pulling against a powerful magnet. But when she saw him stir uncomfortably, as if he missed her warmth, she fled down the hall to the bed in the other room. And because it was barely dawn, she crawled under the covers and quickly fell asleep.

She awoke to the sound of his voice, calling her name from the doorway. When she got up and went to open it, he was standing there, rubbing his head with a towel, his hair freshly washed. Still only half awake, she said, "What time is it?"

"Time to rise and shine. Ten o'clock."

When she went downstairs, Jeremy sat groaning on the sofa, his head in his hands—a picture of the classic hangover. Luke came in behind her to offer him some aspirin and a glass of water...she didn't think either of them looked too chipper.

But soon they both appeared in the kitchen, where she was making coffee and toast. Jeremy moaned as he entered, "I'm dying of thirst." She watched as between them he and Luke downed the pitcherful of orange juice she'd just made.

"Do you want something to eat?" she asked, remembering how Jamie had always forced himself to eat the morning after he'd been drinking.

"Can't you lower your voice?" Jeremy whispered huskily. "And no, no food, thanks."

"You'd better eat at least a piece of toast, Jerry," Luke quietly advised. "You'll feel better later." Ravenna suppressed a smile at this brotherly advice. She was waiting to catch Luke's eye, waiting to see how he would look at her after his tenderness of the previous night. Would his eyes show her what she longed to see?

She turned to pour herself a coffee, dreamily aware of him, while Jeremy—looking as if he were about to walk the plank—finally accepted some toast and nibbled at one corner.

"Did you sleep all right?" Luke suddenly asked her.

"Why, yes...that is—"

"Well, I'm glad somebody did. I guess it was you who took off my shoes. Thanks for the kind ministrations." He grimaced, his voice utterly normal.

So he didn't remember.

"What's wrong?"

"Nothing." She turned away, feeling a sharp stab of pain. *He was exhausted, remember? And the whiskey didn't help. So don't be foolish. This makes things easier, after all.*

When she looked back again, Luke's eyes still rested on her, their expression quizzical. He was too good at reading her, and she looked away again, swallowing her grief and saying in a neutral voice, "When are we leaving?"

"As soon as you're both ready."

She nodded, still avoiding his gaze—those cloud-gray eyes trained on the rose stain that burned her cheeks. She would drink her coffee as if she hadn't a care in the world. She would pretend that nothing had changed. Because it hadn't, since he remembered nothing—and this told her it had meant nothing to him.

More fool her.

CHAPTER ELEVEN

WHEN JEREMY FELL ASLEEP in the back seat, not long out of London, Luke told her about the scene at Angela's the previous night—Gilles Lamont's careful attempt not to lose his temper when he returned to the flat, Jeremy's gruff embarrassment, Angela's dismayed cheerfulness as she tried to smooth things over.

"She must have poured half a bottle of good Scotch down Jerry's throat before I got there," he said with a grin. "I call that an excess of zeal."

Luke had taken Jeremy to his club afterward, where Ravenna assumed the drinking had continued. It was there that Jeremy had confessed he'd been in love with Angela on and off for two years, though she'd never treated him as anything more than a good friend. *He* hadn't seen it that way.

"I think it was a classic case of his reading into every little action of hers only what he wanted to read. But Angela's a sensible woman—she's handled the whole thing very well. I doubt she knew what was really going on in him in regards to her—Jerry can be deceiving—although she must have suspected. My impression last night was that she's terribly fond of him and genuinely values their friendship. Jerry will probably appreciate this... when he recovers."

Ravenna was silently pleased to hear Luke admit Angela wasn't the villainess of the piece. But suddenly she remembered Glynis, waiting patiently for news.

"I called her from Angela's, first thing," Luke assured her. "She said she knew he'd turn up all right...she's developed an instinct about her sons' scrapes."

Ravenna wished she'd been as confident. The whole evening had been a strain, one she wouldn't want to repeat...well, except for a few best forgotten parts. But she felt chastened later as she had to admit to herself that her indignant response to the previous night's escapade might have been premature. When Jeremy awoke, she was struck by the tone of camaraderie in his voice toward Luke, one she'd never heard previously. Luke *had* said he knew what Jeremy needed—perhaps he'd been right after all. At least Luke had abandoned the father role for a more natural one of older brother.

Jeremy's sleepy complacency disappeared as they neared Salcombe around four o'clock, and he became very quiet. "Do y'think you could just drop me off here, Luke?" he asked when they reached the street where Salcombe Playhouse was located. "I'd better go in and straighten things out with Jason before he has a fit."

"I believe he's already had it," Ravenna warned, and Jeremy moaned very realistically. Then she added casually, "By the way, someone named

Carole seemed concerned about you last night. Said she'd like to know if you're safe and sound.''

"Carole? Really? Well, I won't know until Jason gets through with me. But I'll let her kind hands pick up the pieces," he promised. "Thanks, old man." He clapped Luke on the shoulder as the car pulled to a stop. "Do the same for you some day."

Both of them grinned, knowing how unlikely this was.

"I'll see you at home," was all Luke replied, and Jeremy left, blowing a rueful kiss to Ravenna.

She was unprepared when Luke turned to her before starting the engine, his arm resting along the back of the seat. He'd been so quiet on the drive down that now, when he smiled fully at her, persuasively even, her eyebrows rose. "Do you remember once saying you wanted very much to see my work?"

"Yes.... "

He turned toward the steering wheel, one hand resting lightly on it. "I'm going away tomorrow—to the continent for two months."

She started, feeling his words like an unexpected blow to her solar plexus. Luke was going away? The next day? Yet she herself was leaving; her British Airways flight was booked for three in the afternoon. What in heaven's name did it matter to her if Luke left Rathbourn? "But, why?" she blurted out despite this.

"Business," he murmured, still not looking at her. "Something I have to see to in the south of France. But the point is this—I'd like to take you to

Cornwall this afternoon, instead of going back to Rathbourn. I want to show you...the house I've been building.''

The one thing that flashed upon her was that there was no other place she'd rather be than at Luke's side on this her last day in England...for tomorrow she would have Daniel drive her to London. They would have to leave early—there would be no time for long goodbyes. In fact, she planned to tell only Glynis of her departure and write later to Jeremy. Luke, she wouldn't tell at all.

"When are you leaving tomorrow?" she asked carefully.

"Quite early...likely before you're up."

"In that case, perhaps I...I should see the house today. As long as we're back this evening." She had to be, to say goodbye to Glynis and to pack for her flight.

"Of course," Luke murmured. "We can stop in Plymouth for something to eat," he suggested, turning the key in the ignition. His voice had lightened, she noticed. With...relief? She stared curiously at him as he trained his eyes on the road.

"Is it far?"

"The house? No, very near Fowey. Not that far. You'll like Cornwall, I think."

Telling herself she preferred to be surprised, she leaned her head back against the seat and asked no more questions, content to be near him as he drove through the narrow streets and across the high hills out of Salcombe.

Less than an hour later they were in Plymouth—

seated in a quiet restaurant near the magnificent Hoe, with its glorious stretch of greenswards, terraces and seafront looking out over the blue waters of Plymouth Sound. Daniel and she had walked there as recently as Wednesday, and now as then, the Sound was dazzling with the white sails of ketches and sloops and the solid stateliness of expensive yachts.

But she was in no mood to think of her day with Daniel as she watched Luke eat, still as taciturn as on the drive from London. Something must be on his mind...unless he was still tired. Yet he was hungry enough to polish off a large plate of fresh mussels and clams. Although Jeremy had followed his good advice and manfully swallowed a piece of toast that morning, Luke himself had eaten nothing at all, and they'd only grabbed a bite of lunch. Ravenna could hardly touch the delicious seafood she'd ordered. Her appetite—for food—faded as she let her eyes touch his hair, his face, his lips.

At that moment his long lashes lifted and his eyes met hers. "Not hungry?"

"No, not really."

"Shall we go, then? I'd like to get there by six if we can."

"Six? Do you think we'll be back in time for dinner?"

"I thought you said you weren't hungry." He smiled, but a moment later, when he went to call Rathbourn to tell them their plans, she realized he hadn't answered her question.

Oh, well. If they missed dinner, she would still

have time to pack...and make her goodbyes. The less time, the better, really. It was these moments now, with Luke, that mattered most.

They crossed the estuary of the Tamar out of Plymouth, the border of the Duchy of Cornwall and Devonshire. At first Ravenna saw no difference between the two, but as they drove through the quaint towns of East and West Looe and then on to the sea-perched fishing village of Polperro, she began to sense Cornwall's unique charm. When she asked about the strange crosses that leaned by roadsides and in old churchyards, Luke told her they were Celtic, that the Celts had come from Wales and Ireland as missionaries in about A.D. 450, leaving these behind them, as well as place names such as Saint Ives and Saint Just. And after that had come the Roman invasion.... But Celts and Romans aside, there was an almost Grecian air to parts of Cornwall, she thought.

Luke grew silent again as the Lincoln climbed an unpaved road that narrowed to a rough track through steeply wooded hills. He concentrated fully on navigating this, until five minutes later she caught sight of a gleam of glass among the trees, and they pulled to a stop above a glimpse of roofs.

"We're here," he said, turning to her. "You can't really see it yet, though, until we climb down a bit."

At first she could barely make it out, so much a part of hill and wood did it seem. But as he helped her down the hillside, taking her hand firmly in his, the house slowly emerged—a very beautiful creation of wood and glass and stone that seemed to spring from the rock. As they came through the firs, past a small cliff, she saw how it thrust itself out in three layers toward a shining estuary, gleaming in the evening sun. She turned. In the distance shone a harbor mouth, stirring with boats...from tiny dories to graceful sailing sloops and even a big ship drawing near, attended by two fat tugs.

And the air...it smelled of tar and tidal water, and from down harbor came the sharp breath of the open sea.

"Why, it's beautiful, Luke!" she exclaimed.

"Wait a minute," he complained. "That's just the view—you haven't even seen the house!"

She pulled her gaze from the magic of the scene to the house itself, which seemed to climb the hill quietly, triumphantly, and her eyes widened in silent excitement. Its projecting terraces, the top one a roof terrace, were of cypress wood, left to weather outside, Luke said, but waxed inside. The bottom terrace rested on a stone plinth that jutted from the side of the hill.

"Is it for a client?" But even as she spoke the words she knew it was not.

"No. I built it for...myself," he answered after the slightest of pauses. "Come on. I'll show you the inside."

Despite the fact they were on level ground now and that her ankle was well enough to walk on, he still hadn't let go of her hand. She didn't protest as he unlocked a door on the lower level and let them into a square entry hall that opened into a long dramatic living room, with a wall of plate glass overlooking the view she'd already fallen for—the harbor and nearby Fowey and then the far green hills. A massive slate fireplace took up most of the wall facing the outdoor terrace that wrapped around the house. Immediately Ravenna found herself imagining sitting out on it in summer evenings such as this one, dreamily watching the boats.

Everything smelled new, she noticed at once... the wood freshly sanded and waxed, the carpets newly laid. The outside grounds, too, were still very rough and muddy, as if workmen had left only days earlier... or even hours.

Luke led her through to a kitchen of cypresswood and stone, with open shelves acting as the only divider to the dining room beyond. A slate fireplace, smaller than the one in the living room, opened to both kitchen and dining areas. Glass doors allowed access to the hillside at the rear. Everything was of simple natural materials, but of the finest quality and workmanship... with the whole main floor designed in a flowing plan that was sheltered yet open, intimate yet free.

A memory of the drawings she'd seen in his study came back... this was the modern house she'd wondered about, the one she'd never have believed to be in Luke's tastes.

"Luke, it couldn't be more different from Rathbourn!"

"That's exactly the point. I love Rathbourn and always will, but for a long time I've wanted to build—and live in—a thoroughly twentieth-century

home, something in the spirit of your famous Frank
Lloyd Wright. Do you like it?''

The eagerness in his voice didn't escape her. He
was deeply proud of it, she could tell. "I...I love
it," she said with complete honesty. "I've never
seen a house that feels so much a part of nature.''
She looked at him, tall and fair and bronzed, and
thought, too, how very much a part of him it felt. A
passionately realized work of art, she thought. To
live in it would be like living in a work of art, a sort
of sculpture. And its rawness, its rough mascu-
linity—what would it be like with a woman's touch
to temper it? Awkwardly she turned away, catching
the drift of her thoughts, sliding her hand sensuously along the satin surface of the wooden shelves.

"I'm trying to come up with a name for it.''

"What about...oh, Seahaven," she said lightly,
smiling with delight as she opened the plentiful cup-
boards in the kitchen and then crossed to look out
at the view from the dining room.

She was more than surprised when he said quickly, "Seahaven? Seahaven, it is. Thank you, Miss
Jones. Consider yourself to have christened it.''

"Oh, Luke!" she said with a laugh, pleased and
embarrassed. "Really?''

"Yes, really. I like the name. It suits the place.''

A warm glow spread through her, a sense of being at home in the beautiful, very personal house
she'd just named as if it were hers. She was beaming
still as Luke led her toward a wide stairwell behind
the fireplace in the living room.

As they climbed to the top floor, she wondered

idly how long it must have taken him to build it.
Surely he must have begun it well before he left for
Africa. And then she realized: he'd built it for
himself and Kristen! And they had never lived in it.
Some of her excitement for the house dimmed,
thinking of it this way—as a monument to Kristen.

"I suppose you built it before you went to
Africa," she murmured, her eyes on the burled elm
wood of the lovely curved banister.

"Yes, but I left before it was finished—come and
see this, Ravenna." And he drew her to a floor-to-
ceiling window that looked down over the back of
the hill into a cleared area flanked by tall firs. "This
is where the gardens will be—a sort of planned
chaos. I want to continue the plantings down the
sides of the hills. Do you think Glynis would let me
steal a few briar roses?"

"She'll rush right over to plant them for you if
you ask her, I'm sure. It's...it's going to be so
beautiful, Luke." She tried to smile, wishing now
that she hadn't come here.

He took her arm and steered her along the spacious second-floor hall, with its clerestory windows
letting in light and air along the top of the wall.

"This is the first of three bedrooms," he said as
she walked into a medium-sized room with a quiet
contemplative view of trees and hills and a corner of
what would be the garden. Had this been meant as
the nursery?

The next bedroom caught a tantalizing glimpse of
the estuary, but only the third one—past the storage
closets and luxurious bathroom—showed her what

she wanted to see: the full view of the distant harbor again.

It was a magnificent room, with its own full terrace and ensuite bathroom and one wall of rough stone that housed the inevitable fireplace. Another was of glass, opening to the terrace—much as the living room below did, yet with a more intimate feeling.

"The master bedroom," Luke said. Unlike the other rooms, to her surprise, it was already furnished, with a king-size bed, a sofa, a desk and built-in shelving for the omnipresent books.

Luke stepped out on the terrace, and she followed, feeling the slight breeze that sighed in the firs caress her hair. He leaned with her to stare out through the trees at the far-off bustle of sea life, and both of them grew silent.

They were leaning very near each other, she suddenly realized, her hammering heart registering the heat of his arm and shoulder, barely an inch away. The power of the view, of the house, to distract her diminished; it was Luke who was distracting now.

She was wearing only a skirt and a short-sleeved pullover, and the evening air as much as her nervousness at his nearness made her suddenly shiver.

"Are you cold?" he asked, his gray blue eyes turning to drink her in.

"A little."

"Then let's go back inside." He led her into the bedroom again, and her eyes alighted irresistibly on the large bed with its woven wool spread. Through a rush of images of lying there wrapped in his arms she heard him say, "Sit here, I'll start the fire."

He sat her down on the deep leather sofa—the color of dark honey—that faced the fire, and she watched as he bent to ignite the firewood that waited there. Odd, she thought, he was quite prepared for company! Suddenly she remembered to look at her watch. "Luke, don't you think we'll be very late getting back to Rathbourn?"

"No, we won't be late," he said calmly, straightening up as the fire flickered alive. "Because we're not going back."

Had he really said it—clearly, slowly, his eyes intent as he stood there watching her? It took a full moment for his words to register, and then he simply moved toward her, his meaning very clear.

"I thought we might like time to ourselves tonight." His voice had deepened, a rich dark timbre to it. "We're going thoroughly to explore the nature of the 'mere biological urge' we have for each other. Don't you think that's a sensible idea?"

Despite her amazement, her heart began to pound, and her eyes darkened with arousal. A very sensible idea.

"When I called Glynis," he added, "I said to expect us...in a day or two."

A day or two! So he had planned to bring her there all along. The fact that she would miss her flight barely dawned on her. All that mattered was Luke before her, wanting her, and the sound of her heart racing like mad at every step he took toward her. This, after all, *was* her heart's desire.

When he reached her, he simply touched his fingers to her hair, watching her riveted eyes. Then he trailed them to her cheek, to her mouth, smiling as her lips parted for him. And as the fires flashed upward in her, she was kissing his fingertips tenderly, passionately, knowing her eyes told him what his asked to see.

In a second his arms surrounded her, his lips burning on hers, and he was lifting her off the couch. He lowered her slowly, purposefully to the bed, kissing her with deep insistence, his hips molding hers as they fell together. She pulled him closer, meeting kiss for kiss as rapture rose within her and every fiber in her burst into ready flames.

He lifted his head, and she heard him say softly, "Then I wasn't dreaming last night, was I?"

He *had* remembered. "No, Luke." Her face was a soft mist of desire, as she looked at him. "You weren't dreaming."

"Shall we continue where we left off, then?" he said gently, his hands belying that gentleness.

"Yes," she whispered. "Yes."

And his mouth came down on hers with a fierceness that ravished her, kissing her until she lost all sense of everything but a wild need to taste him more deeply, to drink at the well of love.... While his hands still cupped her breasts beneath her sweater, their touch sending her into arching gasps, she heard him whisper, "You don't love Daniel, do you?"

Her eyes hung on his, telling him how much she wanted him, how desperately she wanted him.

"Say it!" he commanded roughly, his hands tightening on her possessively.

"I don't love Daniel," she whispered huskily, swaying toward him with longing. "Is that what you want to hear?"

"Damn you," he breathed. And slowly, so slowly she thought she would die from the torture of it, he pulled her sweater over her head and removed her skirt and bra, sliding her silk panties down her long legs. His eyes devoured her while she lay wanting him, willing him to touch her again, to end her torture by making it worse.

Then he stood up beside the bed and removed his own clothes with a slow measured pace, his eyes never leaving her. He watched her ache for him, watched her breasts and thighs arch toward him wantonly, her arms reach to draw him down as finally he stood there, naked and powerful, as beautiful as a Greek statue but burning flesh and blood. Burning for her just as she burned for him....

The hot contact of his body on hers was sudden bliss, and then she was moaning beneath the exquisite onslaught of his hands and lips and thighs, of his mouth telling her in every way that she was his. She responded with the same fevered passion as his own.

And then she lay naked beneath him and felt the hot length of him mastering her, sinking into her.

He took her as she wanted to be taken, in a long arching ecstasy that made her cry his name, a cascade of sound on her lips, and then she realized she had said over and over the one thing she'd tried to keep from him: "I love you, I love you, I love you." They clung there together, one at last, until he collapsed against her softness, melting into her.

"That's what I wanted to hear," he breathed in her hair. "The truth. It's the truth, isn't it, Ravenna?"

"Yes, Luke, yes...I love you." And his arms as they held her were more tender than she had ever dreamed they could be.

For a long while they lay there like that, naked but warmed by their own fires, completely at peace. Ravenna listened to the wood crackle and felt the dark come down outside, casting the room into shadow, while Luke kissed and caressed her slowly and lingeringly, as if he couldn't get enough of her. She was experiencing a complete surrender to him—his least wish was her highest pleasure, his love for her freeing her as she'd never been freed before. For it was love. Surely he loved her if they could possess each other like that, though he had not said it in so many words. His body and his lips told her in an ancient language that she was his...and her world revolved around the power of his need.

Once he carried her to the fire, and on the deep fur rug before it they again made love, their sweet torment mounting to another crescendo—as deep, as endless and impassioned in her as it was in him. She wondered why she had ever been afraid of losing herself in this, when her whole being cried out for him.

Near dawn they slept exhausted in the wide bed,

wrapped closely in each other's arms, with only a thin blanket over them, her head buried against his chest and her long hair tangled between them like a fiery net. He still hadn't said that he loved her....

She awoke to his lips tracing hers, light as a butterfly. Slowly she parted them, opening to his kiss, and his long legs twined with hers. One hand reached to caress the curve of her hip, an instinctive pleasure for both of them.

She couldn't resist reminding him with a seductive smile, "I thought you planned to leave for the continent before I was even up."

His lips beckoning hers, his eyes still closed as he rubbed his unshaven jaw against her shoulder, he murmured, "I did. Looks like I'll be a little late." And he bent to kiss her.

But even as the heady wine of his kiss carried her willingly into ecstasy, a small voice reminded her that he *hadn't* said he loved her. "Luke?"

But he thought she meant that she wanted him, and his hungry arms pulled her against him. Again passion flared between them, its sweet intoxication sweeping away her anxious thoughts. But when their love was spent, Ravenna found the spell of her ecstasy quickly broken. Now, when he'd finally won her, when she was completely, irrevocably, his... he was going away just as planned.

He lay beside her, his face buried against her shoulder, asleep once again. Ravenna turned her own face away, staring unseeing out the full-length windows. She wanted to cry aloud, "Why? *Why?*" But his words had been so matter-of-fact, as if his going meant little to them both. Her own fears froze on her lips, held back by pride. She couldn't ask him to stay for her sake—not if he didn't offer. . . .

She had been willing to pay the price of loving him. Now she was doing so. Like a fool she'd given everything—herself, her future—to a man who shook her to the core of her being. . . but who didn't love her.

And even as he lay in her arms in the aftermath of passion she began silently to grieve.

To all appearances she was calm as they left Seahaven—although she allowed herself one long last look at the house in which she had loved him, a look filled with private pain at leaving it behind forever. But she wasn't allowed to linger, for Luke took her arm impulsively, intent on escorting her to the old town of Fowey for breakfast at the Ship Hotel. He couldn't wait to show her its Elizabethan paneling and vaulted plaster ceiling, he said with an eagerness Ravenna found heartbreaking.

Once there, seated in the exquisite dining room and still numb with the realization that he was leaving her, she made the decision that allowed her to go on: she would enjoy every moment to the full with him, her only vengeance on fate. And then she would fly home to Kentucky as soon as she could get a flight out of London.

They had eggs Benedict and delicious homemade scones and coffee, but although everything appeared and smelled ambrosial, she could hardly taste a thing. Luke, however, ate with an excellent appetite. Now he looked at her searchingly over the rim of his coffee cup, and his fingers reached to lace with hers. "What is it, my lovely one? You're being very quiet."

She opened her mouth to speak—but what was there to say? *You're going away and I can't bear it.* She said nothing.

He lifted her palm to his lips, the touch of them making her feel weak. "Are you still afraid, Ravenna?"

Yes, she wanted to cry at him. *Afraid of losing you.* But she only smiled.

"Don't be," he said gently when she didn't reply. "There's nothing to fear, I promise."

She almost believed him, gazing into those bottomless gray eyes. Almost, but not quite. He was leaving for the continent. And hadn't she had enough of promises...on Daniel's lips?

He looked as though he had more to say, but she interrupted him. "Luke," she whispered, smiling quickly, feeling her heart break for every moment that she sat there. Suddenly she wanted to be alone to collect herself, to steel herself for the inevitability of their parting, knowing that at any moment he might tell her he would be leaving...when? The following day? Perhaps even later that day. No, she didn't want to know.

Squeezing his hand, she leaned across the table to touch her lips to his, saying, "I think I'll make a trip to the ladies' room to freshen up. I'll just be a few minutes...."

The restroom was large and old-fashioned. Ravenna stared into the huge mirror above the basins, feeling unreal. Her lips looked soft with loving, her eyes enormous, still numb with the pain of Luke's leaving.

Applying fresh lipstick, she slowly realized that a partly open window was reflected in the mirror before her, and visible through that window was a taxicab, waiting for customers at the side entrance to the hotel.

She powdered her nose lightly. A taxi. It could take her to the nearest train station, couldn't it? She might never have to go back to Rathbourn.

But Luke—

Luke would know why she'd gone. He had his appointment on the continent to keep. He would let her go, surely, aware that it was for the best. Perhaps he'd even feel relief when she had gone without making a scene. It would be so simple this way.

Why not take the cab? She might just catch her three-o'clock flight to New York.

She slammed her compact shut and hurried to the door. Down the elegant hall she could see him waiting for her, his back toward her across the dining room.

He would never forgive her. But there was nothing left to say to him when he didn't love her, so what did it matter?

In five steps she was at the side entrance, her

mind made up. The cab was waiting, the driver engrossed in reading a betting sheet, as if business were slow.

"Can you take me to the nearest train station that connects with London?" she asked hastily.

"Hop in, miss," was all he said, and then he pulled slowly away from the curb, passing the parked Lincoln at a snail's pace. Ravenna was in an agony of anxiety that Luke would glance out one of the restaurant windows and glimpse her passage. Shrinking against the seat of the cab, she rummaged in her purse to see if she could actually afford a train to London and still pay for her flight home. Just barely.

They picked up speed out of Fowey, and she began to breathe again. But what had she just done? She might never see Luke again...and she hadn't even said goodbye! It was an utterly childish thing to do, but she felt too frantic with grief to care.

The cabbie took her north to Lostwithiel, and there she had to wait an endless twenty minutes for the train. But finally, miraculously, she was safely seated in a comfortable compartment heading for Plymouth, and eventually Exeter and then London. She sank back, knowing it was her longest journey. Every mile took her farther from Luke's arms. She prayed he'd simply return to Rathbourn, thinking that she would go there, too, to see Daniel. She didn't want to be found by him, not now, not ever again....

Yes, he would surely think she'd gone to Rathbourn, because he didn't know about her flight ar rangements. So she was safe. . . wasn't she?

Rathbourn. That's where she should be going, to see Daniel, to say goodbye to him and Glynis. It was cruel of her to leave England like this. . . but she could at least call from the airport in London if she had time. Yes, she dared not return to Rathbourn, for Luke would naturally go there first.

But by Exeter it was miserably clear she would miss her three-o'clock plane. A quick call from the station told her the last flight out, at 6:30 P.M., was fully booked. But there was one available at 11:00 A.M. on Sunday. Would she like that one?

"I'll take it," she said, and hung up, rushing back to the train just as the boarding whistle blew.

It was only when they were en route again that she suddenly realized she didn't have enough money for a hotel. There was just enough to cover her plane fare and possibly a light meal that evening. She'd even have to have someone fly in from Elk Creek to pick her up when she reached New York. Damn! No one at Elk Creek had any idea she was even coming home. . . her last letter had been full of plans for the August wedding.

The town house? On a note of pure relief she remembered that Daniel had once given her a key to it and had never asked for it back. She searched her purse, and sure enough, there it was.

Should she spend her last night there, just as she had her first? The idea had appeal. . . but finally she decided it would be too dangerous. Luke might go there after Rathbourn if he bothered to look for her. Or he might be staying there, anyway, before he flew on to the continent.

She closed her eyes in despair, ready to weep with frustration. Where could she possibly go? And suddenly the answer presented itself: Angela. Why not go to Angela? Surely she would help her...and Ravenna would make her keep it a secret, just in case. She sank back against her seat once more, beginning to relax a little.

But a small voice inside her reminded her ruthlessly that Luke wouldn't follow her. He was going away. So it hardly mattered where she went.

She stared out the train window, trying not to think.

"LOOK, DARLING, are you sure you know what you're doing?" Angela, sitting before her dressing table, swiveled in her chair to face Ravenna, her hazel eyes concerned. It was seven-thirty, half an hour before she was due to go onstage in *Walk Softly*; Ravenna had had dinner at a small café off Shaftesbury Avenue, stalling awhile before coming to the Globe.

"Yes...of course I do," she said now, trying to keep her misery from her telltale eyes. "My flight's booked, Angela, and...and I really need a place to stay tonight. I thought perhaps you might—" She stopped, embarrassed.

Angela's eyes narrowed shrewdly as she slid a cigarette into her jeweled holder and lit it. Ravenna could almost read her mind—she was probably wondering where her coat and luggage were. But all she finally said was, "Jeremy recovering?"

Ravenna jumped. Jeremy? "Why, yes, he is." Heavens, had it been only two nights ago that Luke had gone to Angela's.... "He's at home—I mean, at Rathbourn, though I guess he's acting tonight in Salcombe. But he's surviving." She fiddled with her purse. Of course Angela would want to hear about Jeremy.

"And Luke?" Angela blew a perfect smoke ring.

"Luke is fine," Ravenna grated.

"Hmmn. Well, *he* may be, darling, but *you* look terrible." At Ravenna's loud silence she raised one hand in protest. "All right, all right...no more questions asked. I'll give you one of my extra keys to the flat—you can sleep in the little study. The sofa pulls out, and there are blankets and sheets in the closet." Her eyes softened, and Ravenna realized this was hardly the first time Angela had doled out lodgings to a friend in need.

"Thank you, Angela." She couldn't stop the tears that welled into her eyes, and quickly she looked away.

The actress stood up as if she hadn't noticed and picked up a brunette wig. "Help yourself to whatever's in the fridge, love...I should be in about one. I expect you'll be asleep, though. What time's your flight tomorrow? Eleven? So we'll have time to talk in the morning—that is, if you feel like talking. It usually helps.... Now I want to be alone. Have to psyche myself into this part for the 785th time. Here's my address.'' She scribbled it on the flap of an empty cigarette pack.

Ravenna smiled her gratitude, then reached over and gave her a quick heartfelt hug. Angela raised her heavily madeup brows, then patted Ravenna's arm, her eyes on her distraught face. "Now scram, love. And stop worrying.''

Ravenna paused by the door as Angela waved her out. "You won't tell anybody where I am, will you, Angela?'' she asked, her throat dry.

"Anybody in particular in mind?'' Angela drawled, watching her in the mirror.

"No,'' she muttered, and hurriedly left. Angela was not being all that sympathetic when you came right down to it. One would almost think she didn't approve of her going home. But Ravenna felt immediately ungrateful—hadn't the woman just given her the key to her flat? And told her to make herself at home? It was natural she was curious. Only Ravenna had no intention of satisfying that curiosity that night or the next day.

Angela's Mayfair flat was a sophisticated but comfortable arrangement of five rooms: a luxurious purple-and-gray living room, a tiny kitchen, a large dining room with a table that looked like it opened to seat a dozen people, a huge study with its sofa bed piled high with colorful cushions. Ravenna stowed her purse there and wandered back into the living room, feeling at a loss now that she was actually at Angela's. For a while she stared numbly at the framed photos of Angela and her fellow actors and actresses, which were scattered about the room.

Her eyes sought out the phone next, and she sank down on the sofa beside the little end table, gripped by a sudden need to call Rathbourn. She was leaving without a single word.... And what had Luke told them when he'd arrived?

The French-style phone with its elegant gold handle seemed to accuse her as she picked it up and then put it down again. Better to phone tomorrow from New York, and her family then, too, she decided. What possible difference could it make, waiting till then—when she had already waited so long? But her hand hovered over the phone once more.

What stopped her was a vision of Luke; his eyes seemed to penetrate suddenly, reproachfully, even to Angela's, blaming her for her deserting him. And what if—despite her belief that he would let her go—he had instead followed her to London, wanting to prolong their affair a little longer? Whoever picked up the phone would certainly ask her where she was, and she could hardly say, "At Angela Heyward's place—but don't tell anyone." Anyone meaning Luke.

She wasn't going to call, and that was that. Nor would she phone her family. Time enough for painful explanations in New York. So what should she do instead, then, to pass the hours until bedtime? It was barely eight—Angela's play would just be beginning. Dinner would just have been served at Rathbourn...Glynis would be there, Fern and Daniel. Garvey would be handing around the soup, doing his stint as footman, and Peters— She stopped, a wave of longing for what had come to feel like home washing through her. As for Luke? Perhaps he'd already left for the continent.

At that the tears came in a rush, as if the dam had broken, and she collapsed full length on the sofa. She had really lost him; she would never hold him close to her again. Her whole body cried out in aching grief.

When the tears were over, she was sore and numbed, her face stiff from crying. She stumbled to the washroom and splashed cold water on her eyes, then dried herself and went to the kitchen. But she wasn't hungry, so she wandered to the dining room and then the living room, pacing up and down like a listless caged animal. She turned on the television and turned it off, then examined the titles on Angela's bookshelves. They blurred before her in a meaningless jumble. After a while she went into the study and made up the bed, then returned to the living room, still restless, still haunted by images of Luke...his face, his eyes, his hard demanding body. But especially those accusing gray eyes. Why did they accuse her?

She removed her shoes and lay down on the sofa again with just one lamp lit, trying her best to blot the imprint of Luke from her being—an impossible task. Finally, in despair, she closed her eyes.

When she awoke, the electric clock on the bookcase pointed almost to eleven. The streetlights cast yellow oblongs through the high windows, and she could hear an echo of voices below in the soft summer darkness. She sat up, thinking she should close the curtains and go to bed.

Then she started. Had she heard a slight sound at the door? Yes, there it was again.

Her mind slowly registered what it was—a key turning in the lock. Angela was home early then and would want to talk. And she didn't want to talk, not at all.

But a second later, when the door opened and the light of the hall poured in, she shot to her feet as if she'd been struck by lightning.

"Luke!" The word was torn from her throat.

"Of all the damned idiotic things to do," he exploded, advancing on her like a cannon blast.

"How. . . how did you find me?"

"How the hell do you think I found you? By driving halfway across England!" His rage collapsed, and he sank suddenly, heavily, onto the sofa.

"Ravenna," he whispered like a man exhausted, pulling her down beside him, "don't ever do this again to me. I swear I won't survive it if you do. You little idiot—what possessed you to run away from me like that?"

She stared at him totally at a loss.

"Don't you know how much I love you?"

Those three small words she'd waited so long to hear. . . .

She must have looked her shock, for his hands cupped her face, his eyes searching hers, and then his head fell to her shoulder. She felt him shudder against her. Her arms went around him slowly, unbelievingly. . until she was holding him as tightly as he was her, rocking back and forth with him.

"I thought I'd lost you, my love. I thought you'd gone back to Daniel," he said hoarsely. "I went to Rathbourn first, and when you weren't there, to Gordon Square. I . . . I thought I'd never find you. I was at my rope's end when I thought of Angela, and I went to the Globe, caught her between scenes." He rushed on. "She told me you were here."

So Angela had betrayed her. "She promised . . ." she began, and then suddenly realized Angela had done nothing of the sort. And thank heavens.

"She took one look at me, said, 'It's a good thing you got here in time,' and handed me her house key. But I wouldn't have given her a choice, Ravenna. I would have made her tell me . . . I realized when I saw her face that she knew where you were." He stopped and looked at her. "Tell me you won't run away again, Ravenna. Tell me," he said simply, his eyes more vulnerable than she had ever thought possible.

"Not if you want me to stay, Luke," she whispered, smoothing the hair from his forehead. "Not if you love me."

"Yes, I love you and want you to stay!" He almost shook her. "Always. I thought you knew that after last night . . . how could you have ever thought otherwise . . . when I was telling you in a thousand ways."

"But I thought you were going to the continent for two months. You sounded so certain."

He looked at her blankly. "The continent? Oh, blast!" He sat up straight. "It's all my fault. I thought you understood this morning—" Suddenly his face melted in a smile, and he touched his lips to hers, then took a long breath. "I think we both have a lot of explaining to do. Do you think you could make me a coffee, though?"

And she realized he was tired enough to drop after two days of driving, plus their almost sleepless night at Seahaven.

"I think Angela can stretch to a coffee," she said, still stunned, "if you promise not to fall asleep on me while I get it."

"Ravenna...." His voice was ironic. "I'm not about to let you out of my sight for one single second, even if it means propping my eyelids open."

And true to his word, Luke was wide awake when she brought him a steaming mug of the gourmet blend Angela kept in her fridge. Lifting her onto his lap in the one large armchair and drawing her close against his chest, Luke began. "As I was about to say at breakfast when I was so rudely interrupted, I am *not* going to the continent. But I wasn't lying earlier. If you hadn't made it clear to me last night that despite your words, and I quote, 'I could never love a man like you, Luke,' that you do in fact love me and are not going to marry Daniel, I had every intention of leaving for France at dawn. I told myself I couldn't stand another second at Rathbourn, watching you throw away what's between us, going off to marry Daniel next week. I've been going mad ever since."

She twisted in his arms, the pain at his quoted words giving way to amazement. "Next week? But Luke, the wedding isn't—wasn't—till the end of August. What are you talking about?"

He looked at her long and steadily, then said quietly, "The night you came back from Plymouth Daniel told me privately that you'd agreed to move the wedding date up to the end of this month. That's what I thought when we went to get Jerry . . . and why I carried you off to Cornwall yesterday. I'd been hoping to show the house to you, anyway. But after Daniel convinced me you were marrying him early, I decided that keeping you with me was the last chance I'd have to convince you how you really feel."

So Daniel had gone to such desperate lengths. "I had a flight booked home for today at three. It's funny—Daniel was lying, since he knew everything was over between him and me—but it really was your last chance, Luke. I would have left today if you hadn't made me miss my plane."

He smiled, his gray eyes encompassing her. "And I'm going to make you miss the one tomorrow, too, my love."

She looked at him in surprise.

"Angela," he explained. "I'm becoming very fond of Angela. The least we can do—"

But she interrupted him, as slowly it sank into her that his arms would continue to hold her, that he loved her and wasn't going to the continent. "But you're really not going away?" she whispered as a deep warm joy burst within her.

"In mid-August I do have to see a client in Nice," he admitted, "but *you* are coming with me...."

She smiled, adoring how he gave her no choice.

"My love," he murmured, his voice once more intense, "how could you ever think I'd let you go?" His arms tightened as if they hardly yet believed they really held her. But when he bent his head to kiss her, his lips touching her forehead, eyelids, nose, cheeks and then finally her mouth, she sighed against him, feeling she was at last sure of him.

"You know," he whispered when he'd lifted his mouth from hers, "you did such a good job, Ravenna, convincing yourself our love was only physical...that you really loved Daniel."

"But I thought that you thought—"

He laughed. "Yes?"

"I thought you were still grieving for Kristen," she said simply. "That you must have built...Seahaven for her and couldn't forget her."

The laughter died from his face.

"Kristen? I did grieve for her in Africa, but it seems a long time ago now. And I certainly didn't feel about her the way I do about you. Mostly I think I wanted to protect her." His face dimmed, and his voice grew slightly harsh. "But she didn't need my protection, I found out. That was the last thing she needed. Never mind. And...Seahaven, no, I didn't build it for her. I actually began it two years before I met her. It's true I thought we might someday live there. But Kristen loved the city—she couldn't stand being at Rathbourn for long, let alone a place as peaceful and isolated as Fowey. It took me a while to see that, but I did. I never showed her the house...."

Silently Ravenna laid her head on his shoulder, admitting to herself she was glad. There would be no ghosts to haunt her there...nor any at Rathbourn, either. "Oh, Luke," she confessed. "I've been so jealous!"

His arms wound more closely. "Jealous?" he whispered. "Then that makes two of us, my love. The tortures I've gone through, thinking of you in Daniel's arms...."

Her lips close to his, she murmured, "Luke... there was no need. Daniel and I were never lovers."

He stared at her, then pulled her down to him. "I'm glad," he breathed. "I couldn't believe you'd make love to me like that at the same time as.... But when I saw you with him in my bedroom that morning—"

"Then you believed it."

"Yes, I did. It almost drove me mad." His eyes told her the agony it had cost him.

"Daniel was just getting something out of his bags." She drew his mouth down to hers, knowing what they had to make up to each other, and kissed him until she felt his kiss match hers, drowning her in sweetness. The intensity of it mounted, igniting the center of her, and she felt him draw her closer, closer....

Both started violently at the sound of a key turning noisily once more in the lock, and they quickly drew apart.

Angela entered, her arms full of roses and a broad smile sweeping her face as she caught sight of the two of them. Ravenna was still on Luke's lap, with her arms around his neck and his clasping her waist.

"So...when's the wedding?" she asked in her deep mellow voice, beaming at them.

Luke turned back to Ravenna. He said slowly and firmly, "Soon. Very, very soon." And his gray eyes touched hers, soft as dawn.

Ravenna smiled, still drowning in those silver pools, and then turned to Angela, her smile widening so that it wreathed her face. "Of course you're the first to be invited, Angela."

CHAPTER TWELVE

IT WAS LATE MORNING when Ravenna awoke in Luke's bed at Gordon Square. She lay watching him sleep, remembering their first meeting...thinking how this had been her destiny from that moment. Their night of love, broken by frequent confessions of how they'd doubted each other and despaired, had made many things clear that still amazed her. Luke had confessed he'd fallen for her almost the instant he opened his eyes to find her in his arms... how nevertheless he *had* gone off to Cornwall in a rage that second night at Rathbourn, determined to forget her. He'd become obsessed with her instead...and at the cottage, after they'd made love, he'd determined to go back to Rathbourn and have it out with Daniel. *She* had been the business she'd despaired of! It all seemed too incredible yet.

She watched as Luke's long lashes flickered on his cheeks, and then he was looking at her, the gaze of his eyes as deep and clear as crystal. "Mmmn," he said, reaching for her, his mouth seeking hers, and it was quite some while before getting up held the least appeal. But when they did, Luke suggested they cart their breakfast up to his third-floor study to eat before the fire.

This was the first time Ravenna had penetrated to this inner sanctum, and she gazed in delighted surprise when they reached the top of the stairs. Luke had renovated the whole floor into one long rectangular carpeted room—with a marble fireplace at the far end and carved bookshelves inset on the other three walls. Three fan-shaped windows opened on opposite sides of the room, above the shelves, and a skylight shed morning sunlight over a huge, intricately carved Jacobean desk, which filled one corner. There were other Jacobean pieces, too—a gateleg table holding marvelous old folios on architecture of the eighteenth century, a beautiful wooden globe mounted on an iron pedestal and some high-backed stools with carved legs. Some of these, circa 1600, were of museum quality...Luke said they had once been at Rathbourn.

Her eyes lifted to him as he arranged their breakfast on the coffee table in front of the deep Victorian sofa that faced the fire. She thought of him at Seahaven and then at Rathbourn and now here—of the many sides of this interesting complex man, of all the years ahead in which she'd be able slowly to explore them. But when he looked up at her, she merely gave him a soft captivating smile.

His eyes traveled over her tumbling red hair and her beautiful glowing face. "Come here," he commanded, and she complied, sitting near him with her feet curled under her, watching him as he poured her a coffee and handed her a plate laden with eggs and toast.

She was still thinking of how far this happiness

was from the agony both had endured, each believing the one didn't love the other. And although they knew differently now, it would still take time to get used to the miracle.

Somewhere in the middle of that perfect breakfast Ravenna remembered Daniel, and for an instant a shadow crossed her face.

Luke caught it and, brushing aside a curling strand of hair from her forehead, said, "Daniel?"

She nodded.

"You know, I'm almost sorry for him. . .but I'd be dishonest if I said I was. So recently I thought I was in his shoes—and I know how he's going to feel."

"I'm sure he knows about us," Ravenna said a little sadly.

Luke said nothing to this, his eyes caught in hers.

"Darling, don't you think it's time you forgave him for Kristen's death?" she ventured. "It would be such a relief for him."

"I never really thought he was responsible for the accident, not after the first shock of it," he answered in a low voice, turning his gaze away.

His words could not have surprised her more. "But Daniel told me—"

"I let him think that, Ravenna." The dark note in his voice stopped her from interrupting. "It wasn't that that made me hate him. Daniel and Kristen were. . .lovers—that was what I couldn't forgive. That's why I stayed in Africa so long. I couldn't bear to go back to Rathbourn with Daniel coming and going all the time."

Ravenna sat very still. So this was the poison that ate at Luke, the source of his bitter anger toward Daniel...what had almost made him lose his faith in love. But Daniel had told her Kristen had only been flirting with him that summer at Rathbourn...and his confession that day on the terrace had rung true.

She lifted her hands and turned Luke's face to hers. "Luke? Who told you they were lovers?"

"It was Fern."

Fern.

"I wouldn't have credited it but for my own eyes—Kristen always acted seductively around Daniel."

She leaned her chin on his shoulder, saying, slowly, "Daniel tried once to insinuate to me that something *had* happened between Kristen and him. But later he apologized and told me Kristen really did love you and had only been flirting with him—there was nothing more between them."

He looked unbelieving. "But Fern said—"

"No doubt she believed what she said. But I think her motive might have been to get you to confront Daniel. I think she was very jealous of Kristen's beauty, Luke, just as she's been jealous of my relationship with Daniel. I'm sure Daniel was telling me the truth."

He still looked reluctant to accept this. "It was easy to believe Fern's accusations because I knew she had her reasons. She and Daniel have been off and on for years."

"Actually, darling, I don't believe they were ever

lovers. Fern told me as much one day when she was furious at me, and she can't have been lying about a thing like that. Did she persuade you she and Daniel were involved?''

"Well, it certainly looked that way at times. And there were all those hints she let drop. . . .''

Suddenly Luke's words that night when they'd first met came back to her. "Another of Daniel's women!'' Now she understood—he'd been thinking of Fern. . .and of Kristen. And he'd been wrong on both counts.

"It's amazing how you and Daniel have given me the idea that the other is a playboy. I doubt it's true in either case,'' she said with sudden insight.

"A playboy?'' He almost laughed. "And did Daniel explain how I had time for all these women—with my teaching, not to mention my even more demanding architectural career?'' His expression sobered. "If what you say about all this is so—''

"I know it is, Luke.''

He paused, his eyes searching hers. "Then I've been very unfair to both Kristen and Daniel.''

She sighed. "He hasn't exactly been easy on you, either.'' She was thinking of all the traps she'd almost fallen into. Simply by believing others, rather than the proof of her own eyes. . .and heart.

"It's strange,'' Luke said now, putting down his empty coffee cup. "This means I've been accusing him of taking Kristen from me when it was untrue. But now I'm taking you from him. . .and he's the one who may never forgive me.''

"It doesn't have to be like that, Luke. If you two would only try.... I don't suppose you've ever really made an effort to get to know each other."

He smiled wryly. "It's true—we've been at logger-heads ever since...oh, as far back as when Glynis first married dad. Neither of us would give an inch. Well, my love, if you keep this up, the Rathbourn brothers won't have any feuds left worth fighting!"

She laughed, leaning back on the sofa. "About time, too. Imagine, Glynis could have married Harold Moreton and save you all a lot of trouble!"

"Harold who?"

"Never mind, darling. Eat your breakfast."

Instead he took her coffee cup out of her hand and kissed her thoroughly, lingeringly.

It was only after they'd finally returned to the business at hand—their rapidly cooling breakfast—that Ravenna remembered her British Airways flight and hurried to the phone to cancel her reservation.

"But we will eventually fly home for the wedding, and we'll have it at Elk Creek Ranch, won't we, Luke?" she said when she hung up.

"If you like, my love. Shall we call your parents today?"

Her face fell. "How am I ever going to explain...." And it was only then that she realized what an awful lot of explaining she had ahead of her. Starting with Daniel.

SHE WAS GIVEN NO TIME to prepare herself. Luke and she, fresh from London and hand in hand, had barely entered Rathbourn when Daniel appeared, a newspaper folded under his arm; he stopped dead under the archway from the gun room when he caught sight of them, his face a wary mask.

"Daniel?" she said softly, but he'd already turned and disappeared back into the library.

Luke gripped her hand reassuringly, his eyes asking if she wanted his help.

"No," she said. "Give me fifteen minutes alone with him first. It will be easier that way."

And soundlessly she followed Daniel, amazed at how calm she felt now that the moment was at hand.

He was waiting by the fire, stubbornly unfolding his newspaper, when she crossed the library. She sat down in the chair next to him. "Daniel?"

He didn't reply at first, and for a second she foundered, wondering how on earth she was to begin. But he saved her the trouble. "You're going to marry Luke." A statement, not a question.

"Yes. You know."

A ghost of a smile crossed his face. "I've known for a while. Longer than you think." He paused, his face and voice resigned. "When did you... decide?"

She knew he meant between Luke and him. "The night I was trapped below the cliffs, when I saw our marriage wouldn't work. I knew then. But I really did plan to go home."

"Luke persuaded you otherwise."

"Yes," she said simply.

"I suppose he told you that I lied to him?" He looked ashamed as he glanced away. "I'm sorry."

"Oh, Daniel! It doesn't matter now." She reached to take his hand, and he let her. "I didn't plan for it to turn out this way. I tried so hard to hang on to what we had. Forgive me."

"I didn't help you, did I?" he said softly. "I'm too absorbed in my work."

No, he hadn't helped her. But even so, would it have made a difference? She realized now it would only have made it harder to face the inevitable.

"Well, I'm glad at least you're not going away. You belong here at Rathbourn. It's funny, though—I'm the one who doesn't."

"How do you mean, Daniel?"

"I've never really felt at home here—all these years."

Yes. She sensed that, too, from the beginning. Rathbourn was Luke's.

"I'm flying to the States tomorrow—to join Fern. Her foster mother died yesterday."

Her eyes flew to his. "I'm very sorry." But she felt little surprise at his decision; mostly she was struck by how Daniel was always there for Fern when she needed him, just as Luke had been at her side when *she* needed *him*. Did he realize how much he cared for Fern? "You're very fond of her," she said.

"Yes...yes, I am. It's taken me a long time to see it. She'd had a hard time in life," he added, as if he'd been thinking about this.

Ever since that day on the lawn, when Daniel had flared up at her after her talk with Fern, she'd known that he had been quietly in love with Fern for some time without being aware of it. He at least suspected the truth of this now.

"Will you stay with her in Syracuse?"

"I don't know. It depends on her. I guess I was never very good at getting along in anything but my work."

"People can change," she said encouragingly.

"Yes," he admitted. "I'd like to. Speaking of Fern," he added, "she asked me to give you this before she left." He reached into his vest pocket and handed her a note.

She opened it curiously, surprised that Fern would want to write to her about anything. It began bluntly enough:

> Ravenna, if I caused a lot of trouble between you and Daniel, I'm sorry. It's just that I've loved him a long time and couldn't bear finally to lose him. I've decided to go back to Syracuse and probably won't see any of you again, as I'm leaving Daniel's employ. I hope the two of you are happy—I really do.
>
> Fern

"Is Fern still working for you?" she asked Daniel in surprise.

"As far as I know." He looked puzzled. "Why?"

"Oh, nothing." She folded the note and placed it in her handbag. The two of them would sort it out in Syracuse. And the note was obviously a little out of date, now that she was marrying Luke. As for never seeing Fern again, oddly, it was much more likely they would meet in the near future—perhaps actually as sisters-in-law. For ironically, with Fern's decision to give up Daniel, had come his determination to join her. If she could only learn to trust him, she would undoubtedly get the happiness she had thought denied her, after all.

Ravenna was unexpectedly glad that Fern had cared enough to apologize. She looked up, smiling at Daniel. "Say hello to her for me," she said. Then, she inquired, "Will you continue to manage the Rathbourn interests?"

"It depends very much on Luke." After a pause he added, "Ever since Kristen's death it's been difficult. I have to deal with him on so many business matters—and it's obvious he'd prefer to have someone else handling things. Perhaps it's time—"

"That's not true, Daniel."

Both of them turned to see that Luke had quietly entered the room.

"You might as well join us," Daniel said half-heartedly.

Luke came over and sat down, ignoring Daniel's lukewarm welcome. "As I was saying, it's not true that I'd prefer to have someone else looking after Rathbourn's investments. No one could do a better job than you have, and I hope you'll continue to want to do it."

Daniel's eyebrows rose in genuine surprise, but both Ravenna and Luke saw the swift flash of pleasure he felt at this unexpected compliment on his work, a pleasure he immediately hid. He said cautiously, "Things *have* been going well lately. I don't suppose I'd like to abandon my work with Rathbourn...I've put rather a lot into it through the years. But...perhaps I should say something here that's been on my mind."

As Daniel cleared his throat, Luke said casually, lighting a cigarette, "If it's about the accident with Kristen—I know it wasn't your fault," and he looked up as Daniel's jaw dropped, their eyes meeting.

"You know?"

"Yes. I'm afraid I misjudged you. I'm sorry, Daniel." Luke reached for Ravenna's hand, as if he wished openly to state their relationship.

Concentrating on the mantelpiece now, Daniel said, "There's something else. I've been meaning to get this off my chest ever since you got back, Luke. Last summer—before the accident—I think you somehow got the impression that something was going on between me and Kristen. Well, you were wrong."

The effort to get this out was obvious, and Ravenna was silent, feeling only Luke's grip.

"I know, Daniel. Ravenna told me. But...thank you."

No one said anything for half a minute, until Daniel, with relief in his voice at broaching the subject of Kristen openly, finally murmured, "You know...I felt so badly about Kristen, the accident and all that. I felt that in a real way I did take her from you. So there's a certain poetic justice in your taking...." He stopped. Then he sat up abruptly, his tone light, "Never mind. I'm off to Syracuse tomorrow, and then Fern and I are on to New York again. I'll be back in a few weeks, I guess—although I'm planning to look at some land near Poughkeepsie. Fern told me of a deal I might be interested in.

"By the way, Luke—" his voice was casual now "—I'm thinking of selling our copper shares and maybe getting right out of commodities, too. What do you say to our trading in the international money market in a big way?"

And watching Daniel's eyes light up as they discussed this, Ravenna smiled, knowing that he would survive their breakup. His hurt, she suddenly saw, was likely more hurt pride than grief, although he didn't know it yet; losing her might be a blow to his male ego but not to his soul. His soul belonged to his work...and surely someday soon he'd share it with Fern. Yes, Daniel would more than survive.

"Well, shall we hunt up Glynis?" Luke suggested when Daniel left them. "Might as well face the entire firing squad at once." He grinned at her.

Ravenna made a face, and just then the roar of a motorcycle came to their ears, subsiding slowly when it reached the garages.

They stood up and glanced out the terrace door to see Jeremy and a slender, brown-haired girl in blue jeans and a T-shirt coming up the steps. Ravenna recognized the girl who'd spoken to them that night backstage in Salcombe—Carole. Without her makeup and costume she was a surprisingly contemporary-looking young woman, with a sensitive face and huge madonna eyes; at the moment both she and Jeremy were loaded down with books, and Jeremy looked rather proud of himself.

"Good lord!" Luke breathed as they advanced toward them. "Do you suppose Jerry's converted?"

"You mean to schoolwork... or Carole?"

She laughed, but the next moment Jeremy and Carole were upon them, entering the library with such determined energy that the doorjamb rattled behind them.

"Hello, Luke. Scarlett." Jeremy turned to present his companion. "Friend of mine, Carole McKenna."

"Hello," Ravenna smiled, and the girl reached out shyly, balancing her books on one hip, to shake hands.

"Actually, I'm Ravenna. You talked to me on the phone the other night. Scarlett Ravenna," she added in deference to Jeremy's nickname.

"How do you do." Carole's eyes were frankly grateful. "Thanks so much for your help the other night."

Jeremy looked curious at the smiles they exchanged but turned from them to his brother. "Say, Luke, d'ya think we could use your study? We need a place to spread out a few things. Carole here's going to help me with my French and German. She's a language major."

Luke's eyebrows rose in surprise, but he recovered to say, "Oh...certainly, Jerry. Help yourself."

Carole was explaining in her soft clear voice, "We're starting by reading Molière's plays together. Good practice for our RADA auditions next year."

"Oh?" Jeremy flushed as Luke smiled. "That's nice, Jerry."

"Oh, Luke!" Ravenna broke in. "Tell him you've already checked it out. You know perfectly well he'll be going to RADA!"

Luke finally dropped the facade and grinned. "I rather thought you might be planning on it. The school prospectus is on my desk in the study."

"It is? Say, that's great, Luke." Jeremy looked momentarily stunned. Then he recovered enough to say, "We'll be upstairs, then. Oh, I kind of thought we could stretch to dinner for Carole, too. Good idea to feed the tutor, don't you think?"

"I'll warn Peters," Luke promised as they left.

When they'd disappeared around the corner of the gun room on their way to the hall, Ravenna turned and asked, tongue in cheek, "Does she meet with your lordship's approval?"

"Carole?" His eyes pinned her impertinent glance to him.

"Mmmn."

He looked about to make her pay for this in the most pleasant of ways, but first he murmured smugly, "Pity. Just when I was becoming so fond of Angela. But at least Jerry's finally studying." He sounded very pleased.

"Yes, even if the subject is Carole...and not Molière!" she corrected with a laugh, until she found herself in Luke's lap, learning a few lessons herself.

The hubbub caused by their announcement had begun to die down by Tuesday. Jeremy had taken the news in stride, his grin wickedly cool when they told him quietly the day after Daniel's departure for Syracuse. "Figured as much," he said to an astonished Ravenna.

"But you said...you told me...you said you thought that Angela—" she sputtered.

"Did I?" he said innocently. "Oh, well, you know how it is. That was ages and ages ago."

And she realized that he *had* finally guessed, probably after their rescue mission that night in London. He'd insisted on toasting their happiness, making a comic little speech about kindness to actors and patronage of aspiring stage artists, and then had asked Luke to spot him a few pounds to take Carole out to dinner. Luke had grumbled something about taking advantage of a happy man...and had complied.

Even Glynis had been quietly pleased for them, despite Daniel. "I've seen it coming, my dears," was all she said, kissing them both and then picking up her needlework. But later she added, watching them sit by the fire, Ravenna nestled against Luke's chest, "I knew it that night when you woke me up, arguing about children just like your father and I did, Luke. And Daniel *would* go to New York." But when she reached over to squeeze Ravenna's hand, a look of understanding flashed between them.

"Thank you, Glynis," was all Ravenna whispered.

IT WAS ONE of those golden, sun-hazed mornings a few days later, with the birds caroling bucolically in the trees and the scent of roses heavy on the air, when Ravenna looked up from her desk in the small study off Luke's, officially hers now. She'd been researching her book again—Luke had critiqued it the previous night, and she was all fired up about pulling an outline together and getting it to John Hadley before the wedding—when the phone on Luke's desk rang. At first she thought it was her parents, calling back. She and Luke had had a long chat with them that morning, and her mother's chief worry had been no greater than having to have the invitations reprinted. . . .

She crossed to answer it. "Hello?"

"Miss Jones?"

"Luke! Where are you? I thought you said you were going to work with me all morning."

"My sweet, we're going riding, instead."

"We are?"

"Be down at the stables in ten minutes." He paused, his voice like velvet. "That's an order, darling."

She laughed. "On the double, Sir Anthony."

When she arrived a few minutes later, the sight of two horse vans parked in front of the brick stables made her catch her breath. Had Luke bought the two Arabians and had them shipped to Rathbourn at last? If so, Jessie would have some competition for her daily rides.

Ravenna could see O'Reilly almost beside himself with excitement, marching up and down and issuing orders at the two drivers, who were inching the vans closer and closer to the stable courtyard. Young Kevin was racing back and forth, uncertain about where to station himself for the best view, and Luke was leaning against the wall, dressed in riding breeches and fisherman's sweater—and apparently quite nonchalant. He smiled at Ravenna.

"Aisy, lads, aisy now!" O'Reilly cried. "Watch me fence posts there. . . a little to the left, that's it, that's it!" He turned to Kevin as Luke moved forward to lower the unloading doors of the first van.

"Now stand back, Kevin. They'll come out dancin' like as not, and the huge craitures'll be on top of you if y'don't give them some room. Aisy now, lads. C'mon, baby. C'mon. . . ."

Ravenna stood riveted, watching Luke unfasten the door, waiting for the first Arabian to emerge. She could hear both of them snorting and stamping impatiently.

But the horse that stepped nervously down the ramp, blanketed and hooded, his bridle held by Luke, was no stranger to her. She recognized that gray Arabian body and the large protruding eyes that gazed out so spiritedly at this new world.

"Coyote! Luke, you bought Coyote!" And then her arms were around the horse's neck, and he was nuzzling her bright hair with loud snorts of startled recognition.

Meanwhile O'Reilly was murmuring endearments to the creature, patting his flank with a soothing hand and fiercely motioning Kevin back from the skittish forelegs. As O'Reilly took the bridle from Luke and led Coyote into the stables, Kevin in tow, Ravenna's arms went next around Luke's neck.

Aping O'Reilly's soft brogue, a teasing light in the depths of his blue gray eyes, he whispered tenderly, "Second, is it now? Am I going to have t' be after being jealous of a horse, then?"

"You could try," she murmured. "But I think it's Coyote's turn."

One lazy eyebrow rose, and his tone changed. "You wanted a firebrand, my love." He smiled challengingly.

The long hot glance from blue eyes to gray told him she knew that she'd found one.

And still smiling, he lowered his mouth to hers.

ABOUT THE AUTHOR

Kathryn Collins has traveled widely in the British Isles. She chose to set *The Wings of Night* in Devon because of the coastal scenery and sweeping moorlands, which seemed tailor-made for a romantic novel.

At university she studied English literature and fine art. Presently she's pursuing both writing and art in a variety of media.

Although she was born in Southern Ontario, her father and mother's family hail from Ireland. She lived there herself on the west coast for a time and will be setting her next Super-romance in the haunting environs of Connemara.

Enter a uniquely exciting new world with

Harlequin American Romance™

Harlequin American Romances are the first romances to explore today's love relationships. These compelling novels reach into the hearts and minds of women across America... probing the most intimate moments of romance, love and desire.

You'll follow romantic heroines and irresistible men as they boldly face confusing choices. Career first, love later? Love without marriage? Long-distance relationships? All the experiences that make love real are captured in the tender, loving pages of **Harlequin American Romances.**

What makes American women so different when it comes to love? Find out with **Harlequin American Romance!**

Send for your introductory FREE book now!